Balloon Theater

Short Stories and Personal Essays

Steve Moncada Street

Contingency Street Press LLC

Author: Steve Moncada Street (1955-2012)

All characters appearing in the short stories (Sections One and Two) are fictitious. Any resemblance to real persons, living or dead, is purely coincidental.

Library of Congress Control Number: 2024905604

ISBN: 978-1-958015-06-3 (pb)

ISBN: 978-1-958015-07-0 (eb)

Logo art: Janet Glovinsky

Cover design: Suzanne Hudson

The publisher gratefully acknowledges *The Missouri Review, The Quarterly, Cimarron Review, Palabra, Great Lakes Review, Another Chicago Magazine,* and *Intima: A Journal of Narrative Medicine,* where some of these stories and essays previously appeared.

Foreword

On the Short Stories and Personal Essays of Steve Moncada Street

1. *His Own Particular Frequency*

Steve Moncada Street had a genius for capturing the foreigner abroad/expat ethos—not just on a vivid perceptual level of sights, sounds, and smells, but with the humanity he brought to the page as he captured the anxieties, complacencies, and, most strikingly, the occasional recognitions that are so immense, in their lyrical moment, as to suddenly redeem all the tedium and indignities:

> The extremes of Cairo—the bombs and the balconies and the elevators fixed with string, the sidewalk smells of jasmine and piss, grilled meat and gasoline, the new tourist towers jutting up out of grand, neglected architecture, the curtain-windowed Mercedes passing lepers on the sidewalk—had finally depleted him. He didn't want to go home, exactly, but he wanted something *more like* home. He wanted to go where life was smaller, or where there was less of it, so that it didn't seem to dwarf his own so much ("Balloon Theater").

We find the same elusive clarity in the startled gratitude of Morton, the rootless diving instructor in "Voyage Exotique," as he recalls a woman he'd previously found ordinary, who had eagerly motioned to him from a coral reef:

What she'd been trying to show him was what he'd been
looking all over the world for, not a place or a thing at all
but a way to look at places and things and people, too.
It had been there all along, everywhere he'd been and at
home as well, and it always would be, if he could remember to keep sight of it. . . .

For Street's characters, engaging "the other" to find those moments
is an ethic of the first order. But what the narrator says of Susan, in
the harrowing story "Understanding Yemen"—"The Paul Bowles stories
she'd read had inspired in her a notion that breaking down barriers, both
cultural and gender-based, was not an option but a duty for any truly
free-thinking individual"—could as readily be found from a Buffalo city
bus: "I felt the same sort of alert calm that can set in abroad, when you're
on your way to another culture's holy sites, along with a kind of startled
thankfulness that I could see this. It was a trip indeed, in the perspective
it gave me on my own place in life, and it cost only a dollar and a half"
("Take the Bus").

His characters are always breaking down barriers to find their own
place in life. In "What Have You Got? Where the Words Are" Steve
Street, after unnerving interactions with both the angry husband of a
Russian émigré, with whom he's had a revitalizing affair, and an overwhelmed elderly neighbor, reflects:

I felt glad to recognize at last my own particular frequency,
the territory I've staked out for myself, the zone in which
I'm going to have to live and make my way: neither mean
nor entirely compassionate, attached nor entirely transient, of a place nor gone too long from it, foreign nor

entirely domestic, clueless nor absolutely sure, happy nor entirely sad.

2. *The Sweetest Days*

In *Balloon Theater*, an expat couple decides their future in an outdoor Egyptian café, as a dead body lies nearby; an overeducated white attendant beholds a "shocking man" who frequents the inner-city laundromat where he works and bides his time; a lawyer meets his long-disenfranchised brother at a Saratoga racetrack; a college-bound Midwestern kid is enthralled by a brilliant townie waitress, another kid is overwhelmed by the humanity and generosity of a strange classmate he'd bullied.

Across the more than two dozen settings, Steve Street's subject is often the star-crossed search for love, usually the beginnings and the endings—"the residue," as an émigré calls it (echoing a joke from her former country) upon meeting her ex-lover in "Native Tongues"—after the quest to break down barriers has crossed class or cultural strictures:

> He knew too what her answer would be, not from memory but from his recent return to futile dating, online and otherwise, with defensive or overeager women his own age, scornful younger ones, the tentative in-between. Even hard-eyed women who knew all about him from his first utterance might negotiate a wary shot at it until the daily weight of the world or the culture—he never knew which was heaviest—flattened any brief pleasure or feeling or possibilities they might have been able to work up together. Love as logistics, as sit-com, as game show ("Native Tongues").

But if "the daily weight of the world or culture" too often flattens the possibilities for intimate connection, for Street the self-knowledge salvaged from the "game show" can be fortifying. And heartbreaking for the reader:

> But when a woman came into my life talking about children and marriage, permanence and attachment began taking on a whole new appeal for me. She was from another country, another culture. . . . [U]ntil the crisis that brought about the end of our relationship, she was fine about coming to my apartment to betray her husband three afternoons a week. . . . And the other night, three months since I'd seen the married woman or heard from her husband, my cell phone rang, and it was her husband again, dialing from a restricted number. "What you did is despicable," he said. But it wasn't. It was as beautiful as she was, and he'd been neglecting her, and the time I spent helping her get his attention were some of the sweetest days I've had ("What Have You Got? Where the Words Are").

3. *His Own Particular Frequency (2)*

Though Street's vision never flinches, his characters are often modest, vulnerable, humorously self-deprecating. And so was he. You wouldn't know from reading these pages that Steve Street was famous, among the most prominent contingent academic labor activists of his time. After teaching for four years at the American University in Cairo, Steve returned to find himself in adjunct purgatory, where part-time professors, who teach the majority of classes in the United States, are usually hired semester-to-semester, paid poverty-level wages, have no academic freedom, can be fired at the whim of their directors, and, worst of all, are often disrespected, disregarded, and condescended to by tenured colleagues and administrators—all at a terrible cost to the quality of higher education. According to his aunt, Corinna Moncada, in a memorial pamphlet compiled by Mark Street, Steve's brother:

> [R]ather than deciding to get credentials that would give him prestige and privilege in higher education, Steve responded to these conditions as a social justice issue. He continued to teach as an adjunct professor while working with intensity as an activist . . . and writing of the injustices he saw and experienced.

After his death, a major obituary in *The Chronicle of Higher Education*, where (among many other publications) he'd been a frequent contributor, noted that his academic labor essays "often expressed the frustrations he and other adjunct faculty members felt in seeking decent pay and benefits and equitable treatment from their employers" (August 18, 2012).

On September 9, 2011, Steve had responded on the Coalition of Contingent Academic Labor listserv to an open call for panelists from the organizer of a regional Modern Language Association conference. He'd be happy to speak if certain "health issues" were resolved by then. I immediately contacted him. Steve wrote back:

> The health issues are pretty bad: a recurrence of the melanoma I beat back twelve years ago. Now it's up to tumors in the lungs, w/spread elsewhere. After two weeks in the hospital to stop a fluid buildup that caused the shortness of breath I went in for, I've got an appt. tomorrow at a good cancer center here to see about what treatment plan's possible. It'll be tough and iffy, but all

doctors so far have been impressed w/my strength (I've told them I climbed the Vail Pass), so I hope to be able to withstand it. Also tumors in the lungs is as good an explanation as any for being behind the peleton, isn't it? Bright side to everything, along with the new free reading and email time."

Steve died on August 17, 2012. He was 56. According to the *Chronicle* obituary, "He died in a hospice in Buffalo, in the company of his brother, after receiving expressions of support from many of his colleagues and friends."

5. Prepare to Live

In 2002, two years after his initial bout with melanoma, Street published "Skin," a short story about an ex-pat teacher who falls in love and abandons his former life: "Anson chucked everything—wife, friends back home, even his grown kids after they'd helped him straighten out his complicated international paperwork—to marry an Egyptian woman, a registrar at the exclusive international prep school he worked for in Cairo."

Not long afterward, his new wife notices a discolored mole on Anson's shoulder. After the growth is diagnosed as a melanoma, Anson returns to the States for a second opinion, near the small Midwestern town where he grew up. At the cancer clinic, the oncologist, Marrins, "held out his hand, which felt warm and solid in Anson's cold, clammy one. 'I know you've got a million questions, Mr. Anson. With some luck we'll have about five hundred thousand answers for you.'"

As he's being treated, Anson spends "much of the time between tests and results in a branch library, researching this disease. . . . Every trend in the research data was contravened by dramatic exceptions: people who should have been dead were alive, and vice versa. As Marrins put it, 'Frankly, we've amassed a vast amount of data that in any given case might or might not apply.'"

Anson returns to Egypt where he abandons his treatment, eventually alienates everyone, loses his job, and is divorced by his new wife. Eleven years later he's back in the small town near where he grew up, working in a used bookstore, when the Gulf War breaks out. The radio plays all day on the counter near the register, broadcasting news from the Middle East:

> As the grief stretched into war . . . Anson heard about the global rages and disparities, duplicities and truths, complexities and misunderstandings he'd experienced as pathologies of his own. Some of what was being articulated now he'd known, and some of it he was learning, but he absorbed it all with the growing feeling that what was most important hadn't been said yet.

If knowledge is elusive, just beyond reach, and in any event might not apply in a given circumstance, by 2012, when Street wrote his final essay, "Hey! Hey! Hey! Hey!" he had discovered a tentative accommodation to the disparities and complexities, ironically enough in the "small, quiet, unexceptional moments identical to moments that have bored, frustrated, embarrassed, and/or angered" him for years. Now he sees them "for what they are: great moments. . . . It's the clichés that capture my new outlook, an antithesis, not to say an anticlimax, to a life spent vilifying and bending myself out of shape to avoid them, in my behavior as well as my work."

Two weeks earlier, his oncologist had halted his ipilimumab regimen, a treatment that "after a year of variously effective others" he'd "developed high hopes for." He knows that he's probably in his "last few inches" of life. At times, he "makes himself" face it:

I still get down. I get sick of myself, discouraged. I worry how much pain there'll be. . . . And sometimes I'm dismayed by the remote attitudes of friends and family, even when they're trying to be sympathetic or thinking they're being supportive. . . . So I get angry, suspicious, susceptible to all my old bad attitudes. But not for long at a stretch, now, nothing like the days, weeks, months. . . . Now it's about facing the light, so easy to do I can't believe all that time I couldn't tell where the sun rises from where it sets.

He likens his heightened receptivity, his euphoria, to the repose a fighter pilot might feel in the midst of combat, as embodied in James Dickey's poem, "The Firebombing." Like combat, "cancer strikes away the bullshit."

He engages the paradox. If cancer is speeding him toward "being less than nobody, maybe," his new outlook allows him to "slow down at the same time." To feel "brand new." He signs a lease for a new apartment across town. He begins to move his possessions:

Prepare to live is my two-week old motto, possibly another tattoo (larger, around the elbow). Bucket lists: sky diving, dune-buggy racing, seeing the Alamo at last—well, fine, if the opportunities arrive, but just living—taking out the garbage, reading a thick book, being awake to hear the first bird at dawn, a twenty-minute walk—all these are enough to make me bust. I'm cooking, finding my own meals delicious, chewing slowly, listening to music I've never understood. I am OK with everything.

Just living, even the "sudden dislike" on the face of a retail cashier as he quarrels with her about a store policy and feels "suddenly sick" of himself and his indiscriminate contentment—"you just shouldn't be so happy, so fine with everything"—is a "kind of relief."

"Just get out of here, her face said. And I did."

Soon afterward Street is told by the "highly informed nurse," to whom he describes "feeling in many ways the best I'd felt in my life": "Oh, that's the steroids. . . . That'll pass as you taper off." And it does. But as euphoria deflates, knowledge won't. As with many of Street's stories and essays, fraught circumstance inspires—or provokes—lyrical clarity in the midst of paradox and complication. He never stops trying to locate his place.

In *Balloon Theater*, Steve Moncada Street doesn't give instructions about how to live, or preach that he has a better idea. All he does is report from the front, in ways that are singular and unforgettable.

———◆———

Over the course of a long (if not nearly long enough) writing career, Steve published many academic labor essays (accessible online) and book reviews. He also published several short stories. He wrote many other short stories, several novellas, and at least two novels. Each (or at least of those he kept) is fastidiously constructed and infused with an ethos that seems to notice everything, particularly the myriad self-deceptions of imperfect but well-meaning people trying to live with themselves. Steve had a gift for expressing moments of lyrical clarity that redeem everything, momentarily. Everything he wrote, he gave his all.

Balloon Theater is divided into three parts. The stories in part one mostly explore and express the experience of ex-patriots. The stories in part two are more domestic and fall into two categories, often dealing with teenage boys in the upper Midwest falling for girls from the other side of the tracks, or adults coming to terms with who they are. In part three are personal essays. As there is some overlapping in concerns, I'd like to note that some of the personal essays may have been intended by Steve to be short stories, and vice versa.

Many thanks to Mark Street for his heroic efforts on behalf of his brother, and to Mark and Ed Taylor for their work in completing "Hey! Hey! Hey! Hey!"

Don Eron
March, 2024

Contents

PART ONE

SNAKES

Lovo tells this story in a venerable old bar downtown, now a cramped and sour-smelling place with a high, pressed-tin ceiling, dark paint on its windows, and two huge television flat screens, one over each end of an ornate walnut bar. Fumes and traffic noise come in the open door. A guy with a gray ponytail stands in a tiled alcove there, murmuring to pedestrians, occasionally coming in to sip from a glass on the corner of the bar. It's so dark inside that the wall lamps are on, though outside is sunny. A fan suspended from the ceiling wobbles as it turns; during lulls in traffic, you can hear it squeak. The screen visible from the sidewalk shows an ice-skating competition; on the other, over the heads of two women who greeted Lovo when he came in, is war news.

He orders with an eye on the news, then takes out a legal pad from a zippered plastic folder he sets on the barstool beside his, uncaps a pen from his breast pocket, and begins checking off items on his pad, drawing lines through some of them, flipping the yellow sheets forward, then back.

"How's the job search?" says the bartender, serving him. Lovo makes a face, evoking with his eyebrows and lips and a hunch of his shoulders fatigue, disgust, resignation, and humor, somehow all at once. He's in shirt sleeves, a wrinkled white dress shirt that sticks to his back; his wide, synthetic-looking necktie, with a pattern like upholstery, hangs loose but stiff to his sternum, less neckwear than breastplate. He sets his pad aside, rubs his eyes with thumb and forefinger on either side of his nose, and nudges his tumbler around by its cardboard coaster, contemplating its shimmering contents until an image on the news screen catches his attention. The sound is off, but closed captioning is on. He nods at the TV.

"I've been there," he says, pointing, his posture straightening with interest. "That exact spot."

"You were over there? I didn't know that. You don't look—"

The bartender, stooped over the sink, flashes up at him a quick and earnest grin. He's a big, good-looking blond kid in a clean black T-shirt tucked into clean black jeans. Lovo's got a good face, too, but he's overweight, sweating, shaggy and gray around the ears.

"You don't look *young enough*," calls out the darker of the two women below the screen, her smile wide and perfect. "He was *going* to say you don't look *young* enough, Lovo." Her eyelids and cheekbones shimmer purple; the make-up accentuates her heavy features instead of softening them, making her large face look uneven, rough. Her bare shoulders are broad; her chest swells the bib of her flowered sundress.

The thin woman beside her speaks without turning, straight out over the bar, as if to anyone. She's sitting very straight.

"Is there an age limit? What's the age limit? Taking everybody they can *get*, is what *I* heard. Accosted Worthy in a mall, two white boys in shiny shoes and belts, shiny visors on their caps, no hair left at all. Told him he could be a musician if he signed up." Her own hair's a cave to her shoulders, her face barely visible in it but for tinted eyeglasses with huge, squarish lenses. Her skinny forearms rest against the edge of the bar like the handles of baseball bats, her wrists decorated with multicolored hoops.

"They'll let him play 'Taps,' maybe. They'll say anything."

"Worthy's forty, I'm saying."

"He don't look it."

"That is true. He's in good shape, Worthy."

"He does a hundred push-ups every morning," the bartender puts in. "Or so he says."

"Of course, Worthy too will say anything," says the woman with the big hair, not a reply but another general declaration.

"Casey," says the larger woman, tucking her chin into her shoulder and pouting her purple lids at the bartender. "Give me a cherry, honey. I've got to keep my strength up. Oh, come on. I spend enough in here. You know I do. Gimme cherry. Gimme cherry. Gimme cherry."

She bounces on her stool until he sets out the stainless-steel dish. Felicia, he calls her. Felicia deposits several cherries on a bar napkin, nibbles at one off its stem. She's drinking beer. In a sudden traffic lull, you can hear the voice of the guy in the doorway. *"Beans? Reds? Footballs, man?"* He's stocky, his clean calves muscular; he wears creased Bermuda shorts and sandals, solid leather ones with padding around the straps, their thick rubber soles planted firmly on the dirty green-and-white tiles in the doorway. His ponytail is neat, his nape shaved. *"Oxy? Whites? Clarity, my friend?"* He comes back to his glass, which Casey fills from a large tin can with a black-and-white generic label: TOMATO JUICE. On the war-news screen, flames billow, orange and black. Felicia's watching skating. "Look at those sequins," she lisps. "What I wouldn't give."

Lovo, scooting his drink around, still not lifting it, clears his throat.

"It was years ago. Before all this." He indicates the war news.

"Right," Casey says, considering him again. "I remember those days. What were you doing over there?"

Lovo crosses his arms on the scarred edge of the varnished bar. "Working, believe it or not." His voice eases up. "Seeing the world, also. Travelling."

"Must be nice," remarks the woman with the exemplary posture. She wears a basketball outfit, matching satiny shorts and shirt, red with white piping. White block letters on the chest say SIN QUEENS, and in an arc of white script over the number 69 on the back: *Auxiliadora.* "Must be very nice."

"*Nice* isn't the word," Lovo says. "It was more than nice but at the same time worse. It was more complicated than nice."

Felicia drops her voice. "Was it *awful* over there?"

"It wasn't awful, either. That's what I'm trying to *tell* you, how it was."

At his tone, Felicia blinks, and Auxiliadora demands, still straight out over the bar, "Why is there skating on when it's ninety degrees out?"

"Question asked and answered, honey: it's a rebroadcast to help us deal with the heat." Felicia has the reassuring voice of an older sibling.

"I can switch it," Casey offers, though he doesn't rise from his position against a cooler. "I can switch it, if everybody wants to watch something else."

"Leave it, leave it. I like the sequins."

"*Thrusters, folks? Ts and Rs? Chicken powder, before I take my break?*"

The ponytailed guy comes in and sits on the stool nearest the doorway, at an angle of the bar, two stools up from Felicia and several down from Lovo, who's scowling down at his full drink as if a contact lens, not his, might be floating on its surface. Felicia looks across at him.

"Aw, Sam. We're listening. Tell it, baby."

"We're all ears, my friend." Casey settles against the cooler, folding his arms across his chest; for the ponytailed guy he ticks his head up at the war news. "Lovo's been there. The very same town they were showing." The ponytailed guy nods and holds his juice glass out in Lovo's general direction for a second before sipping from it.

Lovo, shoulders bunched, is pushing his coaster around with his fingertips again. He looks as if he's got it almost exactly where he wants it now.

"Actually, it's not the town itself I remember so much as a wadi nearby."

"A what-y? Hawaii?" Felicia clowns, making wondering faces until Auxiliadora tells her to settle down. "*What?* It was a genuine question."

Lovo smiles thinly. "A wadi. A dried-up riverbed. A feature in a desert, basically."

"I thought deserts didn't have any features." Auxiliadora's not heckling: she's in school, a serious student.

"Besides sand. I know what you mean. And rocks. But get out in one, and after a while you start noticing things. Blacks, grays, purples. Even some green mixed in with the shades of tan. Shapes, textures. A desert can be beautiful."

"Dehydration," Felicia says. "Hallucinations. Didn't see any burning bushes, did you?"

The guy with the ponytail laughs along with her, but Auxiliadora slaps at her, connecting with flesh to still as well as silence her, all without moving off center.

"We saw cliffs. Lumpy, reddish cliffs on both sides. Without anything else around, at first it's hard to tell how big they are, or how far away. Or how big *you* are, after a few hours of walking."

A man in a suit pokes his head in the door, squinting around in the darkness until the ponytailed guy slips off his stool and goes over to him.

"Outside," Casey warns, and that's where the two of them go. Casey casts a dark look at their backs and begins fiddling with a bottle opener, twirling it around a finger like a gunslinger with a pistol, first one way and then the other. Lovo purses his lips. "Well, go on," Casey tells him, twirling away. "And so?"

"So, well, as it turned out, the cliffs were even bigger than we'd figured, and further away. We realized just how *much* bigger and further when two small, dark specks broke off from the rock to our east and began heading our way."

"Ants," Felicia says.

"That's what they looked like, all right. Crawling straight for us."

"Oh-oh."

Casey's bottle opener stops. "What did you do?"

"Nothing." Lovo looks up with mild irritation. He takes several cocktail napkins from a dispenser on the bar and begins sopping up condensation from his glass that's trickled onto the bar top. The glass itself is still brimming. "Why turn back for a couple of ants? And we wouldn't want to look like we were avoiding them, whoever it was. Anyway, it was a couple of miles before we could even see them."

"Could you tell who they were?" Auxiliadora's hands are clasped on the bar now. They're elegant hands, her long nails works of art, tiny designs and multicolored swirls. "I mean: men, women? Walking, running? What kind of clothes?"

"Were they armed?"

This from Casey. Lovo grimaces.

"They were a couple of girls. Maybe twelve and eight. Maybe ten and six, I don't know. I'm no judge. When they were about a hundred yards away, we veered toward them. Desert etiquette: all very slow and gradual. Neither of us were on a road or even a path. I hadn't seen a right angle since we left the Jeep."

A particularly pungent gust of bus fumes enters, and a cry goes up. The bar patrons cough and protest, but nobody moves to close the door. The ponytailed guy comes back in for a sip, toasting the assembly first. Lovo waits, patient now; even his face is dry. Soon he has his audience back.

"What were girls doing in the desert?" Felicia says. She looks around. "Is that a stupid question?"

"They lived there. In the cliffs, or beneath them. In the vicinity, anyway, because it was clear they were our hosts. The older sister opened a striped shoulder bag and took out tea, sugar, a pot, spoon, and cups. No two cups matched. One was a dish, in fact. Then with a single lens from a pair of glasses she started a fire in a handful of dry grasses and twigs her sister had gathered."

"How did you know they were sisters?" Auxiliadora asks with triumph, as if she might have caught him out.

"They told us."

"How'd you talk?"

"The person I was with spoke Arabic. Speaks it." Lovo looks down, fingers the base of his tumbler.

"He was Arab?"

"*She* was Egyptian, actually. But she'd grown up in England. She lives there now, though. Lived there then." He looks at his drink as if he might be ready for it now, but he still doesn't lift it.

"Lived in the wally? Spoke that wally talk?"

Felicia snickers as she says it. Auxiliadora pokes her.

Lovo sighs. "In the region," he says quietly. "In the region. The language is called Arabic, and it's spoken all over, in different countries in the region."

"With some differences," Casey puts in, looking to Lovo for corroboration. "With some differences, right? But they can understand each other. Like Spanish for Mexicans, Puerto Ricans, and Dominicans. Right?"

"Don't forget Honduras," Auxiliadora says. OhnDOOras. "Serve me another spritzer, bartender. How hot was the tea, on a fire made with grass?"

Lovo laughs, a dry and rusty sound from him. "Hot enough. Sort of tepid, actually. But it was the best tea I've ever had."

At his sudden warmth of tone, the others peer at him. Auxiliadora moves her hands to her lap, facing him.

"That's your story?"

The guy in the doorway's murmuring: *"Cat in the hat? Gagglers? Dex? Snow, my friends?"*

"My story's coming up," Lovo says. "While we had our tea we conversed. My story's our conversation."

"Through your friend who spoke Arab. Your *girl*friend?" Felicia wonders, but Lovo ignores her.

"Through my friend. Through my friend, we told them how much we liked the wadi, how quiet and restful it was, how beautiful the cliffs were. 'Yes', the older sister said, solemnly. 'But they're dangerous. You have to watch out for snakes.'"

"Same here." Felicia's laugh pops. "Seems like every day I meet another snake."

"*Shht.*" Auxiliadora turns, the reflections on her huge lenses bright. "What else did they say?"

"They wanted to know about our homes. My friend had lived in Manchester, which meant nothing to them. Even London didn't."

"How about New York?"

"New York rang no bells. The older sister thought she might have heard of America."

Amazement bubbles. When it dies down, Lovo continues, his voice surer than it's been.

"We tried to tell them about buildings, streets, traffic." He gestures at the open door. "They knew what buses were, but mostly they just listened, absorbing, their eyes like pools of oil. You could see them imagining. At one point the little girl whispered something to her older sister. She had a gold tooth already, the older sister did—a front tooth, but her smile was glorious, her face like the sun. This whole time, they'd shown no fear of us, no hesitation. Nothing but pleasure and curiosity. They were little . . ." He gropes, shrugs. "Little people."

Everybody's listening now, facing Lovo. Even the man in the doorway has turned around. Felicia swallows.

"What did she whisper?"

She's whispering herself. On the TV she's been watching, a spinning figure slows down and glides off.

Lovo looks at Felicia, then the others. "She wanted to know if there were snakes where we lived. My friend said yes, we had snakes, but not where people lived, usually. The girl turned to her sister and said, 'Imagine that! No snakes!'"

He sets the heels of his hands against the lip of the bar and smiles around. Casey's still leaning against the cooler, arms across his chest, still looking at him expectantly. The ponytailed guy has been leaning in, listening closely, but now he shakes his head, faces the street, resumes his murmur: *"Bennies? Bottles? Ticklers, folks?"* Felicia, ignoring the skating scores, cranes around at the others.

"That's *it*?" she says.

"That's it," Auxiliadora tells her quietly. "This time, that's it. Right, Lovo?"

"Yes. That's it."

He lays bills beside his untouched drink, slides his carrying case off the bar, and stands down from his stool. He looks rested, refreshed—even thinner, somehow.

"Drink up," Casey tells him. "Hell of a story. Next one's on the house."

Lovo shakes his head. "Not tonight, thanks."

"*That's* a first." Felicia looks startled. "It's not even dark out yet."

Auxiliadora's square lenses swivel toward the window like coin-operated binoculars at a scenic overlook.

"Good night, all." Lovo doffs an imaginary hat all around and backs to the door, where he claps the dealer on the ponytail as he sidles past. His step is brisk.

"'Bye, Sam!" Felicia stands on the rungs of her stool to wave down at him through an unpainted strip at the top of the plate glass.

When she resumes her seat, no one's talking or even looking at each other. No one's watching the TV screens, either, where skating is over and the news channel shows a commercial. People are looking at fixed points at different heights on different walls. Then Casey gets busy rearranging bottles on the back bar, and Felicia discovers a loose thread on the hem of her dress and begins tugging at it. Auxiliadora, erect as ever, stares straight ahead, maybe smiling a little now under the thick cliff of her bangs.

Outside, even traffic in the street seems to have paused.

ALL THE THINGS

"... [T]hese third world cities where millions and millions of people are crushed in together are a completely new phenomenon on earth. There seems to be no structure in them. Yet this was ... precisely where the mystery lay. The city did work. There was a structure, but it was hidden, internal, because the people in such cities were adaptable, resourceful, compassionate—in short, alive . . . ." (Susan Brind Morrow, *The Names of Things: A Passage in the Egyptian Desert*)

About a decade after the tour of pharaonic artifacts that inspired the hit song "King Tut," not long after weekly EgyptAir service between Cairo and JFK had been established, on the day before Marty Eubanks was to take one of those flights home by himself, he and Susan Fisher ordered lunch at a wobbly card table set in the dirt somewhere between the Mosque of Sayyidah Zaynab and Oasr al Sham, the ancient Roman fortress of Babylon, on the eastern side of the Nile. Across the street was a low mound of dry grass and rubble where back streets and alleys met in what was obviously a public square, though right now it was quiet. In fact it was empty, except for Susan and Marty and two other people, and one of those, lying wrapped in a white sheet not fifty feet from their table, was dead.

Marty couldn't see the body, because his view was blocked by a large metal fuse box beside their table. He was looking mostly at Susan, anyway, and Susan was mostly aware of that. They wouldn't see each other again for four months, if then, because the successful outcome of the TOEFL and Arabic courses she'd come here to take would be a job far from the university town where she'd been working—for Marty, in fact, who owned a book-and-video shop that was just beginning to make money. They'd joked at the irony of his business success coinciding with Susan's quitting her job as clerk/bookkeeper, but career goals were the least part of her decision, and as Marty's departure time approached, they were both feeling a need for her to continue trying to articulate the most part.

That was one reason her mind didn't register the corpse, though she was facing it, sitting sideways to their table. Sometime during that morning's walk, the blue bandana she wore like a headband had slipped to her eyebrows, and she hadn't pushed it back up. She wore an old cardigan sweater over a T-shirt and faded bib overalls, an outfit she'd never intended to wear in public here; her air-freighted trunk had arrived the day before, with a wardrobe of practical, conservative clothes she'd bought for this trip, but the breathless poverty she'd seen all over had made her self-conscious about wearing new clothes, though of course it was her blonde hair and freckles that would prevent her from ever blending in. Even Egyptian albinos—and she'd seen more albinos this week than ever before in her life, along with cripples and crazies and a boy pacing a median strip on all fours, smiling—looked swarthier than she was, tougher as well as darker, the women as well as the men. Already the sensitive skin on her cheeks had blotched, though the sunlight was often filtered by smog, and people said it was only half-strength now in January, anyway. The bone-cold of mornings and nighttime, actually any time but mid-day in the sun, had been a surprise—one of many, though she'd been preparing for this trip for months, reading everything from *Let's Go* to Mahfouz to as much of T.E. Lawrence and Pickthall's *Meaning* (not translation!) *of the Glorious Koran* as she could plow through. But the only reading that came anywhere near doing justice to the amazing things she'd seen and heard and smelled and felt in the hammering assault of Cairo was somebody's remark that no preparation for it is possible. She and Marty had left JFK the day after Christmas, after an eleven-hour delay in a hanger and no sleep the night before, and even now, a week later, she still felt out of sync.

She tried to keep smiling as she surveyed the square, chin cupped in her palm. Marty had his Cubs cap and his Ray Bans on. He wore a wine-colored nylon windbreaker over a plain pocket T-shirt, with khakis and a beat-up pair of Stan Smiths, a nondescript enough outfit at home that made her cringe here, where even the tourists had more sense than to slouch around like a slob. Egyptians looked as good as they could afford to, not worse. The fabric on Marty's Cubs cap was frayed along the edge of the visor, where the plastic showed through, and she knew exactly how much pride he took in that.

The sheet was peppered with flies. It was pulled snug over a head. A leg protruded from the other end, the foot extended, the ball of it huge. Beside the body knelt a turbaned man in a green galabeya; his back was straight, his knees and thighs together, his palms flat on his thighs. Every once in a while he passed an arm over the sheet to scatter the flies.

Susan took in these details along with others in the square, absorbing them all in the same way she'd absorbed what she'd seen that morning and the day before and every day since her arrival: always new and astonishing things to see, one after the other. A simple walk around the block was like the midway at some huge, century-spanning fair: a donkey cart might be passing a Mercedes in front of a TV store beside a tinsmith's or tentmaker's shop; outside Marty's hotel she'd seen a man with a tray full of digital watches and turtles for sale. From the air the desert had looked like caramel-colored velour, the occasional oasis like scattered chunks of bone, and touching down, their plane had taxied past an airliner abandoned just off the runway, its markings faded, its landing gear either collapsed or buried in the sand. It had looked to Susan like a bird stuck in tar, flapping to get out, and her first thought had been, *What IS this place?* Nothing she'd seen since had provided any answers, and the more clues she gathered the less relevant the question itself seemed, though the clues continued to promise something she'd never known before.

So she'd settled into a numb and watchful wonder, and the dead body in the square became just another item in the collage of pyramids and water buffaloes and people, mobs and mobs of people, and a brown dust over everything that made building construction indistinguishable from ruins, and shifting street-smells of jasmine and sewage, gasoline and bread, grilled meat and urine, and honking cars and amplified calls to prayer and the ululations of women in the alley that she and Marty had just emerged from, where preparations for a festival were being made.

There they'd drunk sugary mint tea and watched two ropey-limbed old men squatting against the low wall of a tiny green mosque, one shaving the other with a disposable Gillette. The cross-eyed boy who'd served them said that the name of both mosque and festival was Sidi Ali, a saint's name, and Susan had felt triumph at managing this exchange with just the Arabic she'd learned from a cassette at home and a three-hour "survival session" at the Cairo Language Institute's orientation meeting. Marty's reaction to the saint's name had been a pun—Seedy Alley—and the two of them had barely spoken since.

"So have you confirmed your flight?" she asked him suddenly.

She intended simply to resume conversation, but he nodded curtly, hurt. They'd get into it right here and now if she wasn't careful, she told herself. In their last few weeks at home, their discussions had increased in intensity, including the discussions themselves and pre-discussions, about whether conversation was in fact turning into a discussion and if so where they should hold it (his apartment or hers, a restaurant with memories or a new one, burgers or tablecloths), and then post-discussions, about how the discussion had gone. Their best talks—their clearest, most straightforward and honest ones—had come when outright argument flared up before they could realize it, but still nothing was too clearly resolved between them.

A different waiter from the one who'd taken their order arrived with their salads; inside the wide-open doorway he'd come from, probably the kitchen, Marty, aloud, counted six more silhouettes. The salads were plates of chopped onion and tomato and something like overenthusiastic parsley, and more plates of lumpy gray baba ganoush, which Susan identified from a taste off her forefinger. The waiter's hands were fat; on one pinky he wore a heavy silver ring with a huge turquoise stone. He set a cardboard dispenser of tissues—for napkins, Susan finally realized—on the plaid oilcloth beside the tiny joined dishes of salt, pepper, and a green spice she couldn't name. A grinning boy with ears protruding from a new haircut brought coarse, brown flatbreads in a pink plastic basket. No two plates matched, nor did silverware, chairs, or salad size.

Marty poked suspiciously at the small one.

"Well, off the beaten path is where we headed," he said, but before Susan could answer she was distracted by yet another waiter, who stationed himself beside her chair with his arms clasped behind his back to ask them something; she tried to figure out what. This guy himself was beautiful, his shiny black hair parted clean and curled in locks over his collar, his skin the color of a new penny, his features even and sharp—delicate, really, but at the same time strong. He wore a white V-neck sweater that he'd tucked into blue trousers with about twelve pleats. He stood close, his eyes dark and steady on her, and the soft but guttural sound of his voice as he repeated his question thrilled her. The sounds of Arabic were so different from any language she'd ever heard before that she hadn't been able to tell whether people on the streets were happy or furious, but the waiter's voice as he repeated his question a third time—she felt dumb, blinking up at him—gave her a definite impression of calm, of solidity. He was smiling, too: a thin smile that seemed somehow both shy and insolent, even more complicated than that. In his face she saw at once sadness and delight, cruelty and compassion, acceptance and strength, humor . . . Susan couldn't have named everything she saw in this face.

She still couldn't understand what he'd said, either, so she tried thanking him, and he seemed satisfied with that. *I know you*, his parting smile seemed to tell her, without insolence but without doubt, either.

When he'd gone, she said aloud to Marty, "There's no shame attached to service here, is there?"

Marty finished chewing and swallowed.

"Guy's glad to have a job at all, I imagine, from what I've heard about the economy here. But I'm sure you're right," he added quickly, as eager as she was to avoid an argument.

What Susan was actually wondering was whether she could have come to this restaurant alone, whether she'd have been able to get this far from Mohandeseen, where the CLI and her apartment and relative civilization were, by herself at all. How to be a Western woman here had been the first item on the orientation agenda, and the warnings were unsettling: hissing in the streets and even grabbing, according to one personal account, while policemen looked on and laughed. The general barrage of harsh suggestion she'd already felt, though most women who'd been here any length of time admitted they felt safer on any given street here than back home, whether U.S. or U.K. Here, apparently, the sticks-and-stones principle applied. But from the grim look of several older women who'd made lives here, intercultural marriage was nothing to be undertaken lightly. And most of the foreign guys, apparently, were gay. Susan didn't know quite how she was going to handle sex yet.

Marty, misreading her worried eyebrows, gave her a conciliatory smile, and seven goats ran out of the kitchen, their hooves scrabbling on the cracked marble floor tiles, the tops of their heads spray-painted pink. A flustered boy in filthy pajamas scuttled out to chase them into the street, switching at their legs with what looked like a radio antenna. The restaurant staff crowded the doorway, all laughing except for the fat waiter, who was shouting angrily.

When the goats were gone, the good-looking waiter approached. "Soddy," he said. "Soddy. Soddy. So soddy."

Telling him there was no need to apologize was beyond Susan's Arabic, so she beamed and gestured, and Marty did the same: they shook their heads and their hands, palms out, in an erasing motion until finally the waiter smiled—showing black teeth.

Susan winced before she could catch herself. Abruptly, he stopped smiling and returned to the kitchen, head down, kicking at a scattering of goat turds with the side of his foot. One rolled under the table beside them.

"Oh, nice," Marty said, watching it come to a full stop. "It'd be just my luck to take home a case of hepatitis as a souvenir."

"At least at home you'll have the latest medical technology available to treat it," Susan snapped, immediately wishing she could take it back. But she was tired of his lame jokes in the face of a world he couldn't understand, dammit! She didn't understand it herself yet, but at least she knew better than to mock it.

But Marty was looking so pained and baffled that her anger turned to guilt. After all, he'd come eight thousand miles for her sake, professing cultural curiosity, but she knew better: Marty wouldn't cross a street unless he knew what he wanted on the other side. He'd come this far with her because he thought it would increase the chances of her returning to him some day, and about that he was probably right. An airport parting at home would have seemed more final—Marty left behind—but now her first days in Cairo would always be days spent with him. They were some of the most intense days of her life so far, too, and they hadn't been unhappy until the strain of right now.

"Just kidding," she said, but their smiles were awkward: his irritated, now, hers self-conscious and false—two of several qualities about herself she'd hoped to change here, as a matter of fact. So far, people here seemed more genuine than at home. Smiles seemed like smiles and scowls like scowls, rather than calculated moves or professional responses or—one of her pet peeves—imitations of some movie or sitcom star. Maybe life was simply so hard here it was pared to its essentials. She didn't *know* what it was, this feeling she had about life here, but she meant to find out, and to learn from it. The possibility was exciting, and on impulse she smiled at Marty for real and reached across the table for his hand. She'd heard the injunctions against public displays of affection, but she'd seen couples on the Corniche nuzzling in the evenings, too. She gave his hand a little squeeze. On his fingers she felt bread grit and oil, and Marty smiled at her as if she'd given him an elaborately wrapped shoe or can of tuna fish.

Pops like firecrackers came from the square, and their hands squirted away from each other.

Not far beyond the dead body was a shooting gallery on wheels, a shallow wooden box with one open side strung with what looked like bits of clay on rows of wires. A thin young man in a black leather jacket, jeans, and white loafers was standing a few yards away, aiming a single-barrel rifle into the box. Marty craned around until he could see. Earlier that morning they'd jumped at a motorcycle backfire, then relaxed when they knew what it was, and Marty had identified the phenomenon: the way figuring out even small causes and effects could be a real toe-hold in the chaos here. *Like a psychological crampon*, he'd said.

Back home, Marty was a rock-climber, a man who rose bit by bit, and Susan realized she would have to give him something definite about their relationship, either promise or plan, before he left, maybe even before they got up from this table. She would rather have parted on a note of flexible understanding, a mutual belief in letting things work out. Marty had once accused her of not thinking much about their future, but it wasn't true. She'd imagined it often, sometimes as more and more time between increasingly forced letters of diminished longing and affection, and then one—from either of them, it wouldn't matter—that was shorter than the others. Other times she'd envisioned—just as vividly, if not moreso—returning to him, changed and clarified and stronger after facing the challenges that now lay just ahead. Only then, she thought, could she appreciate the calm life of steady comfort and gain that Marty wanted. It was basically the life she wanted, too, once she'd done some things for herself, by herself—and maybe *to* herself, too.

A group of boys on bicycles entered the square from the street alongside the restaurant. They stopped by the man kneeling beside the form wrapped in white. The largest boy straddled his bicycle and spoke, and the kneeling man looked up and answered. The bicycles had loose, pressed-tin fenders decorated with small flags of horizontal red, white, and black; on a wire affixed to one set of handlebars was a plastic daisy that trembled as the boys pulled back out into the rocky street and rode off. Over the crest of the square rose a TV set. Beneath it a woman's head appeared, then her shiny purple-and-black robes. The TV twisted in the air when she turned to laugh with another woman who appeared behind her, then twisted again when she called out to the smallest of the boys on bicycles, who was struggling to keep up with his friends.

Susan watched it all, and Marty watched Susan, who was thinking that she didn't want to cut herself off from everything she'd known before here, but at the same time, now that she was here in Cairo, she wanted to *be* here in Cairo, not with one foot back home.

The jug-eared boy brought their meat, sausage-shaped kufta on a bed of chopped greens.

"Thanks," Marty said loudly, with an exaggerated smile. "Oh—please. Do you have a minute? Where are we?" He opened his *Blue Guide* to a map page, and the boy obligingly leaned over it. Susan read aloud the transliterated names of landmarks, and all three of them looked around, pointing in various directions and examining the map again, until the boy waved the book off with such a comic shrug that even Marty laughed.

"So Seedy Alley's unmarked," he said when the boy left, propping the book open under the edge of his plate. "But here's Santa's Sleigh Knob or whatever, that mosque where they wouldn't let us go in, and I'm pretty sure we turned south when we came out, maybe a little east, down that market street with the painted drums for sale, and the hubcap store. Which should put us right about here. So when we leave we'll head west, toward the river. *That* way." He pointed to a spot across the square, his smile triumphant, as if by locating the cardinal compass points he'd neutralized everything they'd seen that day that was unfathomable.

Then he noticed the look on Susan's face and shrugged. "Or we can just wander around until we see something we recognize. Hop in a cab. Whatever." He cut into the glistening meat with a bent fork and chewed thoughtfully. "Hmmm! Wonderful! Is there thyme in this?"

"I think so. And cumin."

"And"—his eyes widened—"is that cinnamon?"

It was the most delicious meat Susan had ever tasted.

Marty claimed so, too, but too enthusiastically for Susan to believe he meant it. *He's trying so hard,* she thought. And he'd *been* trying hard, and so had she, not just on the logistics of this huge undertaking of hers but to understand exactly why she wanted to do it, ever since she saw the CLI ad in *Harper's* last summer. She'd just finished a Paul Bowles novel, so that was one explanation. But even angry, Marty had never just written her off as a romantic. And once he'd seen that she was serious he'd supported her fully. He'd read what she'd read, and some of it he'd suggested.

He'd read things she hadn't, not only finishing *Ancient Evenings* but reading even more about the pharaonic period, which tended to leave her cold, though she did like thinking she was moving from the newest civilization in the world to one of the oldest.

But Marty wasn't moving at all, physically or any other way. He was a man who liked reasons, explanations, clarifications, and specifications; he liked to know the names of things, the way he'd wanted to identify the spices in the meat, which, she noticed now, he'd stopped eating. She asked him why.

"I seem to have lost my appetite," he said. "It's funny. I was starving when we stopped. Not literally *starving,* of course, like . . ."

They both remembered people they'd passed who looked as if they might have been.

"We'll have a good meal tonight in the Sheraton," Susan said. "That's one advantage right there: back home we could never afford dinner in a five-star hotel."

Then she froze, because *one advantage* implied others and the trade-off she was making, *him* for *here,* a way she'd thought but never spoken aloud before. Now she wasn't sure he'd caught it, or if he had whether it seemed like anything new. Had he been aware of being an alternative in her life, an option? He was leaning back in his chair to watch a bird, a dove, like a pigeon but skinny and brown, that had flown from the restaurant's roof to the fuse box and was looking down as if also wondering about Susan's decision, and she realized that Marty deserved an answer, finally, to the great unasked question of why she was here. She put her fork down and pushed her plate away. She had no idea what she was going to tell him. She opened her mouth.

"It's not that I don't love you," she said. "I just need some perspective before"—his eyes moved from the bird to hers—"before returning to resume our lives together, if that's how it happens."

She bit a thumbnail, not a regular habit.

He laughed. "It's not that I don't love you, either. It's not that you're unsweet."

"You know what I mean. This is not about love, Marty. It's about more than that."

He studied the last chunk of meat on the tines of his fork, then lowered it to the metal plate. "*What* more?" It was a request for information, his voice mostly curious.

Susan tried again. "Well, there's that net bag of mangoes hanging in the doorway of that shoe store over there. There's the way our waiter balked at our map, and those two soldiers we saw holding hands, and a city of sixteen million where you can walk in the dark, and those bearded men playing with their children—remember?—in that park, and the huge date palms we saw there. This is about another way of living, before I lock myself into the only way I've ever known, and it's about doing something tough, and seeing if I can handle it. It's not just about love, Marty. It's about life."

"Isn't it *all* about life, Susan?" His voice had that control to it, that infuriating patience. "Can we maybe try to put a little finer point on things? Isn't this really a way of *avoiding* life, and avoiding love, and avoiding the difficult things that have to be done to maintain them both?"

He knew her so well. Avoidance was in her, she knew that. She'd always been a dreamer. But she'd always been a talker, too. In that respect she could give him as good as she got.

"Some things *need* to be avoided, Marty. You've avoided them yourself, or you used to. The things we've found so stifling back home—you *know*," she added with some urgency, because she saw him poised for an interruption. Why did he make her redefine terms they'd already agreed on? "Everything we think we know in the West, all our talk about quality of life and how to improve it, all our calculations. All the books you have to stock, on everything from careers to cholesterol to the cosmos, all the self-help books on how incomplete we are, how unfulfilled and un-whole, how less than human we are unless we buy what somebody else is selling."

Waiters had gathered in the doorway.

"Self-help books," Marty said. "You've come eight thousand miles because you don't like self-help books? Just don't read them. That's what I do."

But he knew what she meant, because they'd talked about it all before, not just the books but climate control and virtual reality and dating companies and all the other ingenious inventions that seemed designed to bring people back to where they were before they'd gotten so damned smart.

"All the *things,*" she insisted, "that prevent us from enjoying plain life anymore, so that we've got to relearn how to be happy."

Marty was squinting just above her head, probably considering what part of what she'd said to take issue with first, looking pained but pleased, too, because her talk would have revealed mental errors he could now reveal to her.

But he surprised her.

"I," he said quietly, taking his sunglasses off, "have been happy at home. I have been happy with *you,* Susan."

Behind him, a taxi hit a camel, which tilted away while the car horn blared. A man in a blue *gallabiyah* grabbed the camel by a foreleg, bent it back at the knee, and slipped a loop of rope over it so that the animal couldn't run, since it had to hobble on three legs. Marty turned around, and he and Susan saw the animal's head in profile, upper teeth arching away from lowers like ice tongs; when the horn stopped, they heard its scream. A flat mule cart pulled into the square and stopped behind the taxi. The cart driver lit a cigarette and waited for the owner of the camel to finish arguing with the cabbie through the window. Arms waved up and down.

Marty turned back and continued in the same calm, earnest tone of voice, as if the interruption had been some sort of false alarm, "You know, a lot of women have agendas. A lot of women either want to fit you into them or cut you out. Not you, though. Maybe it's why I'm so—I don't—I mean . . . You don't know exactly *what* you want, do you, Susan?"

She shook her head, fingertips at her lips. She couldn't remember the last time she'd heard Marty grope for words.

He folded his hands on the plaid oilcloth and studied them. "Anyway, I've thought about it, naturally, and this is how I've got to have it. I'll wait until after your courses here are over. Then you'll know if you've gotten a job out of this, or where that might be. You might end up hating teaching, for all we know now, all *you* know, or hating Arabic. You might not like living abroad." He was talking to himself now, as much as to her. "So if you still want to get together at that point, we can work something out. We'll pick up where we're leaving off now, or whatever. But if you're still not sure then"—he looked up at last, his blue eyes clear—"then it's over. Then I'm not there for you anymore, Susan. Fair enough?"

Even this, she hadn't been able to call on her own, a realization she took as confirmation she was doing the absolutely right thing. Her hand dropped from her mouth. "Fair," she said. "More than fair to me, actually. Are you sure it's fair enough to you?"

"I'll be fine." He shrugged. "But whatever happens between us, I'm concerned about you. I won't say worried. I know you can take care of yourself. And people are people all over, I know, good and bad. But this city's not even fully *mapped* yet. I don't want anything to happen to you. So for these four months at least, will you stay in touch? You don't have to give me emotional updates every week. Just tell me you're all right, at least."

While he spoke, the mid-day call to prayer started up from a mega-phone dangling off a lamppost, and a second later another started up, close by, and then another further off. Susan had read what the words meant—God is great, God is great, and she could never remember what came next, but already she recognized the sounds, the syllables. The first voice she'd heard just now, the loudest, was different from the amplified voice near her apartment: this muezzin sounded older, his voice more ragged and off-key, cracked and mournful and tired. But it struck her as beautiful, and it spoke to her in her own vernacular: *life's a mystery, a wonderful trouble, we don't know why and we can't, all we can do is live it, because life's a mystery, a wonderful trouble . . .*

"I appreciate," she told Marty, "your concern."

He nodded and started to speak but didn't. Instead he began figuring the bill, converting the charges to dollars, calculating aloud. It came out to a total of less than three, and he made a happy comment about that. They paid the man in the white sweater, thanked him, and debated a little more which street to take out of the square. Marty rose like a man with new confidence in his sense of direction.

That's when they saw the body on the square.

The man who'd been kneeling and the mule-cart driver were loading it on the cart. The body was stiff, and the driver, a cigarette in his mouth, dragged it by the shoulders up the flat bed of his cart while the man in green stood on the ground, pushing the legs. They left it with the bare foot dangling off the back. The driver climbed into his seat and hit the mule with a stick. When the cart moved, the foot bounced.

"That's a dead man," Marty said.

Susan had been watching the procedure along with him, but not until she heard it spoken aloud did she recognize the body for what it was, a recognition that felt to her like sudden turbulence.

"Right," she said quietly, but her thoughts were wild: *hold everything. Grab on. Fly back with him. You've made a mistake.*

Even afterwards—back in the hotel room, when they'd calmed down and cheered up with showers, gin-and-tonics on the patio over a discussion of what they'd seen and what it indicated about public health standards, overpopulation, and differing cultural emphases on privacy and the sanctity of an individual life—Susan's mind was full of second thoughts, reconsiderations, half-measures, alternate plans. It took a real exercise of will not to mention any of these before Marty's plane left.

But she exercised it.

A QUIET VOICE

At the Mosque of Sayyidna Al Hussein, grandson of the Prophet, a boy was dancing with a five-foot bamboo stick. He was serious about it, deliberate and vigorous, winding the stick behind his neck, along his arms, down his side, hooking a foot over it, holding it above his head as he jumped. Four belled flutes and a drum made the music, a simple tune with endless variations on a climbing, winding theme. "We have heard this music in Paradise," wrote Rumi in the thirteenth century. "Although the water and clay of our bodies have cast doubt over us, something of this music drifts back into our memory."

A dense crowd of men, somber and attentive, watched the boy dance. Some sat on wooden chairs and others stood, all of them relaxed but intent and very, very still. The edge of the oblong clearing their feet made was even. Nobody smoked. It was about eleven o'clock at night, the street lit by white fluorescent tube lights from nearby shops and a few fruit vendors' gas lamps glowing yellow on the cobblestones. Between tunes, you could hear the lamps hiss.

"It's like the Middle Ages, isn't it?" whispered one tourist to another as a group of them left.

"Not exactly," said a quiet voice, accented but clear, at the speaker's elbow.

But all the men had their eyes on the dancer, and the tourist who'd spoken thought he'd imagined the voice.

Away from the lit area, the street narrowed between high stone walls and branched into other streets. The tourists wandered forever before they saw something they recognized, though they worried about it less and less.

ZBORT GLUBB

"In the name of Allah, the Beneficent, the Merciful.
Praise be to Allah, Lord of the Worlds, the Beneficent, the Merciful.
Owner of the day of Judgment,
Thee (alone) we worship; Thee (alone) we ask for help.
Show us the straight path,
The path of those whom Thou has favored, Not the path of those
Who earn Thine anger nor of those who go astray."
(Sura 1, *The Meaning of the Glorious Koran, an Explanatory Translation*
by Mohammed Pickthall)

At first the trainer, Mahgoub thought the American to be hopeless. He knew how to hold a racquet but had no sense of stroke: he either flubbed the ball into the net or rocked into it from the wrist, lopping it over the fence. Mahgoub asked for fifteen pounds for the hour, and the American simply paid it. Obviously not a serious man. With some of the extra money, Mahgoub bought ball-point pens for his nieces, celebrating his luck.

But a few days later he received a telephone call at the club, something that had never happened before. Mahmoud, who took the call, had no American language, but the man said *Mahgoub, Mahgoub, Mahgoub,* until Mahmoud sent a ball boy to find him and bring him to the ticket kiosk at the front gate, where the telephone was. Several ball boys gathered around the windows of the kiosk to watch him talking. *Yes,* he said into the heavy black receiver. *Five o'clock on Thursday.* One hour, maybe two. *Yes. Yes. Yes.*

Thursday evenings Mahgoub visited his father, but he could take a later train.

In three weeks, the American had developed a reliable forehand and a surprising crosscourt backhand, flinging his racquet up and over in a way that delivered deadly topspin. The ball would skid when it hit the clay, bouncing no higher than your socks. The American could control the ball more often now but not his smile, his shoulders, his heart. From the way he walked back to the baseline Mahgoub knew what to expect on the next point.

"Gud," Mahgoub would call. "Very gud." He had taught Englishmen before, and Mahmoud had told him that Americans spoke a similar language.

The American perfected an outrageous service motion: he would dangle his racquet from a loose wrist, then cock his arm back and bring his racquet around over his head, elbow bent like a hook. Mahgoub showed him how to draw back the racquet with his toss so that both arms were extended, then bring the racquet up, out, and over, like a whip. But the American couldn't do it, or wouldn't, and eventually he made his own serve work. It took advantage of surprise, because his jerky motion was like a mechanical toy, so ingenious and engrossing as to catch you off guard when the ball came over the net, faster and faster as the weeks went by.

Sometimes they drank *lemuun* in the wicker chairs between courts, sipping and watching others play. "Gud," Mahgoub would say, pointing to a player, or, "Not zo gud." His vowels were deep, his consonants thick, and he knew that what he said sounded nothing like things the American said, but the American seemed to understand and would agree, smoking a Cleopatra that Mahgoub would have declined, fist to breast. Foreigners could afford better cigarettes, so he was puzzled. A Marlboro he might have accepted, or a Winston.

The next time it would be he who paid for the drinks.

During Ramadan the American neither offered nor ordered any drinks, though Mahgoub told him to go ahead if he was thirsty. The American was no Muslim. In the sudden absence of traffic sounds after *adhan* he laughed but not with joy, as if the silence was something he alone had discovered. Of course it *was* rather funny, but it was expected: Mahgoub tried to explain that after fasting all day, at sunset everyone began eating and drinking instead of driving and honking. But the American had so little Arabic that talking was difficult. He laughed again, and they resumed play. They'd just started a set, which meant that Mahgoub would be taking his own *iftar* late. His tongue felt like chalk in his mouth, but he won enough games to give the American his money's worth.

By the time Mahgoub got back to his uncle's house the new street-lights were on, but there was still plenty of food left. The meat was gone, but there was still plenty of food.

In winter the American began bringing guests. He'd become a member himself, Mahgoub discovered, one of the few *xawaagas* allowed to join. A few years ago, Abdullah had trained an Englishman who was a member, and who, upon leaving, had given Abdullah a radio. Now Mahgoub had his own foreigner. He pointed this out more than once to Abdullah, who had had none for some time, until the American began bringing others.

Some of those he brought he knew well, and some he didn't: Mahgoub could tell from the way they acted together and the sound of their voices. Some returned on their own, working with Abdullah or even Mahgoub but usually playing together. Some of them were women. Some of the women could beat the American, and still he continued to bring them. It didn't seem to bother him.

But no other *xawaaga* came as often as the American did, and he kept his Thursday evenings with Mahgoub, though usually not for more than an hour now. He'd ask to work on specific strokes, such as his backhand, not the slice but an ordinary two-handed one that they worked on until it became dependable, or his forehand, which still wobbled a bit. Or Mahgoub would feed him volleys at the net.

The American lost weight. At first he'd been fat.

On one of the Thursday evenings, over *lemuun*s he had paid for, the American reached over the wicker table between them and patted Mahgoub's head. It did not seem like a sex pat, though with foreigners that was always a danger, but more like the pat one might give a dog, while thinking of other things.

"La," Mahgoub said, drawing back.

He could see Abdullah, between points on the next court, looking over. He could feel the indentation in his hair left by the foreigner's hand, and the sweat from it. The sweet smell from a corn cart outside the front gate soured and took on substance, like fingertips to his nostrils, choking his air off.

"La," he said, shaking his head at the clay between his feet. "La. La."

The American brought his arm in, looking at him curiously. Then he shrugged and finished his *lemuun*. He pointed at the court with the head of his racquet.

"Yallah?" he said.

"Yallah," Mahgoub said, launching himself from the wicker.

By the call at sunset, their habitual quitting time, he had played up from 0-2 to 4-3, though they would finish the set, also a habit. Mahgoub, serving, took every point but one and in the last game took them all, and the American never touched him again except to shake hands over the net.

Mahgoub felt cool spots where the water was evaporating between his fingers and toes and on the back of his neck. Shoes in his left hand, sole to sole, he stepped over the wooden sill, right foot first. Facing the *mihrab* he spoke. *Bism-allah wisallahtu wisallahmu rasulallah allahum*, he began. When he fell silent, he bowed from the waist, his hands on his knees. Standing, he brought his hands to the sides of his face. *Allahu akbar*, he said aloud. His lips moved silently. *Allahu akbar*, he said again. He bowed and knelt and placed his palms on the ground, then his forehead. In the center of his forehead was a spot the size of a lime, where the skin had darkened and roughened. After a minute he rose. *Allahu akbar*, he said. He did all this several times. He said other prayers. Then he turned his head to the men on either side of him. "Salaam," he said to them.

He felt fine.

Ticket prices were raised for foreigners only. No one said the reason, but everyone knew it was the bombs. They were far away and had stopped for now, but Muslims had died.

The American was not pleased. He held up fingers like angry suns to show how many more pounds he'd paid, but Mahgoub could see that he was scared, too. He was with three other *xawaagas*, one with red hair that Mahgoub recognized and two women.

They played mixed doubles. Mahgoub had no lessons, so he watched from the shade of the banyan tree in the raised, tiled patio behind the courts. The American, used to covering his own backhand, kept running into his partner, a yellow-haired woman who was playing in blue jeans but knew better than the American where to stand. The second time he knocked his racquet into hers she whirled around, her mouth in an angry line, and brought her head up. Through the chain-link fence her eyes met Mahgoub's, his glass of tea halfway to his lips.

Her face changed. She was very beautiful.

Then she turned toward the American and began laughing. He laughed too and divided the court with a mark in the clay he made with the rim of his racquet head. The mark was much closer to her sideline than to his, and she rubbed it out with her shoe and made another mark with the rim of her own racquet, closer to the true middle of the court. The other two were laughing as well, with a good laughter that was joyful, not mocking, and when a breeze came off the river a dove on the tiles flapped its wings and rose over the pool, and Mahgoub thanked God.

Despite the price hike they kept coming. The yellow-haired woman became the American's most frequent partner, often twice or more a week. She wore shorts. She would arrive in the shorts, and she would leave in them, waiting on the patio while the American dressed before their game or, afterward, showered.

"Hello, Mahgoub," she might say, smiling.

"Hello, Madame," he would answer. She would laugh.

Faransaawi, Abdullah said: she was French. On the court she was good, and the American was playing with confidence now, his strongest game yet. His service motion was no smoother, but he could place his serve now, making the chalk rise. At the net too he'd become very quick. If he won the first set against the yellow-haired woman, he'd win the second. If he lost the first set, however, then he often lost the second as well. Rarely did they play three sets. As the weather became warmer, they spent more and more time in the chairs, sometimes as much as on the courts, asking ball boys to bring them *lemuuns*.

Unforeseeably, Mahgoub had a very good summer, *AlHamdulillah*.

When the American missed two Thursdays in a row Mahgoub couldn't buy his train ticket, so he missed seeing his father that week. The next week his father didn't say anything, but his mother was angry. He told her about the American, but still she was angry. The American came the next week, but not for lessons and not on Thursday, and Mahgoub had to begin saving for his ticket as soon as he had any money at all. Winter was coming, and the courts were often empty, and people were drinking tea again instead of *lemuun*.

He began delivering drinks courtside, like a ball boy. Usually by Wednesday he had enough for the ticket. The American still asked for him sometimes. Maybe once or twice a month they played together.

Once that spring, on his service, the American tipped a ball from the edge of his racquet into the schoolyard on the far side of the courts. Mahgoub went to the fence to ask somebody to return the lost ball, but it was a Friday, and nobody was in the schoolyard. The balls were the American's.

"I will go," Mahgoub said.

He set his racquet against the fence post and began to climb, fingers through the wires of the fence. The toes of his old shoes were too soft, one of them already split wide open, and several times he lost his footing, landing once with both feet. The fall didn't hurt, but his stance when he landed reminded him of something, he couldn't remember what. That bothered him.

Again he tried to climb.

"Mahgoub!"

The American was beneath him, shaking his head as if he were addressing an infant. He held up a canister of new balls he'd taken from his bag. *"Mish laazim,"* he said. *"Andi gideed."* His Arabic had improved. He wagged the canister from side to side, smiling widely, and Mahgoub dropped to the ground.

His stance was a crouch, and now he knew what it reminded him of: a cartoon he'd watched on television with his young nephews. It was on juice cartons, too.

"Zbydair Mahn," he told the American.

At first the American didn't understand.

"Zbydair Mahn. Zbydair Mahn." Mahgoub jumped onto the fence again, then off, crouching, extending his wrist to shoot an imaginary web from it. "Zbydair Mahn."

When the American did get it, he laughed hard, looking at Mahgoub in a new way. Abdullah, coming over from an adjacent court to see what the commotion was, understood immediately and stomped into a crouch with his wrist out. Ball boys ran over and did the same, crouching with their arms out. "Zbydair Mahn! Zbydair Mahn! Zbydair Mahn!"

Everybody was pleased—especially Mahgoub, as it had been his joke. Several minutes later he and the American resumed play.

Before the American left, toward the end of summer, he sought Mahgoub out. The yellow-haired woman waited by the pool, bathing her face and neck with her towel. Until the manager had spoken to the American about it she had liked to wet her towel in the pool, dipping a corner in. Now she either carried a bottle of Baraka with her or ordered one, then poured the water into the towel and bathed her face and neck and arms, sometimes even her legs. Members looked away and ball boys hid behind trees, snickering. Some of the members laughed, too, at the way she raised her limbs to scrub them. Then from her bag she'd draw a blue plastic bottle and rub white liquid into her skin. By the time the American came back from his shower she'd be glistening like a roast chicken on a spit.

On the day the American said goodbye she was doing all this in the background when he came down the steps to the courts. Mahgoub was playing fourth for Doctor Mustafa and his two sons, and the American waited by the net post, watching until they switched courts. Mahgoub was afraid the American wanted a game, and he began to cross by the opposite post until he couldn't pretend he didn't hear his name.

The Doctor and his sons stopped and waited.

"I am leaving," said the American.

"Goodbye," said Mahgoub.

"To my country. Not return. *Xalaas.*" The American indicated *all over* with his hands: spreading them, palms down. He had learned a few things.

"Ah." Mahgoub waited. In addition to the radio, Abdullah had received a pair of shoes. He shifted his stance so that the American might see where the sole had come loose.

"Goodbye, Mahgoub."

It was the Frenchwoman's voice. He saw her shiny teeth through the chain link. She waved down at him.

"Goodbye Madame. And Messieu. Goodbye."

Still, he waited. But all the American had to offer was his hand and smile.

Full of resentment, Mahgoub muffed two points. His partner, the doctor's son Ahmed, glanced over, displeased. Mahgoub bounced on his toes, preparing to receive service.

"Yallah," he shouted buoyantly to show that he had recovered, then shouted it again, for his own sake. "Yallah. Thirty love!"

BALLOON THEATER

"Je voulais sortir de chez moi, de mon moi." ["I want-ed to get away from my home, from myself."] (Gustave Flaubert,*Voyage en Égypte,* journal entry of 6 February 1850)

Jan called Norton and told him to dress nicely, because tonight was going to be a special occasion. They'd both been aware enough of the approaching ends of their contracts and their work visas, a decisive time for their relationship, to have been avoiding any behavior that might be construed as intrusive, so he asked what kind of special occasion she meant. "I don't know," she said. "Just look good." He hadn't even want-ed to go, particularly, but her abruptness surprised more than offended him, and he got out a washable khaki suit he'd bought expressly for bringing to Cairo, though he hadn't worn it twice in the six years he'd lived here. But the pants he'd washed often enough that they'd faded, as Jan noticed by last sunlight in the cab she had stop at their usual spot on the Corniche to pick him up. Then traffic clogged in Tahrir Square, and she began flicking at his lapels.

"Will you relax about my appearance?" he snapped. "What *is* it about tonight?"

Two dirty girls were approaching with packets of tissues for sale. Jan gave them the Egyptian gesture for No, shaking an index finger instead of her head, and turned to him with a tremulous sigh. She'd worn peach-colored lipstick, and even through his annoyance Norton was aware of how good she looked.

"Vesna's so fragile," she said. It was Vesna's dinner party they were going to. "She's been through so much. I'm just worried."

He relaxed. It would be no worse than he'd expected: another strained expat evening, everybody trying to make up for the impermanence of their circle with the intensity of their delight in and concern for each other. He liked Vesna fine, though her scrambled Balkan accent had precluded talking to her much; he hadn't met the man she'd moved in with, but the guy's name came up in expat gossip so often they might have roomed together. In a way, Norton was actually looking forward to the night's predictability, and as traffic moved again, he reached out and bought a fistful of crushed flowers from another kid who'd approached their window.

"Take her these," he said, handing them over. "Fix her right up."

Jan gave him the look the remark deserved and didn't speak again until the routine argument with the cab driver over the fare to Zamalek, which started halfway over the 26th of July bridge. Norton was so tired of such quibbling he'd have paid the extra pound, but Jan came to life for it, as did the cabbie, a skinny young guy with gold front teeth and a pressed Michael Jordan T-shirt. When they'd reached an agreement, he held the money Jan gave him to his forehead and kissed it, then stuck his palms out his window for Norton to slap, rolling out into traffic with his steering wheel a-spin, teeth a-glint.

"Can you dig it?" Jan said, holding up her sixteen-cent triumph: they'd ended up paying foreigner's fare, but not *ignorant*-foreigner's fare. And their several-block search for the address—unnumbered as half the buildings were, street signs obscured with whitish dust—Jan played like a shell game, pulling him into side streets, where the sounds of traffic receded like a flock of geese, then back to the first place they'd considered, pausing occasionally to laugh. She hadn't been here as long as Norton had, and, all else being equal, he thought she'd be happy to stay. He didn't like to think about how he might figure into that "else," and right now he didn't feel like thinking about his own renewal, either.

In the lobby they faced another delay: the wooden-cage elevator wouldn't start until a Nubian bawab came to rig the contraption with a piece of string. It was just the kind of improbable miracle that Norton used to love about this place as much as Jan still did, but when the car stopped on the twelfth floor, after a wobbly ride up, he couldn't relax his grip on the wooden slats. On the landing, holding the scissor-grate door for him, Jan looked back. "What's the problem?"

"I don't know whether it's nerve or fury," he said. "Who the hell owns this building? We'll be lucky to make it home alive."

Apparently, the sound of voices was all his muscles needed to un-clench, but Jan looked at him with the same kind of baffled resentment he'd directed at her in the cab. He buttoned his jacket, trying to recover some dignity, and she stepped up to the doorbell with a move like a fencing thrust.

"Wonderful," he muttered to no one in particular, but it was Jan who scowled back.

The door was opened by Vesna's new boyfriend, the infamous Ray-mond Veneer, who turned out, in the first surprise of the evening, to be enormously fat. Norton had pictured a small, fit guy with a rigid grin, an image he became conscious of only now that the reality clashed. Neither Raymond nor anyone else was dressed up, but both his manner and his apartment were lavish. He kissed Jan's hand and introduced Vesna, a petite redhead who'd either forgotten Norton or pretended to; the young couple-about-town Rania and Mohammed, whom Norton had met at other parties; and a guy closer to his own age in a fringed suede vest, Yehia, who'd brought his cousin, a calm-faced woman with hair to the back pockets of her jeans: Ibtissam, whom apparently Jan knew from the high school in Maadi where the two of them worked, and they embraced as if it had been more than a few hours since they'd seen each other last. With that much of his hostly duties discharged, Raymond caught Norton's eye, stuck a Glenfiddich scotch in his hand, and commandeered him for a tour.

The apartment was huge. Raymond named his possessions as he pointed them out, and Norton responded, "Wow!" or "Nice!" to a collection of masks from Swaziland, a zinc ouzo bottle from Naxos, a computer with a new gazetteer program whose data included number of dentists per thousand inhabitants and national anthems, lyrics and tunes both, and an original-edition owner's manual for a 1944 B.S.A. M20 motorcycle that Raymond kept, fully restored, in a garage he rented two blocks away. "Want to go see it?"

Norton thought of the elevator. "Maybe later."

"Come out and see my balcony, then. No exhaust fumes up here, you'll notice."

In fading pink light he breathed deep and explicated his spectacular view of the Nile: among palm fronds across the river they could see the striped tent of the Balloon Theater in Agouza, a kind of permanent puppet show, and the white-and-gold minaret of the mosque in Kit Kat Square, named after a nightclub near a British army barracks that had stood there during the war, as Norton happened to know from a guidebook. But he acted otherwise, and Raymond was encouraged to turn him around by the elbow and point out seventy-five meters of stout new genuine-hemp rope wrapped around a huge iron bitt he'd had bolted to a wall in case of fire. He called the bitt a *bollard*. "The building's got an alarm," he said, "but I wouldn't trust it to wake me for tea around noonish on a Saturday. As for the bloody lift, don't make me laugh."

Norton didn't, not only because he agreed but because he thought any unexpected exertion at all might be dangerous for his host, whose consecutive sentences seemed to have brought on heavy breathing. The man's throat was a bag, a full wineskin with a chinstrap of sandy beard, his voluminous pants multi-pleated, his shirt opened to the middle of a hairless, waxy chest. All his clothes were slightly different shades of plum. Hard to believe that this was the guy who, according to rumor, had not only propositioned every foreign woman in town, single or married, after his wife left him, but had met with a good deal of success. The worst story involved a woman who wouldn't, a quite famous poet, a widow, invited to read at the British Council, where Raymond worked: while driving her in from the airport he was supposed to have told her that if ever she felt the need of a man during her stay, he was available. "And he didn't mean for moving furniture," Jan had said.

The big man rapped a pinky ring against the bollard to show how solid it was. The stone in his ring was plum-colored, too, and Norton wondered if he had others for other outfits. "You've heard 'em get into a lift an' say, 'Fourth floor, God willing,' haven't you? Buggers can't make a bed. Whole country needs a back-up plan, dunnit?"

They'd strolled the length of the balcony, and on the other side of a sliding screen door, some of the Egyptian guests sat within earshot. But everybody inside was deep in a conversation that distracted Norton, too, now: apparently another bank had been bombed, this one in the Garden City district, where Norton lived. A month ago at work he'd heard one go off, and if this one wasn't just a rumor, it meant the government's crackdown wasn't working. Some of the guests were pooh-poohing the fundies' feeble efforts at overthrow, but Yehia was lambasting government corruption. Both reactions were familiar, neither too reassuring. Norton and other foreigners stayed at the government's behest, and each slight shrinkage of their comfort zone felt like saltwater drying on his back.

Raymond slapped it, his eyes like the heads of nails driven into his fat.

"Subject change—host's prerogative," he announced as they stepped inside, and everyone but Yehia laughed.

Vesna appeared in the doorway of the dining room.

"Deenair is sir-r-r-rved," she announced with a bow, and conversation throughout dinner was light. Jan and Norton had been seated at opposite ends of the table, and her laughter floated down to him with the music of silverware on plates; between courses he heard it with Vesna's in the kitchen, and he stopped thinking about anything beyond the glow of the centerpiece candles and the duty-free Czech wine, a real treat after Rubis d'Egypte. Good food helped: Vesna, half-Italian, was an excellent cook.

"Which was the special occasion, the wine or the clam sauce?" Norton whispered to Jan as they left the table.

She looked around to make sure no one had heard, then whispered back: "Probably neither. I think they eat this way all the time."

Next came a fashion show: Jan and Vesna disappeared and returned in short, tight dresses. Vesna's was the color of her hair, with a saucer-sized hole on one shoulder and another that showed the opposite waist and hip. Jan, who designed costumes for school plays for a living, had made it from a photo in a French magazine and brought it to the party in her purse. Vesna was supposed to pay her 300 L.E. for it, but now they were dancing, Jan in a dress of Vesna's that was as short as the new one but striped like peppermint, and intact. With their arms around each other's shoulders, they kicked their legs in approximate unison, laughing their heads off, a parody of girlish delight. Jan's full blonde hair still offset the gray that had set in, and Yehia, who had brought the cassette tape they were dancing to, seemed to be falling in love with her, his eyes watering like Omar Sharif's. Vesna was dark, trim, and at least ten years younger, but Norton's eyes, too, kept returning to Jan.

He was going to leave her. The founding principle of their relationship had always been *No claims*, her own phrase, and he knew how tough she was; he knew she would be all right. She'd survived her husband's departure two years before, to marry their next-door neighbor in Ann Arbor. And her school here had a quota of foreign faculty to fill, because bringing new people over was such an expensive and high-risk proposition that anyone who could stick it out was pretty much guaranteed work for the foreseeable future, barring some socio-political cataclysm that even the war hadn't brought about yet.

But it had ruined his own nerves. At the language institute where Norton was a teacher trainer, by now he'd been promised a raise if he signed up for another hitch, but he'd put in for transfers to branches in Turkey and Romania and on Crete, and now, watching the fashion show, he resolved to take the first one to come through. The extremes of Cairo—the bombs and the balconies and the elevators fixed with string, the sidewalk smells of jasmine and piss, grilled meat and gasoline, the new tourist towers jutting up out of grand, neglected architecture, the curtain-windowed Mercedes passing lepers on the sidewalk—had finally depleted him. He didn't want to go home, exactly, but he wanted something *more like* home. He wanted to go where life was smaller, or where there was less of it, so that it didn't seem to dwarf his own so much. And Jan herself was the one who'd once wondered how much of what they had together had to do with them and how much came from what was all around them.

"Everybody!" she cried now, oblivious to him. "Let's dance! Come on!"

"Dance! Dance!" Vesna beckoned around rapidly with both index fingers. "Everybuthy rise!"

Norton begged off, pleading clam sauce, and Jan, after a second of hesitation in which he thought she somehow knew what he'd decided, held her arms out to Raymond, who protested from the depths of a cordovan armchair everyone else had instinctively avoided. At his flattered brays Norton was embarrassed for him. When Vesna stepped in to dance for her man, Raymond laughed louder than anyone.

The other guests' appreciation was restrained, though Yehia and Ibtissam rose to dance. Such festivities wouldn't be seen in any of *their* homes, Norton knew or thought he did, though as a single man past the proper age for marriage, he'd rarely been invited to an Egyptian home. Other intercultural barriers he'd come up against included dating, let alone sex: both happened, but even mixed couples of long standing seemed to cause anxiety for all concerned, including strangers on the street. Even Egyptians who'd lived elsewhere seemed likely to obey the social codes at home, though those who'd spent time abroad made much of their distinction. "Hear that guitar?" Yehia asked over the song's final flourish, spinning his fringes to address the room at large. "That's me, if you believe it. We recorded this one in Nashville."

"This is you?" Norton recognized the tune from radio airplay fifteen years before, not one he would have recalled unprompted, but he was impressed.

Ibtissam paused to lean down to him, holding her hair back against her clavicles. "My cousin," she confided, winking. "The wonder of a single hit."

She sailed away, just her feet and hair moving. During dinner she'd mentioned attending a design school in Denmark, and he'd placed her from Jan's previous talk: engaged to a Dane at one point, she'd broken it off because she missed her family, and now, according to common wisdom, a match here would be difficult. Mohammed and Rania were married but still living with their respective parents until a suitable apartment could be furnished: they were *maktoob kitabnya*, Mohammed had explained with irony and pride at the same time. He'd gone to medical school, but instead of practicing he was modeling for a fashion magazine that some friends in Mohandeseen were starting up. Rania, who'd studied philosophy at the Sorbonne, never raised her eyes or lifted a fork that

Norton noticed, her index fingers tracing invisible patterns on either side of her plate.

Norton himself, the son of a high-school principal in Gas City, Indiana, had adjusted to the automatic social privilege of expat life easily enough. But cynics said that the only three reasons for a foreigner to stay were religion, sex, or money, and now that he'd decided to leave, he could admit that for a long time for him it had just been the money, and not even much of that. He made enough to travel and live comfortably, certainly better than he'd be able to afford without a great deal more effort in the States. Even the money, though—the currency itself: the small brown pound notes and larger blue fives, the green twenties that almost matched the inflated new hundreds—never seemed quite real to him. But foreigners who made their lives here sure did. As Vesna's rich sauces worked their way into his bloodstream he noticed that Raymond seemed to have fallen asleep: feet extended in front of his chair, he looked in profile like a plum-colored mudslide. Another tune ended, and Vesna sank into the huge lap.

"We're all so very *mad*, aren't we?" Norton heard Ibtissam murmur to Rania as host and hostess rubbed noses and Jan sprawled out on the rug, exaggerating her breathlessness for comic effect. Yehia laughed appreciatively while the Egyptian women reddened and looked away. Still clowning, Jan blew him a kiss, then blew Norton one, which he returned. They could have several more months together, but he promised himself that he'd tell her of his decision soon, though probably not tonight. *Better on our own special occasion*, he thought.

"I hop you *doan* think," said Vesna, on her feet once again, "that *thiyus* was the special occasion. I will catch my *breaths,* and you will get lee*querrrs,* and *theyun,* you *will* zee." Her small jaw worked out the vowels as if she were chewing; she stressed too hard and often wrong, flattening her r's like a Brit mocking an American, her accent veering between the exotic and the ugly.

"*Raymond has*," she said when they'd all been served and she'd settled in a chair of her own with a cigarette in an ebony holder, "been transferred to Singa*pore*." She looked at Jan. "Sing*a*pore ?"

"Well, maybe," bellowed Raymond, enormously pleased. "*May*be. At this juncture it looks likely, but we'll have to see. It would certainly be a boon if it happened, and the London chief's an old friend of Dad's from Nairobi, which of course never hurts." He chortled. "That's not the *main* announcement, though, is it, darling?"

Suddenly he stood up, amazingly agile, without spilling a drop of amaretto from his tiny tinted glass. Holding it out to the assembly, he cleared his enormous throat.

"She's only known him a few weeks! I can't believe she'll go *through* with it," Jan said when the taxi driver ran out of English to practice on them. It was almost three in the morning. Rumors of bombs made cabbies nervous, and Norton and Jan had spent twenty minutes in the street before this guy stopped—partly, apparently, for a vocabulary drill. In the daytime he was an accountant, he'd told them, and to support his family he drove all night, though he was hoping to land a job with an American firm someday. It was far from the first such story Norton had heard, but he encouraged the conversation, anxious to avoid the one that suddenly felt imminent with Jan, about how the wedding announcement might relate to their own case.

But she didn't seem to be thinking about that. "I can't believe she doesn't *know* about him. Then again I can't think of anyone who would have just come out and *told* her, either."

Norton didn't know what to make of this, after the way she and Vesna had hugged. They'd gone to change their dresses and emerged from the bedroom arm-in-arm, laughing through tears, and the gathering had become warm and intimate. Even Rania's effusive congratulations seemed genuine, and by the end of the evening, Raymond himself hadn't seemed so bad.

"People change," Norton offered, but Jan bit a thumbnail and shook her head.

"Of course *I* never told her anything, but I never thought it would go this far this fast. Now I don't know how I *can* tell her."

"Tell her what?" The way she'd said it made him think she meant something specific. They were crossing the island on Mohammed Moktar Street, between the Japanese-built opera and a new sports arena, its walls painted with featureless figures representing tennis, basketball, and soccer, but in spite of their action poses and modern design they looked stiff and sad. Norton noted the absence, at this hour, of the crippled hunchback who usually wheeled his chair into traffic to sell bread along here.

A possibility that had never occurred to him before suddenly did.

"Raymond never put the moves on *you*, did he?"

The ordinary brick wall around the opera seemed to fascinate her. She opened and closed her mouth twice before sound came out.

"'Moves'?" she said weakly. She tried to laugh.

It was not a fidelity issue or even a how-could-you issue, considering the anxious nights they'd all spent during the war or after an assassination or a demonstration or last year's earthquake, rumors flying like tracers around town. At worst this was none of his business, at best a kind of solution, and he thought it would be easy not to touch. They spent that night at her place in Maadi, fatigue a handy buffer, but in the morning, Norton realized that he was not going to be able to leave it alone. After a distracted cup of coffee, he said he had tests to grade, and they'd probably last all weekend. Jan bit her lip. She'd been talking.

Back at his own apartment, every time he finished one paper and reached for another, he recalled something he'd only half paid attention to when it happened. Occasions came back to him, and looks and tones of voice did, and when he calculated time spans, he thought of a time, after Jan's husband had left and Norton was just getting to know her, when she must have been sleeping with Raymond. The fact of it floored him. He spent the afternoon telling himself he couldn't hold what she'd done then against her, but by evening he was back in their first tentative weeks together, feeling revolted and duped.

At about nine o'clock he called her. The line was busy until after ten. He didn't know what they would say to each other, but he thought it might go better face to face. He suggested dinner the next night, naming a fancier place than they usually went to. "Fine," she said.

But he saw Vesna again before he saw Jan, the next afternoon at Sunny's, the cramped Japanese supermarket in Zamalek where foreigners shopped. Norton had gone there mainly for the walk from Garden City, the most exercise he'd been getting since his latest tennis partner, an engineer with the French company that maintained the subway, had returned to Paris. The half-dozen items Norton usually picked up at Sunny's he could buy anywhere, but he liked being able to take them off the shelves himself. And he liked just looking at the Fruit Loops and Camembert and freeze-packed coffee and wrapped meat with no tails attached and now, he saw in the cart ahead of him in the checkout line, even Johnny Walker Red, at a hundred L.E. a fifth. Somebody must be getting paid off, he thought, idly counting not one bottle in the cart but three before looking up and recognizing the back of Vesna's head.

Surprised, he nudged her elbow with the jar of peanut butter he was holding, and she whirled around already smiling, her dark eyes shining: she'd known he was there. He thanked her for the previous evening. "The bride-to-be does her own shopping, I see."

She shook her hair back and grinned. "*Wayull,* the wedding hasn't *hop*pen yet!" People in line ahead of her turned; her voice was as loud as it had been to address her assembled guests. "But insha'Allah nothing will go wrong. The question is, when will you marry my girrrl? *Haaaah?*"

More people turned, and Norton lost his grip on his peanut-butter jar. It didn't break but rolled under a rack of German tabloids, and when he'd stooped to retrieve it Vesna grinned down at him, one hand on her cart handle and the other on her hip.

"When? When? When? I *want* to *know!*"

He tried to disarm her with a smile, pointing to a space ahead of her as the line moved up. But even when she'd paid, she waited, dangling her two full bags at the door, until he'd paid for his own items and joined her.

"*When?*"

"Shhh, Vesna. Listen. Have you got a few minutes for a cup of coffee? I think the President Hotel is open."

Vesna nodded once, as if satisfied. "Tea," she said. "At the Marriott. It is clo*zayrrrr*."

The Marriott Hotel was where he and Jan had agreed to meet that night. It had once been a palace for three wives of the khedive Ismail Pasha; during the opening of the Suez Canal, Empress Eugenie had stayed here. What Norton noticed this time was how much security had tightened up. Vesna, who'd sent her groceries home in a cab, walked in with her hands in the pockets of her camel hair overcoat, stalking through the metal detector as if it didn't obstruct the ornate cast-iron porticoes. Norton had to stop and hand over a thick pocketknife, which the guard opened to examine every blade and implement. When he got to the tiny magnifying glass, he raised it to peer at Norton suspiciously, then laughed heartily, closed the knife, and handed it back, all jovial smiles.

Vesna lifted an elbow for him to take her arm, but it was she who steered him across the richly patterned lobby carpet toward the marble steps at the back. "We will try the patio," she said. "I think it will not be zo *warrrm,* but!" She raised her black eyebrows and smiled. Her bright red lipstick was perfectly applied, and after his first impulse to somehow talk things out with her, now he didn't know how he could or even why he should.

The patio was sunny, but menus flapped in a chilly wind on the round marble tabletops. The only other patrons besides Norton and Vesna were an Arab family strolling in the garden. Vesna sat in a round-backed wicker chair and turned up her collar. At least it was quiet out here, Norton remarked pleasantly when they'd ordered from a waiter who carefully placed their cups on their napkins. Vesna stage-sighed. Under the table, apparently, she'd put on a pair of olive kid gloves.

"Nor Tone, please. No non*sinse.* I tell you now about Jan Ice." She gave each syllable in each name equal weight. "These are think you thing you know, but you don't know. Zo I tell. Jan Ice is a forty-year-old. Yes? Thirty-nine, forty-two—" she waved a rapid hand at the surprise that must have shown on his face. "I call forty. And you?"

He had a feeling of pleasantness past, but he told her.

"Zo. Close enough. Unless you want children, but you don't. Am I true?"

"Too small. Easy to pack but easily misplaced." These were his standard lines.

"Nor Tone. You are funny man. But Jan Ice is unable, since a time when she was young. You know this?"

He knew.

Vesna shrugged. "A problem for her husband, always-always, but not for you. And never married. Are you gay?"

He looked at this woman Jan had called fragile.

"Zo, fine. You decide. Many men come here, they want boys. About you, Jan Ice thing no, but we *voo*man never know."

"Wonderful."

"Zo, zo, fine, OK. But what I want to tell you iss not so much for you." She held up a leathered index finger. "Iss for Jan Ice. It will be very difficult for her to marry now. It is always difficult because of the age, but I have read magazines from your country, you are very hard people, though you seem so soft. Zo. Some like alone, some doan. Jan Ice is a *doan*. She *doan* want to be finally alone, I doan thing you know thiyus how much. *Me*, she tell." An olive thumb thumped her chest. She dipped into a pocket for a drawer-pack of Dunhill's, lit one with a marbled red lighter, and clacked it shut. Blowing smoke, she raised two fingers.

"Two. She is a good work. She has millions of taste, she can do many think. She can go anywhere, she will have job. She worries, but she will have. She will have job because she wants job. That is maybe another think, but zo." The third finger popped out. Vesna set her elbows on the small round tabletop and looked him in the eyes and waited, as if she didn't already have his attention.

"What?"

"Three iss loff. She *loff* you."

Norton's heart jumped like junior-high. He looked around for the waiter and made the wrist-chopping motion that indicated he wanted the check.

"Thank you very much for your concern and advice, Vesna. I will certainly consider the things you have said."

Vesna half-rose, scraping her chair legs on the salmon-colored tiles. She stabbed her cigarette into the ashtray and ground it out, her black eyes boring into his. "Nor Tone. She will *not* loff you always. You must *do*."

The waiter arrived, and Norton reached for the check

"More *tea!*" Vesna barked.

The waiter hesitated. In bow tie and striped vest and tailed jacket, he had an obsequious smile and mocking eyes for any man who would sit still with such a woman, and Norton felt a flush of anger until, looking down, he saw ripped seams in the man's shoes. "More tea for Madame," he said then, and Vesna smiled. Dark stains between her teeth made them inverted points, like the teeth on some creative child's jack-o-lantern. When the tea came and she'd steeped her bag and sipped, Norton leaned across the cold marble and asked her quietly who she thought she was, to be setting him straight about his own life like this.

She nodded once, as at a fair question. "I will tell you who I am. Do you know why I am now in Cairo?"

He shook his head, though Jan had mentioned a few things.

Vesna's wicker creaked. "I was visiting my sister in Ridyah. She married a Saudi, our mother is Muslim. I loff my sister but in Saudi I had to be covered, there is nothing to do, I left early. In Cairo I change planes. I wait. Four hours, five, six. *Seven.* Do you know what has happened? My country disappeared. Zagreb, Dubrovnik, Sarajevo—airports closed. My town was Split. I phone my mother, I hear guns. Thanks God she lives, my aunts, we are alive. But we lost houses, cars, our money. We lost the future. And *position*!" She sat up even straighter. "Our friends were the best people. Then nothing. I have a passport from no country. Now, with the help of Raymond, I have papers. Without him— who knows? I don't say to make you cry. I am lucky. We are. But I have *learn* what a person must do to be what a person is."

Norton didn't say anything. He believed everything she'd told him. Jan had mentioned some of it. But the satisfaction Vesna took in telling her story made it all seem false. He felt mean and low and petty, but he remembered the bottles in her shopping cart and wondered how much she drank herself. Maybe it was her accent, or the green gloves, or the jaw-jutting way she was clamping her ivory holder and lighting another cigarette, but what struck him was not the pathos of her story but the tired realization that he'd heard a pathetic story either *from* or *about* every foreigner he'd met since he'd arrived. Was it the distance they came or what they became when they got here—a few pale, pudgy faces among the masses of gaunt copper, brown, and black—that made their lives so spot-lit? No matter what we were at home, he thought, here we're like bad mimes, gesticulating in greasepaint.

He told Vesna about Raymond and Jan. He told her the dates he'd figured. He spread his hands. "I have no proof. But Jan admitted it, more or less."

Vesna's throat moved. Her lips parted slightly, closed, and parted again.

"I see."

She was quiet for a long time.

"I wondered," she murmured at one point. "May*be*, I knew."

Her eyes sought Norton's, her chin small in the lapels of her overcoat. Her lipstick suddenly seemed too old for her face, and he couldn't look at it. He turned to the octagonal fountain. Its water pump wasn't working, but it was a stately thing, its salmon-colored marble elaborately carved: on every side was a roaring lion. Around it a small, black-haired boy walked beside a woman in slacks with a sequined hijab over her hair. They walked slowly, their demeanor formal, but the way they were together made Norton think the woman was the boy's mother. The boy matched her steps, his hands clasped behind his back like a grownup, his face serious as a grownup's, too. He wore a blazer and creased trousers and black shoes like lacquered blocks. Then woman and boy made a turn and snuck a grin at each other, and Norton got a glimpse of the precarious place in the world of most of what he still assumed to be plentiful and free.

"I'm sorry, Vesna. I'm sorry it happened, and I'm sorry I told you."

"No." She stood up. "It is better that I know. Raymond has cried in my arms, at the size of his stomach. He will be difficult."

She removed her glove to shake Norton's hand, her own warm and smooth and dry, and then left, her posture perfect.

He had a drink in Harry's, a facsimile English pub in the Marriott complex, then called Jan to suggest they meet there a little earlier than they'd agreed. Or else he'd get a cab out to Maadi and they could go to Pub 13, a smaller and more casual place. The fact that she heard him out told him Vesna hadn't called yet.

"I'll come there," Jan said quickly. "Why the switch? I'm already dressed, and I haven't looked this good since the fashion show."

It was a familiar kind of quip from her, though her voice was strained, and the best he could manage was an imprecise answer: he said he'd gotten held up in Zamalek that afternoon and didn't want to cross the river just to change, then come all the way back. A few days earlier, he wouldn't have thought twice about telling her the whole reason for a delay, and now he wanted to tell her something, any small thing that was true. The rest could wait for another hour, at least.

"I'll be here," he said, hearing a strain in his own voice now. He slid into an accent like Vesna's: "Don't *vooorry!*"

Then he listened, hoping she'd . . . what? Laugh?

VOYAGE EXOTIQUE

Lunch was a tuna the captain had trolled behind the boat for that morning, which the mate chunked and fried with onions and tomatoes on a Butagaz burner in the wheelhouse, adding Sport Cola when the mixture boiled down. It turned out to be so unlikely good that afterwards Morton, the older of the two American men aboard the *Nidia*, wanted to sleep for about three days. But when Ahmed, the dive leader, came around with the news that the current had slowed, so they'd try Jackfish Alley that afternoon, if nobody had any objection, Morton made sure to sit up and say what an excellent pick he thought Jackfish was. He had dive-leader certification himself and a notion that Ahmed, who wore Florida Tech track shorts and drawled his English, was more than just an employee at the dive shop, and Morton would be needing a job soon.

Ahmed seemed flattered, and Morton thought that so far he'd played this one just about right. No one else seemed to care which site they dived, though the skinny British girl, Pooky, claimed to have dived Jackfish before and wanted to talk about a hammerhead that had swum right at her there once. Her friend, a Californian somewhat less obviously in her forties, seemed to have heard it before and changed the topic to men. The two of them were sitting on the foredeck with their backs against the angled cabin windshield, towels over their shoulders and legs stretched in the sun toward the Italian couple, who were snoozing side by side in matching purple suits. The German girls were sunning in the stern, profile to profile on the dive rack: too young, so Morton stayed on the bridge and eavesdropped on the rapid, flouncy British that funneled up in the wind along with intermittent hums in Californian. He gathered that these two were leaving the next day, returning to Cairo for teacher-trainer jobs that they didn't like much. Just the time, he thought, for a dinner date.

He'd chatted with the Californian enough already to have learned her state of origin, but he didn't like to hit on a woman until he knew they both wouldn't be stuck on the same boat the next day. Tonight Buster could take the Brit, because Buster, who'd glommed onto Morton in a weight room in Dahab, had said himself that his philosophy of life was to take what he could get. Right now Buster was in the cabin, professing interest in the Arabic names of things in order to bum cigarettes off the mate, who had a pack of Marlboros. Buster had developed his intercultural concerns quick.

But this part of Sinai didn't even seem like another culture anymore; it was more like International Playland. Every time now, Morton noticed more dive shops, bars, and walled tourist villages strewn like litter beneath the creased brown sheets of mountain that loomed from the Red Sea, which he could imagine parting these days not by miracle but by technology, in some seafloor reclamation project funded by the IMF. Sharm el Sheikh had a mosque, but from the beach you didn't even hear the calls to prayer, not that Morton could have answered them, or would have if he could have.

"But the best one," Pooky was saying, lolling her head toward her friend, who closed her eyes and smiled at the sun, "the absolute love of my life was Jean-Yves, a Frenchman who worked for the UN in Singapore. I was teaching for the Council, and we fell in love a month after he was married. At first I didn't know, but by the time he told me I couldn't help myself, nor could he. Soon he was transferred to Hong Kong, a promotion, but he continued to shuttle back and forth, making excuses to come back to Singapore to see me. He would set up a three-day conference, then never leave my bedroom except to go to the loo. When he went back to Hong Kong, he'd send me cassettes about how lonely his life was. I listened to them over and over on a wicker settee, until the shadows from the mangrove trees outside my window fell on the birds of paradise he'd have brought me on his last visit. Always birds of paradise. That's what I remember, those shadows on those flowers and his voice, which I heard mostly on tape. But finally his *wife* got a tape telling her he'd made a mistake, he wanted his old job back and a life with me. Then we were intensely happy for about three days until his superiors got into the act and changed his mind for him. Also his wife had money, I think. So for the next eighteen months I cried and worked, worked and cried, cried and applied for any job in the world that would take me away from those shadows on those flowers. I suppose I should have simply stopped buying birds of paradise!"

Startled at her own joke she laughed, her pointy knees rising in convulsion, but the Californian's slightly narked smile didn't change. This one wore wraparound shades, mirrored space-warrior glasses, so Morton couldn't tell if her eyes were open or not. In case they were—and aimed up at him—he smiled, but her face stayed the same.

"Oh, but then he'd ring me up," Pooky carried on. "I'd answer the phone in the middle of the night and he'd be crying. God. So finally I told him *enough*, he had to choose. Well, he chose, all right."

The Californian did say something now, rolling her head against the cabin window: a question.

"No. Sometimes, maybe, the way you think of a particular toy you liked as a child before it broke, and you laugh at how much it meant to you—but nothing like daily. Last I heard he's in New York, king of the UN or something, with his wife and two point three children—and her money."

"My ex used to play the same kind of games," said the Californian, sitting up. "My second, Jim. He was all hot and cold agony, so eventually I just chose *for* him. I must have told you about that. I mean, a seven-*teen*-year-old!"

She was laughing. Underwater she was something to see, her long blonde hair streaming from below her mask strap, her arms held properly across her chest and her good legs flexing Tusa Liberators as if she'd been born in fins. Around the crotch of her suit her pubes were brown, but Morton didn't think the hair on her head was bleached except by the sun. Her one-piece suit had a low back and leopard stripes, black on dayglo yellow; she had angular shoulders and nicked-up skin on her back but a nice waist and butt. Now she pushed her shades up on her head, and he noticed again the way her green eyes widened when she talked to people. That morning they'd dived the toilet-bowl wreck, a ship that had gone down with a hold full of plumbing, and from the way she described it afterwards you'd have thought it was Atlantis. She couldn't get over the barnacles on the porcelain.

"The bastard," Pooky said—*bos* tud, it sounded like—and talked on loudly in the expatriate illusion that nobody else around can understand, and Morton quit listening so as not to lose interest in them both. Wedging a cushion under his armpit he noticed Buster grinning across the bridge at him, half a Marlboro in his teeth and a full one sticking out from under the red bandana he'd tied on his head, pirate style. Buster was in his ninth week here on a construction bid that was supposed to have taken two; so far he'd regressed to about high-school age. He was from Kansas, neighbor to Morton's state of Missouri, a coincidence Buster had made much of.

"Salami LAY coon," he said. "Which I just learned."

"*Aleekum issalaam,*" replied Morton, who'd learned the greetings on his first visit, over a year ago now. The captain, a chubby old man in a dirty T-shirt and herringbone pants, turned around from where he was steering the ship with his feet. With his toes on the wooden wheel spokes he grinned and unleashed more Arabic than either of them caught.

"*Hold* on, *hold* on." Buster waved his arms in ferocious mock protest, and the captain shrugged and turned front again, disappointed but unsurprised.

Morton told Buster about his plan for dinner and asked if he wanted in.

Buster grinned. "Pooky and Sis? Okay, but I'd rather go with Greta and Hilda back there. I'd let you have Hilda."

These were the German girls, one of them a stunner, with platinum hair and melon breasts and big child-bearing thighs. The other was strong-bodied too but with a face like cactus. Buster was yukking it up, and Morton was slightly ashamed of himself.

"See what happens," he said. "It's just a thought."

Jackfish Alley was a drift dive: the *Nidia* would drop them off at the southeast tip of the reef and then motor northwest to wait. Ahmed, sounding like a schoolteacher, kept repeating that he wanted everybody to stay together. Morton didn't like the way organized diving was tightening up, though he supposed it was a necessary thing. A lot of the new divers were yahoos like Buster, who liked the scene but not really the water: he got very quiet before a dive and very talkative afterwards. But the group's staying close might give Morton a chance to get to know Sis a bit. When he held her tank for her to grapple into her stab jacket she smiled over her shoulder, and Morton thought, *Hey.* He pulled her hood up, but she shook her head.

"I'd rather be cold and free," she said, smiling again.

What crap, Morton thought, but he liked the white flash of her teeth, and he answered, "I hear ya."

When they hit a cold patch about twenty meters down he tried to distinguish her from the other divers, to see how she was doing. His depth gauge had sand in it and didn't work, but he estimated twenty meters because the reds and yellows of their suits were turning black and gray, everybody's alike now except the Italians' Scubapros, which were pink in the sun and lighter-colored than the others undersea. Sis was ahead of them and her dive partner, Pooky, he thought. She seemed to have changed her mind about the hood.

Then they were all in the alley, gradually descending single file into the crevice, Ahmed in the lead, their breaths lifting and lowering their bodies like nine frogs on a kiddie-go-round. An orange nylon line had been affixed to the face of the reef since Morton had last dived here, the huge eye-bolts still shiny. You were supposed to hold onto the rope. But Buster was already struggling, with too much weight on a belt he'd also hooked up wrong. He kept tilting to his left.

Morton helped him adjust the belt and hopped over him, then over the Italians, until he was one back from Sis. Between them, Pooky seemed to have spotted a head of fan coral, and she dropped another three meters to examine it. Sis didn't seem too interested, but she descended to wait for her partner, and Morton cleared his ears and dropped too, below Buster now, who kept flailing, the dipshit. All you really had to do was give in.

That was what Morton loved about diving: the letting go and going down, weightless. Underwater felt to him not just relaxing or enjoyable but right, *true* to be incommunicado beyond a few broad hand signals, breathing through a tube, your every breath an audible reminder of how close you are to death. More noise than that, even much faster movement than you could manage underwater had come to seem to him like fraud, its urgency exaggerated, a panicky thrash. At eight meters down, the speed that signified was of a whole different order: the quickness of a fish emerging from deep blue, a suddenly recognizable shape in startling color before it was gone, and Morton liked the sure knowledge that such glimpses were all he could expect.

But more and more now, he did need that glimpse. After a few weeks of airports and buses and both sides of hustling in strange languages he would head to a sea, where the fish didn't want so much from him, and he didn't want much from the fish. With the fish it was fine if he was there, but it would be fine without him, too, fine if he lived and fine if he died—which was basically the case with people as well, Morton thought, though people liked to pretend otherwise. So with people he kept thinking it was going to *be* otherwise, ongoing evidence to the contrary. Back home one day, his wife had just told him she wanted a different life, no offense, offering by way of explanation phrases she'd read in magazines and heard on talk shows, as near as Morton could figure, because he'd heard them many times before, just never before from her. Even his kids didn't seem too surprised, and when he'd asked for a leave from the Postal Service to get his bearings his supervisor of fifteen years had just said that if Morton didn't want to work, many others sure did. So he'd sold his share of the house to his wife in a perfectly civil transaction and taken off to see if he, too, couldn't find another kind of life, one where people and emotions didn't seem so much like commodities with a money-back guarantee: full refund or exchange if you wanted it. He thought he'd try some of those places with the interesting stamps.

Well, now he'd seen them, and he'd met the new people and done the new things and come to believe that no, places might look different but were basically the same, some prettier than others but all backdrops for the same old life. Nationalities and names, faces and races might vary, but what everybody wanted was food, sex, and money, in one order or another, and maybe, like Pooky, a story to make things seem otherwise. Morgan knew he'd been on the road longer than was good for him, but he still hadn't found any place he wanted to stay longer than any other.

He *had* found diving, though, off Geraldton, Australia, where the reefs were bigger than Sinai's, and not as dead yet. The coral everywhere was dying, of course: all the divers said so, and all the divers killed it. Morton could see, or could imagine he could, the colors dimmed every time he returned to a site, the fish straying further from the reefs in search of food. Even the populations seemed visibly to change: more goldfish, he'd noticed here this time, ordinary goldfish like you could buy in a plastic bag at Pets Plus back home, and more of the poisonous puffers, since nothing ate them, and fewer parrotfish. He couldn't really work up much indignation over it, partly because everybody tried to and partly because he knew he wasn't going to stop diving. And partly, too, because it wasn't the natural world that he loved about diving most of all. For all his contempt for Buster, Morton had to admit he didn't know much more about marine life himself, not to mention the finer points of scuba. He was into diving for the feel of it, the silence, and the danger ever-present but actually remote, if you were moderately careful, with a nark buzz afterwards as a bonus.

Pooky turned and waved to catch his eye. At first he thought she was having trouble with her regulator.

But she was just hovering, legs and fins down straight, to point at the fan coral. He followed her finger, expecting to see a big grouper, maybe, that she feared was a shark. When he didn't and motioned *All OK* she waved her arms and pointed again, lips bulging around her mouthpiece as if she were trying to talk. Her skin was yellow, her eyes blinking above an inch of water in her goggles. Now she was using both hands, fingers spread, to indicate something, and Morton looked at the coral again and saw the stream of silver fish: thousands of them, a large, dense school, almost transparent at this depth except for black eyes and a shimmer to their scales, all of them swimming down through the fan coral. Pooky was bringing her hands together in slow-motion applause.

He signed that he'd seen and noticed Ahmed finning back to investigate the holdup. Pooky was still trying to tell him something, and he wished she'd leave him alone. Sis, for some reason, had faced around toward deep blue, sprawled out in an awkward-looking fashion, and he reconsidered his plans for the evening: dinner by himself in his room, white cheese with flatbread and Stella beers, maybe later go down to watch Superchannel in the lobby or somewhere he wasn't likely to run into Buster. Or find a shop with a night dive, which was the closest thing to what he really wanted to do: *stay down here.*

Then he looked up and saw Buster gesticulating wildly, extending both arms and jerking his thumbs backwards at his tank, and Ahmed swam back to read on Buster's pressure gauge what Morton should have kept an eye on and might have expected: that Buster had breathed too fast and was down around 40 bars already.

So they'd all have to go up. Even through two pairs of goggles, Morton could see reproach on Ahmed's face, for having ignored a dive buddy like this.

⚬

The German beauty surfaced mad at the short dive, her words indistinguishable to Morton from her cough. Ahmed came up with Buster, who promptly floated on his back. Morton paddled over and apologized.

"I coulda *died,*" Buster told the sky. "Jeez, I coulda *died.*"

"You were never going to die," Ahmed said, but when Morton hastened to corroborate this Ahmed shot him another sharp look. No mistake: he'd fucked up. Ahmed twisted around in the water to count heads, blew water out of his whistle, and signaled for the *Nidia*, two longs and two shorts.

Next to Morton, Pooky was inflating her stab jacket, still trying to tell him something. Then she snatched her hood off and he saw that it wasn't Pooky at all but the Californian, Sis, who'd been beside him all along.

"Didn't you love those glassfish!" she hollered across the waves. With her goggles off he could see her eyes widen. "Weren't they beautiful?"

When he tried to respond he got a mouthful of saltwater, and Sis spun around in the water and paddled off, still exclaiming, toward Pooky, who'd surfaced ten feet further on, and Morton floated on his back and watched his dreams of job and girl float away with the clouds. He could tell when the boat was approaching by the diesel fumes, which made him slightly sick.

Word of what he'd done, or hadn't, got around the boat like blood in the water. The German beauty shivered him with a look, toweling a backside that *he'd* certainly never touch now, and when he sat on a bench in the stern beside the Italian couple, they stood up and moved to the bow. Nobody was talking to Buster, either, except Ahmed, who took him up to the bridge.

Morton stretched out on his back, draped an arm over his eyes, and listened to empty tanks thokking into the wooden storage racks and suits being hung over the gunnels to dry. From beneath his arm he saw tea glasses on a tin tray that the barefoot mate was offering, but Morton pretended to be asleep. He heard Pooky and Sis installing themselves on the bench opposite him. Pooky was still oblivious that anyone else spoke English, and he couldn't avoid a tale about a Jamaican boyfriend who'd insisted on packing her bags whenever they took a plane trip until she finally wised up: to escape his smuggling network she'd had to cut off her hair and her pant legs in a Houston airport loo. Morton tightened his arm around his head and faced the sea.

After a brief silence he heard Sis's voice.

"Weren't those glassfish in the fan coral amazing, though? The way they switched and cut, all together, like they'd rehearsed or something? Like a ballet! Like they were performing, and for *us*, because I saw them just swimming along before they veered and converged on the coral, as if they hadn't seen us before that moment. Two schools of them came, thousands from each side, and at first they all just hung above it, quivering, like dancers waiting in the wings for the orchestra to start up. Then they dropped, flowing down into the fans in groups that split, almost symmetrically, two and then four, then eight . . . and at the bottom they gathered and split again and streamed up the sides to start over, like a second movement. But *this* time . . ."

Morton didn't even think he was narked after such a short, shallow dive, but the bright energy of the voice entered him, with its familiar inflections from home, and beneath the black weight of his arm he began to see again the glassfish ballet, the lines and the curves and the rhythms and the colors of it. And then he saw the two divers hovering nearby—Sis, pointing, and himself, blind—and the excitement he felt now took the form of the thought that what she'd been trying to show him was what he'd been looking all over the world for, not a place or a thing at all but a way to look at places and things and people, too. It had been there all along, everywhere he'd been and at home as well, and it always would be, if he could remember to keep sight of it, and the mountains behind Sharm were still umber cones in the distance when he sat up and interrupted a new story by Pooky to ask Sis if she'd have dinner with him.

"Just the two of us."

"Oh!" she said, bringing a hand to her breastbone, fingertips just below her clavicles. She had freckles on her chest and blunt thumbs. He couldn't see her eyes because she kept her space shades on to consider him, cautiously, not smiling yet. "Tonight? Well . . ."

Just dinner, he thought. *Please.*

ORACLE: The Oracle

Owl's wife went home at Christmas and won't be back, according to her airport declaration and frequent calls and e-mails since, so Owl has to find someone else to go with him to the Siwa oasis, a trip he's been planning all fall. The advantage to Beth's leaving is more fun for him, he tells people who seem about to express concern, a quip that works best with an audience who likes them both, but it's true he's been losing himself in Ptolemy, who documented Alexander the Great's trek to Siwa to consult the oracle at the temple of Amun. At sixty-eight, Owl has no sense at all of duplicating the young warrior's mission, but he's never seen Siwa, and he's always wanted to, and he'll be damned if he'll stay home just because Beth's afraid there's going to be a war. He'd go alone, but the Western Desert might be a bit rugged even if he were twenty years younger. None of the people he works with now, TOEFL teachers half his age or less, will even deign to hear out his itinerary, though he can barely stand a workday with most of them anyway, let alone twelve hours in his Fiat.

Finally, the day before break starts, he sees two backpackers in a tourist restaurant, Felfela's on Talaat Harb Street, which has been almost empty this year. A boy and a girl—Americans, he can tell from their posture across the dimly lit back room, which is actually quite crowded this evening, but that's not why he takes the table next to theirs.

"Just say the word and we'll stay strangers," he says, sliding in against the wall. "But you look like you could use some help with that menu."

They're holding it between them like a map with no marked north, though everything on it's either translated or described, to the extent that "herbs and bean fried patty under oil" indicates much. They thank him, still blinking and baffled from the streets of Cairo. Their packs, huge constructions of foam, brightly colored nylon, and aluminum tubing, are arranged around their table like sandbags.

He provides some description of the entrées, and when everyone's decided (for himself he orders the pigeon, to the amazement of his new friends) he finds out that they're year-abroad students, on break from what he thinks must be a fairly delightful course of study in Florence. They've come south from Crete, which turned out to be colder than some travel agent had promised them, and in Egypt they've found nothing but dirt, cancelled tours, and stomach trouble.

"Have you got a hotel yet?"

They look at each other and hesitate. Then the girl, Gwen, faces Owl and spills. "We *thought* we did. But we gave the fax with our reservation to a guy who offered to take us there, and we forgot to ask for it back when he dropped us off here. In between he took us to a building with no glass in the windows. He got out there and talked to some people, then got back in and tried to tell us something sad, judging from his eyes. The Hotel Fun Duke, it was supposed to be called. I remember the name, because we joked about it before we left. We knew we were taking a chance at a hotel called The Fun Duke. Especially Keith."

The boy grimaces, and she pokes him. *Funduq* is the Arabic word for hotel, but Owl decides not to bother. "I'll get you set up," he says. "I know a few places. Don't worry."

"You can't even read the signs here." Keith makes it sound like the sign-makers' fault. "And the next ferry back to Crete doesn't leave Alexandria for a week. We don't mind roughing it . . . but *this!*"

He waves a hand around one of the most reliable places to eat Owl knows, without paying big-hotel prices, though it's true the plastic vine décor is overdone. Keith has longish hair tied with what appears to be a bootlace around his head, but his squint and jutting chin make him look less hippie-like than car-salesman or ball-player-like, Owl thinks: someone who thrives on controlled aggression. Keith's vigilant eyes are far apart, and he has a way of pushing his face forward as he talks, as if he's daring you to take a poke at his jaw.

Gwen looks as if she's considering whether to take him up on it.

"This whole trip was my idea, you see, and he won't let me forget it."

Her freckled complexion provides Owl the mnemonic *Gueneverean*; he knows his own memory. He also knows a little something about tension among traveling companions, too, and he thinks he can save these two, not just from spending a night on the streets but from each other.

"Nice packs," he diverts, gesturing to their fort and thinking that what they'd really like is the Maniel Palace, where Club Med rents out rooms around a pool and runs a disco at night. Some of the people he works with go there every weekend, just for relief from traffic noise and smog. But instead, once the bread and baba ganoush have arrived and they're all safely munching, tummies and tempers padded, Owl mentions Siwa.

"I'm planning to drive out tomorrow," he drops, aware that he's making the oasis sound more like a suburb than the trek it'll surely be. But the part about planning is no lie. "Hey! There's room in the car! You guys want to come along?"

Again the kids look at each other. Owl's a big man, and he knows he can seem imposing, with his veiny beak of a nose and tufts of white hair around his ears, carcinoma scars on his bald pate. *Here's a possibility—but we don't even know this guy,* Gwen tells Keith with her eyes, and his respond: *Well, what* else *are we going to do? But you decide, as usual.* The expressiveness of their private communication in public reminds him of Beth, and so does the way Gwen composes herself, deciding on her approach as she turns to say, "Oh, I don't know if we—*thank* you, of

course, and for your other help tonight, but I *really* don't think we can
. . ."

Owl's on familiar ground.

"You're quite right, of course. Plenty of adventure for you right here.
If you let me see your guidebook, I'll give you some ideas." He points
to a *Lonely Planet* in a windowed pocket of one of the packs, withdraws
half-glasses from his own breast pocket, and, when Keith has gotten the
book out and handed it over, adopts his most grandfatherly tone, licking
his fingers as he pages through.

"Nice section on Siwa here, actually. Beautiful, isn't it?"

The kids examine the pictures, huddled against the commotion of a
family of eight installing themselves at the next table. "Is it *quiet* there?"
Behind the busy arms of waiters setting their orders down, Gwen's eyes
show the answer she needs.

"And *clean*?" says Keith, staring with dismay at what the waiter calls
his hamburger. "Is this a *clean* oasis, at least?"

The broiled bird on Owl's plate looks like exactly what it is, only
greasier, and he wishes he'd ordered the lentil soup and felafel-and-egg
sandwich he came in for, instead of showing off. He leans across the space
between his table and the backpackers'.

"Clean as sand, my friends. Quiet as sunlight."

The look they share this time is hopeful, and by the time they've agreed
to a departure time the next morning, Owl believes he's invited them
more for their sake than for his own.

He's at their hotel (they said they didn't care about money, so he
dropped them at the Semiramis, where the same doorman in epaulettes
who unloaded their packs from his old Fiat loads it up again now) at five
o'clock sharp, because that's how he likes to travel, wider awake than he's
felt in the mornings for weeks; he was up past midnight, too, packing the
car, which he'd had tuned up and equipped with new shocks and struts

the week before, thanks to the Boy Scouts a half-century ago. What he'd really like to show these kids is the delta road, with its water buffaloes turning *sakia* pumps in the fields and cabbages the size of shrubs, with maybe a stop for tea in Tanta, but there's no predicting the roads beyond Alex or how long they might take to navigate in the heat of the day, so he heads out to the desert highway.

On Rodah Island he avoids passing the Maniel Palace rather than risk the kids' recognizing it from some Club Med poster somewhere and having second thoughts, not that they seem awake enough to do anything but bounce along and blink out the window at the already active Sharia al Ahram, once they've crossed the Gizah bridge. When he asks, they each say they liked the accommodations, but they do it separately, taking turns to speak, as if the tension from last night re-mains unresolved. Even the pyramids—which Owl can't see himself as he searches for the turn-off but which should be visible, he announces, out the back window once he's turned, backlit by a brightening sky if not the actual sunrise yet—don't animate them much. Gwen, in the front, glances over her shoulder and reflects politely that they're probably the oldest thing she's ever seen.

"How about dirt?" Owl winks, but she looks put-upon, her eyes slits and her head at a quizzical angle, the ends of her copper-colored hair grazing her lap. She's worn shorts, which might become a problem be-yond Alex or even there, given fundamentalism these days, but he wants to wait before bringing up that particular topic of conversation. The sun comes up on billboards and plastic bags choking the rocks beside the road.

"Oldest *man-made* things," she says. "I knew we shouldn't have agreed to travel with a teacher."

That's what he told them last night, and it's true that teaching has kept him abroad for thirty years, though about all it brings in now is pocket money and visas. And the term seems so inadequate to the possibilities that a road trip represents that by the time they reach Sadat City, which looks like a huge, empty parking garage beyond the highway, he's deep into the whole complex story of his life abroad, or at least the most entertaining parts of it (though Keith, who's begun snoring in the back, will have to be filled in later). Owl's been teaching abroad since his own kids were in school: first at the Lycée Américaine in Paris, then the Roberts School in Istanbul; then in Libreville, Gabon; then Manilla, for the military; for a business school in Tokyo; for Aramco, in Saudi; elsewhere. And for every place a story. "Name a spot," he likes to say, "and if I haven't lived there I've lived within a twin-engine flight of it."

Gwen's head's on that angle, her hair to her lap.

"Buenos Aires."

"Except South America and Australia. And the USSR, as we knew it fondly. And Tito's Yugoslavia, Hoxha's Albania, and so on."

"And Mao's China, I suppose. How about Bombay?"

Owl's impressed. "I considered a school in Delhi. But most people there speak better English than I do."

"Bangkok."

"I spent some time in Saigon, when it was called that. Why don't we move around the alphabet a little?"

She came so close so soon that he's moderately rattled. He doesn't talk about his years with the State Department, though wherever he goes, his first career usually comes back at him in some way, either factually or in some wild rumor straight out of Graham Greene. On his own, he rarely looks back at it.

"Zimbabwe," Gwen says.

He's spent some time in Swaziland, visiting friends one summer, but that twin-engine line is like anything else: hold it up to the light too long and it's going to fade. Owl begins fussing with the air conditioning. Even working properly, it's about as efficient as an ice cube in the vent;

he forgot to have it checked when he had the tune-up. But there's no distracting this gal, who's like a dog with a bone.

"Is the Kalahari like this desert?" The hair around her face is damp already; darkened strands stick to her forehead and cheeks.

"In some ways they're quite similar. No water, for example. Want some, by the way? You're very knowledgeable, Gwen."

She accepts the compliment along with the still-cool plastic bottle of Baraka from the floorboards behind him. Pointing out the window at the sign for Wadi Natruun, Owl tells her what he remembers about the seventeen-hundred-year-old Coptic monasteries while she leans forward, head to dash, and ties her hair up off her neck with an elastic band Owl thought was a bracelet. They finish at about the same time, she tying and he talking, and he's thinking of a next topic when she reaches over her shoulder to lock her door, nestles against it, and says, "Nap time."

In a minute, as if she and Keith have agreed not even to occupy the same state of consciousness, the boy's jaw juts between the seats.

"What were you two talking about?"

Exceptionally, Owl doesn't feel like summing up his travels again, after the grilling Gwen gave him. "Nothing, really," he says. "Deserts and monasteries. And which do *you* prefer?"

He's just trying for some banter, but Keith's eyeballs fairly quiver in an attempt to tell what Owl means and whether he, Keith, is being made fun of. Today he's tied his hair back in a tail so tiny it looks like a bun, a style that suits his angular, go-getter features no more than the headband did, and in a reversal of the kind of speculation Owl himself often invites, he wonders if Keith is CIA; maybe the war on terror has lowered the age for recruits. He hopes it's the vibration of the rearview mirror that makes the boy's scowl seem so ferocious, but as they rattle on—*did the jack come loose under the trunk, or what?*—Keith settles back with his arms crossed, positioning himself as if to keep an eye on the front seat.

Owl looks at Gwen. The air conditioning is definitely kaput, and he hopes she's comfortable. She does look it: her eyelids are translucent, and air from her open window ruffles strands on the top of her head. Her posture against the door reminds him of all the times Beth—or Toni, his daughter—has ridden beside him like that, and he drifts off into places where no air conditioning is needed.

In al Amiriya, outside Alex, the gauge is at half-full, but from now on everything will be less certain, so when Owl is sure he's on the coastal highway, not his first turnoff by any means, he stops at a station whose red, white, and yellow tiles look brand new. The fumes wake his passengers.

Do they need to use restrooms? Stretch their legs? Buy Sport Colas, Rocket Bars? Owl's in full tour-guide mode, his smile wide, but when Gwen straightens up beside her open door and stretches, a uniformed attendant at the next island turns to gawk: her arms and legs are golden in the sun, and Owl feels he has to convene a little conference. Gwen says she's been "culturally cautioned" before, and from a pocket in the backpack Keith's been leaning against she pulls out a rainbow-colored scarf, gauzy but huge, and wraps it around her waist before heading toward the station—where, thinking of cultural caution, Owl can only hope she finds more than a porcelain-edged hole. He unloads the trunk and battens down the jack, tightening the oversized butterfly nut as tight as it'll go. Faithful Fiona, at least, is traveling as well as ever: over two hundred klicks, and not a half-liter of oil down.

Then they're spinning along the Khalig el Arab, the Mediterranean sparkling on their right. Sometimes it's no more than a ribbon at the horizon, striped in multiple shades of brilliant blue, but they can smell the salt, and the suggestion that the water lapping against these shores must have also bathed the shores of Europe infuses the car with a new sense of optimism that even Owl, who loves this other part of the world best, can feel. Gwen's in the backseat now, trailing her scarf out the window. She and Keith launch into a repertoire of songs Owl's never heard of, so they teach him. Traffic thins, each vehicle more and more of an event. He teaches them "Mares Eat Oats"—first the tune, then the spelling—and even Keith smiles. The scarf is so long Owl can see it through the back window. Some of its threads are metallic, rippling and glinting in the sun like a sparkler.

For a good way, they don't see the water, and the gaiety dies down. The nature of the sand changes. No gold dunes here but streaks, white and gray, like blistered paint on old wood. The sky becomes white. There's an occasional rock.

"Rommel country," Owl shouts over the engine noise at el Alamein. It's been some time since anyone spoke. "Rommel and Montgomery. Ike was here, too. Due west we'll hit Sidi Barraani, which was taken and retaken by Italians, Brits, Germans, maybe some Free French in there too before we Yanks arrived—taken by everyone but Arabs. Even now, it's a Swiss developer, I believe, who's building condos on the old battlefield."

Sure enough, in a few miles they can see a row of arched white balconies facing the sea like a line of skulls.

Keith has a question, Owl can tell in peripheral vision, so he turns.

"When's lunch?"

"Marsa Matruuh. Another hour. No sweat."

But he nudges the speedometer needle up, because besides food there, they'll need permission papers, and the office might close at noon, for who knows how long. It might be closed anyway, for any reason, and without papers, they'd just have to turn around and go back. All this information would be in the kids' guidebook, though Owl doubts they read it; he himself hasn't exactly been forthcoming on this particular point.

So to keep his own mind as well as theirs off this potentially volatile topic he brings up another: current events. The last thing Owl paid attention to was a Security Council timetable that went nowhere, but Keith proves to be up on all the particulars, from the number of that resolution through 1441, explaining them all like college-basketball play-offs. He knows all the players' names—Jack Straw, Hans Blix, Mohammed el Baradei, Ahmed Chalabi, Ari Fleischer—and all the background. "*Every*thing's involved in this decision," he says, animated now. "The Shoe Bomber. Bali. North Korea. Chechens in Moscow. Even those snipers in D.C. Everything has a bearing, and it's all coming to a head. Do we wait for the UN or go in now?"

In the streets of Cairo in recent weeks, Owl's caught everything from cheers to hisses that he imagines stem from the debate, but from this particular point in the Western Desert, the likelihood of war seems remote to him—not so much the likelihood as the *concept* of it, the whole point of such trips, in fact.

Now it's Gwen's chin between the seats. "In Florence we can stroll piazzas, tour the Uffizi, and shop for cheeses, wines, and vegetables, but most evenings we've been spending in front of CNN."

Owl asks why they risked coming at all.

"Tickets were so cheap!"

They say it together, united in delight.

Luckily, the offices of Wadi el Giddid Province are open, and clearance comes through with the usual suspicion-fraught delays but no real hitch, thanks in some degree to the bureaucratic patience that the developing world has taught Owl. He collected the kids' passports and paid the fees himself, less out of generosity than worry they'd gum up the works, while they shopped for lunch in the market across the street.

From the steps of the police station, he spots them between two carrot carts, carrying a huge, multi-colored wicker hamper between them. Across it they seem to be arguing. Gwen, who needed no reminder this time about covering her legs, has wrapped her shawl so tight she can only take tiny steps, and Keith seems to hold her pace against her. Owl gets to the car first.

"What's that?" he says when they arrive, both stony-faced and sweating.

"Lunch, for starters." Keith drops his side of the basket in the dirt, but Gwen holds onto hers.

"And a souvenir to carry it in."

Owl opens the lid and sees newspaper-wrapped bundles inside. The hamper's the size of a small bathtub. "The perfect souvenir for backpackers," he remarks. "Where are we going to put it?"

Keith pushes his face toward Gwen. "See?"

"Fine." She gets in the passenger's seat and slams the door. "Leave it here. It only cost seven dollars."

Robed and grizzled men gather to speculate loudly on what these foreigners' problem might be. Owl puts the documents in the glove box, hands the wrapped food to Gwen, and unlocks the trunk, where he looks around for something to lash the hamper to the roof with. Finding twine, he enlists Keith and someone from the group of commentators beside them, a cross-eyed man in a dirty galabeya, and they get to work. The job itself isn't hard, but it takes some time, because periodically they have to stop to fend off suggestions from volunteers and resolve disputes between them and the cross-eyed man. Finally the hamper's secured, and Owl passes out a fistful of blue twenty-five-piastre notes and starts the engine. He's sopping wet and worried about the time.

So he passes up Cleopatra's Bath and the beach at Agiibah, which under different circumstances might have made for a pleasant place to eat, stopping only to fill up the tank and add a half-liter of oil at what might be the last station they see until they pass it again on the way back. Before the road turns into the desert for good, he points out their last look at the aquamarine sea, but Gwen is busy tearing into the newspapers on the dashboard and sniffing at what's inside. Then she speaks the words that echo in the otherwise silent car for the next hour and a half:

"They call this *cheese?*"

A dot on the horizon turns out to be a tent, square and black.

"Made of goat hair," Owl says, pointing as they approach it. "By Bedouins."

The sound of his own voice is strange. He tells them about the Bedouins he knew in Jordan, who resisted refrigeration and indoor plumbing when the government relocated them, but his passengers watch the tent pass with no apparent interest. Keith has affixed himself by the ears to some sort of electronic device. In the rearview mirror, whose vibrations are worse than ever on the patchy road, his red face blurs.

"Fuck you!" he shouts suddenly, very loud.

Reflexively, Owl's foot comes off the accelerator. He's startled, then incredulous: the invective seems a sudden resumption of Keith's previous spat with Gwen, whose left arm rises like a charmed snake, her middle finger rising like a smaller one from her fist, aimed over her shoulder. Keith leans up to grab it and twist.

"Ow ow ow!" Gwen says.

"Reminds me of a story," Owl says desperately, but it works: Keith lets go and slams back in his seat, and Gwen, her hand recovered, turns to Owl.

"What does?"

"That tent." He has no idea *what* story yet, but the kids wait, apparently glad to be kept from each other's throats, and between the engine drone and the vast, empty sameness of the desert, what comes to the forefront of Owl's mind is the time Beth bought that silk in

Damascus. Maybe the goat hair triggered it, he doesn't know, and now he doesn't care who listens: he's given himself over to his story already. He accelerates, and his shoulders relax. He grips the steering wheel at ten and two o'clock.

"I'd landed a job in Tehran," he begins. "This was just before the Shah fell, which is what happened to *that* job, but for a while I made an obscene amount of money teaching the kids of Rockwell and Bell Helicopter technicians, so I didn't want to believe the unrest would amount to anything. Anyway, on our way back after one of our paid visits home, we had a layover in Damascus. We went to the *souk*, and Beth fell in love with a certain silk. She bought a whole bolt of it—for gifts, was her original intent. But a few months later, when the trouble got so bad that we couldn't go out to a movie, Beth took up sewing. She wasn't an experienced seamstress, and she hadn't packed any patterns. But she *was* an experienced expat, so she knew how to make do. Most of her clothes were durable, practical, style-less things, and she had this pantsuit from an L.L. Bean catalogue—woods attire, with roomy pants and breathing vents in the shoulders of the jacket—that she copied exactly. Well, by the time we were evacuated she had not one but *three* of these pantsuits, all hand-sewn out of a gorgeous green silk with a design like a peacock's tail."

Owl laughs. Gwen's listening: her head's on that angle, her red hair catching all the milky light there is to catch. Keith's got his arms crossed, but he's removed his headset.

"Thing was, though: she just looked ridiculous in them. She wore one on the Galaxy transport that airlifted us to Athens, and the airmen were laughing. When we landed at Edwards, Beth's sister, who'd flown in from Wisconsin to meet us, was convinced I'd finally driven Beth nuts. She wasn't, of course, but she'd been shaken up more than I realized, and she wore a green silk pantsuit to every cocktail party in Madison that summer. I had to convince her to wear something else to Clark's wedding. Clark's my son.

"Anyway, soon enough Beth was laughing about our time in Iran, but when those pantsuits wore out, she kept wearing the jackets, and when the elbows on the last jacket shredded she patched them with felt, and she wears that thing still, sitting out on the porch of our cottage on Lake Monona. She always wanted a place in the States to return to, you see, so back when I thought I was going to be teaching at the Roberts School forever, we put a down payment on that cottage . . . geez, thirty-five years ago now."

He's forgotten Gwen and Keith.

"It was just after I'd renewed my contract in Paris. We were going home for the summer, but first we took a road trip to Brittany, and on the way, we stopped at the cathedral at Chartres. I remember standing in the blue-speckled light of that amazing rose window, and Beth turned to me and said, 'It's like the light on a screened-in porch. Someday, Owl, I want a house with a screened-in porch.' Seven centuries worth of architecture, and she was thinking about an all-weather porch. Well, now she's got it."

He's hunched over the wheel, squinting through his driving glasses at a picture of Beth he can see in the road ahead of them: in a rocking chair in her suit, doing something in her lap—knitting, which she took up recently, or solving one of the crossword puzzles she used to bring by the suitcase-full whenever he got a new assignment. He can see her face so clearly he's *not* seeing what's actually there in the road ahead of them until Keith pokes his shoulder with a forefinger and shouts, "What's that? Owl, what's *that*?"

It's a roadblock. Some fifty yards ahead, a bent cattle gate sags across the highway beside an outhouse-sized guardhouse with hand-painted stripes, diagonal red on white, which leans back toward the desert as if blown by wind. Owl brakes to avoid hitting a soldier who comes out, and

Gwen braces a hand against the dashboard. The Fiat's engine dies, the car windows fill with dust, and everything's suddenly very, very quiet.

On a stool inside the hut sits a fat man in a black woolen uniform and white loafers. The guard wears parts of three uniforms, drab and khaki with a camouflage cap; his black leather boots fit like galoshes. At Owl's window, he speaks over the roof of the car to the fat man in the hut. Their tone is serious.

"Something's happened," Gwen whispers. "I just know it. The bombing of Baghdad. It's started."

"Nothing's happened. This is what we got the papers for." Owl takes them from the glovebox to hand out to the guard, who carries them to the hut. "Just keep smiling."

They do, but due to various misunderstandings and points of obtuseness, it costs them thirty more pounds and Keith's music machine to get through, for which price they receive not only free passage but a bulging black plastic bag that the fat man, smiling now, runs out of the hut at the last second to insist they take.

"Three cantaloupes!" Gwen discovers as Owl, waving out the window, stomps on the accelerator before there's another delay.

The fruit is delicious, but Keith's full of bitter remarks about blackmail, and when Owl tries to set a context of relative wealth—in six months, the guard might make what one of their backpacks cost—Gwen's still-scared face tells him that's not the point.

"It'll be all right," he says, almost reaching over to pat her chiffon-scarfed knee, but with her untouched fruit in her lap she crosses her arms across her chest, and when Keith's diatribe is over, silence fills the car the way the dust did, the engine sounding ominous now.

Owl notices no telephone lines anymore (*When did THAT happen?*) and has to admit: *This is FAR*. He checks his watch and drives for what he thinks is five minutes, but when he looks at his watch again, a half-hour has passed. Sometimes it's the other way around. Other times he thinks he smells smoke, but he never sees any.

The Fiat spins on.

An old bus comes from where they're heading, the first vehicle they've seen since Matruh, its sheet-metal sides flapping. Dark faces look down at them from every window. Keith turns to watch the bus recede, then bounces up between the front seats, rocking the car a bit. This time he stays between the seats, watching the road with Owl and Gwen.

Eventually it begins a slow descent through cut limestone, and then, around a curve, the tires change pitch. The pavement's stopped: they're entering the oasis. Arching the road is a rusted tin sign in several languages. "Welcome to Our Toun," says the English.

Siwa is small yards and gardens, fences of bound reeds, stands of palms, flowers in ditches: sudden lushness out of nothing, and Owl imagines how Alexander must have felt, after not a twelve-hour drive but weeks on horseback, through a dust storm that almost swallowed half his men and a rainstorm that saved them. Ptolemy says they were guided by serpents with human voices. *Easy to believe, in the desert,* Owl thinks. Easy, too, upon reaching the oasis, to feel that your troubles are over for good.

So he's caught off guard when Gwen lifts her head from where it's eased back against her door and says, "I was dreaming about silk, Owl. Green silk. Why isn't your wife here *now,* anyway? I mean with *you*?"

The upstairs stinks a good bit, though the guidebook called this the better of the two rest houses, and the doors are so loose in their jambs that they rattle when people walk past. Rooms are on one side of a long corridor whose other side looks out over a heap of old tires. An old man who insisted on toting the kids' packs walks gracefully ahead of them, one pack on his back and the other on his head. Owl carries his own supremely efficient travel kit under his arm. Keith and Gwen's room—the man at the front desk said nothing about their different last names, which Owl had worried about—is the next one down from his, and when they've peeked inside, they look back at him with dismay.

Owl all but jumps inside his own room and shuts the door, after a fashion.

Sewage from toilets causes the smell, but at least each room has a toilet. There's no soap in the sink, though there is on the cracked mirror of Owl's dressing table: white script in the snake shape of "Allah." From next door comes a brief, sharp squabble, but then the quiet is so deep Owl can hear the convulsive braying of a donkey tied to a palm tree half a mile away, as he can see when he steps out onto his whitewashed balcony.

"We can't stay here."

Owl doesn't turn around. He knows it's Gwen, and he knows the look on her face in his doorway. But he's not as annoyed now as he is weary and embarrassed, even humiliated by the way he answered her question in the car. *My wife's not here because she hates me* is what came out of his mouth.

"In our room there's a—"

"We can't stay anywhere else, Gwen. I'm sorry. Let's wash up and rest a bit before we take a look around. Meet on the veranda in a half-hour, say."

In a few seconds he hears the sound of the door closing, then the donkey again.

In the lobby a Danish archaeologist, according to a dated signature in the lower left-hand corner, has left behind a map he made of the entire oasis, which includes several villages and lakes and smaller bodies of water; beside it is a sign in larger, rougher handwriting: "Please respect our Siwan customs. Avoid shorts, alcohol, or public shows of affection." Owl forgot to remind Gwen about the scarf, but she and Keith come downstairs in jeans, observing the last item to the letter, and they pull wicker chairs to opposite sides of the veranda's marble steps.

Owl—lightly, he hopes—suggests checking out downtown Siwa: "The main drag, so to speak." The other two nod, once apiece, and on the dirt road toward what looks to be a central square a few hundred yards in, they maintain their distance from each other.

He tries to forget everything but Siwa. A turbaned Berber is sweeping a yard with a twig-bristle broom. Two robed men walk past, their little fingers linked. Under a date palm, four pink-uniformed schoolgirls are playing a game with a piece of string. None seem self-conscious or even aware they're being gawked at. By comparison, the travelers seem awkward, clumsy, too big. Gwen lopes, her hands in her back pockets, her hair in a loose braid now. Keith strides, lips compressed, looking skeptical of everything he sees. Owl, for the first time he can remember, feels self-conscious, out of place.

At the near edge of the square they see bicycles for rent, three wobbly contraptions in front of a corrugated-tin lean-to. Keith suggests they rent them before somebody else does, and Owl admits it's a good idea: they're not quite the only guests at the rest house, and beyond the square he can see other foreigners on bicycles, weaving among the Siwans like trained bears in a wax museum. In the lean-to a barefoot kid with a denim jacket over his galabeya and an Air Chief transistor radio in his breast pocket has such surprisingly good English he can hold his own with Keith, who finds fault with the gears on the bike he gets, as if he'll need more than one on these flat roads. Owl's own machine doesn't even have a seat but a seat-shaped plank covered in fringed plastic.

They pedal toward the fortress that dominates the square, its bricks made of mud so saline that rain has melted them.

"Cool!" Keith says. "Let's explore it." Gwen wants to see the sunset, which her guidebook recommends watching from a certain shore of the largest lake. Owl's watch says five-thirty; he suggests splitting up for a while, with a rendez-vous at the rest house a half hour before sundown.

"Fine," Gwen says, and, free at last, he leaves them both there to ride off in what he thinks is the direction of the Temple of Amun.

It's supposed to be a couple of kilometers out, near a village called Aghurmi. The wheel ruts in the road are like petrified ropes. He passes donkey carts, ox carts, and a Daihatsu truck full of taro, he thinks, though he doesn't know if fall is taro season or not. Siwans raise a hand or nod to return his greetings. On either side of him is more greenery than he's seen in months: date palms and reed fences and flowers in ditches he thinks are Turban buttercups—*Ranunculus asiaticus* pops into his head from some textbook or article he can't place. The road winds and crosses other roads, sometimes marked with cardboard arrows, sometimes not: it's a maze, but Owl's in no hurry. He ambles along, the top speed of his knock-fendered klunker about matching his own top speed. The foliage becomes denser: branches canopy the road. Half hidden in vines, a mud-brick house appears, its doors and windows dark. The courtyard is vacant but strung with washing, and Owl figures he's taken a wrong turn somewhere when he sees, in a clearing across the road, the hearth-shaped facade of what must be the Temple of Amun.

He stashes the bicycle and climbs. Parts of stairways remain, and parts of walls, with parts of windows in them; no trace of a roof. From part of a landing, he makes out what must have been a courtyard, and behind it the sanctuary. He scrambles up to a shelf that must have been a floor, until the middle caved in, and sidles toward a jagged window in the back wall. The masonry he's gripping changes texture. Between his fingers are inscriptions, lines and curves and symbols he can't read. There's a man with the head of a ram. There's a woman, he thinks, in a double crown.

He remembers what he's read. Twenty-two hundred years ago, Alexander stood on this spot, or feet from it. He'd just consolidated his empire from Macedonia through Gaza to here. But he came to Siwa in a time of trouble, to ask the oracle for advice before confronting an enemy, Darius of Persia. Not even his friend Ptolemy knew the questions Alexander asked, but the scholars Owl's read have imagined their gist. Alexander was twenty-four, and he wanted to know what Owl can wonder still: *who am I, and what should I be doing?*

No one knows the answers he got, either, but Owl fills them in along these lines: *there's god in you, boy, so you'd better act like it.* Because from then on, that's what Alexander did. When Darius ran, Alexander wouldn't even deign to chase him, pushing on instead as far as India, half conquering and half exploring, sometimes leaving local leaders in place and adopting native clothing himself. He had his weaknesses—mainly drink and women, liking one too much and the other not enough, to Owl's mind—but they didn't stop him. Even when he finally turned back, it was only for the sake of his exhausted men.

Owl could teach a class on him. Through a hole in the back wall, he sees stands of palms, fronds stirring like a whole classroom full of kids with the right answer. But there's no one in front of him now, and the long song of a Hoopoe lark makes him realize how alone he is. Beyond the trees, the clean cliffs and sands of the Libyan Desert drape like linen. The air's so clear, the sky so blue, that it all seems fake. He's sweating from the exertion of his climb, and his mind drifts eight thousand miles away.

Beth hates me so much she stayed home, he told Gwen in the car.

Immediately he tried to laugh, but when something he'd been trying to avoid popped out like that, fast and true, he was too dismayed to do anything but swallow. Now it strikes him that Beth's fear of war was just a good excuse to leave him: the truth is she resents him for the life he's led her through. All the adversities they overcame to form what he thought was such a unique bond were just that for her, adversities.

"Clark has seen the Taj Mahal but never owned a baseball mitt," she screamed at him on the way to the airport. "Antonia can speak five languages—one for each husband."

Well, Clark did have a hell of a time of it for a while, but Owl doubts it was for lack of sporting equipment. The boy's been clean for seven years now, and Toni and number five, the dentist, have three kids already.

Beth wants to watch them grow up. In a letter that arrived last month, she asked him to choose: life with her and the family or life abroad by himself. "What are you after? Where has it gotten you, this incessant travel bug?" Her tone can cut across time zones and generations and bloodlines, too, less a wife's than a disappointed mother's. He hasn't answered her yet. And now, staring out at desert, he considers that she might have a point: where it's all gotten him is bending the ears of hitchhikers and clinging to old rock.

But just then the sun enters a new atmospheric level, the panorama in front of him turns the color of caramel, and light pours through a saddle-shaped ridge to the west like streams of coins.

Two women in the square are watching Keith climb the fortress. Faces hooded, they clutch gray robes around themselves, fists at their chins. As Owl approaches, he can distinguish a herringbone pattern in the cloth and at waist height embroidery, narrow bands of red and orange. Keith's a small figure three-quarters of the way up. Owl stops, whistles, waves. The figure turns and raises an arm to pump a fist. Owl pantomimes, rolling his arms like a referee, clasping them above his head, pointing west: *Where's Gwen? Hurry back to the rest house, or we'll miss the sunset.* The two hoods face him, then each other, and he hears giggling before the women run off. One of them is wearing pink canvas shoes with blue labels on the heels: Keds. The figure on the fortress waves, turns, and climbs.

Back in his room, Owl has stretched out with Ptolemy when he hears rattles and between them a knock, and when he opens the door, there's a freshly showered Gwen, in a terry-cloth bathrobe he can't believe she packed. The dread look she shoots him is left over from his answer in the car, he thinks at first. Then he sees it's worse.

"What's wrong?"

She shakes her head vigorously and makes a grin. She's holding a bottle of Baraka and cradling a bundle of newsprint in the crook of one arm. "I guess we'll miss the sunset, but that's OK. The restaurants looked sort of dodgy, so I bought some bread and fruit and things. Hungry?" Her voice keens with willed cheer.

"Come on in."

Owl's aware of a hole in his sock. He slides on his espadrilles and shuts his bathroom door against the smell. They sit on opposite sides of the sagging bed, where Gwen spreads the newspaper between them. She has bananas, pocket bread, olives, and dates, and seems to have made her peace with feta cheese, too, sawing open its cardboard packaging with a Swiss Army knife twice as thick as Owl's. She tears the bread into wedges to make tiny cheese-and-olive sandwiches. They're not very good, but the work seems to soothe her.

"I found a little store while Keith climbed the fortress. Keith's a climber."

She presses her lips, cuts her eyes away. The rim of one ear splits her wet hair, which is the color of rust in this muted light. She herself smells like some expensive brand of soap, and Owl has certain thoughts, though the age gap here is greater than the length of his marriage. In forty-five years, he hasn't cheated on Beth once, not that he worries so much about virtue, but it always seemed like so much trouble. Take your chances on things that count, he's always thought.

Gwen notices the script across the dresser mirror.

"What's that say?"

He explains. What he doesn't know about Islam is more than what he does, but he's learned a few things. The ninety-nine names of God, however, turn out to be more than she wanted to know.

"Is Owl a nickname?"

It's an acronym, actually, for a name he could never stand, but he won't tell her what it is. "I dis*like* it. That's the point."

She sighs heavily and hands him a date.

"Keith and I are finished, you know. Oh, we'll talk, maybe even study together, but it's over. I can't tell how I feel about it yet." She shrugs and looks away, suddenly fighting sobs. Then she stops fighting. Owl, out of respect, lowers his sandwich. Watching her cry doesn't seem so respectful, either, so he takes another bite, but of course that's not right. "Aw, Gwen," he tries, his mouth full.

The light outside changes: over the palms outside the balcony is the sunset they're missing. It's a color the precise likes of which Owl's never seen in a setting sun before: yellow, pure yellow, the yolk of an egg cracked too soon.

"Look," he says softly. "Gwen, look."

The light deepens the hollows in her neck and gives her age as well as color, and when she looks out the window, her face is brand new. She seems about to say something when the door bursts open.

"That fortress is *mine*," Keith announces. "Whoa—what's going on here?"

In the pit of his mattress, Owl's trying to sleep. The flask on his nightstand was meant to last the trip, but it's already half empty. He turns his pillow over and punches it. *What's going on here is a kind of magic,* he's thinking. He can't name it any more than he can tell Beth what he's been after all these years, but he can feel it, and he recognized it when he saw it happen in Gwen. Keith might be impervious to it, though he ended up joining their little picnic last night, chattering away happily about his climb. But the change in Gwen was something else, something quiet and slight but at the same time rare and great: something people travel thousands of miles for when they think they've lost it, which Owl knows because at various times in his own life he's had it, lost it, sought it, and found it again. When he's got it he knows where he is in the world, no matter what small spot on it he happens to be occupying at the moment, and when he doesn't, the world remains small, no matter how much of it he thinks he knows.

He flips his pillow again. From next door he hears a commotion for which three implausible explanations occur before the obvious strikes him—*Gwen and Keith are having sex*—and then he's on his feet in his pajamas, listening at the wall, now out in the hall. The slamming goes on and on and on, grimly, because he hears no voices or moans, even, through their loosely latched door, and he recalls the golden light on Gwen's face and the jut-jawed red one in his rearview mirror, *that conquering son-of-a-bitch.* The door gives way as soon as his shoulder touches it, though not before he's seen through the crack that she's the slammer, not the slammee, but like the tailback he was fifty years before, he was already in motion.

Before dawn he gets up, shaves in cold water, dons a clean shirt. Nobody's in the lobby downstairs, and two of their three bicycles are gone.

Owl pedals the last one into town, where a man setting up card tables in the dirt brings him coffee *masbut* as if he's been serving shamefaced elderly Americans every dawn of his life; only a slight stiffness of the spine betrays some effort. When Owl's finished his coffee and still hasn't seen the kids, he heads out toward the temple again, figuring they might have gone out to see it. There's not much else to do here: jewelry and crafts cooperatives, more ruins, a few scattered ancient baths. He doesn't know what he'd say to them if he saw them; the best thing would be to find a secluded spot to spend the day reading and answering Beth's letter. Not that he knows what he's going to tell her either, now he's seen Siwa. If war breaks out, he'll have to go back. But until then, if he has to sit on their screened-in porch and watch the lake all day long, he'll be the one looking to declare war, and Beth will be the one wanting him to come back. He knows that much.

The sun's not over the treetops yet. Thinking he remembers the way back to the rest house, Owl pays no attention to the cardboard arrows, so pretty soon he's lost. At a T-intersection he sees a wall and large stones he hasn't noticed before, probably what's left of a second temple he remembers reading about, from the 30th dynasty or so. A nineteenth-century governor blew it up to collect flagstones for steps to his own house, which is long gone, too, but on the pieces left Owl can make out faint coloring and traces of inscription. Peering down a road for more, he realizes he's gone in a circle: he's fifty yards from the central square, where two bright nylon backpacks are propped together like a tent. Beside them Gwen and Keith are talking to the boy who rented them their bicycles, which they're still straddling. The boy's holding something out in his hand, maybe his radio, and they're all three looking at it as they talk. When Keith notices him, all three turn, then turn back to each other and shake hands all around, and Keith and Gwen begin pedaling toward Owl.

"What's the news?" Owl says after an exchange of extremely polite greetings. Last night, he apologized, of course, but his "Oops: wrong room!" couldn't quite cover, and there seems even less to say now.

The radio news was no news, apparently, because Keith's answer is that he and Gwen are leaving. "There's supposed to be an eight o'clock bus," he says, looking none too sure about it as Gwen pulls up beside them. He grips his handlebars near the headset, bouncing the front tire between his feet, and looks at her as if for help. She's looking at a spot about six feet in front of Owl's shoes.

"We'll pay you for gas for the whole trip," she says firmly, "just like we agreed on. Then we're going to splurge on a hotel in Alexandria until the ferry leaves."

"The Palatine," Owl suggests, automatically but eagerly, too, as he hears in his own voice. "This time of year you'll be able to walk right in."

"Thank you," Gwen says in her same resolute voice, her eyes still on that spot in the dirt. It's eight-thirty already, but they seem reluctant to leave, and when Gwen does look up it's to share a glance that Owl recognizes on them by now: fear. Remembering the rickety bus yesterday—*only yesterday?*—he guesses they'd like an offer to drive them back, though maybe not: the mood in the car yesterday would seem like a party compared to the silence he can imagine now.

"Well, have a good trip. You know, I've taken that bus," he adds, and at their hopeful looks in spite of themselves he eases into storytelling mode. "Not that exact route, but that same bus system, in Upper Egypt. There's only the one bus company here. It's a safer way to travel than it looks, and I'll tell you why. If the driver has an accident, the company makes him pay. If he's dead, then they go after his family. So the drivers become expert mechanics, and they check out their own buses meticulously and drive like little old ladies. I wasn't even driving the speed limit when we passed that one yesterday."

"Really?" Keith wants to believe. Gwen's eyes are still at the ground; Owl can't tell whether she believes him or not.

"Sure. It's a cruel system, but it works, like a sort of Third-World regulatory commission. Our accident rate here actually rivals Greyhound's. Your guidebook didn't mention that? Throughout the Middle East, 'an Egyptian bus driver' basically means Sunday driver. One of the miracles of this crazy place."

Gwen looks up. The sun is behind her, so he can't tell her expression; from the angle of her head, it might equally well be *Thank you for saving my boyfriend's face* or *You're lying like this dirt I've been studying*. Both are correct.

"I'll take that hamper off my car, then. Good luck getting it on the bus."

"It's already off!" Keith chirps, happy now. "We took it down."

"We bequeathed it to the rest house." Gwen's voice has softened. She might even be smiling. "What are *you* going to do, Owl?"

He hasn't decided. The thought of three more days alone in the oasis, then the twelve-hour drive back to Cairo by himself doesn't particularly appeal to him. But he'd be driving the last leg solo anyway, and he doesn't want to return in defeat. He might stop in Matruh and hunt up that cross-eyed guy, buy him coffee to play some backgammon with him. As far as options, that's about it.

Behind them, the sun over the temple wall is too bright, and it's drawn sweat on their upper lips already. Every issue of the *Al-Ahram Weekly* reports at least one severe bus mishap: head-on crashes, crushed pedestrians, buses driving into the Nile or off cliffs. *The magic of travel,* Owl thinks, *is that you can't read the newspapers.* And these temples are just rocks, big rocks scattered in a field. Even thousands of years ago, the oracle inside them was just a man with a resonant voice.

But Owl will be damned if he doesn't hear that voice now, not so resonant but clear, and steady, and speaking to him. *Your name's Oliver,* it says. *You've had your chance with the world. Now drive these young people to their hotel, and drive on back to Cairo. Open your door. Set your things down. Pick up your telephone. Call Beth.*

UNDERSTANDING YEMEN

A few days after a splinter group of the furious had declared another war on tourism with a nail bomb in Tahrir Square, two Americans ate dinner in a different part of Cairo, the relatively affluent Mohandeseen district, at a restaurant called Abou Shakra, not exactly a tourist restaurant, and these two weren't tourists. They had the beleaguered look of long-time residents: a bad haircut on him, lines in her over-rouged cheeks; he was heavy in the middle and she was too thin, with whiter hair than his, though it was long and thick and woven into a loose braid. In plastic bags at their feet were liquor bottles from the duty-free outlet across Arab League Street, where they'd just run into each other. As they ate, they showed no interest in the chrome-and-marble décor, the framed calligraphy on the walls, or the leopard-spotted turban on the woman installing her family at the next table. They poked no forks into the kofta they shared and made no excited speculations on what spices were in it.

Instead they talked about their jobs: he was a computer man, contracted by USAID to help consolidate decades of overlapping Egyptian civil laws onto one database, which he said was as frustrating as everything here but paid well, and she was a teacher at a language institute run by the gay British couple who, a couple of weeks before, had thrown the party where these two had first met.

"Susan," said the man when a waiter had whisked their plates away and they'd been silent for a minute, "you interest me. Your independence, your intelligence, your collarbones—I was attracted the moment I saw you."

She stopped chewing, her green eyes widening. "Uh-oh."

The husband of the turbaned woman looked over, and the American man's ears reddened. It was easy to forget how many people spoke English here.

"No offense," Susan told him. "It's just that I haven't been involved with anyone in so long I don't even think in those terms anymore. Romantically, I mean."

"I find that hard to believe," the man said.

She considered him. "I mean it. I don't think I'm ready yet. Especially now, when I'm not even sure how long I'll be here anymore. Does anyone, these days?"

"I thought you were staying. You said you'd just renewed your contract."

"I said I've signed it. But I'm always toying with the idea of going back. Even before recent events, I was. It's just hard to leave a part of the world where you've grown up—I mean not as a child does but a place where you've come to fathom the real—" She reached across the table to touch his arm. "Please, Philip. Don't tell Marvin I might leave."

"Your secret's safe with me." Philip laid a hand over hers—gently, but with the quickness of trapping a fly. "The real what?"

One of her plucked eyebrows arched, and she smiled in a way very unlike her first answer to him. "I guess that's the real secret, isn't it?"

She withdrew her hand to tear off a piece of flatbread, dip it in tahini, and wipe beans from a stainless-steel bowl. On every finger she wore a ring: a gold braid and a silver disc from Siwa, as she identified it when asked, and a white cabochon and, on a pinky, turquoise set in heavy silver, a smaller version of the ring fruit-sellers wear. Before coming here for her TOEFL certificate she'd done graduate work in theater, she'd told Philip.

Now she added, "You know, I do have an ex-husband back in Michigan. And I don't go for women, if that's what you're thinking."

"Oh, it wasn't. It wasn't." Philip started to add something, then shook his head—*ah, these distances between us*—and looked out a window. The dining room was on the second floor, and the reflections of diners in the black glass were dotted with lights from Arab League Street. On the grassy median below, a man pushing a yam-cart waited for a break in traffic, smoke rising from his cart's crooked iron stack. At the curb he flipped one end of a scarf over his shoulder, cloaking himself to the eyes, his breath faintly visible through the wool. The dining room was toasty.

"Maybe I spoke out of turn," Philip offered, turning back. "We all *need* so much here, don't we? All of us foreigners do. What's this?"

A waiter, a smooth-skinned young man with sharp cheeks and laughing eyes, was serving them another plate of kofta on another bed of parsley. His black jacket looked new, but his faded pants were shiny in the knees.

"*Mish ayzeen*," Susan told him crisply. "*Mish ayzeen dilwaa'ti*. Send it back."

The waiter raised his eyebrows and inclined his head in puzzlement. "But Madame ordered *kofta*. Also Messieu." He smiled.

"We wanted them *at the same time*," Philip enunciated. "Never mind, never mind. Might as well eat it," he told Susan. "They'll charge us for it anyway, and it'll be forty minutes to explain. Good thing it's so cheap." He made a hand gesture to the waiter, who beamed at Susan, then glided off. She watched him go, deadpan.

"I wish I'd learned Arabic the way you yave," Philip said as they tucked in, forks poised over the same plate. "When I first arrived, I took a course, but that didn't last long. What is it? *What*?"

The waiter had returned to ask what they might want for dessert. He addressed himself to Susan, but she turned away. The woman in the leopard-spotted turban smiled at her, but Susan turned away from her, too, and shook her head at Philip, who told the waiter to just bring the check.

"No coffee?" said the waiter, miming hurt. "Why not try our Egyptian coffee? Also, *umm-Ali* is very delicious. Two *umm-Ali*?"

"Just the check," Philip repeated. "*When we've finished*. Jeeze," he added to Susan. "Try to have a simple dinner."

The waiter was staying where he was, smiling. "Madame is very beautiful," he said. Susan flinched, and Philip rose, napkin in his fist.

"Look, my friend. Come on. I swear. Have you got a supervisor I can speak to? *El boss*? Who's the manager of this place?"

But Susan waved him down, propping her other elbow on the table and sinking her forehead in that hand. "It's all right. Forget it. Actually, I could use a cup of coffee."

"Mazbut, Madame? *Siaada?* Or *saada?*"

"Just Misrcafé," she told Philip, who ordered two of them, then looked back at her in concern. Her eyes had filled.

"Oh, Philip," she said. "It's been such a long time since I've heard things like what you told me a minute ago. Since I've believed them, anyway."

He leaned forward. "I meant it." He set his napkin on the table, watching her. "How a woman can live alone here is beyond me. It must take such strength."

"It's true!" She said it quickly and lightly, as if surprised to hear it. Then she sighed. "Have I told you about my trip to Yemen? Of course I haven't. I don't tell just anyone."

"I'd be honored," Philip said.

She considered him a moment, then decided, arranging silverware in front of her: an actress preparing a big scene, or a teacher with a tricky lesson to present.

She'd intended to travel with a roommate named Polly, but at the last minute Polly had come down with what turned out to be hepatitis. Polly was emergency-prone and was always pulling this sort of thing, but Susan was mad mostly at herself, for having depended on Polly in the first place, and at a world that made women afraid to be alone. She had just ten days between TOEFL courses; she'd already paid for her plane ticket, and she'd wanted to see Yemen ever since running across a magical photograph book by a Frenchman named Maréchaux: *Arabia Felix*, it was called. Yemen was Sheba, land of Bilquis, the queen. Frankincense grew on trees there; stone bridges linked mountains draped in fog, and salt caked the desert by the sea. Susan wanted to see these things. South Yemen had recently opened up, after Communist rule since colonial days, and she wanted to see the craters of Aden, too. The Paul Bowles stories she'd read had inspired in her a notion that breaking down barriers, both cultural and gender-based, was not an option but a duty for any truly free-thinking individual.

So she went.

A sandstorm in Saudi delayed her plane, which landed in Sana, capital of the North, at one o'clock in the morning. The hotel where she'd reserved a room had given it away at midnight. Across a highway toward town there was supposed to be another hotel, so she headed for that. Like the airport, the highway was full of men, some in coats and ties or shirtsleeves but most in suit-jackets over white robes like the Egyptian galabeya, with long curved knives in their belts called jambiya. Susan had read all about them. Whether their sheaths were solid gold or silver or plating showed a man's social position, but jambiya weren't just for show. In the deserts and mountains, tribes ruled, and half of the men she saw now looked like they were just visiting the city. She didn't see any women until the next day.

A desk clerk at the second hotel said he'd have a room for her in an hour. This hotel was shabbier than the first, with plaster walls lit by a bare ceiling bulb and in a corner a post lamp with a perforated metal shade. The lobby was full of men: standing around drinking tea and talking or waiting quietly on a broken couch—Susan hated to imagine what for, in a hotel that freed rooms at two-thirty in the morning, but she didn't have much choice. Outside, everything was quiet and dark; Sana was indistinguishable, so far, from any airport district anywhere. The only other sign she could see was for Air France, back toward the airport, on a low building whose windows glowed white through humid air. The light from streetlamps looked like balls of gauze. Her hair was entirely wet.

The desk clerk took her money and her passport and let her carry her own bag, but he showed her to her room. She was gaping in horror at pubic hairs on rumpled bedsheets when she heard him say in English, *See you soon*.

"What do you mean?" she said.

"I'll be right back."

"And he said it with such absolute confidence that it didn't sound like a lewd suggestion or even a proposition," Susan told Philip. "Though it certainly wasn't a joke, either. It was a flat statement of plain and ugly fact."

"Western women and Arab men," said Philip, his own voice flattening a bit. "These stories are always so horrible."

An older waiter in a galabeya was setting down stainless-steel pitchers and saucers and cups with paper packets of Misr Café inside, but Susan didn't seem to notice either the waiter or Philip.

"As soon as the clerk left, I tried the key in the door," she said. "But it wouldn't lock. It wasn't even the right kind of key. Outside my door I heard him laugh."

"Uh-oh." Philip reached for his packet of instant coffee and tore it open. "What happened next?"

The clerk returned her passport when she demanded it but didn't speak or even look at her again, and she was too furious and frightened to demand her money back. In any case she'd brought plenty, along with a credit card, but right then money was the least of her problems. She considered returning to the airport and catching the first flight back to Cairo, but she hated to concede defeat this early, and once she got outside again, she told herself that nothing had really happened that she hadn't been able to handle. She headed for the Air France office, intending to sit outside in the light, at least, until someone arrived in the morning. But as she approached, she saw a man inside, in shirtsleeves and loosened tie, working at a computer in a small office. She knocked on the glass.

He turned out to be an Egyptian—Cairene, in fact—and he did indeed know of another hotel, which he called. It was downtown—he would drive her there. "*Oh*, no," Susan said, but he laughed and said that his wife was French, and that Susan would be safe with him. His car had air conditioning, and he carried her bag into the hotel and introduced her to the desk clerk there, another Egyptian, who was also friendly and relaxed. Before leaving, the Air-France guy, Mahmoud, said that if she stopped by his office the next day he'd show her Sana's highlights, along with some areas to avoid.

In her room, she once again considered returning, but after six hours of sleep like a coma she talked to the desk clerk, who said that the hotel employed a guide she could hire to tour the country with, a man named ("Surprise!" she told Philip, startling him) Mohammed. Maybe with a native companion, Susan thought, the harassment would stop. Mohammed turned out to be sixty years old, less than five feet tall, and missing his front teeth. But he was definitely a native: he wore a red-checked keffiyeh and a suit-jacket over his robe, like men she'd seen in the street, though with no jambiya. He said he had daughters himself, so Susan should consider him a father. Susan smiled at him. All right, she said. She showed him a list of villages she'd read about, and they worked up an itinerary in an efficient and businesslike fashion, negotiating prices in the presence of the desk clerk to forestall any misunderstandings later. They planned to leave early in the morning three days hence: she wanted to spend time in Sana, and anyway Mohammed's car was in the shop for air-conditioning repair.

All three shook hands, and Susan took a cab to the Air France office, where Mahmoud was happy to take a break. He introduced her to a friend, a Yemeni called Ali, who wore civilian clothes but was supposedly a colonel in the police force. Ali, like Mahmoud, was in his thirties. He had a savage-looking scar on his left cheekbone but was otherwise harmless looking: pear shaped, balding, and courteous in her presence, so low-key that he gave the impression of not being too bright. Ali would be a great asset to them in Sana, Mahmoud said.

The two men showed her amazing things: the Great Mosque and al Bakriyah and qat dens and open-air markets with booths for lettuce and tomatoes beside booths for hand grenades and machine guns—this was where tribesmen armed themselves. The few women she saw were covered in black to the eyeballs, but as long as Ali and Mahmoud stayed with her, nobody gave any indication that she wasn't an entirely ordinary sight. Before returning to work Mahmoud told her to stick to the main streets, and he marked on her map a few areas he said to avoid if possible, though they weren't really dangerous, and then he and Ali invited her to a restaurant for dinner the next evening, an opportunity to sample Yemeni cuisine and hear Yemeni music that she'd have no access to alone. Mahmoud said that perhaps their wives would be there, too—just one wife apiece, Ali assured her, and both men laughed—and they left her on Bustan as-Sultaan near a park called Saa'ilah, a quiet area with elaborate limed designs around the windows of homes.

Within five minutes, a car pulled up beside her, and a man got out of the back seat and took her arm.

At first she thought she'd dropped something he wanted to return to her, but he tightened his grip and began pulling her toward the car. She yelled to other men who were passing, but no one stopped. She began shouting in Arabic: *Haram*, she hollered, meaning forbidden by the Koran ("I know," Philip said) until the driver of the car said something to the man who had her arm and he dropped it, and the car sped away.

By the time Mohammed and Ali picked her up for dinner the next night, she'd been approached almost as boldly three more times, not counting comments and assorted hisses that she could pretend to ignore.

Philip was decorating his placemat with indentations from the edge of his spoon.

⁕

Mahmoud got out at her hotel, giving her the passenger's seat. He said that something had come up, unfortunately, and only Ali would be able to take her to dinner. Ali's wife, too, was sick. Alarmed at the sudden change in plans, Susan tried politely to back out, but at Ali's charming protests she told herself that she'd just gotten paranoid. On the way to the restaurant she mentioned the men in cars, and Ali was sad, apologizing for the backwardness of some of his countrymen. He said she must understand that all Yemeni men were not like that, and dinner was delightful, with lute music from a balcony and pine nuts in the lamb sauce and a sunset over Hadur Shuayb mountain, then a delicate web of lights falling over the city. The only discomfort she felt was at the sight of the other women diners, who had to lift veils to bring food to their mouths. The first time she mentioned this Ali smiled sadly, but the second time he seemed not to hear, so she concentrated on enjoying her meal—which was not difficult, the food was so good. She was glad she'd stayed.

Then, driving her back to her hotel, Ali said that he was organizing a party for her the next night. He wanted to introduce her to some friends and to more Yemeni food and music in a less formal atmosphere. No strangers would be invited, he said, and the party would be held in his own apartment. When Susan asked whether his wife would be attending, Ali shrugged and looked down, his scar glowing in the dashboard light. She thanked him profusely but said she was due to leave with Mohammed in the morning, hoping hard to herself that the car had been fixed on time.

In front of her hotel Ali insisted, smiling and playfully lifting his foot off the brake pedal so that the car edged forward whenever she tried to get out, until finally she promised to give him a call on her return.

Philip lifted his head from where he'd been leaning on the heel of a hand. "Sounds like a close one," he said. "What a creep."

Susan looked across the table at him as if from a much greater distance. "It gets closer," she said.

The next morning Mohammed was on time, with a yellow, round-fendered Mercedes that felt like an icebox inside. For the next five days he took her everywhere they'd contracted for: south through *wadi*s and lush central highlands to Uthmath and Ibb, across the Scimara Pass to the walled city of Yarim, to Mansouria in the Tihama coastal plain and Jebel Sabir south of Ta'izz, and she saw all the wonders of the Land of Punt.

As soon as they left Sana, though, Mohammad changed. He became remote, talking little and usually staying in the car to let her savor views and snap photos alone. He negotiated whatever she wanted to buy and stood behind her at mealtimes—she never saw him eat—and slept in the car. As per their agreement in front of the desk clerk, she paid him in daily installments when he'd found her a room in the evening, and though she was disappointed that he hadn't become more of a friend, they had no outright disagreements until Aden, where he pulled up in front of a low clay house that he said belonged to cousins of his.

He would sleep there, he told her, and he wanted her to sleep there, too. She thanked him but said she preferred a hotel. Don't insult us, he said. In front of the cousins, who soon surrounded the car, she had to insist. When Mohammed had taken her to one in angry silence, she didn't have the correct change to pay him, but she was so eager to get rid of him for a few hours at least that she paid for half the next day in advance.

The next morning, he met her in the lobby and demanded the rest of what she'd agreed to pay him for this trip. She reminded him of their contract: the last installment wasn't due until he'd returned her to Sana. Mohammed said yes, but one of his cousins was getting married, and Mohammed had had to buy a gift. Susan said she was sorry, but she would give him more money only when it was due.

"You must give me money now," he told her. "We have no benzene left."

"What have you done with the money I gave you last night?" she demanded, but Mohammed pursed his lips and folded his arms, his eyes like macadam. Men in the lobby looked over their way. In a low and even voice, Susan threatened to ask the desk clerk here to place two calls: one to the desk clerk in Sana for a reminder of the terms of their contract, and another to the police.

Mohammed laughed. "All right," he said. "I will take you back to Sana. But because the direct route has been damaged in the revolution, something my cousin told me only yesterday, we must leave immediately, instead of tomorrow. You will not see Aden, and that is that."

At this point Susan did involve the desk clerk, not to place the call to Sana but to inform Mohammed that their contract was cancelled, because she did not want to get into a car with the man again. She was so upset she switched to English to give full vent to her outrage, which the clerk apparently translated extremely well.

Mohammed began to scream and shout, and other men in the lobby gathered around, taking sides. Nobody seemed to be taking Susan's, though, and eventually she paid Mohammed half the remaining amount to break their contract. She told the desk clerk to send food to her room and book her a place on the next Yemen Air flight out of Aden. "Preferably back to Cairo," she told him, "but anywhere away from here will do." She caught a glimpse of the craters on the way to the airport, but she never saw the ancient cisterns or the pumice quarries or Steamer Point or the Tower of Silence or even the Indian Ocean, except from the air.

Philip caught their first waiter's eye and made the wrist-chopping motion that meant he wanted the check. "Well!" he said. "What a shame, Susan! To go all that way!" Glancing at the slip set in front of him on a tiny silver tray he pulled some bills from his wallet and handed them over his shoulder.

"There's more," Susan told Philip, slapping the table hard enough to make the coffee cups jump. "Goddammit, there's more!"

The waiter with the money stopped briefly, then without turning around continued on his way to the cashier with it.

On the plane a Frenchman, an engineer for Total Oil who was returning to Paris after two years of successful prospecting in Seiyun, west of Aden, told Susan that an uncovered woman in Yemen was assumed to be a prostitute and was treated as such. Of course, Susan had read such things before her trip, and out of respect she had not even packed any shorts to wear, hot as she knew it would be, or sleeveless blouses or anything else that could be considered provocative. But she'd refused to wear a hat, much less a scarf. "If that's asking for it, so is breathing," she told the engineer. "So is being alive."

He smiled noncommittally and shrugged. But when she mentioned the colonel, Ali, he told her something she hadn't heard before. Exactly as she'd described, he said, a respectable-seeming man will befriend a female tourist, then offer to throw a party for her, calling it an opportunity to see Yemeni culture at closer range. But if she goes to the party, the engineer said, she is drugged, raped, and held there until the men tire of her. Indeed, on that very flight was a Frenchwoman he had seen in the Embassy. He told Susan not to turn just then, but when she could look unobtrusively, she would know this woman by her stark white hair, though her passport would show her age to be twenty-six. She'd been released from such a party after a month, the Frenchman said, and there was nothing that the Embassy or anyone else could, or would, do about it.

Susan's palms lay flat on the tabletop. Her face was bright red. "Can you *understand?*" she asked Philip, her voice rising. "Can you *understand* a place where this can *happen* to a person's *life?* Can you *change* it, perhaps? Can you *punish* it? Make *peace* with it? Can you just *leave* it?"

He stared. Other people were staring, too, and scowling.

"A steward approached me an hour into the flight," Susan said, suddenly calm again. "The captain wanted to see me. In the cockpit a uniformed man with a mustache rose and bent over my hand. 'I'm told you've had trouble in our country,' he said, and he apologized. He explained the instrument panel to me, and he told me about his friends and family. He said he liked Garfield the cat very much. When we approached Mecca, he asked me to go back to my seat, because he had to fly the plane, to change course. It's forbidden to fly directly overhead, you see."

She sat still for another moment, then began to put her arms into the sequined sweater draped over her shoulders like a cape. The young waiter had returned, and he pulled her chair back for her. He was no longer smiling, no longer meeting her eye. His own eyes were glistening, and his posture was stiff.

Philip, too, had visibly changed. "Susan," he said. "I'm so sorry. I . . . I . . . What can I do?"

She raised an elbow for him to take and stalked past the waiter, who was bowing, expressionless.

"Tip him," she said.

COMPASS

Two old friends run into each other at a mall, days before Christmas. It's been years, decades. They count: two decades, it has been. One of the friends introduces a woman who looks almost that much his junior: Cynthia, his fiancée. He and his wife have divorced, the second bit of news he shares.

"And how's . . . Carol?" he says, snapping his fingers before he comes up with the name. He wears a cashmere coat over a T-shirt and jeans; in spite of the slush outside, his loafers are thin-soled. Cynthia wears a short coat with hair like a goat's. Her tights have a pattern like paint running down her legs, into high leather boots that preserve the shape of her ankles and calves. Between glances at her fiancé's friend she looks around the mall, which between the season and the weather is exceptionally active. She has the eyes of wildlife.

"Carol's dead," says her fiancé's friend. He's wearing a blazer, his tie loose. A lapel pin with the name of a department store identifies him as Jake. "I thought you knew, Stu."

"How would I have known?" Irritation before compassion: a trait Jake remembers now. "I'm sorry to hear it, of course."

The young woman's eyes move to Jake, who's nodding, his own eyes on the floor.

"After a long illness, as they say. We hadn't been together in some time." He shrugs. "Her decision, not mine."

It's how Jake has always been, too: offering up the worst facts of his life and daring you to draw your own conclusions, as if revealing himself were some kind of virtue. Stu's way is to reveal only what's likely to do him some good. But the nostalgia of the moment moves him to offer something in exchange.

"Jenny remarried, you know. She and another guy bought a boat with the settlement. They run a tourist business that makes enough for them to spend three months a year in Florida, doing nothing. I mean, from California, for chrissakes! They live in San Bernardino! You'd think they'd prefer a different kind of scenery, wouldn't you? Alaska or something, right?"

He grins whitely at the young woman, Cynthia. They're both exceptionally tall, Stu with a stiffness that looks like courtliness but is in fact a slight disability: he can't turn his head without moving his shoulders in the same direction. It gives him a posture Jake knew immediately, even across the crowded arcade. Jake himself, as Stu murmured to Cynthia in the time between hearing his name called and crossing the mall to speak, is almost unrecognizable. Cynthia returns Stu's smile in a way that indicates how many times they'd discussed his ex-wife's new life, and Jake remembers something else.

"I saw you on TV a while ago, Stu."

"Which time?"

He laughs in a way Jake recalls, too: an overachiever's bark. Stu's a doctor, and he was on a panel debating a proposed piece of health-care legislation. Jake's forgotten the specifics, but he remembers Stu was against it.

"Some years back."

"Right, right. Listen . . ." He looks at his old friend closely. "Let's all have a cup of coffee, why don't we? Cindy? Cappuccino? Jake? Have you got time?"

Jake can't say he doesn't. He's on his dinner break; it's just started, and he's on a diet. Instead of eating he walks the mall. On less crowded days he can put in three miles before he has to return to his counter at the luggage department.

The mall has the floor plan of a cruciform church. Jake's department store would be the apse, and across from where they've stopped, about midway down what would have been the nave, is a coffee shop.

"Jake, my friend, no offense, but I've got to ask: whatever happened to you?"

They've lucked into a table. On its round, laminated top are their cups and a handful of paper napkins, plastic lids, and mixing sticks. Stu insists on paying. Draped over the back of the one free chair is his cashmere coat; piled on the seat cushion is Cynthia's shaggy one. Underneath she wears a wine-colored knit dress with long sleeves and a collar like an open seam. Stu is in town to meet her parents, she's told Jake. *They're great. Salt of the earth,* Stu put in, apparently with no conception of how this might sound to Cynthia, but her face didn't change. It's a striking face, with full lips, a heavy jaw, and high cheekbones; her bright blonde hair is cropped close, and her neck's long, her ears perfect. She asked Jake what had brought him to this town, and he named a building supplies company that's gone under since. But Cynthia recognized its name, and she looked at him in a quick, open way unlike the way she looks at Stu. Then there was a silence, which Stu broke with a sigh and the announcement that his kids were gone now, the youngest just starting in at—*You? Kids?* he interrupted himself to ask. *Not really,* Jake said. Carol's children he'd loved as best he could, but he'd never thought of them as his, and the distance between himself and them had never entirely closed; he doesn't know where they are now. He explained this as if he were just now realizing it, and Stu didn't respond. But Cynthia cleared her throat and said, as if coming clean, *I have two: Alex and Alicia, seven and ten. Right now, they're with my parents.* Stu's smile was dazzling. Then he shook his head and said, as if following through with the same topic, *Building supplies. Luggage.* That's when he asked Jake whatever happened to him.

It's a hard question to digest, applied to oneself that way, let alone come up with an answer for. But Jake knows exactly what he meant, if not how to answer.

"Failure," he says finally, barking it out and laughing at the simple truth it expresses. More quietly he adds, "Hard luck and trouble. Abuses and excuses. Ups and downs—mostly the latter, recently. For one reason or another, I have not lived up to certain expectations."

"Yours or other people's?" Stu leans forward. At Cynthia's raised eyebrows he adds, "It's okay. We were close. We used to tell each other everything. But deep down you used to hate me, Jake. Didn't you?"

Jake snorts mildly, amused but unsurprised.

"Not hate, Stewart. Disapprove. You did things I would never. Small things, meaningless maybe, but you used to do them all the time. Hurt was a reflex with you. That old janitor in the arithmetic building, what was his name? Melvin. I still think those pranks are what killed him."

"The arithmetic building! Mel! Soap in the keyholes!"

Stu slaps the tabletop and leans back in his chair, hooking his thumbs into his waistband. His stomach is flat, his thin belt ornamental in its loops. He grins over at Cynthia, who's watching the women coming out of a boutique for erotic lingerie across the way. You can tell what she thinks of them by the droop of her eyelids and the lift of her upper lip.

She dangles her coffee cup from three long fingers, elbow on the table. Her nails match her tights.

"And that red puddle leaking out of his broom closet. The guy had kids, too. I don't remember how many."

The front legs of Stu's cane chair clack on the floor.

"OK, Jake. Fair enough. I was probably an asshole. Lots of us were, at that age. I remember an episode in which you didn't behave so well yourself. Over a certain Tabitha, wasn't it, or Sabrina?"

"Samantha I wanted to marry," Jake says. Cynthia's eyes flick over. She raises her coffee cup, watching him over the rim.

"Not after Anderson got done with her, as I recall."

"Ah. Yes. I forgot about Anderson. Talk about assholes." Elbow on the table, Jake flicks at a front tooth with a thumbnail. It's been years since he's said *Ah*. If he said it to a customer now he'd be risking a sarcastic retort, if not a complaint to his supervisor; if he said it around people he worked with, they'd mock him until his nose bled. Stu's tipping his chair back again. His haircut is close but expensive, the same length all over, with no nicks showing scalp. But his hairline has risen a good bit. Jake remembers when hair sprang out of that forehead like wheat.

"You know, though, Stewart: oddly enough, I *don't* resent you. Even still."

"Why should you resent me? As I recall, you never even wanted what I went after. Anyway, I've worked damn hard for it."

"Work was never the problem with you. You always worked. Harder than I ever did."

Stu looks into his cardboard cup, rotating it like a snifter. "Was that it? Lack of effort? What *was* the problem?"

"Failed at what?" Cynthia says. The two men look over as if she'd made them lose their place. When Jake takes too long to locate what she said she turns to Stu. "He said he failed. What did he fail at?"

Stu shoots Jake a glance he seems used to giving: slightly embarrassed, requesting understanding for her. "Well, honey, he was—he was the smartest of all of us, weren't you, Jake?" His old buddy makes a droll face at his fiancée. "But in fact, I don't even remember your major, come to think of it. You were always going on about books the rest of us read in Cliff notes. I remember that."

"I made up my own major. Multidisciplinary—not a single subject, like biology or English. Basically, it just meant three times the papers."

The definition is for Cynthia, whose tongue makes a bump in her cheek. "I know what 'multidisciplinary' means." She checks out the boutique clientele.

"You know, actually, I can tell you guys *exactly* what happened to me, if you want to hear about it."

She turns back to check with Stu, whose eyebrows rise in anticipation. Jake props his elbows on the arms of his chair and presses his palms together, as if either praying or preparing to dive. His necktie angles to one side of his stomach, and the bright mall light shows what an uneven shave he's had. But he's dark and even featured, and Cynthia watches him closely, folding her arms and scissoring her legs, angling herself in her chair.

"I had no specific goal," Jake says.

"Error number one," Stu chortled. "Classic."

"One of many. But *I'm* talking, now, Stu. Shut up."

Stu grins over at Cynthia, delighted, but her profile doesn't move. Just beyond his elbow, a procession of shoppers circulates like lava, and Stu cranks around, the stiffness in his neck making his movements puppet like. He gazes out at the shoppers as he listens to Jake's story as if to music; in fact, gradually the shoppers seem to interest him more, and his face changes. *Livestock,* he might be thinking. *Refugees.* Teenagers especially, with their wide pants and piercings, make him scowl. Then his eyes drop to his coat, and his features become peaceful as he brushes away a thread or a fleck of lint, his fingers light on the fabric. When he looks up at the crowd again, his jaw muscles flex.

"So I went after happiness," Jake sums up. "The big H, wherever it presented itself, and however. Also the big E—experience, and L—life. Life's Lessons, really, and you might think about what all that spells eventually. But before it did, I got my chuckles in. Got my vino drunk, et set er ah. Saw the world, met many interesting folks. Lenin's grand-daughter. Dodi Fayed. On Paros a hundred and-sixteen-year-old man, forty-five of them with one eye, the last decade with one foot."

"You *met* Dodi Fayed?" Cynthia said. "Princess Diana's Dodi Fayed?"

Stu hoots out into the shoppers, but the other two are rapt.

"He drinks Campari with brown sugar. His yacht put in at Nuweba, on the Red Sea, where I was living on the beach. For six months I baked in the sun there and read Mahfouz, Rimbaud, Leonard—whatever I felt like. Ate whatever I felt like, too—twice what I do now, and I was thirty pounds lighter, happy as shellfish. Swam three miles a day in the sea. Now look at me."

He brings his arms together to show how tight his jacket sleeves get.

"Rambo wrote books?"

Cynthia's sitting up very straight now. Her hands are clasped, fingers interlocked, on the tabletop, where the light reflecting on her nails makes her seem to be operating some sort of high-concept Dictaphone.

"Rimbaud. A poet," Stu tells the shoppers. "I remember that much about French literature. Wild and romantic and self-destructive. Also gay, as I recall."

Now he does turn, his eyes sharp and hard. Cynthia's eyes, too, get still, her mouth carefully set.

"It's not that easy, I'm afraid," Jake says. "I've slept with women, and I've slept with boys. In certain parts of the world, it's very common, you know."

Cynthia cuts her eyes away, her lips compressed. Stu's lips buzz.

"'Easy,' he says. Meanwhile *I* was back home, building a life. *I* was doing the things you're supposed to do, not running all over waving my dick around. *I* was feeding my kids and helping sick strangers get well, my friend, so don't be acting like you know something I've missed. And don't begrudge me the meager rewards I've reaped."

His head ticks toward Cynthia, who's been about to shush him, but no shush comes. Except for the snap in her eyes, she might have been blowing him a kiss. The gloss on her lips is like sherbet, her eyes like crushed ice.

Stu swings the rest of the way around to Jake, who blinks.

"You're right, I guess, Stu. It all sounds so selfish, doesn't it? But I never kept a thing for myself. When I had money, I gave it away. I once handed a hundred-franc note to a bum, after which I spent a few nights in a culvert myself."

Stewart looks like he's being rained on, his eyes slits. He folds his arms across his chest.

"What did you do for expenses?" Cynthia says. "On your travels, I mean."

Jake smiles at Stu. "Oh, various things. I cooked. Taught people our language. Learned how to handle a boat. Most of the world lives on skills you can pick up."

"*Not true!*" The flat of Stu's hand comes down on the circular table-top, rattling their empty cardboard cups. The shop is overflowing with customers holding full and steaming cups, all waiting for a free table. "Not true," he repeats in a lower voice, leaning in. "And it's less true now than it's ever been. We haven't even be*gun* to see—"

"–the ramifications of a technology that will transform the world and with it human life," Cynthia finishes, providing a little tune and head-wag for it.

"Right, right," Stewart mumbles. He looks at her, puzzled and perturbed, and crosses his arms again.

Jake gazes at a spot between them. "So I just followed my nose," he says. "If a train was leaving, I got on it. If a ship was, I bought a ticket. If some people had a car, I made friends with them. For a while I had a motorcycle, a cheap one I bought in Czechoslovakia. You put the oil in with the gas, like a lawnmower. But it got me over the Alps all right. I just followed—"

"His bliss," Stewart mutters, holding the *s*. "I *help* people for a living," he repeats. "I'm concerned about *others*."

"Certainly very commendable," Jake says.

"Have you been to China, Jake?"

Cynthia has one fist on the other, her chin nestled on top. Her blonde hair bristles out of a cowlick at the crown of her head and swirls in the trough of her neck. A thickset woman standing above her with full cups in both hands and shopping bags dangling from both wrists looks down as if wondering what shade cappuccino and blonde might make. Stu, glancing up, notices her.

"We ought to go," he says, touching Cynthia's elbow, but she draws her elbow in.

"Have you ever been to China, Jake?"

He shakes his head, then nods.

"Hong Kong," he says. "Once. Briefly, before the transfer. I was on a ship that put in there for a few days. I remember a sulfur smell, from a barge heaped with something that looked like chalk. I bought litchi nuts from a man on a bicycle who was carrying them in a towel on his head. But downtown just looked like Wall Street."

"Wow."

"You're so easily impressed, Cindy." Stu's voice is patient. "You shouldn't be so gullible."

"I'm not *gull*ible," she says, pointedly turning to Jake. "How about Egypt?"

"Didn't he just *say* he met Howdy Doody there? Red Sea—what'd you think, he was in Saudi Arabia?"

"In Alexandria the light's like lemon, Cynthia." Jake's voice has dropped to a murmur. "In front of the Cecil Hotel you can drink sweet tea, smoke shisha, and get your shoes shined—all for sixty-six cents, including a generous tip. Down the Corniche a ways, you can eat fish grilled with cinnamon."

"We are *going*," she says suddenly, raising her head. Her front teeth overlap a bit. "Here's our answer. We've been wondering where to go for the honeymoon."

"Bilharzia, honey. Schistosomiasis. Not to mention all the political dangers. This is no time for carefree travel, darling."

Jake checks his wristwatch.

"We've been thinking Aruba, the Bahamas," Cynthia tells him. "We're not actually calling it a honeymoon, just a trip. But these places *you've* been—now *that's* a trip! I'd like to see the Pyramids."

"Who could you trust there?" Stu insists. "Any cabbie, any hotel clerk, might have sworn to kill you before he ever set eyes on you."

"Can you ride a camel there, Jake?"

Jake nods.

"I want to ride a camel. We've been thinking Hawaii, the Virgin Islands—but either one or both of us have *been* to those places. I've done Carnival cruises four times." She holds up four nails like small murals, the back of her hand out.

"This is no time for carefree travel," Stu repeats but with less conviction in his voice now, and Cynthia ignores him.

"We'll be in town all week, Jake. I've got a million questions. Let's have dinner. Pick a restaurant. We'll bring an atlas. We should probably buy one right now." She leans out into the arcade, looking both ways for a likely store.

"Ah. Well. Oh! Gee!"

Jake looks at his watch openly now, eyebrows shooting. He stands to gather their trash, fussing with the plastic tops and stir sticks. Stu studies him. When Jake comes back from the wastebasket, he holds his hand out to Cynthia first.

"Nice to have met you. I can't really say about dinner, I'm afraid—this week's hectic—but if you give me your number I'll call." He pats his jacket in the vicinity of its pockets. "I seem to have lost my pen, however."

"Wait!" Stu barks.

Cynthia gapes at him. The woman with the shopping bags on her wrists has found a seat at the next table with her companion, a woman holding a big box on her lap. Both of them look over.

"This guy has never left the country," Stu announces.

"Oh, here it is!" Jake smiles, waggling a Bic.

"Maybe to Canada, but I doubt even that much. I don't think Carol died, either, if there ever even *was* a Carol. And he's never had sex with a boy."

The women at the next table bring their heads together, their faces full of shock and puzzlement.

Jake stands with his head down, fists in the pockets of his blazer. The stitches on one of his loafers have split; visible through a seam is a bright yellow sock. "Cut it out, Stewart."

"You know who this guy *really* was, Cindy? He was the campus liar, that's who. His major, whatever he called it, was really talk." Stu's eyes are on Jake as if to pin him there. To another couple standing over them with questioning looks he snaps, "We're not *done* here yet! I mean, it was almost pathological, Cindy. It *was* pathological. What else would you call a guy who'd borrow your stuff and tell you he'd lost it, then a week later you'd see him *wear*ing it, in the case of a certain plaid-lined windbreaker I loved?"

"No. This never occurred." Jake shakes his head. "The jacket was lost. Then I *found* it again. I was bringing it back. It was a cool fall day. We lived at opposite ends of the campus at that point. I put the jacket on to re*turn* it."

"So what was he going to wear home? Answer me *that*," Stu demands, and when neither of them does he makes a noise between taut lips, spitting dry. "He wasn't even a *good* liar, just a constant one. Come to think of it, he could have seen all those places he was talking about on television, couldn't he? Or even"—his dawning thought shows in his smile—"on travel posters."

"What?" Jake looks quickly at Cynthia. *"What?"*

"In the pictures in ads for luggage, say."

Jake's fists go to his hips. "Oh, come on. Who'd make up the kind of stuff I –oh, *man*. You think I made that all *up?* Oh, come *on*. Who'd ever . . ."

"When did you ever need a reason, Jive-o-matic? That's what we used to call him, Jive-o-matic."

"Like that proves anything."

"Proves your reputation, Bud."

"Reputation, gossip—*what* exactly is the difference again?"

They keep bickering while Cynthia stands up, takes her shaggy coat from the chair, and puts it on. They don't stop until, three sharp times, she brings her hands together. Then she puts her hands in her pockets, her weight on one leg, to consider Jake and Stu.

"Grown men," she says. "Supposedly. You guys are like a couple of kids. My *God!*"

Stu, accommodating his neck, watches her from the tops of adoring eyes, a smile twitching at the corners of his mouth. But her own mouth stays grim. Jake's face is on a level with hers, but she doesn't return his smile, either. The women at the next table are no longer pretending to look elsewhere. Even passing teenagers slow and turn, and when Jake notices them he intones from the side of his mouth, "What *will* she do, boys and girls? Everybody gets a choice, but there comes a time when we've got to *make* it, don't we? Anyplace you go can teach you *that* much."

"Come on, Baby." Stu might be trying to talk a cat down from a tree. "Let's go home, where we belong."

Jake's eyebrows wiggle. "Or: come weese *me*, to ze Casbah!"

Cynthia quivers her head back, eyes on the ceiling. "Too weird for me, boys. I've got to run an errand, I just remembered. Don't get up—it's a girl thing, sweetie. I'll meet you back at the car." Without looking at either Stu or Jake she steps out into the shoppers, where she struggles briefly against the tide, turns, and lets it carry her along. The people waiting for a table close in.

She drifts (thinking, "No specific goal, oh, *no*! The bastard!") past the lingerie shop, past a bookstore that sells atlases, past stores for soaps, stores for jewelry, and stores for housewares and clocks, until she comes to an island of varnished benches and potted trees, where only one man is sitting quietly by himself.

As she approaches, he turns to look directly at her in a way that makes her think he's been expecting her: without surprise but with mild irritation, as if she were late, but somehow as if he's used to that from her, too. She gets the unmistakable impression he knows her, not just as someone from the bank or the post office might but knows *all about* her, though she's sure she'd never seen this man before.

At the same time, though, something about him seems familiar. He's sitting very still in the precise middle of a gleaming blond bench, his feet flat on the tiles, knees together, hands in his lap. He's slim but broad shouldered; a loose brown shirt cuffed tight to his wrists gives an impression of strength at rest. His pants match his shirt, like work clothes but of a finer fabric, and his shoes, old-style dress shoes with capped toes, are worn but highly polished. His skin is the color of copper, but his features aren't African, entirely. His wiry dark hair is, clipped close to his skull, and his lips are, a bit, but not his nose. His ears are quite delicate, his hands small, the fingers pudgy but tapered, the nails tiny and cut so close they look bitten, though his hands sit calmly in his lap. Cynthia thinks of the phrase "at home," but his posture is alert, too, in a way that makes her think that the mall must be a new experience for him. His dark eyes on her glisten with some quick, sure feeling—whether amusement or yearning, love or contempt, she can't tell. The way he's looking at her makes her feel as if she's done something wrong, something not terribly wrong but definitely wrong, but she can't tell what it might have been. All she knows for sure is that he makes her uncomfortable.

This happens in an instant, a glance: it's a tiny break in the holiday hubbub. Then the man turns away, and so does Cynthia, and she's staring at a rubber-tree leaf so shiny she can see her reflection in it.

Flushing, she steps back into the crowd and heads back in the direction she came from, double-time. "God," she's thinking. "I hope they're still *there!*"

RULE OF LAW

The guy from the Embassy looked like a man determined to relax. The only one at the party in a tie, its knot halfway down his chest, he was perched on the back of the couch, one penny-loafer dangling, the other planted on the floor. His haunch was as solid as a full sack of flour, and his beefy fingers made his highball glass look like a toy. He rotated it idly, checking out the crowd. That afternoon, a government minister had been shot in a street in Abbasiya, and everyone was talking about that. A drunk jostled his elbow.

"So what's the official word? Is it all going to blow?"

The Embassy guy glanced down as if at a fly near his dessert.

"These things happen," he said. "Life goes on."

"Yeah, but will this government go on? The people who grant us our visas—will they go on?"

"The country will go on. The infrastructure, the systems here . . . things are basically in place. I don't foresee any great disruption. These guys aren't going to . . ." The Embassy guy ran his free hand over his face. "Look. I've been on the phone all day with this. Do you mind if we change the subject? You're not a reporter, are you?"

"Me?" The drunk laughed and raised a large brown bottle he'd been dangling by his leg; on its oval yellow label was printed, in both Arabic script and Roman lettering, "Stella," under a blue star. He extended the neck. "Beer?"

The Embassy guy looked into his own glass and downed what was left. "Why not? I think they're out of gin already. Thanks. What do you do here?"

"Wait a minute," said the drunk. "Less than five miles away a prominent figure gets shot from a motorbike and you want to make small talk? I'm sorry, but what other subject is there right now? I've been here for years, and I still can't get used to it. Every time, it's the same. You hear the news and it's like everything you know is erased, like from one of those tablets where you draw with a bare nib on a plastic sheet, and it's impressed underneath on a kind of carbon copy—you know? Then you"—he pantomimed lifting the sheet away from the tablet—"and poof! everything's gone. You start over."

The Embassy guy rubbed his face again. "Etch-a-Sketch?"

"No, that's the one with the knobs. This was the kind, I don't know if they still make them—anyway, my point is that every time something like this happens, I question all my assumptions from the ground up. Self, country, God, no God, the whole bit. I mean, right now I'm looking for answers I haven't worried about since I was a teenager. In other words, terror works! Doesn't it?"

He had a shaky, pleading sort of laughter, and the Embassy guy didn't laugh with him. The drunk was skinny; his face was pasty, and his movements were exaggerated and out of sync. Even just standing there, he twitched like a marionette. He wore a wrinkled shirt of pale-green silk, and the short sleeves quivered.

"You should think about going home, buddy. And I mean HOME home."

"Can't stand the heat, I know. But it's not the heat, it's the morbidity." This time his laugh popped. "Were the dogs still in the lobby when you came in?"

The Embassy guy snorted slightly.

"Yeah. I think one of them's giving birth."

"Plaster falling off the walls, light bulbs out—it looks like a tenement on the Lower East Side, doesn't it?"

"Except no graffiti, I know. What's your point?"

The other man seemed to have another one, an index finger raised, his face intent. "Then you enter a home like this one and it's like the inside of a crystal." He pointed around at mirrors and portraits, heavy purple drapery, gleaming parquet. Greeting newcomers at the door was a woman in a sparkling gown, a long black ponytail, and earrings like chandeliers. "I can't figure it out. Can you?"

"Sure I can," said the Embassy guy. "Public chaos, private order. That's what I was trying to tell you. Assassinations, corruption, even wars come and go. When the dust settles, there are these people, same as ever. I'm frankly admirous."

"So why don't I feel better? Is 'admirous' even a word?"

The Embassy guy waved a hand.

"Bottom line: we pump billions of dollars into this place, and both sides know it. Every side does."

"What are you saying?"

The big man raised his arms, his blazer gapping open like a cape. "This is exactly what I didn't want to get into, but here you go: the guy in the car knew it, and so does the guy on the motorcycle."

"Did they catch him? Do they know who it was?"

The Embassy guy was surveying the party. "I just saw somebody I've got to talk to. But I want you to consider what I said about going back. Maybe it's time for you."

"Maybe." The drunk raised his brown bottle. "No? To our health."

"Meantime, take it easy. Everything's fine." The Embassy guy seemed to recall something not so fine, then broke into a luminous smile. He pointed at the drunk with two parallel fingers, large thumbs straight up, and moved off backwards, loafers shuffling on the parquet floor. "Just keep a low profile, my friend. And avoid large crowds!"

SKIN

Anson chucked everything—wife, friends back home, even his grown kids after they'd helped him straighten out his complicated international paperwork—to marry an Egyptian woman, a registrar at the exclusive international prep school he worked for in Cairo. He was an American, near fifty when he did this. He'd been just a mediocre combatant in the university wars in his own country, too fond of his subject to be able to hone it into an effective weapon, and when his application to this foreign school was accepted—and again when he saw how far his dollars would go in the Third World, how well he could live there—he couldn't believe his redeemed life. His American wife, actually his second, had come along for an adventure of a couple of years, tops; she'd soon had enough of being light-haired in a public full of dark-haired men, and she said so daily, at least once. So Anson hadn't even brought up the issue of staying until he'd cinched things with Laila, the registrar, and the way he finally informed Ellen of what he'd decided to do was particularly abrupt and ugly. She flew home under sedation, and in their small expatriate community not one person was on his side.

But the expat turnover rate was so high that he and Laila only had to miss a few parties and one Headmaster's annual reception, and by their second attendance as a couple they were regulars, with their own set of mocking but fond names for everybody there. The pounds Laila had put on within what seemed like weeks of their lavish wedding (she had an uncle in a ministry, and her family owned several blocks of Cairo) hadn't damped her trilling voice or dulled her wit, and back in their Zamalek apartment she made Anson laugh in a way he hadn't since—well, he didn't know if he'd *ever* felt so full and glad. He thought of the years he'd spent in anguish and worry, and though he could remember the reasons why and knew them for good reasons, he couldn't imagine getting so wrought up again, over anything.

"I've become an Egyptian," he sometimes thought with satisfaction, though he had enough cultural sensitivity not to say it aloud, even to Laila. This was before the Gulf War and spectacular acts of terrorism linked to Egyptian groups, but what he meant didn't really have to do with nationality or politics, anyway, or even religion. Laila had the country's golden complexion but was Coptic, not Muslim, so he hadn't even had to convert, though he would have. In fact, he'd been quite taken with a demeanor he thought of as Islamic: a certain clear-eyed patience and proud humility, a sort of attentive, invigorated calm. But what he meant by "becoming Egyptian" was another attitude entirely, one somewhere between the Sphinx's smile and the deep, easy laughter of the legless man who sold him his *Herald Tribune* in the morning: a feeling of having been let in on the vast joke of the world at last.

But when he took his shirt off on the night after their third annual headmaster's reception, Laila's laughter stopped.

"What is that?" she said, turning him so that he could see something on his right shoulder blade in the mirror of her dressing table: a mole.

"Oh, that. I've always had it, I think, haven't I?" He pitched his shirt toward a huge woven-grass hamper in a corner of their bedroom.

"Not always of that color."

The shirt missed; he thought he must have drunk more wine than usual that evening. He crossed the room to pick up the shirt and drop it in.

"I'll get it looked at, Lyle. Next time I see Mustafa, I'll ask him."

"You must call Doctor Mustafa tomorrow."

The objection that came to mind didn't seem important enough to voice, and when he'd set up the appointment he forgot about that, too, until his assistant reminded him on the day itself. Doctor Mustafa's assistant shaved the mole off for biopsy, but it was the doctor himself who phoned Anson at work a week later with the results.

"Malignant," he said.

"That bad?" Anson quipped, though he knew what the word meant. He shrugged, as if he weren't alone in his office.

"I'm sorry," Doctor Mustafa said.

Second opinion! Anson was thinking. Serious medical trouble in this country had always been his great fear. Of course, hospitals here saved lives all the time, and babies were delivered smoothly—too smoothly, as the common expat joke had it, considering the population—but how negligible those broad truths seemed compared to stories about primitive needles, flies in the operating room, mix-ups between patient and corpse. Mustafa was recommending a procedure, a surgery he called minor, but Anson barely heard him. *Lysol!* he was thinking. *Television! Jell-O!*

Late that night, so as to catch her in the early evening, he called his sister back in the States. Within the next few days, she called some people she knew, then called him back. It took many more calls between them, and then to the melanoma clinic she'd located, before his appointment was set. This was in the early days of email, before civilian use of the internet became widespread. Anson was no good with numbers, and every time he phoned he had to refigure the time change: did you add seven hours or subtract? Had Daylight Savings started yet? One of the receptionists at the clinic—Debbie, Darcy, or Diane, who seemed to take turns answering the phones, unless now his memory was shot, too—told him to bring slides and samples of the malignant tissue with him. Mustafa knew what was needed, how to package it and get the paperwork for customs. By hand he wrote a detailed letter for Anson to take to his next doctor, like a formal letter of introduction to his disease, and three weeks after his diagnosis, just into a new calendar year—on Coptic Christmas, after Laila had gone to a midnight Mass so she could take him to the airport—Anson boarded a 747 with his tumor in a front pocket of his pants, in a plastic egg that could have come from a gumball machine in the doorway of a discount store. His appointment was with a specialist: Marrins, supposedly the best. An American, just like Anson himself.

The institute was famous, but it was located in the small rust-belt city where Shelly lived, near the town where she and Anson had grown up. In a vague way he'd always known of the institute's existence, but he'd never actually seen it before. Now, due to delayed flights—a day lost in Athens, more hours in Paris, a detour to Ireland for cheap fuel—Shelly had to drive him straight to his appointment from the airport.

Dry flakes slithered on the highway like sand tossed under their front wheels. It was noon, overcast, the light white. They'd been talking about everything but illness: the logistics of his trip and setting the appointment, how long it had been since they'd seen each other, Shelly's new perm. She was younger than Anson but bigger and physically ungraceful, and when she asked him in her serious way what he thought of her hair, he wondered if she'd had it done just for his sake, as a gesture of normalcy and optimism.

"It's very nice," he told her, and she nodded, considering the compliment for a mile or two before bringing up her other news: with a man Anson hadn't met yet, she'd been looking to buy a house. The market offered bargains if you were willing to put in some work on a place, and they were; they just hadn't found the right place yet, though they'd agreed on their neighborhoods of choice. The local references in her conversation, along with his own jet lag and the impression of cleanliness and order that always stunned him for a while on coming home (even the traffic here was so quiet!), made his own contributions to the conversation seem less and less necessary.

Then at some point he realized that Shelly, too, had stopped talking. At first he didn't know why. He noticed her grip tighten on the steering wheel, and then he noticed that the houses around them had been boarded up, whole blocks of them, on either side of the highway. Even a church tower had plywood on it. Trash clogged the chain-link between tiny backyards and the highway, which was gradually descending. From a bridge, a lone pedestrian looked down as Shelly drove under, arms spread against the rail like some bleak charcoal sketch: a Black man, and when white Anson caught a glimpse of the man's grim face through the windshield, all the tense American connotations for the word *color* returned. Where he'd just come from, his own race was in the minority, but a thousand other differences—in language, dress, outlook, even ways of walking in public, not to mention the difference between a diet of beans and one of meat—tended to diffuse the notion of otherness somewhat.

Shelly was reading from a sheet of directions she'd unfolded against the steering wheel. She took an exit named Locust, and at a light they saw their second pedestrian in some miles: another Black man, with a beard and a runny nose, who stepped off a curb and walked inches from their bumper with no turn of his head or hitch in his stride, no sign of having seen them at all. He wore a fatigue jacket and a bright orange knit cap. A sign below parking regulations on a lamp post read "Economic Development Zone," and that was when Anson fully understood where he was and what he was doing there: *I am sick,* he thought. *I am very, very sick.*

Then they turned into the intersection that was the cancer institute's address and saw huge wreaths and candy canes hanging from streetlamps, above human activity galore. At a steaming hot-dog cart stood a long line of people, some in doctor's coats or blue scrubs, people of all races, smiling and chatting, apparently neither hurried nor cold. A uniformed security officer waved Shelly up a ramp to an open parking space, and when his jacket gaped open Anson saw crisp laundry creases in his uniform shirt. A first-story walkway connected a red-brick building to a yellow-brick one across the street. Over the door of the main entrance was an art-deco visor like a gigantic cement tiara, and Anson remembered an episode of a TV show he'd once watched with his sons: as a set-up for some bad guys, operatives had constructed an American town deep inside some glum, repressive country, complete with ranch houses and kids shooting hoops in the driveways. His first impression of the famous cancer institute reminded him of that. But the signs of order, stability, industry, fellowship, and good cheer—these were what he'd come home for.

Inside were more such indicators. Windows and carpets were clean. Everyone he was directed to—seven people, at reception areas progressively deeper within the red-brick building—smiled and called him Mister. When he was sent for tests, receptionists made sure Shelly knew where the magazines were. Within a couple of hours, he'd left her with *Newsweek* for a windowless, beige-tiled consultation room in the Melanoma and Soft-Tissue Sarcoma Clinic, where two cheerful interns and a nurse practitioner asked him similar questions, almost as many about his life abroad as about his disease. One by one, they excused themselves or were beeped.

Then Marrins came in, an ID card clipped to his breast pocket, and held out his hand, which felt warm and solid in Anson's cold, clammy one.

"I know you've got a million questions, Mr. Anson. With some luck we'll have about five hundred thousand answers for you."

His wide smile showed spaces between his teeth. He might have been five years older than Anson, or he might have been ten: he was in better shape, but his crewcut was white. An old Navy man, Anson guessed, which he took for a good sign, though he himself had never had to serve, and before this, he'd tended to think of the military with a combination of mistrust and amusement. When he'd removed his shirt, Marrins fingered the scar where Mustafa's assistant had cauterized the skin after shaving off the offending mole.

"Shaved!" Marrins murmured. "That will make staging it a bit tricky for us now."

"What? Tricky? *What?*"

"Shhhhhh. It'll be OK. We'll take care of you."

Anson believed it. He relaxed, feeling the rest of his back being checked.

Marrins reappeared in front of him, smiling again.

"Good news, then?" Anson said.

The doctor waggled a hand: so-so. He sat on a stool in a casual posture, heels drawn in toward the casters, hands propped on his knees. He said he wanted to do the procedure Mustafa had described. He wanted to do it the next day.

It was the beginning of six months of up-and-down trouble: good news and bad, logistical errors and communication glitches, setbacks and delays. In the first operation, Marrins took out an oval of skin around the spot where the mole had been removed, to examine it for more melanoma cells. Anson was left with a six-inch scar on his back and a pucker he was promised would stretch. A smaller scar beneath his right armpit was left by another procedure, a nuclear one called a sentinel-node biopsy, which was meant to tell whether the cancer had spread to his lymph nodes. When the results proved trickier to interpret than expected, Anson called Laila to tell her he'd have to postpone his return.

"I should be *with* you," she said, as she'd said since the beginning, but he was firm. *Because I say so* still carried a good bit of weight in her culture. But the notes of her voice over the crackling telephone lines moved him so much he had to put his hand over the receiver. He didn't think he could handle seeing her here.

Marrins gave him pamphlets to read, with bibliographies for more books. If the disease hadn't spread, depending on various measurements, it was considered curable. But survival statistics in the other case took a huge dive. The very compilation chilled him—the word *survival* did.

Only the older of his two sons ever called. Naturally, he heard from neither Ellen nor the girl he'd helped her raise. Shelly eventually quit apologizing for being so busy with her job—she evaluated grade schools for the state, and it was spring-deadline time—and the minutiae of home financing, though Anson thought something else was going on with her, he had no idea what. Even before he'd moved abroad, their relationship had become distant, and she hadn't responded to his wedding invitation, though he'd offered to pay her airfare. But he hadn't held it against her then, and whatever her reasons now, he figured it was just as well she didn't want to be more involved. Their parents were dead, and he was happy that at least they'd been spared this worry. And the man Shelly lived with, a big, quiet guy who owned a house-framing business, expressed some curiosity about Egyptian foods but beyond that seemed glad to let Anson go his own way.

So he spent much of the time between tests and results in a branch library, researching this disease. The more he learned, the less he knew. Every trend in the research data was contravened by dramatic exceptions: people who should have been dead were alive, and vice versa. As Marrins put it, "Frankly, we've amassed a vast amount of data that in any given case might or might not apply."

Naturally, Anson had always known that life comes with no guarantees. He'd known he would die. He'd always known that. But *this!*

About *this*, he'd had no inkling.

He discovered the cancer literature of the spirit, human and divine: the connection between attitude and health, between living and wanting to, between life, love, and belief. He examined his pre-diagnosis self. *Cancer as character*, he thought. *Cancer as punishment*. The concept returned to him unbidden, with the precise and insistent regularity of electrical current through tungsten filament, and he couldn't look at it for long.

Other possible causes were genetics and the sun, or some combination of them, though Marrins said it was too soon to blame the North African sky. The literature most often mentioned sunburn in childhood. Not even constant sunburn—intermittent exposure actually seemed to be worse. And did the depletion of the ozone have a bearing here?

"Very possibly," Marrins said. "Perhaps."

Anson waited for him to say more, but there wasn't any.

He was walking back to Shelly's from the branch library one day when he slipped on black ice and sat down heavily in a snowbank. It was old snow, grainy and dirty, and he could feel it seeping through his pants, soaking his underwear. He was deliriously happy. Faces mocked him from a passing car with a bad muffler. He waved.

Another time he was overcome with the beauty of a tune in a radio ad for stainless-steel sinks.

Eventually he had to have another operation: pathologists had found melanoma cells in his lymph nodes—not many, but enough to have to check for more. This operation was bigger. He would have to stay in the hospital for a while.

The morning after his surgery Laila phoned his room at five o'clock. "How *are* you?" she breathed, her intonation pulling him across eight time zones. "I should be *with* you."

Thanks to morphine, he felt great. "Everything is going to be fine, Lyle," he murmured into the receiver, and in one way it was: no more cancer was found in the nodes that were removed. But the safest course of action then—the standard of care, as Marrins called it, the best recommendation known to medical science—was for Anson now to begin an adjuvant therapy of interferon, a protein that would either kill any stray tumor cells that might be left or stimulate his immune system to do so—or else do both, no one could say for sure. It was a seek-and-destroy mission that would last a year, but it would significantly alter the survival curve. Anson deliberated for about eight seconds.

He took the first month of intravenous injections at the institute, 40 million daily units that left him tired and feverish for the rest of the day. Then would come a series of less frequent, subcutaneous injections, lower dosages he could give himself, and he was told that if he wanted to, he could return to Egypt to finish those. Marrins had recognized Doctor Mustafa's name from a conference in Geneva they'd attended, but for overseeing the final treatments he recommended a doctor at the British Hospital, where he called the care "top-notch." This was a tougher decision, but Anson didn't have too long to deliberate. Shelly surprised him by trying to talk him into staying, offering him a room in the new house they'd decided on.

Anson declined, though. He wanted to live out the life he'd chosen. Now that the worst seemed over, he wanted to choose how he'd interpret this illness, too, which except for the mole had, after all, been symptomless: a matter of test results, diagnoses, and treatment.

Now it was over, he decided. He'd sought and received the best advice, and in a few months he'd be finished with his adjuvant therapy, which would then become only a thrice-weekly inconvenience. He'd resume his good life.

But it didn't turn out that way for him. The shots were more difficult than he'd imagined. He'd been instructed to pinch the fatty tissue of his thigh before injecting it, alternating thighs each time. The needle didn't bother him; even its puncture didn't. But the worst he felt all week was on the days when he knew he was going to have to shoot up at night. His anxiety worsened in the evening and peaked when he measured his dosage: his hands would tremble, and he'd sweat. The moment before injection would be a paroxysm of anxiety, nothing he could think himself out of or through. Right afterwards he was calm. Then in the middle of the night he'd wake up, drenched in sweat again, clenched in worry.

A little over halfway through his treatment, the Gulf War broke out. Tensions in the region ran high: would the trouble spread this far? How bad was it going to get? Whose information to believe? Strangers, friends, the local press, the BBC, and CNN were all spreading rumors, from mail bags floating in the Nile to imminent airlifts, one source apparently as reliable as any other. People in the streets seemed to be going about their business as usual—or were they? Anson couldn't tell, and he couldn't tell whether his periodic shuddering was caused by interferon, the war, or his own loosening grip.

He called Marrins, who said that reactions to interferon were indeed unpredictable: some people had more difficulty with it than others. His voice was so clear he might have been next door.

"Difficulty?" Anson said. "You didn't tell me about that. You gave me to believe this part would be easy."

The silence too was clear, but finally Marrins spoke again. "I'm sorry, Mr. Anstett," he said.

So, about the time Saddam Hussein's retreating forces were setting fire to the oil wells in Kuwait, against the advice of the doctor at the British

Hospital, Anson controlled what he could and quit his medicine. But the tremors continued, like a low-grade fever. Though sometimes he felt fine, lucid and calm, those times came to seem to him like the aberrations.

A book in the branch library around the corner from Shelly's had recommended parties to mark treatment stages, and a month after Anson went off his treatment, Laila threw him one, a surprise. Even the Headmaster and his wife showed up. But Anson didn't speak to them or anyone else.

"Who am I to deserve a party?" he asked the empty room when the guests had left—early, because he'd made them so uncomfortable. "What have I done worth celebrating? Does the newspaper vendor get a party for making it through another day with no legs?"

Laila was helping Madiiha, their servant, to clear the table. Anson had spoken in English, but Madiiha's eyes showed she understood there was disagreement afoot. It was not his first such outburst. Laila, holding a stack of dirty dessert plates, looked him full in the face for a few seconds, unsmiling, then stepped around him toward the kitchen.

"Excuse me," she said.

The anguish from the days of his career troubles returned to him tenfold, more and more often and over small, unimportant matters. He'd get furious at students over spelling errors, or at Laila over issues such as toast. When he told her he didn't want any more children, though he'd promised her two, eventually—she divorced him.

He developed a sure sense of chickens roosting. Human accomplishments began to astound and terrify him with their intricacy, from television to crossing a street. Third-World irregularities he'd have laughed at before—a rickety elevator, a cab with no doors, a wedding ring in a restaurant salad—began to fill him with dread.

He was buying lettuce from a blind woman in Tahrir Square when a nail bomb went off in the El Nil Café. He heard the explosion and saw the fire and smoke and chaos, and like everyone else in the crowded square he knew immediately who was responsible, more or less. He knew the gist of their rant: the godless West was craven, sinful, miserable and sick—the rhetoric of extremists, madmen. But he began to feel that, at least in his own case, the charges had some truth to them, and he felt he hadn't atoned fully yet.

He began drifting off in the middle of lectures, in the middle of sentences, gazing out a window with a finger to his lips until the bell rang. Sometimes he'd sleep through his morning class or hand back papers unread, or graded randomly. Other times he'd talk through the bell, feverishly expounding on some inkling that had just occurred to him. He lived on mangos and yogurt and Kentucky Fried Chicken from a new franchise that had opened up downtown, near the smaller, shabbier apartment where he'd moved. Laila had kept the Zamalek flat, with its view of the Nile, but now he lived on the first floor, not quite above traffic fumes, in a building where street dogs slept in the lobby and barked when he came home late. He often mentioned the dogs when declining invitations to social functions, though he continued to receive them. In the expatriate community he'd become something of a legend, the gossip about him wild: he'd once been CIA; he'd converted to Islam; he liked boys; he was working for the Egyptian government. The times he did show up, he wore a yellow linen suit with a string tie. Hostesses loved him.

The daily truth of his life was less dramatic. During the summers, which he and Laila had once spent on Crete, he now stayed in Cairo, writing in a journal he kept sporadically, staring out at traffic, thinking up errands and running them: getting a belt repaired, buying a pen. He was much the same during the school year. Students at the international school were paying a lot of money for their educational edge. After he was taken out of the classroom he was shuffled between administrative tasks for a year or so. But eventually the headmaster called him in.

He'd protected his retirement benefits against Laila's claims in the settlement, but they weren't enough to live on in the rust-belt city he returned to once his visa expired, where the cancer institute and his sister were. He found a job clerking in a used bookstore and rented an upstairs apartment in an Economic Development Zone. The neighborhood reminded him of Cairo, with less-crowded streets. Shelly and her husband—they'd married and had a child now—asked him more than once to move in, but he said no, though he accepted their invitations for holidays. His older son began accepting, too, with his own wife and child, Anson's granddaughter, Nell. Anson would bring the stuffing, or a yam dish, or a new kind of sausage he'd discovered how to fry. "I'm a wizard with a skillet," he'd say. For Nell he'd have candy, toys, books. One Thanksgiving, he just came right out and asked.

"Ellen has remarried," his son said.

Anson lived a few blocks from what he thought was the same church he'd spotted with Shelly on their first drive to the clinic. As it turned out, only the steeple windows were boarded up, to discourage bats from nesting, and he went to services twice a week. The denomination he didn't recognize or fully understand: the pastor referred to himself in the third person and threw dice during his sermons, rattling them on his lectern and pulling his arm back in a great gesture heavenward; the peach-colored silk robe he wore was the brightest thing around for several blocks. On the Wednesdays Anson had off from the bookstore, he did volunteer work at a soup kitchen in the church's basement.

He no longer believed the world to be any kind of joke, but he learned to meet it smiling.

By the time the twin towers fell, he was into his eleventh year without a recurrence. That very afternoon, he saw a woman in the romance-paperbacks section who reminded him of Ellen. Nobody else was browsing: all day long, people had been wandering in off the street to listen to the radio behind the counter that Anson had turned on when the second plane hit; they'd stare at him or at each other, ask a question or make a few remarks, then leave. In the normally quiet bookstore the day had been like a long conversation, disjointed but community-wide. Perfect strangers would finish each other's sentences. But this woman had disappeared immediately down the H-L aisle, and Anson sidled down his counter to see her better. On this day, the uncanny resemblance seemed acceptable and unsurprising, though worthy of a closer look.

Her size and coloring were unlike Ellen's, but the similarity in mannerisms was strong: the angle of her neck as she read books' spines, the way she held her hair against her shoulder. When she came out with three thick selections she kept her eyes down, fumbling in her purse. She'd fixed a hinge of her glasses with a tiny gold safety pin. The books she was buying weren't to Anson's former taste—few in the store were, though he didn't read much now, anyway—but he recognized in her a serious reader, as Ellen had been, as he himself had been once. People on the radio were saying things they'd said before, as if to convince themselves that the things were true. Anson looked around to make sure neither of the store's owners, overweight brothers who'd begun feuding over every dime, was within earshot, and when he didn't see them, he told the woman to put her money away.

At first she didn't understand; she seemed alarmed. Other people looked over. Everybody was jumpy.

"Just take them," he said, sliding the three books back across the counter. "My gift. Please."

Then she did take them, though she was hesitant. She left without thanking him.

But in the weeks afterwards, when he thought about her reading those books, maybe on a bus or at a fluorescent-lit break table somewhere while headlines streamed across a screen and co-workers jabbered at her elbows, he felt better. Not great, but a little better. At his counter now the radio was never off, the multiplying accounts of death and loss like the heavy, dark curtains that drop in folds in old theaters. More than once, handing back change or asking, "Bag?" Anson looked up into eyes as full as his own. As the grief stretched into war news and the strand-by-strand extrusion and examination of causes and possible remedies, Anson heard about the global rages and disparities, duplicities and truths, complexities and misunderstandings he'd experienced as pathologies of his own. Some of what was being articulated now he'd known, and some of it he was learning, but he absorbed it all with the growing feeling that what was most important hadn't been said yet. He watched for the woman who looked like Ellen, but he never saw her again.

Ah, well, he thought.

EYES

Say you're a xawaaga, a foreigner, and you come home some evening during Ramadan, just after the cannon shot from the Citadel has echoed across the city. In the lobby you interrupt your building's bawab, FatHi, who's breaking his fast with a plate of seasoned beans, scooping them up with a piece torn from gritty flat bread. On the stone floor with him are soldiers from their posts outside your building and from embassies, banks, and elsewhere in the neighborhood where xawaagas live: seven or eight young guys with bad teeth and bruised faces who wear black uniforms that don't match or fit, one or two still in dirty summer whites, one in a white coat with black pants and another the opposite, gappy boots crumpling around their ankles. Russian-made rifles (Raskolnikovs, you always think first, so far are they from any reality you've ever had to know; they're rumored to be unloaded, though other rumors have them going off, inadvertently shooting pedestrians or the guards themselves in the foot, as that rumor usually goes) lie around like dropped toothpicks. At the moment, the lobby's free of dogs.

As soon as the men become aware of you, their faces light up, and they lower their food from their mouths and indicate their plates, spreading palms like leather on either side of the stacked metal pails in which their food's been brought to them.

"Itfaddal," they chorus, meaning, Here, have some. Share my food.

You don't, of course, but the next time an opportunity arises for some return gesture, some small indication of generosity or goodwill, even if not toward FatHi in particular or the very same soldiers outside your door, you make it. Say it's the guy who sells bread in the souk, or the date seller there. You offer him a cigarette.

He might accept it. Or he might decline with a hand to his heart, wrist to breast, fingers curled in a loose fist. Or, if your own gesture has especially surprised and touched him, he might lean toward you suddenly, intently, smiling faintly, and with an index finger touch first one cheekbone, then another, meaning, "I'd give you my eyes," which are glistening.

Nor do you take them, of course.

PART TWO

AGE

"**I** am *sitty*-nine years ode!"

The number would come out more quickly than the words, which were never contracted: always "I am," never "I'm." But otherwise it all came out differently each time, amazingly expressive: sometimes of wonder, other times of anger, pride, defiance, triumph, or regret. It was always spoken loud, though, almost a roar, and usually in some larger context, each one a mini-rant. I'd seen people leave with their clothes still damp rather than listen to any more.

"Don't tell me that! Everybody knows that! *I* am *sitty*-nine years ode. *I* know that. I am sitty-nine years *ode*!" People smiled, nodded, tried to move away.

"I am *sitty*-nine years ode! Raised by my mother, in the church—ain't nothing wrong with that! I am sitty-nine years ode, and that eighty-nine-year-ode woman taught me everything I know."

He had several motifs, delivered with slight variations each time, enough that you could be half-listening for twenty minutes before you'd notice a recurrence. If you weren't watching you might think it was single conversation, but he'd be moving around, buttonholing first one person, then another. You didn't like to stare, just as you didn't like to make any movement that might catch his attention and draw him your way.

"*You* always talking about money." Nobody'd have said anything. "Money *don't* help you live! Money don't help you *live*! I am *sitty*-nine years ode. You think I *paid*, to get to this age? Money ain't living, I can tell you *that*. I can *tell* you that. I am sitty-nine years ode. Money *ain't* living."

He'd come in three or four times before I realized he wasn't addressing a good friend or long-suffering relative. Strangers would answer him the way you will with someone you think is a lot simpler than you are, though he ended up outsmarting them—or trapping them, at least, because there was no ignoring him. You'd see people turn to each other, their eyes staring in disbelief, their faces in pain. They'd come up to my window, exhausted: *Hey, man, is there anything you can DO about this?*

Well, no, there wasn't. The old man was plugging his quarters in, just like everybody. What was I going to do, call the police? I had other responsibilities, big ones: to check for dirty needles, for example, not just in the bathrooms but in every washer and dryer whenever I got a free minute, part of my job description ever since a lady reached in after a sock and pulled back with a hypodermic stuck in her thumb, dangling off it like a transparent ferret; on the sidewalk out front, people have been shot. *Officers, this man won't keep his voice down!* I don't think so.

By this time, you see, I'd already learned a few things. The idea had been to stay in town and keep loving Lenny (incidentally sharing his cheap rent upstairs) while I finished my thesis—in sociology, though I was still yearning for the theater, which I'd switched from as an undergrad. But as it turned out, I was spending half my nights at Acrobats with Lenny, then in the mornings stumbling down to man my counter in the laundromat, where my real education was taking place.

"People today, they always lying. Always a put-on, with people today. Me, no. You see me today, you see me tomorrow, I am the *same man*. I am sitty-nine years ode."

At one point I tried to predict the days he'd come, so I could reschedule my shifts to avoid him, but he didn't have a pattern. Sometimes weekends, sometimes Wednesdays or a Friday. He was retired, another theme:

"I have *always* worked. *Always*. I am sitty-nine years ode, had my first job at twelve. Collecting bottles for a penny apiece. Worked for the post office all my adult life. I am sitty-nine years ode. Rain, sleet, all that. Not no more, though. Retired. At sitty-five, like God intended us to."

Even now, every time I think about him I remember something else he said. At the time, annoying and un-ignorable as he was, I did my best to shut him out. When I first "met" him he was sixty-six. "I am sitty-six years ode!"

But it was what he said at sixty-nine that I've got to thank him for:

"You see that boy on the TV news, that thirty-six-year-ode man shot his wife and self? Oh, you don't watch the news. I see. Well, that was my son. I am sitty-nine years ode, and if I live to be a hundred I'll never know what happened. Nobody does. That was my only son. Except God. *God* knows."

He'd said it at least once already that day before its enormity registered on me. I looked out. A woman had her arm on his, a gray-haired white woman in a pink cardigan sweater. I don't know whether he'd unburdened himself directly to her or she'd come over to him, but I rarely saw him speak to white people—he never did to me—and he wasn't looking back at her: he was looking at the floor, his head at a quizzical angle. He had on a new-looking corduroy snap-brim cap, wine-colored, like his old Buick, as I'd happened to notice in the lot. He wore a lined windbreaker and saggy brown dress pants with laced leather shoes, cracked but polished. "*God* knows," he said again, more quietly.

The maybe half a dozen people that were in that day were either looking at him appalled, like I was, leaning out of the office, or, like him, staring down at the floor. Or else they were going about their business, pretending not to hear. Maybe they hadn't. But "shot his wife and self"—who could ignore *that*?

Then he squinted up in way I couldn't see but that made the woman in the pink sweater draw her arm away as if she'd touched something hot.

"You always talking about money," he said. "I am *sitty*-nine *years* old!"

He turned. His face wore the mouth-ajar expression of concentration and puzzlement of someone having difficulty with some small but delicate task, like threading a needle or fitting two pieces of broken china together.

"That eighty-nine-year-old woman . . . All these put-ons, today . . . I am the *same man*. Unh . . ."

It was an unraveling. A woman two tables down from him turned his way, the sheet she'd been folding pressed to her mouth. An eye-glassed young man in a gray hoodie under a leather jacket called out.

"Hey, old man! What eighty-nine-year-old woman?"

That snapped his head up, and it's what brought him around.

"My mother! That eighty-nine-year-ode woman taught me everything I know, and I love her to this day for it. Ain't nothing wrong with that!"

"*Nossir!*" said the man in the hoodie.

"*Noth*ing wrong with it!" somebody behind them said.

He didn't turn toward the voice—it was difficult to tell the extent to which he was aware of others more specifically than as moving shapes to address, his own voice like a heat-seeking missile—but now he was moving again, head bobbing, a boxer. He crossed to a dryer that had stopped, took out the clothes like raked leaves between his hands, and dropped them in the low plastic basket in which he'd brought them. His clean clothes going out looked just the way they did when he brought them in, accounting no doubt for the crumpled state of the pants he wore. He didn't fold anything.

"Ain't got no wife. I live with my mother. Ain't *nothing* wrong with that! That eighty-nine-year ode woman will bury us all. All right, I'll see you! I'll see you! God bless you, now. God bless!"

Somebody got the door for him. The woman who'd been holding her sheets to her mouth beamed and waved. When the door closed behind him people sagged, looked at each other, shook their heads. Somebody who must not have heard the bit about his son laughed. Washers and dryers were still going, but the relative silence was like a vacuum in which I kept hearing him:

"Shot his wife and self. My only son. But God knows. God *knows!*"

That must have been in the early spring, the long and painful stretch of ugliness we have in March and April and sometimes into May, when light and calendar are spring but temperature and wind aren't. I place this episode there thinking he might have bought the corduroy cap both for celebrating the *idea* of spring and, in the actual instance of what the season means here, keeping his head warm. I could be wrong, of course, but it's important to me to place when I first heard him speak about his son. He must have been back several times afterward. I know I heard it again, because I began paying closer attention. His every visit was as compelling as a performance, with a rise and fall to it, but at the same time spontaneous and genuine. He was like a musician who knew his material so well he could play with it. Sometimes he told about his son, and sometimes he didn't, but for the time he was there his voice controlled the laundromat, drawing from his audience the full gamut of reactions, from annoyance to hilarity to horror.

That fall, Lenny moved out—not, as we'd been planning, with me to Boston but across town with Nate, a bartender at Acrobats. For a long time, I thought my world would end and my thesis wouldn't. I had three hundred pages but still didn't know where it was going, and on what my job paid I couldn't afford rent without Lenny, clean clothes notwithstanding (you get four Big Mouth-loads a week, plus all the drying time you want). I went on full-time, which helped with the rent but not with my mood or my thesis. By Thanksgiving I was in a tailspin and was *this far* from moving back to Indiana with my parents when I realized it had been a while since I'd seen the shouting man.

The chance he'd be in became my reason to rise in the morning. Even just thinking about him helped: if he could stand his pain, I could mine. For the longest time I'd had no interest in anything. Now I did.

But I couldn't just come out and ask people—*Hey, whatever happened to the shouting man?* I did mention him to some of the regulars when they came up to report no heat in a dryer or whatever, but nobody'd seen him in a while, though they immediately knew who I meant by "the shouting man." *Thank God!* they'd laugh. *Peace and quiet!*

Then, around Christmastime, the white woman in the pink sweater, which she was wearing still, said he'd died.

"Mr. Phelps shot himself in the stomach a week after his mother died, on his seventieth birthday. The police called it an accident." She knew the details because his mother had gone to her church. In fact, it had fallen to the woman in the pink sweater to bring him chicken that afternoon; she knew the woman who'd found him the next day.

A week later she brought in his obituary, an inch of newsprint carefully torn out with fingertips. I asked her to watch the desk for me and took it to the UPS Store across the parking lot to have a copy made, which I posted on the bulletin board, then returned her original. People squinted up it, but there was no picture and no mention of his mother, and nobody ever reacted that I saw. There was no mention of gunshot, either, only "Terrence Phelps died at home." I'd never heard his name before.

I unpacked. I'd been taking everything I owned to Indiana for Christmas, intending to stay on to see if I could concentrate on my thesis there. But I stayed only three days. All through school it had been a personal point of honor not to borrow money from my father, but now I asked him, and he lent me three months' rent and a little extra, probably figuring he was getting off cheap compared to my moving back in. So I returned to Lenny's apartment, as I had never stopped thinking of it, though his ghost was no longer there for me. Because on Valentine's Day

I met Aaron at Acrobats, and by the next thin days of spring, he'd moved in. I'd abandoned my thesis and written a first draft of "Age," which the Studio Arena didn't want, finally, so now the new dramaturge at the Alleyway has the second draft. Meanwhile I work the counter, and I'm paying my dad back. I am thirty-four years old.

IT'S A PRIVILEGE

Toward the end of Bevin Rand's junior year at Hondecker High School, a senior named Tommy Fondell burst into French class to get Nicki Mills. He hustled her down the carpeted hallways of Modular 3, and when Mr. Henning burst out of the administration office Tommy knocked him down, according to kids who'd watched from the Learning Materials Center. This was years before Columbine, video cameras, or emergency plans, and Tommy dragged Nicki across the front lawn, past the new mallards-on-a-stick sculpture by Hank Boggs, a colleague of Bevin's father's at Hondecker College, and toward a stolen Camaro in the weedy vacant lot across from school; but before he could get her inside Nicki fainted, giving a squad car enough time to arrive. Everyone in Hondecker was shocked and excited by the episode, but in Bevin it stirred something he usually found in novels or movies or headlines of the war and war protests: a sharp sense of the glorious urgency of life that he felt lacking in his own.

Tommy Fondell had been to Wales School for Boys once already and never came back to school again. Nicki Mills returned in time for the French final, two seats up from Bevin in the next row, her white-blonde hair newly permed. She arrived late and finished early, and that summer Bevin heard that she'd gone back to live with her mother in California, where she'd come from at the beginning of the year. That left southeastern Wisconsin without a most beautiful girl at all, Bevin told his friend Findley, though later in the summer Bevin lost his virginity to

Susan Harris and she to him, after long friendship and discussion. But in September Nicki Mills was back, in Advanced French, and Mademoiselle Peterson announced that the highest grade on the previous year's final had been Nicki's—meaning to integrate her among the class, Bevin understood, because Nicki'd belonged to no real group of them. After class he waited until she'd disengaged herself from girls clustered around her, then caught up to offer his own congratulations. Over the summer she'd stopped perming her hair and let it grow: it had streaked, and she wore a short yellow skirt with no hose and an olive-colored blouse, her skin gold in the fluorescent light. She had eyes like crushed ice, and when she turned to him the congratulations caught in his throat and came out, "Way to go, Nick-o," though he'd never heard her called that or, for that matter, called her anything at all before.

Her look seemed to hone in on him from a great distance. Then it changed: she gave him a small, V-shaped smile and thanked him, and in a voice he could barely hear, she said she hadn't expected to do so well. To see a person in her now, a person looking at another person like him, startled Bevin so that in a giddy rush of intimacy in which he assumed that most people had the same ironic perspective on themselves that he had developed on *him*self, he said, "I always thought you were more than you seem to be."

Horrified then at the flash of anger in her eyes, he laughed, and the next day, she dropped French.

So from then on he knew her mostly by reports: she'd modeled for Weise's and her father'd hit a man in a bar and she was going out with Arnold Vogelsson, a drop-out older brother of Mike Vogelsson, who had once drunk grain alcohol at a homecoming game and fallen off the bleachers on his head. Nicki wore Arnold's jacket, the gray letter-jacket parody with black leather sleeves, and in the mornings of late fall, as Bevin locked his Raleigh in the rack beneath the mallards, he could see her in the lot across the street with the smoking group, both Vogelssons looming in the center. Clouds of tobacco and pot smoke drifted from them but not from Nicki; Bevin had heard she never drank, either. The huge dark jacket hung to her slim thighs, its ribbed collar flipped up over her blond hair, and Bevin thought of a gull stuck in oil. By Christmas he heard that Arnold had given her to Mike, then joined the Army and gone to Vietnam, though newspapers were using terms like *scheduled reduction* and *Vietnamization* then. In spring Bevin heard that Nicki was pregnant, that she'd had an abortion, that she'd fucked herself with a Southern Comfort bottle at an outdoor party in Lathers Woods.

But by prom time the people Bevin knew had other things to think about than Nicki Mills. He and Susan Harris had been accepted to different colleges in the East and were preparing for a smooth separation. His friend Findlay had been accepted to UW-Madison but wanted to work for his father's trucking company instead, a safe move because in the draft lottery his birth date had been drawn 358th. Bevin, eleven months younger than Findlay and at no immediate risk from the draft, shared his friend's scorn for the artificial sanction of institutional education: learning, he thought, was an essentially human, individual endeavor. But the pictures and course descriptions in college catalogues looked like fun, and he never really doubted that he would go. So Bevin and his friends savored the last few months of their world before it broke up, and Nicki Mills was someone he'd see across the LMC with headphones on, a hard-eyed girl looking through him.

The week before graduation, the valedictorian came down with mono, and Bevin, ranked second, was asked to speak. Along with what he considered to be obligatory platitudes he felt morally compelled to say something about the war, though McGovern had won 271 delegates in the California primary and 65 in New Jersey, and Bevin's excitement was such that saying something brief was a problem. Finally he said this: "The *New York Times* reports that the last American ground-combat unit, the 3rd Battalion of the 21st Infantry, which was guarding an airbase at Danang, was deactivated yesterday. We can only hope we're going out into a better world." His notecard shook as he read it until he saw the look of approval on Susan Harris's face, and he finished his speech with a more conventional wish and a mild joke that he and Findley had developed over a bong. The speech brought him glory among his own crowd for weeks and several angry letters in the local newspaper the next day. But right after the ceremony, in the chaos of hugging and returning purple mortarboards and gowns to the wrestling room, he spotted, near his parents' beaming faces by the steel gym doors, Nicki Mills. She stared at him for what seemed like a minute before walking out, alone. And before Fourth-of-July weekend, when Findlay was driving a truck to Milwaukee and Susan Harris had the flu, Bevin rushed nostalgia by opening his yearbook and read an entry he hadn't seen before, in an even and graceful script: "You have no idea. Nicki Mills."

The phone book listed seven Millses, two in the Ledges that he discounted right away and the rest on the West Side. Two of those were disconnected, the third and fourth no help, and the fifth and sixth were busy. The voice that answered Walter Mills's number had a Spanish accent. "I'm sorry," Bevin said. "I'm trying to locate Nicki Mills."

"Neecki not home." It was a woman's voice.

"So she does live here?"

"Who djou?"

Bevin identified himself as a friend from school who'd just called to chat, and what might be a more convenient time to call back? He wished he'd said "better" instead of "convenient," but after several seconds of silence he heard:

"BAYbeen. O.K. Eeb Neecki want to talk to djou, Neecki geeb djou a telephone call."

Two days went by. Bevin wondered if she'd gotten the message or understood his name if she had. He was working forty hours a week at a cement plant for the summer: from six to three he toted a three-foot wrench and in the evenings combed white pea-sized balls out of his hair, which he was letting grow. He still didn't know exactly how to interpret what Nicki had written in his yearbook. Sometimes he thought she'd called him naïve, and other times he thought she meant she'd harbored secret feelings for him.

Either way, by the end of June, he felt ready for her, and after work on a Wednesday, he called her again. She said she'd gotten his message but had forgotten it, but when she laughed at a self-disparaging quip he made by way of reply, he plunged right in: would she meet him at Riverside Park, by the bandstand whose basement was used as a warming house for ice skaters in the winter, at one o'clock Saturday afternoon? At two the boat races would begin, an annual event, and Bevin thought afterwards they might drive elsewhere for dinner and some better music than they'd hear at the park. His parents and younger brother and sister were camping in Ontario; he had full use of the Plymouth Valiant, and not too far into Illinois, Dave "Snaker" Ray was playing in a coffeehouse in a converted barn. Bevin asked Nicki if she'd ever heard Dave Snaker play.

"Let's see how it goes at the boat races," she said.

But she was there before Bevin was, in braids and a headband, perched on a scarred picnic tabletop overlooking the lagoon to watch shoehorn-shaped hydroplanes doing time trials. She wore faded denim cut-offs to the tops of her tanned thighs and a work shirt with the tails tied above her midriff, and Bevin swallowed. He'd worn his favorite pants, baggy seersuckers he'd found at St. Vincent de Paul, and a Hawaiian shirt with blue parrots on it. On the rear-window ledge of the Valiant was a wide-brimmed straw hat that at the last minute he'd lacked the nerve to wear in public.

"Hello, Nick-o," he heard himself say.

He'd almost forgotten her V-shaped smile. An Evinrude whined, and she turned toward the sound. She had clavicles, and Bevin watched the tendon in her neck and the smooth twist of her waist. But when she turned back to him, he couldn't help but notice that the two peace signs on her beaded headband had lined up just above her eyes. As if she could see her reflection in *his* eyes, she snatched it off.

"I feel stupid in these braids," she said as they walked along the river bank, and she began undoing her hair. The weather was sunny and not too hot, and the narrow strip of park was crowded; cars parked the length of Riverside Drive, which was choked with more traffic. People had brought blankets and lawn chairs and radios and grills, and the air smelled of brats and beer. Black people and whites had attended the races in about equal numbers, but they kept apart. Many of the Blacks had dressed up, and many of the white women wore curlers. Bevin noticed quite a few police. Above the park, on a bluff across the drive, were rows of painted factory windows behind grillwork, some of them broken or missing; he could see the top of a router he'd worked on the previous summer. Further down was a new outdoor mall called The Plaza, whose sign was supposed to rotate but was already broken, stopped at an angle on its pole. Bevin's parents had never expected to stay as long as they had in this town, and he'd been raised to believe that the world started outside it. He was glad to be leaving but sorry to know that the town wouldn't miss him. Guys were gawking at Nicki. He asked how her summer was going.

She ran her fingers through her hair, which swayed off her shoulders when she shook her head back. "I don't know how to answer that, I guess. I miss some things about school already. Some of those counselors were pretty cute."

Bevin didn't think he'd ever heard her laugh before, certainly not like this: she let out a sudden burst of a guffaw, big and merry, that stiffened her back and brought her head up, as if a spring inside her had been released. It was a whole new side to her, and it was fairly alarming, like walking in on a teacher picking his or her nose.

Then she touched his elbow and smiled. "Just kidding. I'm working at Ciaffa's"—this was a supper club with rumored links to organized crime—"and the tips are decent. I'm reading *Johnny Got his Gun*, which is not exactly cheery, so I'm sort of making myself finish it. Luckily, it's short. Looks like all the benches are taken."

"I should have brought a blanket," Bevin said. He'd quoted Dalton Trumbo in his graduation speech, and the thought that Nicki was trying to impress him was like a gift of cologne: nice gesture, but what to do with it? He couldn't think of a good way to ask whether she was going to college in the fall, either. "We've got some L.L. Bean camp stools in the garage I could have brought, except my parents took them to Ontario. Want a Sno-Cone?" He paused in front of a vendor.

"Ontario," she said. "No, thanks. You're thoughtful, though."

"Well, no, I'm not. Thoughtful would have been to bring a blanket, wouldn't it?"

Susan Harris would have laughed, but Nicki seemed annoyed.

"Let's try the bridge," Bevin said. Underneath it were cement ledges on support columns that would put them close to the boats, which would turn before the bridge. With satirical buddies, Bevin had attended the boat races several years running. He asked Nicki if she ever missed them before remembering she'd gone away the previous summer.

"I've never seen one. I used to know a guy who raced in them." Her voice was bored.

"Is he racing this year?"

"He's dead." She shrugged. "To me, he's dead."

She must mean either Tommy Fondell or Arnold Vogelsson, Bevin thought, though he'd probably have heard if Arnold had been killed. The morning news had reported another break in the Paris peace talks and Hue shelled with 122-millimeter North Vietnamese rockets; commentators had doubted Thieu's promise that Quangtri Province could be taken back soon.

"I'm sorry," Bevin said.

Nicki shrugged again. "This particular guy wanted to die. At least that's what he used to say all the time. 'Blaze of Glory' was the name of his boat. And he couldn't wait to go to war."

"The war's just awful." Bevin said. He still didn't know who she meant, but the war was familiar ground for him; he knew it was being fought by guys who really didn't have much choice, whether they'd signed up or not. He mentioned the previous summer's Senate debate over the Selective Service bill to extend the draft, reminding Nicki about Hatfield and Mansfield and their defeated amendments, warming to his topic until he realized by her face that his voice had turned strident.

"I don't really know about all that," she said. "All I know is, this particular guy was a bastard."

A gun started the first race. People were already sitting on the ledges underneath the bridge, so Bevin and Nicki climbed a dirt slope and wedged into the crowd on the bridge to watch from the rail. The Rock River looked like spinach. Bright fiberglass hulls skittered and whined toward them and veered back, chased by white arcs.

"Pick a winner," Nicki said.

Bevin pointed out a boat at random. For as much and as long as she'd been on his mind, he couldn't think of what to say next. Standard getting-to-know-you questions bored him. Before Susan Harris, he'd once ruined a date by asking *What's your favorite shape?* He figured five more hours before Dave "Snaker" Ray took the stage, maybe six with a local opening act. Nicki had worn a perfume that smelled like strawberries, and the cement underfoot was hot. Traffic roared across the bridge from a stoplight, the exhaust mixing with the fruity smell.

"This is nice," Nicki said, and, wildly, he agreed. She put four fingers on his forearm, her nails perfect. "I mean it's O.K.," she said. "Buy me a hot dog."

She took his hand, and they headed back toward the concession stands. Racers were idling toward the dock, shouting to people onshore. Bevin hadn't noticed who won.

"I guess this means no dinner," he said, mock-glum, handing Nicki one of two foot-longs he'd bought and thinking she might take the chance to cut the date short herself. Susan Harris wouldn't have let him pay for the hot dogs, much less asked him to buy her one. Not that the money bothered him. But Nicki's request was like her headband and perfume and political void. Susan would have laughed at the ambiguity of his remark about dinner, too, but Nicki's face had set.

Then she whirled and crouched over her hot dog, her eyes shut.

Bevin thought she'd broken a tooth until he recognized Mike Vogelsson among pony-tailed guys at the beer booth. They all wore shirts with the sleeves ripped out and baggy shorts with work boots, and a couple of them carried shiny black canes like a magician's prop; Mike was leaning on one, his free hand raising a Pabst cup in their direction. His voice was rocks.

"Whore bitch," he hollered. "Cunt sore. Who's the twerp?"

His buddies laughed.

"Let's go further down," Bevin said.

Nicki let him lead her. To circumvent the beer booth, he headed for the sidewalk alongside Riverside Drive, which led back to the bandstand and the lot where he'd parked the Valiant. The jeers receded and then followed, and when Bevin looked back he saw guys trotting, no sign of any limps: those with canes carried them like spears, parallel to the ground. Nicki dropped her hot dog in an oil drum they marched past, cursing in combinations and rhythms new to Bevin. When he touched her elbow, the cackles behind them exploded.

"You don't have to do this, you know," Nicki said with no break in her stride. "You can just go."

"Don't be silly. I'm having the time of my life." He laughed at the truth of it, then heard a clatter on the pavement behind them and barked, *"Run!"*

They made it to the Valiant, Bevin's chest jumping. From inside he heard hoots and saw Mike and pals in the middle of the parking lot, dancing around a black cane. Nicki looked in another direction, her hands in her lap. Bevin started the car and stomped on the accelerator, crunching his tires in the gravel.

"What the hell are you *doing*?" Nicki cried.

Mike and his friends scattered.

"No harm done," Bevin said, but he could barely get the words out, and then the back window popped.

Safety glass, it crumbled, but Bevin didn't realize what had happened until he looked in the rear-view mirror and saw his hat bouncing off the trunk. The empty window framed Mike Vogelsson in a pose like the comic-book hero Thor's, hair wild and legs splayed, one arm across his chest in follow-through from his throw. His cane clattered beside the hat, and Bevin wedged out onto Riverside Drive.

"Well," Nicki said to the windshield when the traffic picked up. "I guess we're on for that banjo music, if your invitation's still open. Frankly, I can't go home just yet."

Bevin was calculating that the back window would cost a week's pay at the cement plant, but he could probably get it replaced before his parents returned. Trying to breathe normally, he pointed at a Dairy Queen sign ahead and suggested a cone for the drive. Nicki shrugged. Inside, she studied the menu with her arms wrapped around herself against the air conditioning, her fingertips lightly scratching the taut skin over her ribs. A girl working the grill glared at her from under the stainless steel smoke vent. She ordered a small plain cone, then at Bevin's urging decided to have sprinkles on it. He paid, ordering nothing for himself, because he felt sick with nerves and desire.

She might have been riding a public bus. They passed the Holiday Inn and took 51 South, and after ten silent minutes on the highway Bevin cleared his throat and admitted that driving at Mike like he'd done had been wrong.

"Wrong? Oh, Mike." She grimaced, then touched his arm and pointed out his window, her eyes wide. "Look! White cows!"

Half a dozen Charolais cattle were grazing beside a corrugated aluminum silo. Nicki turned to watch until they'd passed, then leaned against the dash to keep an eye out for more. Around one forefinger the DQ napkin was wrapped tight, with its red logo like a bandage on a deep, brand-new cut. The Valiant had no AC, and air from the window raised wisps of her hair.

"God, I love the country," she said.

Bevin whiffed. "Stout. Pungent. Rich."

She sat back, focusing a look on him from across the bench-style seat. She asked if he had brothers and sisters, and he told her a bit about his siblings. He thought he'd heard that Nicki didn't have any, but she turned out to have a sister married to a mechanic in Long Beach and a half-sister just divorced, a dental hygienist in Fort Bragg. Her mother had just remarried in L.A. When Bevin asked how often they all got together, Nicki said she wouldn't be going back there again. He didn't know what to say to that, but none of her answers had bored him.

"So. Why'd you call me?" she said.

He felt the question in his spine. He said she'd always interested him, but circumstances had prevented him from getting to know her. He said he studied pretty hard during the school year, which was only partially true, but he had no other easily identifiable sports or hobbies to name. *I would have asked you out earlier, but I was reading the newspaper.* "Also, you were always going out with somebody else."

"How do you know I'm not going out with somebody now?"

"I don't, I guess. To tell you the truth, I was intrigued by what you wrote in my yearbook. What did you mean, I have no idea? About what?"

"Look how high the corn's grown!" She'd brought a hand to her mouth. Then she gave him the V-shaped smile. "Sorry. I forgot about that. I didn't think I'd see you again. What happened to Sue Harris?"

"Luckily, Susan's got the flu," he said, and Nicki laughed. He explained the agreements he and Susan Harris had been reaching, putting them more in the past tense than they actually were.

"Smart girl," Nicki said.

"Smart's relative, though, isn't it?" Bevin pointed out that Susan had gotten only a B+ in French class. He asked Nicki why she'd dropped it.

She gave him a long look and then shrugged. "What's French going to get me? I'm not going there any time soon."

"Why not? How do you know? Do you want to?"

"Sure, I'd love to. I'd love to be queen of the world, too. Then you'd see some changes around here, for sure."

"It's entirely possible," Bevin said. "Current queen gets hit by a bus, you're a shoo-in. Don't give up hope."

Nicki grinned and shook her head. "You're sweet, but you don't have a clue."

"Then why'd you come out with me?" He touched the hang of his hair, clowning. "Cute guy?"

"Extremely cute. But no clue."

He objected comically. "But O.K.," he said finally. "Let's say you're right, just for the sake of argument. So give me one, will you? Give me a clue."

He stopped for a light. They'd reached the mall and food-joints of Loves Park. Nicki grinned to herself and bit a cuticle, considering him. "I could," she said when the light turned green. "I could give you the whole fucking answer."

His stomach dropped. "Tell me. I want to know."

In the next block she said to stop. She was pointing at the pink neon vacancy sign of a motel called Ike's. Bevin couldn't believe he was turning in.

It was sex like he'd read about and dreamed about. Nicki was playful, matter-of-fact, proud. She directed. Bevin's main contribution was to suggest they stop and take off the loud plastic the mattress had been wrapped in. Afterwards they napped, and he awoke to Nicki exploring his body, slow and sure until he knew that what he wanted was all right with her. She responded with enthusiasm and gratitude.

"For what?" Bevin said. "Are you kidding? You're the one to thank. Jesus."

She grinned and propped the side of one foot against the cinder-block wall.

"How long have you been doing this?" he said.

She guffawed at the wall, rocking the mattress, but he thought he could probably get used to that laughter eventually. "Still no clue."

"Maybe by fall."

She dropped her leg and sighed at the ceiling.

"We'd have to see."

She lived on one of the curbless President streets, Johnson or Jackson or Grant, in a square single-story house with yellow aluminum siding and an R in the screen door, which he could see by a bare bulb over it. TV light flickered behind a picture window. When Bevin pulled into an empty gravel driveway a woman in a sleeveless blouse appeared barefoot on the plain cement stoop, holding a glass. "That's Luisa," Nicki said, one leg out the passenger door. "My father's friend. Call me tomorrow, if you still want to. Around noon, say? I go to work at seven."

On Sunday they paddled the Rand family's canoe north of town and made love in a field until a farmer appeared, then drove to Bevin's house and made love on a towel on his parents' king-sized bed, which Nicki couldn't get over the size of; when they'd finished she got up and bounced around its perimeter, turning at corners as if marching around a block. Bevin was amazed at the way her quick interest enlivened ordinary things he'd never considered unless he was stoned: trees and bugs and faucets and a ceramic bedside lamp. Nicki'd tried pot twice, she said, which was enough.

Naked in the kitchen, they were eating a pizza they'd ordered, Nicki rubbing her toes into the carpet, when Susan Harris phoned.

She said her flu was over and that she'd heard he enjoyed the boat races this year. Bevin said he was glad she felt better, paused, and said his job was turning out to be pretty tiring, so maybe they should start putting their agreement into effect; he knew they both had a lot to do before fall, anyway.

"I just hope you're using condoms," Susan said. Nicki was reading *New Yorker* cartoons taped to the saffron-colored refrigerator, chewing pizza and massaging the small of her back. "By the way," Susan said. "Did Findlay tell you about his disastrous truck trip to Milwaukee? Apparently he's reconsidering the college option post haste." They exchanged a few amused but affectionate remarks about Findlay while Nicki moved from one cartoon to the next, and Bevin stretched the cord to point out one he particularly liked: a resentful-looking dog watching a man screw in a light-bulb, a thought balloon over the dog's head reading, *I could do that*. Nicki nodded.

"Well, Susan—goodbye," he said into the phone.

It was Bevin's father who urged Nicki to apply to Hondecker College. Bevin's friends tended to consider his father cool—he had a handlebar moustache and let Bevin call him Cal, and when Bevin had admitted repairing the window in the Valiant and told him how it broke, Cal had just laughed; but Nicki was reserved with him. Cal couldn't get over the fact that when a counselor had made Nicki take the SATs, she'd scored in the 1500's, better in math than in verbal, the opposite of Bevin and in fact fifty points higher overall—but she hadn't had her scores sent anywhere. Cal told her about Hondecker's scholarship for locals and a special late-admissions policy, and finally she agreed to fill out the forms he gave her. The result was an invitation to audit two first-semester courses tuition-free and apply for full admission in the spring, with retroactive credit possible for the audits. Nicki said she'd take the Hondecker catalog home, at least, and Mrs. Rand, who'd never liked Sue Harris much but seemed to have a soft spot for Nicki, advised Bevin not to pressure her about it.

They saw each other almost daily for the three hours between their jobs. Bevin would drive the Valiant to her house in his work clothes, steel foot-protectors over his boots and cement balls in his hair, and when she appeared over the R of her screen door with a cold beer for him or a lime popsicle or an apple she'd half-eaten herself, he thought his life had begun at last. They made love in her bed, because Luisa was at work in the late afternoons and Nicki's father was rarely home. When Bevin did meet him, he was a surprise: a thin, balding man in bifocals and long-sleeved shirts he kept buttoned at the wrists, he seemed more nervous about seeing Bevin in his house than Bevin was to see him there, which was plenty. The few words he mumbled to Bevin he ended up addressing to Nicki. He was a draftsman, she said, between jobs; she didn't volunteer anything else.

And once, at the Plaza, Bevin recognized his own straw hat a few places ahead of him in line at Walgreen's. When he came out, Mike Vogelsson was waiting, tamping a pack of Salems against the heel of his hand. *So be it*, Bevin thought, squaring his shoulders and breathing deep through his nose, if somewhat tremulously.

But Mike, once he'd worked out a cigarette and lit it, grinned and doffed his hat, revealing a crewcut. "Signed up," he said, extending his other hand. "What's the diff. Probably won't be able to wear this, where I'm going. Want it back?"

In August, Bevin told Nicki he loved her.

"Bull*shit*," she said, loud enough that an elderly couple in half-glasses glanced up from their tassled menus at the next table. He'd debated about how to say it, whether to let it rip out in bed or drop it fetchingly at some incongruous moment or treat it more solemnly, which is what he'd ended up doing, in a new restaurant in Madison called the Hands of Thyme. It was on the top floor of a bank building with a view of a clock tower and the lit capitol; they'd eaten crab salad and creamed asparagus in flakey pastry and were waiting for *peches flambées*. In the pocket of his gabardine sports jacket was a small velvet-covered jewelry case with a pearl on a thin gold chain, which he planned to give her during the drive home.

"I know, I know," Bevin told Nicki in a low but urgent voice. "It sounds hokey. But, you know. I mean it."

She'd worn more makeup than usual, and it seemed to have irritated her eyelids; she dabbed at them with her napkin and glared at him. "This is a nice place," she said, "but I've been to places where a salad costs *twice* as much."

Alarmed and incredulous, Bevin managed to keep his voice down. "Nicki, what's the matter? Here, look." He set the jewelry case above her plate, and when she just stared at it, nostrils flared and lips compressed, he reached over and opened it. "Don't you want it?"

"Want?" she said, as if she didn't understand the word or, worse, him. "*Want?*"

She was beautiful, and he loved her more than ever, and he thought that if he could only make her believe that, everything would be all right. He put his hand on the one she was holding her linen napkin in, looped over a forefinger, like the Dairy-queen napkin, but she jerked it back. Then she exhaled, wiped her face, gave the couple beside them an apologetic little shrug, and smiled.

"Whew. Boy. All right. Sorry. Thanks," she told Bevin and picked up the pearl. "It's beautiful. You're the nicest guy I've ever been out with, and I mean that, too. I've been thinking about things also, you know. And I guess I wouldn't mind taking calculus in the fall, like your father said."

Bevin felt himself flush, he was so happy. The gabardine collar of his jacket scratched his neck, and Nicki teased him about the look on his face. "Talk about clueless, boy. *Man.*"

On the night of her birthday, toward the end of the month, Bevin drove to Ciaffa's to pick her up after work, a surprise. He was leaving for Vermont in a week and a half. He knew he'd been manic recently, and the more plans for them he'd tried to make in between logistics of his own—investigating transfer credits, was the main thing, so that they could eventually end up at the same college—the quieter Nicki got. So he'd backed off for a few days, not even calling her. Then he worried she'd think his feelings had paled beside his immediate future, which to his own dismay actually did seem partially true sometimes, though he knew it was just a temporary buzz. Now he hoped to smooth everything out, though she'd never wanted to see him at work. Ciaffa's was across the state line, where the drinking age was twenty-one; long before he'd ever known Nicki, Bevin had once stood in the amber light of its entranceway with a larking group being refused entrance. He remembered dark wood, red leather, high heels, and furs; it must have been in the winter. "Ciaffa's may hold the clue I'm missing," he'd joked once.

"Forget that," Nicki'd laughed. "It's too dark inside."

But from the bar he could clearly see a burly man at a table of twelve, the last to empty, pat Nicki's behind when she brought his change on a tray, and Bevin could clearly see the way she smiled down at the man. Her hair was done in a way he'd never seen on her before, swept up off her neck and piled high; she looked about twenty-five. Bevin was dressed older himself, in his gabardine jacket and a part in hair he'd combed wet, and he hadn't been carded. He waved at Nicki twice before she noticed him.

"Happy birthday," he said when she finally took the stool beside him. He nodded toward the burly man, who was now at the coat-check with his party. "I guess you had to let him do that."

She gave him a scant glance and compressed her glossed lips. "He's harmless, Bevin. That's his wife, and that's his mother." She emptied her change apron on the varnished walnut: an order book, a Bic pen, a pile of crumpled bills that she began to straighten and count. Bevin saw fifties.

"Never mind," he said. "I'm sorry. Can I buy you a drink before we go? I've got the Valiant." Everything that came out of his mouth in this place sounded small.

She finished counting, then turned to him, her face and voice careful. "Thanks for the happy birthday, Bevin. That was sweet. But I asked you not to come here, didn't I?"

Down the bar a ways, the bartender unstuck two long rubber mats from the bar wells with a crackling noise. He lowered them in a tank below the bar and looked down at Nicki, heavy eyebrows raised. He was dark and thick-necked and gold-chained, and when Nicki raised hers back, Bevin thought a huge and ugly truth was being revealed. The gunk from under the mats was sour; even from where he sat, he could smell it.

"I see," he said. "At last. The whole fucking answer. Isn't it? *Isn't* it?"

For Thanksgiving he flew home. The whole Rand family met the O'Hare bus at the Holiday Inn on Wednesday afternoon. Nicki hadn't audited anything, his father had written when he'd asked, early in the semester, and her name hadn't come up since.

After dinner he asked to borrow the Valiant. His parents exchanged glances, Cal debating with himself before handing over the keys, and Bevin could see both parents watching from the bay window as he backed out the drive. He'd tried to talk enthusiastically about college but hadn't been able to hide his disillusionment. He was making C's and D's, and he hadn't liked the East. He'd tried to present himself to his peers as a factory boy on scholarship, but he hadn't fooled anyone. He'd canvassed for McGovern during the last hopeless days and even tried hitting the books for a while, but everything seemed beside the point. He'd written Nicki three long letters, and she hadn't written back.

Ciaffa's carded him, but Bevin didn't care because he'd seen Nicki's back, her hair done up the way he'd seen it here before. She was taking orders in a tight black skirt, and at the sight of her he felt a soaring in his chest that he hadn't felt in months. From a machine on his way out he bought a hard pack of Salems, a habit he'd cultivated in the East. He had the only Valiant in the lot, though among Cadillacs and Mercurys and Chargers he saw one rusty Ford, a Galaxie. On the outside, Ciaffa's was nothing: brown clapboard with a roofed entranceway to the parking lot and a blue neon sign on a pole. To the south was a wall around a salvage yard, across the road a tiny all-night market that wouldn't sell Bevin beer. He bought a six-pack of Mountain Dew, popped one in the car, and lit a joint.

He listened to the radio for a while. Kissinger had met with Le Duc Tho for four and a half hours in Gif-sur-Yvette, no indication of progress; the Packers led the Central Division, and Neil Young's *Harvest* had hit number one. Bevin took a leak on the salvage-yard wall and smoked another joint outside. Back in the car he did another Dew, slouching when bare-legged women in dangling stoles emerged from Ciaffa's with fat, laughing men. From one of these slouches he rose into a flashlight beam over his shoulder.

"Place your hands on the wheel," said a cop with a sharp Adam's apple, eying Bevin's shoulder-length hair. His partner asked Bevin what he thought he was doing.

Tell the truth, Bevin thought. He could not believe how calm he felt.

"Waiting for my own true love," he reported. "We haven't seen each other in months. I've been away. At college. In Vermont." He told them his own name and Nicki's and pointed at where she worked.

The cops looked at each other, then at him, then around the interior of the Valiant. Bevin had replaced the Hondecker College decal when he'd replaced the back window, and he saw its glimmer in his rearview mirror now as the flashlight beam passed over it. The beam dipped to the red-and-green cans on the floor and stopped on his overflowing ashtray, and the cop with the Adam's apple reached in and picked out his roach.

"Looks like you've fucked up," said the partner.

"I know I have," Bevin said. "I'm sorry." Diners were getting in their cars, paying no attention. The radio in the cop car squawked, and the partner went over to it.

"We're going to take a little spin," said the cop with the Adam's apple, tucking Bevin's roach under the pressed flap of his shirt pocket. "And when we come back we don't want to see any little Plymouths."

"You won't, you won't. Not this one, at least."

"Good."

Bevin fumbled with his keys. The patrol car veered toward the shoulder and stopped, rocking on its shocks, its headlights on a thin black man in droopy pants. In the time it took for Bevin to try two wrong keys in the ignition he saw the cops get out, frisk the man, bundle him into their backseat, and drive off. Bevin tried another key, scared to death now.

Then he saw Nicki. She was alone, heading for the Galaxie, one of two cars left. He bent over the steering wheel to watch her through the windshield. She'd changed into jeans and a windbreaker with Hondecker Tech on the back, its collar flipped up, her hair still piled. Her back was straight, her step brisk, her hands swinging free. Girls at Bevin's college usually carried some kind of bag, even if they wouldn't call it a purse. The Valiant honked. "Shit," Bevin muttered.

Nicki moved back toward the lit entranceway of Ciaffa's before seeming to recognize his car. He left it running and got out, approaching her slowly in the weak amber light. He stopped six feet from her, and she smiled, not the V-shaped one but broader, tight and tired; she set a hand on her hip, her weight on one leg. "Bevin Rand," she said. "How *are* you? On vacation?"

"Nicki, Nicki, Nicki," he said. "The cops are after me. In about two minutes they'll be back, and if my car's still here I'm doomed. Quick! Will you come for a ride? Or follow me, and we'll meet at . . . where?"

She looked at him, eyes widening, then dropped her hand and laughed the loose, merry guffaw that had first alarmed him at the boat races. But now it sounded so right to him that in a second he joined in, though he knew she wasn't going to get in the car or follow him anywhere.

ACCIDENT

Over dinner, MacKechnie's mother read him an item from the newspaper: the Barneses were back in town, after a car wreck on their way to Mexico for vacation. The parents had suffered only minor injuries, but Carson, whose name MacKechnie's mother claimed to recognize from some birthday party he couldn't even remember, had spent two weeks in a downstate hospital before he was allowed to come home. The paper didn't mention any other Barneses, and MacKechnie said that it was typical of Carson Barnes to be an only kid in a family that wanted to leave the country. "Too bad he got hurt," he said. "But it's the only fame that guy will ever get. We call him Poindexter, which means loser, or fucking wimp." He was not trying to start an argument but to set her straight about the facts, thinking of which he now remembered he'd once beaten Carson Barnes up. His mother waited until she was sure he saw the way she was looking at him over the edge of her newspaper. "How nice it would be for you to go and see him," she said. "And watch your mouth."

She had fat arms and bad feet, both from her job on the cinnamon-roll line at Shurfine bakery, and he'd heard her cuss worse than he ever did, and the difference between the way she'd insist on talking to him and the way she actually was, and certainly the way *he* actually was, insulted and enraged him. When he'd driven her upstairs by pointing all this out, he called Shackleford and Briggs to see what was doing, but he got no answer at either place. Andy Reno was still getting rabies shots for a raccoon bite he'd gotten down at the creek: MacKechnie and Shackleford had been the ones who'd taken Reno to the hospital, which had been all out of the new vaccine, so he was getting fourteen shots in the stomach, one a day, and MacKechnie wasn't going anywhere near him until he was cured. TV was shit, and MacKechnie sat on the front stoop, razzing the twins next door while they tried to find enough uncracked sidewalk for a hopscotch court, and then they didn't even know how to draw one. After another no-answer at Shackleford's he went upstairs and tried to apologize to his mother.

She and MacKechnie's brother had gotten along even worse, but ever since his brother joined the Navy it seemed like she'd been missing their dead father more than ever. His brother was on a destroyer called Maddox, which a year ago had seen action in a gulf called Tonka, like the trucks, but since then he'd been writing them less and less. "Well, no news is good news," said his mother every day when she'd been through the mail, though MacKechnie knew that even the Navy would do more than write a letter if something happened to his brother.

Through the hollow plywood of her bedroom door now he could hear the ice cubes in her glass. "Mom, come on," he said, but she screamed "Leave me be!" and turned on her radio.

It was too early in the summer to be pissing her off this bad already, and MacKechnie asked himself what it would really cost him to make her happy on a night that looked fairly useless anyhow. He looked up the Barneses' address in the phone book. The street name he recognized, and the number was the year of his birth if he'd been born in the next century, which he took as a sign he should go. From between the garage and a neighbor's back fence he got out his bicycle, which he'd made himself from a Schwinn Typhoon frame somebody'd dumped in the creek. Now it had high-rise handlebars and a banana seat that he'd taken off a bike at the mall, the first real stealing he'd done, *real stealing* distinguished in his mind from *not really stealing* by his having gone out and sought what he needed this time as opposed to just reaching out for what happened to come along. He'd camouflaged the seat with duct tape, and tonight he did half of Atkinson Avenue on the back wheel alone, a new personal best.

He figured another two hours of daylight left, easy. At the top of Milwaukee Road bridge, he stopped and got off his bicycle to see if Shackleford or Briggs or anyone was down there, but all he could see was trees and tracks and creek. The trees were so full now you could only see about half as much creek as even a week ago. In the deepening sunlight the tracks looked copper. He unsnapped the breast pocket of his pinstriped overalls, which him and Briggs and Halverson had once gotten kicked out of school for all wearing on the same day with no shirts, as he was wearing his now, and dug out a Salem hard pack with three cigarettes and a joint left in it. He lit the joint on his first match, cupping it against a light breeze that brushed his hair against his bare shoulders. His hair was getting good now: it would be ready for a ponytail by the time the weather got hot. But tonight the air was cool, and he wished he'd worn a shirt. Holding the joint between his teeth he got back on his banana seat, shoving his butt back against the sissy bar and lifting a heel over the top tube of his bike. He felt fine.

The Barneses lived in the Ledges, near Sally Blake and Jane Capitano and Halverson and those guys, but the Barnes house was not like the others around here. MacKechnie could tell which one it was even before he checked out the address. It was older, for one thing, three stories of brown clapboard like a house in town, similar to the MacKechnies' landlord's house except no weather stains or peeling trim, and more lawn. It was probably the first house ever built out here, set so far back in the trees at the end of Maplewood Terrace it was not really part of the Ledges at all. The lawn had been cut, but high weeds grew through the gravel in the long driveway, as if the Barnses wanted to make it hard for you to get any closer than the street. Other houses around here had asphalt driveways and were more modern and cooler-looking, two-toned with neat shapes of roof and double garages overflowing with bikes and kids' toys and lawn-care tools. The Fourth was a ways off yet, but most houses had their flags out, and dads and kids that MacKechnie didn't know were trimming hedges or shooting baskets or cleaning up barbecues. It was a nice neighborhood. But at Barnes's place there was no flag, no hoop, no barbecue, and the single-car garage door was closed, with no car in the drive, though MacKechnie realized their car might have been totaled, which would not be their fault. He dropped his bike about halfway up the drive and climbed wooden steps to the wide front porch. The curtains inside were drawn.

But when he rang the bell, a tall woman with wavy gray-and-black hair and half-glasses opened up and blinked out at him as he said who he was and why he'd come. "It's nice that the rest of your family's all right," he added.

"Yes, well," said the woman. "We were lucky. Carson's upstairs, I believe, doing something for his father. But I don't see why you can't talk to him while he works."

When she took her glasses off and opened the screen door, he saw the book in her hand and remembered hearing that both Poindexter's parents were teachers, not even high school but college, which was why Poindexter was supposed to be so smart. But he would do stuff like wear white socks with leather shoes, which everybody knew was a hated thing, and if you knew that, why the hell would you do it? Poinie would not only wear white socks but would point them out to everybody, laughing like the fool he was. *In and out*, MacKechnie thought, *and then the old lady can call over here and find out I've done it if she doesn't believe me.*

Mrs. Barnes wore a loose black dress that had orange-and-red stitching on the chest shaped like roosters that a child might draw, and she was barefoot, with orange polish on her toenails. MacKechnie tried not to stare at her feet as she led him through a long living room, which was lit only by a tiny cone lamp behind a big leather chair. Air-conditioning was on, and there was a deep, dark carpet with a snaky-looking pattern in it that MacKechnie could tell was expensive as shit, and against every wall was a bookcase. It was like a cross between a library and a museum in here, with paintings and a stand with a clay pot on it and a bunch of little stuff on the sill of a stained-glass window by the stairwell in back. On the bottom step Mrs. Barnes turned to make sure he hadn't swiped anything, judging from the look on her face.

"How are you enjoying your summer?" she said.

She was older than MacKechnie's mother but actually fairly pretty, in a bony kind of way, and when she lifted the hem of her dress and took a couple of stairs sideways, waiting for his answer, he saw that she had nice ankles. MacKechnie said that summer sure beat school but he'd be glad when he was old enough to get a job next year, which was not entirely true but seemed like the kind of thing to say to a lady like this.

But it was not entirely false, either, because when he was old enough for a job he'd be old enough for a driver's license, and he was looking forward to that, for those couple of years until he'd have to decide whether to join the Navy or chance getting drafted, which would have happened to his brother anyway, as it turned out. But you had that good couple of years. It was just work that he was not looking forward to. Work was what had killed his dad, who as far back as MacKechnie could remember had just about lived at the plant and had literally died there, from a heart attack. The company had had to hire two guys to handle what MacKechnie's dad had done alone, manage shipping, and then it paid MacKechnie's mother about half the benefits it was supposed to, which was why she went to work at Shurfine. So MacKechnie *would* have to find some way to get money next summer, for a car and gas for it, which meant he'd told Mrs. Barnes the truth, so why did her smile make him feel like such a liar?

Whoooa, Nellie, MacKechnie told himself, trying to remember which dope he'd rolled that joint from, because it was even better than he'd thought. *Watch yourself, man.*

"You're all in such a hurry to grow up," Mrs. Barnes said. "Carson's in the back bathroom."

They were at the top of the stairs, in an L-shaped hallway where every door but one at the far end was closed. He smelled tobacco smoke, not cigarettes but probably a pipe, because it was sweet, and behind one of the closed doors he could hear a typewriter clacking away so fast it might have been two of them, like in the office at school. Thinking Poinie was in there he reached for the knob, but Mrs. Barnes touched his arm, and when he turned around he saw her pointing at the open door down the hall. The place where she had touched his biceps felt cool and dry, he smelled her soap, and before he knew it he was wondering what it would be like to fuck her. In the fading daylight from a small window on the landing, her eyes on him were intensely bright and green, and he thought she might have been thinking about it, too. *MacKechnie!* thought MacKechnie. *Jesus Christ!* He stooped to fold down the pants leg he'd rolled up so it would miss the grease on his bicycle's chain.

"Carson!" Mrs. Barnes called, her eyes still on MacKechnie when he stood up. "You have a visitor, dear!" She gave MacKechnie's back a little push with her fingertips that gave him rushes up the spine, and Poinie appeared in the open doorway with an unhappy look on his face. "I know, I know," his mother said, "but you've got all day, you can spare a few minutes for your guest." She gave Poinie the same kind of look MacKechnie's mother had given him about an hour ago to start this whole thing off, and then she went back downstairs. Poinie blinked at him.

His hair was gone, and he was even skinnier than before, if possible. In fluorescent light coming from another door inside the room he was working in, right next to him, his skin looked middle-of-February white.

Geez, MacKechnie thought. Poinie had on white gym shorts and rubber thongs and a yellow collared shirt with a wide brown stripe down one side, like a bowling shirt. In one hand he held a toothbrush, in the other a sponge.

"I'm cleaning the grout from between the tiles in my dad's shower," he said. "Come on in."

"Hey, I'm sorry about that fight we had," MacKechnie blurted. They'd fought in about the fifth grade, and he didn't even know if Poinie remembered it, though there'd been some blood involved, not MacKechnie's. Maybe he'd broken Poinie's nose.

Poinie shrugged. "That's all right. I was a jerk back then anyway. You can put the toilet seat down to sit on if you want."

MacKechnie did that, and Poinie crouched on the floor of a shower stall in the small bathroom, which smelled like pine cones and ammonia and was modern, all green tiles. The fixtures were gold and modern also, the kind that swivels on a ball. Poinie dipped the toothbrush in a plastic bucket of greenish water and examined the tiles to find where he'd left off. In the bottom of the bucket were an athletic sock and an S.O.S. pad and a scrub brush with a wooden handle. MacKechnie wondered what everything was for until he thought that the poor guy must have had tried them all before he thought of using a toothbrush.

"Your dad makes you do that, huh?"

"Grouting is an ideal location for micro-organisms to hide." Poinie flushed, MacKechnie could tell. "Also they don't want me to make the accident an excuse for getting lazy, which I have to admit I've got a tendency to be." He braced a leg against the tiles and began scrubbing. On his calf MacKechnie saw a scar shaped like the blade of a sword.

"Wow," he said, pointing. "How many stitches?"

"A hundred and eighty-seven in the leg, fifty-two in the head." He tipped forward so that MacKechnie could see. The head scar was straight and about four inches long. It ran along the left side of his head, Poinie's left, from one corner of his forehead to about six inches above his ear, like a part in the stubble that was growing back. It reminded MacKechnie of Shackleford's part, which Shackleford said he had a barber put in. Shackleford wasn't touchy and would talk to you about stuff like that. After they got Andy Reno to the hospital that time with the raccoon bite, Shackleford was the one who made the joke: *a coon on the East Side! There goes the neighborhood!* Unless somebody meant something by it, though. Then Shackleford would say, "Back up a second, my friend." Usually the guy would back up about a mile. Shackleford was all right.

"Really, it's a cool-looking scar," MacKechnie said. Without that hair flopping in his eyes like some kind of faggot pony, Poindexter actually looked a lot better.

"You think *that's* cool." Poinie broke off scrubbing and pointed his toothbrush at the wide stripe on his shirt. "This is what I was wearing at the time of the accident. See these stains? I used to hate this shirt, but now it's my favorite one."

MacKechnie looked closer, saw that blood was what the stripe was, and felt light-headed. "Man," he said, impressed. Maybe there was hope for this kid after all.

Poindexter was grinning. His teeth were crooked, the huge front teeth gapped and the others crammed in on both sides. Poinie still looked about twelve years old, which was about the last time MacKechnie had seen him this close. But you couldn't really hold how young he looked against him, could you? You couldn't hold it against him any more than you could hold it against Shackleford for his color or MacKechnie himself for being on the short side, because what could they do about it? MacKechnie grinned back. "You look like a rabbit," he said. "How about we call you Peter from now on?"

Poindexter stopped grinning and hung his head.

"Hey, man. I didn't mean it bad. Really. I meant it *good.*"

But Poinie was scrubbing away like a motherfucker, and MacKechnie thought, *Shit*. This was the whole problem with Poindexter. Even as a kid he had never just been a kid. He always thought everything was about something else. If he'd ease up on that, he wouldn't be any worse than anybody else, really.

"Hey, man, Carson, look. Sometimes I just say a thing that don't come out right, you know? Like I mean one thing but you hear another."

Poinie relaxed a little. In a minute he said, "They want me to get braces."

"Braces," MacKechnie said. He leaned back against the toilet tank and interlaced his fingers in his lap. He knew that Halverson's braces had cost a thousand dollars. Shit, MacKechnie had told him, for half that price we can rearrange your face right here in the parking lot, be done with it. Halverson said he'd once locked his braces with Sally Blake's out at Riverside Park, and they walked half-way downtown like that, heading for a dentist's, before they broke apart. Halverson, however, was in general a lying sack of shit. MacKechnie set one ankle on his other knee and saw some grease that had gotten on his pants leg even though he'd rolled it up. "Damn," he said.

"That's sort of how *I* feel," Poindexter said. "I mean who wears braces that's any cool? Halverson, I guess. But braces are like hanging a big sign around your neck, 'I Expect To Be Perfect.'"

"What?" MacKechnie said.

"I mean the world's far from perfect, isn't it? So why don't we just admit that, instead of putting steel bands around everything and yanking it around so that it looks better? Because looks don't tell half the story, as we know. Looks are less than fifty percent."

"Hunh," MacKechnie said.

"It's like this Platonic ideal of perfection as defined by the powers that be." His *p*'s were popping. "It's like saying people *are* their careers, which is another one of my pet peeves these days." He dropped his toothbrush in his bucket and began clawing at the air with his fingers forked, two on each hand. "'Doctor,' 'lawyer,' 'teacher,' 'college graduate.' Not everybody fits into these neat little categories, do they?"

Poinie's eyes were green, like his mother's, and about as bright. MacKechnie didn't know if Poinie was literally a faggot or not, and he looked away. The tiles on the bathroom walls were the same as on the floor and ceiling, like a sound studio or something. It was a really nice bathroom. When Poinie began scrubbing again he squinted like he was trying to figure out what he'd just said, which was pretty much what MacKechnie was trying to do. It began to seem like some time since anyone had spoken, and when it looked like Poinie wasn't going to say anything else until MacKechnie did, he guessed and said, "Yeah, I guess I hear you about doctors and lawyers and shit. Most people aren't really anything like that."

"Right!"

Poinie looked up at him like Mr. Coomis in Biology, who was also the track coach. MacKechnie couldn't do biology and couldn't run, either, unless somebody was after him, but no matter how many times you fucked up with Coomis, he always looked at you like this time you were going to get it right. Poinie was holding that same look, and MacKechnie said, "Matter of fact, a lot of guys have two or three different jobs, so what do you call them? Other guys are just, you know, a fat guy. Or a dumb guy, or a guy with a bad temper and shit. A guy who likes to fish, or a real fine chick with a funny name."

"Exactly! Women, too! And it's not like they're nothing, is it? I mean they're still people, aren't they? Even if they don't get into the best college?"

"Like a woman works at Shurfine but she's also somebody's mother. A guy who stutters but can play the piano real good. A bow-legged chick who drives a pink Camaro. A Black guy who'd do anything for you, even if you're white." That was Shackleford: MacKechnie was talking about the people he knew. Poinie was like amazed at him, and MacKechnie grinned and kept on with it. "A freckled guy who can hit right-handed or left. A rich guy who doesn't give a shit. A dead guy. A big-toothed little guy who *almost* died. Oh, man, I'm sorry. It was another joke."

Poinie'd blinked away and ducked his chin in, but then he looked up like Coomis again. "No, no, you're right! Those are the things that make people, not their jobs! And we're all still people, aren't we? Whole people?"

MacKechnie didn't really know what all the excitement was about until he realized that he'd just had a conversation with Poindexter Barnes and his mother, too, and hadn't been called stupid once. He wanted to be careful now, so he said, "Speaking like you said about whole people, you know Amos Shackleford? His dad only has one arm. Lost the other in a scrap-metal crusher."

Poinie looked like Coomis when he was disappointed, too. "That's terrible," he said, fishing around in his bucket for his toothbrush again, and MacKechnie knew that whatever they'd been talking about before was over now, because he'd blown it. He realized that he wasn't that high anymore, either, and he put his hands on his thighs and got ready to stand up.

"So anyway then, I guess you were in a coma, huh? Got knocked on the head pretty bad?"

Poinie spun around on his ass and started talking again, scrubbing in an entirely different corner. "Well, that's true, but I've been doing a lot of thinking about it, and what the accident really was, I think, is an opportunity. I mean I was incredibly *lucky*, right? I stared death in the face and here I am, with all my pieces intact, as far as we know at this point. So I can be *diff*erent now, after staring death in the face like that. I mean all my life I've been kind of buying into the prevalent socio-economic structure with good grades and all that, and I've been missing a lot. I mean I've always *known* I was missing a lot. Hell, look at *you* guys. Look at the fun you've been having. *You* know there's more to life than getting ready for college. So what's the point of being spared, you know, after staring death in the face like that, if I'm going to go back and live for college? I'm actually kind of pleased it happened."

"Hunh," MacKechnie said. Poinie looked at him like he wanted something, but MacKechnie didn't know what that could possibly be. And when you got down to it, he didn't really know about any big *diff*erence in Poinie, either, let his hair grow back. "So you're all better now, great," he said and stood up—too quick, because Poinie flinched. "I mean, so I guess you can go out and everything, right?"

Now Poinie actually looked scared. Maybe he thought MacKechnie wanted to beat him up again. But he said, "I'm OK. I do my physical therapy exercises outside when the weather's nice. I still take lots of naps. Anyway. Thanks for coming by, Don. You're the first one that has." He stood up in the shower and held his hand out. When MacKechnie took it, Poinie pumped, grinning like a little kid again and MacKechnie saw that the green eyes were wet, not dripping but definitely teary. *Like a girl*, he thought. *I'm sorry, but exactly like a girl.*

"Awright, then," he said, dropping Poinie's hand. "You take care now."

He was at the top of the stairs when the typewriters stopped and one of the doors burst open and a bald man with a little black beard around his mouth and chin came out. He blinked at MacKechnie the way Poinie had done at first.

"Hello!" the bald man said.

"Your wife let me in. I came to see Poin—Carson. I was just leaving."

"Hello!" the man said again. His eyes opened very wide, and he rocked forward and then back on his heels like one of those inflatable dummies you can't knock down when you were kids. He was shorter than his wife and fatter, and he wore his pipe in a leather holster on his belt. A little thread of white rose from it, then cut off.

"Me and Carson had a nice talk. He's looking good. I can find my way out."

"Carson!" The man cupped his hands to his mouth to call the whole fifteen feet down the hall, his voice like he'd called many times before. "*Carson!* Aren't you going to see your friend to the door?"

Poinie came to the door with the toothbrush in his hand. "He knows the way out," he said. "Same way as he came in, basically, only in reverse."

Poinie's father blinked again and then looked down at MacKechnie and winked. "Do you sass your old man that way? Carson, come on downstairs with us, Son."

MacKechnie had once hit his father in the shoe with a baseball bat and broken some phalanges—in self-defense, though, he wouldn't have done it if he'd known his father was going to check out about six months later. But before he could think of something he could actually tell Poinie's father, he felt a hand on his neck, and when Poinie came over he got a hand on *his* neck, too, and his father took them both downstairs like that. MacKechnie didn't like it, but he didn't see what he could do about it. Poinie kept his eyes on his feet. At the bottom of the stairs his father let go, and Poinie's mother, in the leather chair with the bright little lamp over her shoulder, closed the book in her lap and beamed at them. Between MacKechnie and the front door was about six miles of funky-ass carpet.

"Our son has a friend in this town, Mother," boomed the father. He wiggled his eyebrows at MacKechnie and said, "It's more than we can say for ourselves, let me tell you. What's your name, friend of my son's?"

"MacKechnie," said MacKechnie, wondering how he could tell Shackleford and Briggs about all this so that they'd believe it. It would keep them going all summer long.

"Well, MacKechnie," said the mother in a voice like he'd said something funny that she wanted to get in on, "We were planning to go out for some ice cream right about now. Would you like to join us?"

"He rode his bike," Carson said from the front window, where he'd parted the curtain to look out. "He wouldn't have time to get ice cream with us, come back, get his bike, and ride home before dark. And he doesn't have a light."

"We could put his bike in the trunk and drop him off afterwards. That's a possibility, isn't it?" The father talked like he was daring you to listen. "Have you ever ridden in a brand-new Volkswagen square-back sedan before, Mac?"

"Ben," said the mother to the father. She told him something else with her face, and his chin bobbed back as if she'd jabbed at him. Then he looked at MacKechnie and wiggled his eyebrows again.

"Your bicycle would have the honor of being the first thing we've carried," he said. "You know, ours is one of the first square-back sedans in this part of the world."

"I've got to run some errands for my mother," MacKechnie said, backing toward the door. "I've got to pick up some milk." In fact she could probably actually use some, he thought. He knew he had a couple dollars on him.

"They sell milk at the ice-cream place, don't they, Mother?" Both of the Barnes parents were coming at him now, the father's eyes popping and Mrs. Barnes at his side, looking worried. "Don't they sell milk at the ice-cream place? All dairy products in the same store? Isn't that the way these things work?"

"He doesn't want to go, Dad." Poinie was holding the screen door open. His voice wasn't smart-ass, the way it had been before, and he gave his father a nice, easy smile. "He just doesn't want to go out with us. He's got to go home."

"Oh," the father said.

Both parents stopped at the edge of the carpet.

"Well, thanks again for coming," Carson said, following MacKechnie out onto the porch. Carson's voice was steady, his eyes dry now. In the deep sunlight from the west, the stain on his shirt was even darker, a thick braid running down his left shoulder from somewhere on the back of his hairless head, like the Chinese guy in a Western. He fixed MacKechnie with a flat look, then gazed out across the Ledges.

"Look. Carson. I'm glad you're all right." MacKechnie meant it this time, and he said that, too. "We'll see you in school, okay?"

Carson shrugged. His parents were standing a little ways inside the screen door, like they knew they weren't supposed to come out but couldn't make themselves move back. The father was blinking like a house afire now, and the mother had her hand over her mouth.

"Hell, man, Carson, I'll see you before that. Summer's just started. Listen, we're probably going to be playing a little ball over behind the stadium. You get a little stronger, stop on by. Afternoons, mostly. How'd that be?"

Carson looked as if he could imagine *exactly* how it would be, and MacKechnie had to admit he could, too, but the father burst out onto the porch. "Boy, Carson, did you hear that? Thanks! Thanks!" he said to MacKechnie. "Did you hear that, Son? Baseball! Baseball, right? Baseball!"

Then Mrs. Barnes came out and began thanking him, too, and MacKechnie pretty much leapt off the porch. When he'd landed he scrambled to his feet and ran down the weedy gravel drive to where he'd dropped his bike, snatched it up and pumped off fast, not looking back.

But he could picture them watching him from the porch, the father's hands on the necks of the other two, and though MacKechnie's gear ring tore his pants leg he kept on cranking all the way down the dead center of Maplewood Terrace, his eyes straight ahead so that nobody could tell he was bawling, shit, like a motherfucker, nothing to tell Shackleford or Briggs about, ever, or even his mother.

YOU PETTY THIEF

With Carter in jail, it was just Russell and Eddie, middle and youngest of the Nash brothers, who moved to Illinois when the millwrighting and heavy-hauling company their father worked for did. Their new house had a yard with a brand new tree in it, corrugated paper still wrapped around its spindly trunk, but no grass on the lawn yet, and Eddie was so homesick that he just stayed high; only reason he got up for school at all, Russell thought, was to sell a little dope before the bell rang. Russell still considered himself a possible U of M student at some point in the not-too-far-off-future, but he didn't know about his Massachusetts residency status now. Then the new high school decided not to accept all his credits, which, together with an eighth grade lost to bronchial pneumonia, was going to set him two years back. He was going to have to retake algebra and some other things he'd actually done all right at, not because of grades but because of some problem with semesters versus the modules they had out here, which was such bullshit he didn't even want their fucking diploma. He could pick up those credits anytime, anyplace.

Where he really wanted to be was Boston, but he didn't know anyone to stay with there. He knew people back in Worcester but nobody well enough to move in with except his aunt, and he didn't want to live with his aunt. He liked his aunt; he just didn't want to be a guy who lived with his aunt. So he paid what rent and grocery money the old man asked ("Don't quit school," he'd said. "I already have." "All right," the old man said and named his price, which was fair.) and for the time being stayed where he was, getting his bearings.

He grew a little moustache and tried a few things that didn't work out too well, then got a job at an old resort north of town, near the Wisconsin state line: the Carriage Wheel, where apparently a lot of wealthy people from Chicago and Milwaukee used to converge during some unspecified heyday of the past. The highway sign out front was a white carriage with a neon back wheel, its pastel spokes twirling in the dark, one of the few things left in the place that worked. A ballroom and formal dining hall were boarded up, and in the building where Russell worked, rips in the upholstery were patched with clear mailing tape. A few people still pulled in off Route 2 for a night's sleep, but the Interstate exit was five miles east, and now the biggest draw was local, from bands that played the bar on weekends.

That's where the real money was, the bar, and that was where Russell aspired to, so he bought a used paperback drink-recipe book at a library sale to study when he could. Meantime he worked the basement, collecting fees from six regulation pool tables, five old leather-pocket slate ones and a fairly new Olhausen with blue felt. Plus, in a separate room behind the desk where Russell sat was a mini-bowling alley, four lanes another half-level down from the poolroom, where the ceilings were low and the walls were red, with a flocked, striped paper above wainscoting. Apparently the basement had been considered a real state-of-the-art pleasure palace at one time, but now people laughed when they came downstairs ("A *bowling* alley! Look!") and a whole room was devoted to video and pinball machines that were emptied and maintained by an independent operator; Russell didn't even have a key. But from the rest he developed a nice little scam for himself. Nothing huge: cigarette and gas money, incentive enough to stay alert for whatever else might turn up. So Russell stayed alert.

The guy he reported to was in his thirties, five feet tall, and wanted to be called "Shank." He had a squashed-looking face in a squarish head, as if somebody'd put a normal-shaped one in a vice lengthwise when it was still soft, then flipped the screw about twice. The Carriage Wheel was a family business, but Shank was unrelated. He was like Russell, except for his clipped blond hair and sideburns and a squint when he talked from the corner of his mouth, as if what was at stake here was national security or dynamiting rock rather than a stuck ball in lane #3 or whether to reorder talc today or wait till next week.

Or wear jackets, another big issue with Shank. Everybody on entertainment staff was supposed to wear black shoes and pants with a white shirt and a Carriage-Wheel-issue maroon polyester blazer, which hung off of Russell's bony frame like a smock. He tried rolling up the sleeves, but Shank said no. He tried to wear it like a cape, but the fabric was like an umbrella's, so light and slippery it wouldn't stay on. Once he tucked it in his waistband like a second shirt, but Shank, who didn't have to wear one himself because he was management, had a fit. "Of all the cockamamie bird-brained—Russ! Mr. Tanner likes a professional appearance, I've told you that!"

"*I* like Russell, and I guess I've told *you* that."

Best defense being a good offense, since Shank was the man to trip his little scam up, if anybody could. How it worked had to do with pool-ball rentals, which were by the hour: punch a party's card out before they quit playing; then, when they did return their rack, charge them by the clock, pocket the diff. No way to tell unless Shank also timed them somehow from his "office" upstairs, which was essentially a clipboard at the bar, so it seemed unlikely. Or if a customer examined the clock-face stamp on their receipt real close, but they never did. If they worried at all it was about what they paid, which was correct, the whole beauty of the scam. For insurance you could stamp at a slight angle and smear the ink. Similarly with bowling: who kept their receipts? If they bowled four lines, charge them but write up three; just make sure to get rid of any score sheets they might leave behind. Shoe rentals were good for a quarter here and there, fifty cents.

It was no gold mine. Three days might go by with no bowlers, maybe a few pool players in to practice bank shots alone. But give Russell a steady weekend and he could get his hourly up to a respectable level, which otherwise it wasn't. The key was to focus: watch for opportunities, think, and block out extraneous stuff, including thoughts like *Should I be doing this?*, which at first Russell had more of than he'd have liked to admit. What he was doing here was not something he'd done before, this systematically and deliberately; but once he'd smoothed it down to the point of habit, it felt as easy and as natural to him as breath. After a long time when he'd been holding it, in fact.

Just before Thanksgiving, when he'd been at the Carriage House about six months, the amount of change that arrived in the cash box at the beginning of each shift began to vary. It had been twenty-five dollars, give or take a quarter or a dime or even a whole dollar every now and again, but now one day it'd be twenty-three, the next twenty-eight and a half. Or odd penny amounts: $23.06, $27.44, though taxes were built right into the entertainment charges, and even pool-ball rentals you didn't calculate any closer than the dime. Russell halted all skimming and kept track of the box for a month, charting deviations from a mean of twenty-five dollars and looking for a pattern. (If it didn't work out, he thought he could maybe save his figures to petition the high-school for some kind of mail-in math credit, motherfuckers.)

But no pattern seemed apparent, and the best he could figure, unless he was being set up, was that somebody didn't care too much. The bar manager was Janice, who had waist-length hair parted in the exact center and a posture to keep it there, so all the office hours Shank put in probably didn't mean he was counting change boxes down to the penny. Russell could never tell whether Janice's low voice and steady gaze indicated fascination with him or "Please keep this raging affair I'm having with our boss a secret." Odds were against the first possibility, considering his bad skin, but you never could tell.

That was something Carter often said, about any given situation: *You never can tell, so don't write anything off*, and Russell imagined him living by it still, where he was now. After a long silence that turned out to have been due to confusion about their new address, they'd had some postcards from him, arriving all at once just in time for Christmas. "Russell, you hang in," he'd written on one of them. Carter hadn't killed anyone, but a guy he was moving air conditioners with had shot a warehouse guard, so Carter was going to be where he was for a while. But if he'd done like the old man had wanted him to and joined the Army, he might never be coming back at all. His postcards were light. "Winter's holding off here this year," he'd write, or "How about those Sox?"

Russell's contribution to the family card, after deliberating for days over the wording, was, "You're the one who needs to hang in there, Carter. You are missed." He hadn't received an answer yet.

———— ◆ ————

For a week after taking his first dollar directly out of the change box, he kept the money in the drawer of the rental desk, so that he could always look down and find it nestled between a receipt book and the ink pad: hey, right here, must have slipped out! Things never came to that, but even as he gradually resumed his other scams he continued the policy, always holding a few dollars, whatever he'd skimmed the day before, in the drawer beneath the cash box, which Shank made a point of coming down to collect personally at closing time, one-thirty, just before last call at the bar.

That was the only sticky part: Shank would often be there while Russell totted up tickets and counted the day's cash, so on a busy night he had to have all his personal computations done beforehand. Shank thought too much of his own subtlety and sophistication to actually eagle-eye Russell's every move, but while playing pinball or wandering around flicking lint off the pool-table felt, humming along with the band upstairs or talking about much-needed improvement projects such as *Sweep this shit off the floor*, the angle of his head would be ever-vigilant, as if he might dart over at any time to grab Russell's hands. Forget three strikes: this guy believed in the deterrence value of his own mere presence. Only level look he'd give Russell all night was when he reached across the desktop for the cash box, his burning eyes all the lie detector he required: "OK then?" Or all the arithmetic, Russell thought, and more than once it crossed his mind that maybe the reason Shank finished out every night this way and the reason for the varying amounts in the change box at start of shift were one and the same: maybe Shank just didn't know how to count. Or else maybe he just found it easier to browbeat his employees than do his actual job.

It all gave Russell more reason than ever to continue what he was doing rather than contribute to the perpetuation of this sloppy, hypocritical, and mismanaged world as if he believed in it, which would make him a hypocrite himself. So he didn't have any trouble returning Shank's look. In fact, he excelled at it. And Shank would saunter over to the carpeted staircase, the cashbox propped between a hip and dangling arm as if it really meant not so much, on his way up brushing the fingers of his free hand along one of the varnished walnut banisters as if he was not a runt but tall and slim, as if old *de luxe* were his very own style. Russell would sweep the specified shit off the floor and shut off lanes and lights and arcade machines before coming upstairs himself to hang his maroon jacket on a hook in the bar-supplies closet, then punch out on a clock that was also in there.

At the bar he'd get a soda from the gun and chat with Janice, who eventually began chatting back, unless Shank was around, not as if she wanted him but as if she liked him all right, which was good enough for Russell for the time being. On weekends he might catch the tail end of the last set if the band was any good, which it usually wasn't. Once in a while, there'd be swipeable bar change, though most people weren't that careless, and even if they were, you couldn't automatically go for it, as you didn't want some overnight guest waking up in the middle of the night, going, "Hey!"

It was easy to identify the overnight guests, as they'd be the ones blinking around with road fatigue or else snickering to each other at the fake gas lamps in the booths, the moldy deer head over Janice's cash register, the staff's wine-colored coats. Of course those marked Russell, too, when he came upstairs for his dinner break, but he felt a kinship with them, these travelers from out of town. The others were just plain local and looked it, some as if they'd already tried every other roadside tavern and no-event lounge on both sides of the state line, saving the most hopeless for last. Some he recognized from week to week or even from elsewhere around town, though none to talk to, and of that he was just as glad. To Russell, any fun that customers had or pretended to seemed puny, and he felt that his position behind the scenes here gave him a kind of privilege. At U of M he had planned to major in philosophy, which meant to him something like the insights into human behavior he was able to have here. He thought he might eventually make some contacts here, too, meaning he didn't know exactly what, but he'd know them when he made them, and meanwhile there were people to watch: people meeting, falling in love, fighting, breaking up, falling in love again. No one had actually given birth on the blue felt yet, but it wouldn't surprise Russell too much if it happened.

He got interested in a group of repeat customers he thought of as slummers: they wore hammer-loop jeans and similar feathered haircuts but arrived in worthwhile vehicles, one a Corvette with Indiana plates. College kids, Shank said, and by light from the neon spokes above the parking lot Russell saw dashboards with sound systems alone that must have cost what his used Maverick had. Slummer women were wild dancers, their hair like fool's caps in the strobe. When the slummers showed up even disco could turn the dance floor into a box of eels, and Russell, watching from his stool at the end of the bar, guessed he knew why.

He was right: during a band break once he heard the word *hash*, turned, and saw two slummers standing one tier back from the rail, where he was, looking around as if for a third who hadn't showed. They wore thick flannel shirts and suede vests and cologne, their chins so smooth they must have just shaved. Russell caught the eye of one of them.

"I can get you that," he said.

They grinned at each other, and while people talked and laughed and reached beers over his head Russell negotiated for twenty up front, hoping Eddie was home.

But when he called from the lobby Eddie wasn't, and after twelve rings Russell hung up and went outside and with his pocketknife cut a chunk of tread off a tire of a pickup truck parked well away from the sign. Between the foundation of the building and a snowdrift he shaped the rubber lump and peeled the foil from the liner of his cigarette pack to wrap it in, and when the bar emptied he met the guys not ten feet from the truck, inventing "Barberia Black," which, he didn't know if it was a place name or not, but it sounded far. And it worked: they paid him another thirty bucks, no questions asked. A couple of weeks later he had a bad moment when he saw one of the guys eying him across the bar, until the guy burst into a goofy grin with a big thumbs up, such a candy-ass motherfucker the parking-lot purchase alone must have copped him his buzz.

It was more or less the end of Russell's serious expectations for nightlife around here, at the Carriage Wheel and in the entire state of Illinois, though he hadn't been to Chicago yet, which he thought might present some possibilities for the future. By the depths of February, after closing up and saying goodnight to Janice and Shank, he would usually just go home. He was saving up for his own place, but he hadn't seen anything just right yet. Sometimes Eddie's friends were over, and he'd sit around with them for a while. He'd envisioned a different life for himself, but he didn't need a high school diploma to know that nothing lasts forever. Whether things changed for the better or for the worse was mostly a matter of being ready, he thought. "Oh, no thank you," he would say when Eddie or one of his friends passed a joint to him. Even his beer consumption he kept to a minimum. He wanted to stay sharp.

———◦———

"Hey, it's Oh No Thank You," said one of Eddie's friends when Russell opened the Nashes' hollow-core front door one cold Saturday night in March. All over the living room, kids were sprawled on rug and furniture, mostly paired. The house was warm and smelled like chocolate through the two kinds of smoke. Eddie appeared in the lit kitchen doorway with no shirt and hammer-loop jeans on, cupping a hand under a dripping wooden spoon. His hair was in pigtails, and on the point of his left shoulder was a Li'l-Devil tattoo, neither of which had Russell ever seen on his brother before. Around the New Year Eddie had seemed to make his adjustment here, more or less all at once.

"Mom went to Molly's," he said. Molly was the Worcester aunt, and going to stay with her was an often-heard threat, occasionally acted upon. "Took the Buick."

"For good this time?"

Eddie shrugged and licked the spoon. "Maybe a week, she said. Maybe two."

That meant she'd be seeing Carter, Russell thought, but Eddie was like their father in this one respect: neither liked to hear Carter's name, though their reactions if they did were approximately opposite. Eddie's was sad.

"Dad's at work?"

"Loves Park and then, I forget. He gets to fly back afterwards." Their father had moved equipment either to or from as far as Mexico before, and when he wasn't on the road he was out of the house by dawn and home after midnight.

"We're talking about the guy with the goatee, right? About yea tall?"

Eddie rolled his eyes at the ceiling with a certain smart-ass gesture Russell remembered from his time at the high school here: the heel of your hand to your forehead, then head back in a slow-motion snap. Eddie executed it all with relish. Then he smirked at his brother.

"We're going out for breakfast later, Russell. Want to come?"

In an apparently conscious decision to talk like the people around here instead of where he came from, Eddie had developed a sing-songy bray that set Russell's teeth on edge. Russell himself had never talked as if he came from anywhere in particular, as they'd lived in three different states when he was small; until this one it never seemed to make much difference. Now it occurred to him that Eddie was growing up in ways Russell knew nothing about. To answer his brother's question he smiled, raised his arms like an orchestra conductor, and pointed at the kid who'd greeted him.

"Oh, no thank you," said the kid, taking his cue.

Everybody laughed, the high point of Russell's night.

Shank came down with a stack of three-by-five cards. He leaned on the rental desk while Russell got receipts and cash in shape. Highly unusual for Shank not to be wandering around edgily and impossible to slip a dollar out, but Russell was just glad he hadn't adjusted any bowling or pool receipts yet. He wrote down totals on the slip, so accurate and aboveboard he felt like something was wrong, rubber-banding the receipts and fastening the steel cashbox clasp. Shank took it without his usual fiery look. Something was definitely up.

"Mr. Tanner wants to hire you a partner," Shank said eventually.

Russell tried to laugh. "I don't need a partner. There's barely enough work down here for one, as it is."

"I know that. But Tanner says the summer's coming up, and he's got big hopes for it. What happens you get sick?"

"I don't. And what happens now, on my days off?" What happened was that Shank would cover, or Janice would. Or Shank's wife, Connie, would come in.

Shank pursed his lips and shuffled his cards. "I've got to pick five or six for Tanner to interview, and you're supposed to help. But he's the one who'll make the actual hire. Tanner."

The name hung between them like cigar smoke, though Russell had never seen the man and known it, and he said so. He himself had been hired by Shank, apparently a policy that was undergoing a change, which was not lost on Russell, either.

"Well, *I've* sure seen him," Shank said. "*I* see his sour-ass face so often it wakes me up, sweating."

This time Russell's laugh came easily.

"Say, Shank. Question." Russell touched his temple with a forefinger and lifted it away. "Speaking as you were about reinforcement staff, what do you think about my spelling Janice every so often—just as needed, I mean, up at the bar? I make a pretty tasty banana daiquiri, and people have been known to inflict casualties for my vodka martini."

Not strictly true, but Shank laughed at the phrase, actually less a laugh than a snort. "We'll see." He split the deck of index cards like a Vegas sharp. "You pick three, I'll pick three, and we'll send them to Tanner."

"What are we looking for, in an applicant?"

Shank sighed, scowling at his cards. If he hadn't been so crushed by his responsibilities he might have been an all-right guy, Russell thought. He stayed an hour to help Shank go through the cards and decide. No overtime, though, since the workweek was based on only thirty-eight hours, for just such eventualities. And as it turned out, Tanner didn't hire anyone they'd nominated but a college kid, Adam Tallwood, with the feathered hair and smooth face of a slummer.

"So what are you studying up there?" Russell asked him on his second or third night, once he'd settled in a bit. The college was on a hill in the center of town, a campus sort of like a mini-Amherst that Russell had been on exactly twice, once when James Taylor came, but it was sold out, and another time when the place was deserted except for a security guard, who'd walked a hundred yards in broad daylight to ask him what he was doing there. He told Tallwood that he himself had almost gone to the U of M, but—he shrugged—life had intervened. "The *M* stands for Massachusetts, by the way, not Michigan. Or Minnesota."

Tallwood stared at him. He had a high and bony forehead and bulging, startled-looking blue eyes that made it seem like he was either going to laugh in your face or pop you one, though Russell would have done what he could to prevent that last eventuality. But Tallwood's mouth alone was like an uppercut.

"Gee, and here I was thinking Mexico."

He was snotty with the customers, too. A lady about his third night on duty asked him where the powder room was. She was with some bowlers in a wedding party, so well dressed she just watched. Tallwood rocked back in his swivel chair, leaving his feet on the edge of the rental desk.

"'Powder room.' You've got to be kidding in a place like this," he said. "The *toilets* are over there," gesturing with a book he'd been reading.

Russell, returning from a cigarette break, saw the whole thing. *Shank hears that and this guy's gone*, he thought, though the lady herself laughed before trotting off in the direction Tallwood indicated, and when Shank came down for the cash box, he would treat the kid like one of the guests. Russell would be demonstrating procedures for totting receipts and closing, supposedly for purposes of training, but Tallwood would be joking around, and Shank would join in, the two of them hovering all over the desk—no chance to slip anything out of the box. One Sunday when this happened, Russell had eight Salems and a quarter-tank of gas left until payday, on Wednesday, so he was less than charmed.

Then one time Tallwood asked him to please keep the door to the alley shut from now on, because the thunder of balls on board made it hard for him to concentrate on his book! As if the whole operation was set up to enhance his study habits!

This time Russell went right to Shank about it, but Shank, raising his palms high off the bar, just said to work it out between them. "Tanner picked this guy for a reason, Russell. Not that he let me in on what it is."

He looked over at Janice for his laugh, drawing her calm eyes from Russell's, and Russell went back downstairs with a thumbnail between his teeth, worried about how to protect everything he'd worked so carefully to set up. He'd made a mistake by complaining to Shank. He should have known it would be entirely up to him.

What it finally took was some nine-ball with his new colleague during a slow afternoon the same week. Tallwood wasn't awful, but afterwards, when Russell showed him a simple kick system for escaping from a hook, the guy was so impressed it was embarrassing. "That's ingenious!" he said, setting up the shot himself. He hit the three rails all right but missed his target by eight inches.

"Use running English," Russell said, on purpose to befuddle him. "Left. Line up on the diamond."

Tallwood was laughing at himself by now, but after a couple more tries he made the shot, and from then on when the room cleared out early they'd have a game or two on the Olhausen before Shank came down. It gave Russell a little more time alone at the desk, while Tallwood was shooting or setting up trick shots, though Russell was still nervous, and he wanted to work something out before business began to pick up for the summer. During slow times now they had all sorts of new tasks to do, like buffing all the exposed wood with a lemony spray Shank had provided, and there was talk of repainting and replacing the arcade machines with a giant Magnavox TV. One abruptly warm weekend before Easter, customers thronged tables and alley both when the band upstairs took breaks, and Russell made fifteen dollars off a drunken party of six, Tallwood notwithstanding.

"It's getting to be almost like work, isn't it?" the kid said when the crowd finally thinned out, grinning at him. Shank wasn't due for another few minutes, but in a burst of energy after the drunks had left, they finished their chores. Tallwood's forehead was glistening in the fluorescent lights—sweating, Russell thought, probably a new experience for him, but then something made him feel sure that Tallwood, whose physique tended now toward the rangy, had once been a fat kid. His eyes still had that shocked look, but without his defensive hostility he just looked sort of naïve and suggestible. Russell remembered hearing on some talk show that real success is a matter of being able to adapt to change, and now he had another idea.

"Change box arrives with a different amount every day, Tallwood. You ever notice that?"

The grin vanished.

"Nope," Tallwood said. He studied the blond laminate of the rental table as if he were going to say something else, but he didn't.

Russell had four dollars in the drawer he was holding back, pending the clearing of that day's change-box surplus. Now, against all alarms going off in his head, he pulled out the bills and put them on the counter, in two piles of two. One of these he pushed towards Tallwood, who looked back and forth between the money and Russell, only his eyeballs moving in his head. When Shank's feet appeared on the top step, Russell reached out, took the two bills nearest him, and pocketed them. By the time he could see Shank's belt buckle, Tallwood's pile, too, was gone.

That was on a Wednesday. On Thursday there were six dollars to split, on Friday eight, and on Saturday, which was warm but rainy, over twelve, not including shoe and bowling profits. The nature of the talk between Russell and Tallwood changed: it was all business now, though when Russell handed over his take, something about the way Tallwood took it made it seem as if he were doing Russell a favor. But as long as nobody else wondered why they weren't playing as much pool anymore, Russell was happy. Even split in half, the money was better than the sporadic change he'd been able to rake off before letting Tallwood in on it.

⸺◆⸺

Sunday he had off, and his father was home.

"To what do we owe this unexpected honor?" Russell said at dinner. Everybody except Carter, of course, was there. Russell had gotten used to sitting in his father's place, at the head of the table—not that there was a head or foot either, when you were eating by yourself—but now his father gave him the baleful eye Russell knew so well, reminding him that every other seat, when his father had resumed his, was the foot.

"How's the career, Russ?"

"Career's fine. I'm in line for Assistant Manager. Any day now."

"He's doing so well," Russell's mother said. His father ate with his elbows on either side of his plate, chewing behind his fists.

"He pays his rent on time," Eddie put in. It was a common dynamic when the father was present, the others filling him in on each other's activities. Now his head rolled toward his youngest son.

"What in the holy name of Jesus H. Christ happened to your hair?"

"He braided it," Russell said at the same time his mother said frantically, "Molly said to say hi, Arnie!"

For a moment they all four held their breath, and then all four were laughing—for four different reasons, no doubt, but Russell was glad he hadn't moved out yet. If Carter had been there, he thought, he would have been as happy as he'd ever been in this godforsaken state.

On Monday afternoon he went in at his regular time and was fired. Shank waited for him to punch in, don his jacket, go downstairs and seat himself at the rental desk, then came down and told him. He had no customers yet.

"Tanner's known about you for months, as it turns out. Matter of finding and training your replacement, he said. Said to tell you he's got all the figures written down, if you want to challenge him. Guy didn't get where he is by blah blah blah."

"I don't want to see the figures." Russell removed his jacket and folded it neatly over the back of his chair.

"Well, he kept them all. Never told me a thing. Adam either, as far as I know, so don't go blaming him. He don't even know what's happening here now."

For the first time that day Russell noticed Tallwood mopping the lanes in the bowling alley, his head bobbing with each stroke.

Shank gave Russell a variation on the old cash-box stare, modified with a touch of pity now, then consulted his clipboard. "Just as I was getting used to you, too. The three days' pay on your card since last check we'll mail to you, if your address is the same. Pretty generous, considering you've probably swiped that much already."

"Same address." Russell raked through the desk drawer and found his drink-recipe book, nail clippers, a ball-bearing puzzle from a Cracker Jack box, and a solar-powered, credit-card-sized calculator. "This stuff's mine," he said, though the calculator was the last thing some bowler had left behind.

Shank shrugged, just as Tallwood came through the door with the mop handle between his legs like a toy horse, clowning until he sensed that something was going on. From his face then, Russell knew that what Shank had said was true. Shank was breathing deep through his nose, on guard against any possible confrontation, and Russell turned to see Janice on the top steps, stooping to scan the poolroom as if it were a storm cellar she was checking for rats. When her eyes met Russell's, her nose wrinkled.

"You petty thief," she breathed.

Russell's heart felt as if she'd nudged it off a cliff with her foot. He stepped away from the desk, leaving the drawer open, and bowed to her. "Oh, the shame of it," he said, and when he rose he gave the others a jaunty little salute. No doubt about what made Tallwood's eyes pop now: it was fear, and Russell relished the power he held for that moment, not that he would ever bother to turn the pissant in.

He moved for the staircase, ordinarily three strides that he took four to cover, the son-of-a-bitches, then got out of there.

GEOMETRY

They were playing this game, as it turns out—this trick, and it was on me, the last person in the class who deserved it. Mr. Benavides, the teacher, is this small guy in a three-piece suit that's sometimes corduroy, sometimes herringbone, sometimes this shiny fabric with a blue stripe in it, but it's always basically green. No matter the weather he'll have the vest buttoned and the knot of his tie nestled in the wrinkled hollow at the base of his throat, though he did all right by me before this. "Best in class, Rob!" he'd put at the bottom of my quizzes and on papers make remarks, though his handwriting's bad, so I didn't always read them. *A,* was the point. *A, A, A, A.* Then one day last month he runs out of bluebooks and sends me to get some. We'd been discussing initiative, which he no doubt figured I knew all about. Or so *I* figured at the time.

First, who's in the class. Mostly the same bunch I've been with since junior high, but when Westside burned down last summer they combined the districts, so there were some new kids, namely Licia Terranova. It was almost Easter, and I still hadn't gotten her to acknowledge me. A couple of near-smiles at Christmas and a possible glance around President's Day had seemed like progress, but since then nothing. For a while I'd wondered if she was a little dim, but when Benavides returns papers he'll lean down and say a few words to her in a voice other than the one he uses to address the group, a tone he'd tried once or twice with me, except I didn't want any part of it, myself. Some of these teachers, it's like, you don't know where they've been. Mr. Benavides has got to be forty, and I didn't see any wedding ring. Still, you like it when they approve.

Anyway, he writes me out a requisition and sends me to the supply room, not that it's ever much better stocked than the classrooms. Fridays are essay days, and he wanted us to respond to something we'd read in the textbook. Fine: I was done. I had a match coming up with Aquinas, so my mind's on that. I need a scholarship out of here, and the more stuff you do the better it looks, so this year I took up tennis. By sophomore year I'd already broken most of our records in other sports, not that I'm so great but that Eastside's so lame, and I wanted a new challenge. Already I was up to third man, but Aquinas was our first league match, and I was on edge. Edge is good, edge is good, but some of those Aquinas guys grew up in the country club. Plus, from Aline James I'd learned that Licia Terranova had a brother at Aquinas, and he was on the tennis team. For all I knew she'd be there. Our bus left right after Benavides's class.

Plus, the supply room's run by Mrs. Persha, Jennifer Persha's mother, who *is* somewhat dim, as Jennifer will be the first to tell you, and Mrs. Persha let slip that Jennifer was going to the prom with Seth Henderson, supposedly my best friend. This was news to me. Jennifer I've known since we were four, and though she's gotten somewhat pudgy, I'd sort of considered her my backup, though I'd been giving myself another week with Licia. Prom was the twenty-seventh, and this was the beginning of the month.

So I get back to the classroom, preoccupied with all this, and they're in the middle of one of Benavides's quirky lessons about nothing. He does these every once in a while, when we finish early or he can't get our attention any other way, after a bomb scare or something. They're never anything about English, his subject, like when did Boswell live (or why, a better question), or what's the difference between the Renaissance and the Enlightenment (a couple hundred years), or *i* before *e* except after *c.* Sometimes he draws things, like that design you can see as either a vase or two profiles, depending (on what, we never get around to), but not both at the same time. There's never any grade involved, so it's like, whatever. On this day, the board was covered with different-sized lines he'd drawn with the side of a piece of red chalk, all facing every which way like the tracks of that proverbial chicken, and everybody was staring up as if those red lines might tell who'd cut its head off.

"Thank you, Mr. Kidd," he said when I put the bluebooks on the corner of his desk and ducked back to my seat. Aloud he calls everybody either "Mister" or "Miz," and as soon as I sit down he goes on with his interrogation of Mr. Fallon, a.k.a. Michael Fallon, who was talking when I came into the room and who's pretty smart. I don't think he's ever held any kind of ball in his hand, but he outscores me in just about every class and often says stuff that impresses not only Mr. Benavides but, judging from the way she looks around, Licia Terranova, who never says much herself.

"The same," Fallon says now, raising a finger to his dimpled chin. "To me, those two lines look the same length."

Benavides is spread-eagled across the board, his jacket dangling like there's something heavy in his pocket, to point at two of the lines he's drawn, a little one in the top left corner of the board and another, down by the chalk tray on the right, that's like two feet long. The first one's no more than three inches, so I figure I've missed something.

"Class?" he goes, straightening up and turning around. One thing about Benavides, you can never tell much by his face. The square lenses of his glasses reflected the fluorescent tubes overhead, and the deep lines in his cheeks were parallel, perpendicular to the floor. From a certain angle, the way his hair flips up on one side and his jaw cocks to the other makes his head look like a rhomboid. My favorite subject's geometry, not these brain games.

"Michael's right," people are saying. "Same length. Yes." Heads nod. People look front like they're waiting for the next question, the next step.

There's obviously some progression here, so I wish I'd gotten in on the first move.

"Good," Benavides says, turning again, and his coat gaps again and he points to two lines, both up high this time but again: one short and the other long. "Ms. Hardy?"

She studies them. Bev Hardy is this killer blond with an unfortunate skin problem, her only drawback. Her mother runs a beauty school, and Bev's already been through the course and qualified for her license, but she's got to wait for her next birthday before the state will let her take the exam. Meanwhile she does her friends' nails, which means pretty much all the girls in school. Her specialty's the semaphore, the two-tone diagonal. Last fall when I was giving my speech for student-council president in assembly I looked down into the front rows and saw a swarm of bees, which spun my head until I realized it was fingernails painted brown and yellow, Bev's colors of the day. Now she's scrutinizing those lines Benavides is pointing to, everybody else waiting patiently for her answer.

"I think the same length?" she says finally. "Maybe a half-inch difference? It's hard to tell?"

One's six inches, the other's at least a foot. I mean there's no comparison. Remembering that lesson about the profiles and the vase I look for the optical illusion, maybe some effect created by the intervening lines. Everybody's nodding, corroborating what Bev said with glances and nods, then sitting back, resolute. Was it something about the angles, like putting a pencil half in and half out of a glass of water, some trick of the light here instead of liquid? I thought of geometry again, the way the sum of a triangle's angles is always 180; in an animated proof of the Pythagorean Theorem that we watched, all the cut-up shapes fit perfectly into one another. That's the kind of stuff I like. With any kind of closed system, there's always some pattern you can figure.

"How about these?"

Somebody says, "That one's longer," though *these* particular lines look exactly the same.

"These? And these? And these over here?"

Same. Same. Same: everybody's answer is the opposite of how I see it.

Then I saw Licia Terranova looking over at me. Her desk is in the front of the row closest to the door, right under the flag, and she'd turned to sit with her back to the wall. That day she was wearing her hair down around her shoulders like a cloak made from the curly wool of a black sheep. She had on these flat-soled gladiator's sandals with narrow leather thongs to her excellent knees, her smooth calves like new cheeses tied lightly with string, but what really got me was the bright look in her dark eyes and the way she held her hand over her mouth. Green and pink were Bev's colors that day, and over them Licia's gaze at me was shocked and fascinated but impersonal, too, like she was curious mostly about what I was going to do—which, before I could think, was grin at her.

"Agreed, Mr. Kidd?"

Impossible to tell whether he'd been waiting for this moment to pounce, just as it's impossible to tell whether Licia Terranova's superiority to any other living thing in terms of beauty has ever registered on him. He was pointing to an eight-inch line and maybe a sixteen-incher. Maybe ten and twenty—but I mean hugely, hugely different.

"Ah . . ."

I looked around, thinking maybe I could still figure out the operative principle here. This wouldn't be the first time I'd pulled it all together at the last second. Eleven years of public schooling and you get pretty good at reading a classroom situation. But people were looking at me like I'd already given some answer they disliked. I sit in the precise center of the classroom, and almost everybody in front of me had turned around in their desks. Lips were pursed, eyelids lowered. Licia Terranova crossed her legs. Behind her hand, I could swear she'd begun to smile. Benavides tapped the blackboard with the nail of his index finger, making a sharp but hollow sound under the long line first, then the short one. When he hands back papers I've noticed he lets his nails grow, though they're generally clean enough.

Jeez, I told myself, *I've got to concentrate.* I squinted at the lines. The one on Benavides's left extended from his fingertip to the white strip of shirt under the cuff of his jacket. The line on his right went from his fingertip to his elbow. I felt sweat on my upper lip and the back of my neck. The shirt I had on darkens with moisture, and all I could think about is which spots would be visible across the room, where Licia was into what seemed like about her seventh straight minute of watching me; it was more attention than I'd gotten from her since Westside fried but not exactly a boon for my concentration.

"Mr. Kidd, please. It's a relatively simple question."

Relatively. Now I'm thinking that *that* word's the key, and I give it a last few seconds of intense consideration that get me no further ahead. Then I remember what Mr. Benavides himself told us: if you're not sure about how to pronounce a word, say it loud. That way you make your mistake, get corrected, and if you embarrass yourself enough, it'll be the last time for that particular mispronunciation. Always seemed to me it'd be the embarrassment you remember, not the correct spelling, but anyway it was worth a shot.

"They're the *same,*" I said. "Those lines are *exactly* the same length. Of course I'd need a micrometer to be absolutely positive, but even without one I'd lay fifty bucks that there's no more than a centimeter's difference between those two red lines you're pointing at right this minute, Mr. Benavides, sir."

"You're sure? These two right here," he goes, tapping again, but he's drowned out by a roar. People are hooting, stomping their feet on the floor, pointing back at me and leaning on each other's shoulders for support. Licia's hand falls to show her perfect teeth, and Benavides comes as close as I'd ever seen him to cracking a smile. When the noise dies down he steps up to his desk, then pauses and raises a hand like something he was swallowing got stuck, and pandemonium breaks out again. Licia Terranova, who ordinarily looks neither right nor left, is jabbering excitedly across the aisle with Aline James and Carol Randolph. Even Sloppy Joe, the heavy-metalsmith in the desk behind her who in my mind will forever be throwing up at recess in third grade, looks happy.

Eventually, order was restored. It was a lesson about conformity, like we'd never heard of peer-group pressure before. Just because little Johnny Jones says the lines are the same length, do *you* have to say they're the same length, too? If I'd been half the adolescent I thought I was, I'd have stuck to my guns. Order was restored, but my reputation was ruined. Nobody was even looking at me now.

Benavides did try to undo the damage a bit.

"Before we have too much fun at Mr. Kidd's expense, know that he's in the umpty-umpth percentile of similar responders among high-school juniors. [My head still ringing with public humiliation, I didn't catch the numbers.] That includes some of the premier academies in the country, too. So take heart, Mr. Kidd."

Well, too late about the fun, but really, my heart felt fine. "To thine own self be true" is all fine and good, except we're not living in olden times, are we? "Hey, is this iPod mine or thine?" Exactly what job is it that holds interviews at a Round Table? Think for yourself too much in an airport security line and you're liable to end up screaming or back home, if you're lucky. I mean, I'm looking at a world where the rules change daily, but if you don't play by them you're out where there are no rules at all. Just ask my dad, who's on the forty-eighth step of a forty-eight step program, so far; one of his paintings was on the cover of an LP that's been out of print since before I was born, and now he's a Holiday Inn manager.

Benavides said he wouldn't have picked anyone for his little lesson that he didn't think "could withstand it," in his phrasing, like that was supposed to restore everyone's respect for me, and he allowed me to say a few words about what I'd learned, why I'd done what I did, and what was going through my mind at the big moment, just before making a spineless ass of myself, when everybody was waiting for my answer.

"Jeez," I told them I'd been thinking, "if I blow this, I'll *never* know whether Licia's got an innie or an outie."

Just kidding. Just being true to mine own name, trying to get a little of mine own back. Because as it turned out, I had still more to lose. It was Licia's very brother, Leonard Terranova, that I had to play that afternoon at Aquinas, and he beat me 6-2, 6-0, 6-3. *And,* after the first set, Licia was there for my every double fault. At particularly crucial moments I was aware of her green-and-pink nails through the chain link. I'd imagined she might show up, but by the time I'm down four games in the second I'm wondering why. Our baseball team had a home game right then, and even Sloppy Joe was probably there. What was she doing here? What kind of girl is such a fan of her own brother? Licia and Leonard. Did they have some kind of extra-familial relationship going on?

You see, I do not like to lose; but once losing sets in, I can have a hard time stopping it. Soon I was looking around between points to see if Benavides had shown up, too, figuring he'd love this, since he was the one who'd started it. By the third set I was just lunging at the ball when it came over, half-hoping to twist an ankle before the match could end in another bagel.

But then my shot-to-hell concentration glommed onto the thought that maybe she hadn't shown up to watch my opponent. Through the chain link, I noticed that her dark eyes weren't going back and forth anymore; they were staying down at my end of the court. Two games I gave up to ascertain this, but after I had, I won three straight, including my first and only service break of the match. And when it was over and I was heading back to the locker room (which at Aquinas had a hair dryer beside every sink), completely drenched and defeated, Licia gave her brother a wave and trotted over to me.

She'd changed clothes since class. She wore little terrycloth shorts and a sleeveless yellow top, and she'd done her hair in a thick braid down one shoulder. Her anklets had yellow pompoms on the back, and around her neck she wore a tiny gold cross on a chain so fine it didn't hang, just lay against her skin like a trail of coins in untrodden sand. I could smell her shampoo, her soap, and her detergent, separately. I stepped back so she wouldn't whiff my loser's funk, but she moved right in.

"He's been playing since he was six," she said. She meant her brother, of course, but for a second I had this vision of a tiny Benavides in green shorts with a blue stripe and a serve like an AK47, acing all the other neighborhood kids to teach them lessons about character. I must have chortled, and Licia stopped walking. When I turned around she had her hand out, her elbow locked and her fingers veering back from her palm. "I'm sorry," she said and introduced herself, as if I didn't know. "That was my brother you just played. We're in Benavides's class together—I don't know if you've noticed—and I just wanted to tell you I thought what you did in there today was great."

About eight astounded questions popped to mind, not the least astounded of which was, *You didn't think I'd NOticed?* But I went with the more sophisticated, "What I DID?"

She either didn't catch my astonishment or ignored it. "The way you saw what Benavides was doing and played along. That crack about the micrometer. I mean unless you were going to fly in the face of the common wisdom we'd all been instructed to impart, you found the best solution."

"That bastard," I said, but her lids lowered: she wasn't prepared to go *that* far. Even in my surprise, I saw how I might have played this. *Exactly,* I might have said. *But if I'd pointed out the obvious I'd have ruined his lesson, wouldn't I? And where's that going to get any student? So, you're right: I played along. Pretty bright of you to pick up on that. What did you say your name was?* Etc. Any other chick dealt me a hand like this, and I would have picked up my cards and led with the two of clubs, the way you're supposed to.

But Licia's got these dark, serious eyes that were looking up at me. I'm a head taller (Benavides might have you believe we're the same size, but no), and up close, she's not perfect. Her nose is a bit long, her chin on the small side, and she's got a little overbite. Not much, but a word came to mind, *rodential,* which I've looked up since and it's not even a word, and I mean her nose wasn't twitching or anything; she doesn't have whiskers. I did wonder though if she was setting me up the way Benavides had, waiting for my reaction, withholding judgment until it came. The possibility shook me a little.

"Well," I told her. "None of what you said was really my intent, but if it seemed that way, fine. It sure didn't cut down on the laughter much."

Her shoulders relaxed, and I guess mine did, too: if this had been a test, I'd passed it.

"You can take it. That's what Aline told me. I'm a friend of hers." This was followed by a despairing wince. "Sort of. We talk sometimes."

"I've known Aline since before we could walk."

"I know."

I was trying to remember all the ways I'd ever successfully asked girls out, all the coy banter and tricks to get them to ask you first. What I wanted was a sure-fire winner, a lesson-plan that wouldn't depend on sending somebody out of the room. But on a botched overhead about ten minutes earlier, I'd knocked my racket head against my shin, which picked that moment to begin throbbing like a fire alarm, and I couldn't think of a single, solitary line. Licia was talking on about what kind of friends she and Aline were, not best but pretty good, though not as good as before, although recently . . .

"Listen," I finally interrupted in much the same way I'd gone for the ball in the last set. "Prom's coming up. Would you like to go with me?"

Whether from dehydration or whatever, I felt like I was seeing those bees in assembly. Licia's eyes flicked away for a second, then shone at me the way they had across the room in Benavides's class. For a second I thought she was going to laugh.

"Yes," she said. "I would."

I had no idea what had just happened.

And in the three weeks between then and prom, Licia gave me very few clues. That weekend I called her house and left a message she never returned. If you leave more than one, you're a stalker, and by Sunday night I figured maybe her family'd taken a trip. I picked an old Mountain cassette out of my dad's stuff in the basement and on Monday traded it to Sloppy Joe for his seat in Benavides's class. When Licia came in she smiled, but once the bell rang, she didn't turn around. She'd done her hair up with this huge wooden butterfly clip with a brass spring in it. Just above her gold thread of a necklace was a mole that was shaped, no lie, like a tiny heart. Between classes she'd walk with me, but her response to whatever conversation I tried to get going was mostly this lingering tragic look, like she either knew we were going to be horribly disappointed or else thought that whatever had transpired between us had been a horrible mistake. Either way, the common denominator was easy enough to figure.

Finally, a week before prom, I cornered her. It was after school, before a home match. I was up to second man by now; I didn't have any trouble on my home courts. I was on my way back out to them after returning to the locker room for my grip tape when I happened to see her. The hallway lights in the old brick wing beside the gym were off, and Licia was a silhouette heading for the door at the end of the hall. She was walking slowly, head bowed, hair down over her shoulders, in jeans baggy enough that at first I thought she was a nun, which I'd never really seen one of up close, so it was frankly kind of scary. Then I recognized her and called her name. She turned.

"Are you coming out to watch?" My voice boomed off the lockers.

"No," she said sadly, her head going to one side, but she stayed where she was, and I trotted toward her. The custodians had just waxed the cobblestone floors, so the hall was full of that oily lemon smell. My soles squeaked.

"Look," I said. "If you want to call it off, fine with me. I'll understand."

That was the biggest lie I ever told, and I stood to gain the least from it, too, but even a rose gets ruined if you bury it, and I was tired of guessing what was up with her. In a week's time I could find a dozen girls who'd love to go to the prom with me; some would probably ditch their boyfriends for the chance.

"No, no, no," she said, her head going to the other side. "It's just—well, if *you* want out, *I'll* understand. You see, I haven't gotten permission yet."

Hallway passes, assistant principals, and counselors all came to mind before I realized she was talking about *parents.*

"You haven't told them yet?"

"It's not *them,* for me. There's just my father left. Never mind, I was small when she died, it's OK. Not *OK,* but . . . Anyway, I've asked, he just hasn't answered yet."

Again I thought of counselors. I mean intervention strategies are in place for cases of abuse, even psychological, and I mentioned that.

She laughed. Even in gloom, she had more light in her than a halogen lamp.

"He's not a*bus*ing me. He'll come around. He's just—well, you'll see. You'll meet him."

I went out and won in straight sets.

Her father came around, sure enough, and mine lent me his orange Karmann Ghia convertible, which has pretty much stayed in our garage since he drove it back from Brazil, where it was one of the last ones made. My dad's not a real demonstrative guy, so this was his way of saying, "Don't fuck up." But Mr. Terranova never even came out of the basement. They live in this neat, low brick house with a neat, low garden surrounded by a chain link fence, on one of those winding streets in The Acres. Annie Robson-Rand used to live over there, before her father lost his job and they moved to the East Side, and the city manager does, but in between the mansions are plots that used to have carriage houses or servants' quarters on them, and the Terranovas' is one of these. Her dad's a carpenter, Licia told me, with a workshop downstairs.

She looked so good I couldn't look back, let alone answer, and we both peered down at the living-room carpet as if we might be able to see him through the pile. You could smell the wood, and everything in that house was white. The deep carpet was white, and the curtains were white gauze tied back with white yarn, and the wallpaper in the living room was white on white, with a white velveteen stripe. The dining room was white, furniture and walls both, and on one hung a white-framed picture of a woman in a bridal veil—also white, of course. The silence, as if all the white wasn't enough, was like snow.

"Leonard's at the library. He's our big hope. Dad wants him to go to Harvard, you see, so . . ." She winced, then said again, as if conveying his apologies, "Leonard's at the library."

"That's all right," I said idiotically, forgiving him, but it also struck me that I might have bitten off more than I could chew, here. I mean, she'd just told me why Leonard was at Aquinas while she was at Eastside, which was something I'd never even wondered about before. I remembered that wince from her hard-to-express friendship with Aline, and I wondered to what extent the flip side of her beauty was a chance to talk about her problems. Luckily, I also remembered her corsage, and with shaky fingers I tried to pin it on while she held open her cotton cardigan, also white.

That's when I had a horrible thought that must have shown on my face, the mum cradled in my palms like shattered pieces of glass. I couldn't believe I hadn't even considered it before: I mean, I suppose virginity was some of her appeal, but the implications hadn't even occurred to me; the logistics hadn't. She was like some theorem I'd been staring at for hours but only clicked later, when I was brushing my teeth or something, and I realized this night was going to be a whole lot more complex than I'd imagined.

Her smile faltered. "Is something wrong?" she said.

"It's this pin."

Finally, I got the mechanism to work. I did my best to smile, and I put it on her. She was beautiful, yes, but I was wondering when her curfew might be. No later than eleven, certainly. For after the dance, a banquet hall at the country club had been rented; the tradition was to pair up, spread out on the golf course, and spend the night on a green. I figured that maybe after I dropped Licia off I could return and find somebody in the parking lot who'd had a fight with her date, then head out to the country club. The night was like us: young.

But it was a good bit clearer. Outside, we could see the stars. My dad had put the top down.

Gym, balloons, crepe paper, strobe. No pig blood. The band was the same one they hired for every school function, plus or minus somebody's cousin. Seth Henderson had smuggled in a case of apricot brandy, which a few of us spent a goodly portion of the evening passing around the locker room. Others had volunteered to burn off excess rope, and by ten o'clock Billy and Benny were knocking around in the stalls, their violet tuxedo jackets over the door, screaming, "Oh! Oh! Oh! Oh!" When you went to take a leak it was like walking on bubble wrap, from the vials popping underfoot. Everybody was anticipating the night's activities at the country club, on the greens. Seth kept agonizing about having to choose between holes, and the locker room kept cracking up.

What I kept cracking was the locker-room door. Licia and Aline James were standing in front of the band, colors washing over them like crayons scribbling on paper dolls. Aline James had brought a guy from Aquinas who liked his brandy, as it turned out, so I was glad Licia had somebody to talk to. Michael Fallon stood with them for a while.

But I just couldn't make myself go out there. All the way here, I hadn't been able to get a precise curfew time out of her. What if she didn't *have* any? What if she'd told her father she was going to spend the night on the greens with me and that was that? Well, fine, but what did she think was supposed to happen out there, study groups? And what if down in the basement he was fashioning a lance with which to show up at three in the morning and skewer us both? What a morass of possibilities, none of them good. Here I'd been working toward this date since Labor Day, more or less, and the only thing that got me back into the gym was a full flask of apricot brandy that shattered on the tile in the locker room when Seth dropped it. Half a dozen of us barreled out the door immediately.

And just as immediately barreling down on *us* was one of the chaperones, Mr. Benavides. Not really barreling, more like speed-walking, the legs of his suit trousers flapping like green sails with a blue stripe in them. I broke stride and reached down as if to tug up my zipper tab, double-took to see him, waved with huge delight, thinking *You son of a bitch*, and strode on into the ballroom, smoothing my hair back with my palms. He and Mr. Goldman, who taught me all the ninth-grade civics I know, disappeared inside the john. I found in a pearl-gray pocket of my rented tux the Tic-Tacs I'd stopped for on my way to The Acres, as if I'd known all along how the night would turn out, and I passed them out to my boys before rejoining Licia and Aline and a woman who looked like another chaperone.

Licia smiled, either at or in spite of the tongue-tied shell she turned me into simply by extending her graceful left hand to my right, like the first move in some seventeenth-century dance. Whichever, I just took it.

"Rob? I'd like you to meet Ms. Glenda Watkins. Glenda, Robin Kidd."

The age where the gorgeous paired up with the homely had been a few years earlier. Now dumpy hung with dumpy, perky with perky, lissome with lissome. Aline—who was out on the floor now, dancing with her recently dashed-out date—and Licia were like negative and positive of the same photo, in some ways, and this woman was like a blown-up duplicate of the blonde version. If she was a teacher, it wasn't at Eastside, and I couldn't imagine anything getting done in any class she stood in front of anywhere. Her hand was smooth and soft, her nails glistening, her smile more powerful than the strobe. But she was one of those adults for whom everything associated with youth is really just the biggest *kick!* Guys from the hemp squad were chasing each other around and sliding on the hardwood in their leather soles, and when one of them crashed into us she just straightened him up with a "boys-will-be-boys" smile, as if she thought neon-red eyes were a matter of hormones.

"I'm with Al Benavides," she said when she'd sent the guy (Garrett Singh, a total burnout) on his way with a pat on the back.

"Ma'am?" I said for possibly the first time in my life, thinking, *OUR Al Benavides? YOU're with Rhomboid Al?* She was twice as tall as he is. (Again, Al might want you to think they're the same size, but it's a trick.)

Glenda smiled, actually clasping her palms together.

"They've been together fifteen years." Licia said as if I was supposed to take some lesson from this fact. The band announced a break, and girls who hadn't seen each other since two songs ago began shrieking and pattering across the room to hug. "I was just telling Glenda that Mr. Benavides is my favorite teacher."

"Sure is," I muttered in lieu of *Mine, too*, and when Licia squeezed my hand I added, "Great," and by the time Benavides came up, Glenda was beaming as if I'd said the perfect thing. Licia relaxed her grip on my fingers, but she wasn't letting go.

"Hello, Mr. Benavides," she sang out while I mumbled in something like, *Yo-yo, misdemeanor.* As usual, I couldn't tell anything by his face. The eyes behind the square lenses were two crows in two windows, the deep lines in his cheeks perpendicular to the floor. I thought he'd stepped in the brandy: for the first time since my Tic Tac, I smelled apricots.

"Ms. Terranova. Mr. Kidd." He inclined his torso slightly. "Dear."

On the tennis court, my best shots I don't think about, just hit and am amazed at afterwards. I pointed to two black streaks on the floor left by slipsliding stoners. "We were just discussing which is longer, Mr. Benavides. What would you say?"

Glenda laughed delightedly, clueless, but I didn't mean my smile. I don't know what I thought was going to be resolved, but I had an impulse to turn this into some kind of battle-of-the-wits showdown: no one would go down, but when it was over, there'd be no doubt that only one of us was on his feet.

I must have begun squeezing Licia's fingers, because she dropped my hand. When I looked over, she was gazing back as if the true significance of why I'd blown the lines-length lesson was dawning on her, slowly but surely; and surely, too, I was *never* going to get it right.

Benavides's angular face stayed as it was, as usual. Then the head turned toward me, and over the frames of his glasses, an eyebrow rose.

"I'd say they're about the same, Mr. Kidd." It was the classroom voice from the classroom face, but before I could strategize a response he added, "Of course, I'd need a micrometer to be absolutely positive."

That eyebrow rose again, and I could have sworn I saw a corner of his mouth twitch, speaking of micrometers, and Licia laughed and took my hand again. She began to rock our clasped hands gently, almost imperceptibly, her palm like a satin cushion, and something began to dawn on *me*: if Benavides hadn't used me in his little classroom demonstration, would she have even looked at me twice? I mean she hadn't before, had she? And I've been to the blackboard, so I know how people look from up there: you can see whether they're listening or snickering or craning for a glance from a girl in the front row. Maybe the guy was on my side, I was thinking, and in more ways than getting a scholarship.

I'm just beginning to absorb these implications when a metal detector at the far end of the gym went off, and security personnel ran out waving their arms around, hollering to stay put. We couldn't tell whether the beeping was a threat or a mistake, but it didn't stop, and eventually people's concern leveled off at milling around as usual. A chant for the band went up over the beeps; somebody let loose with an air horn they'd smuggled in, and Garrett Singh zoomed up and away like a hockey player stealing our puck, setting off Glenda's "You kids!" laughter again, and when the four of us turned around we were standing in a square, boy-girl-boy-girl, looking at each other like, "Well, what's it going to be *now*?"

Then Al smiled outright, nothing subtle but this huge toothy grin, and at *me,* and held it, as if in full confidence I'd learn this last lesson he had to teach, as he held his hands out to Glenda and Licia. So I did, too, and our little system closed. I still couldn't tell what the pattern was, but Licia was squeezing my fingers excitedly, squeeze and then still and then squeeze, squeeze, squeeze, and it didn't seem to make any difference who'd embarrassed whom a couple of weeks before, or who was still a kid and who wasn't, technically or otherwise, or who got what scholarship to what college or stayed in town and washed dishes at the Holiday Inn for a year, saving money if no scholarship came through.

But I wasn't even really thinking about any of that. I was thinking that maybe after the dance, Licia and I could just drive around with the top down, maybe stop somewhere for ice cream and sit in her driveway and eat it, picking out constellations and getting to know each other across the handbrake, keeping an eye on the light in the basement. And until somebody on the security team figured out how to shut the metal detector off, we all just stood there smiling at each other, holding hands, hoping for the best.

SOCIAL SERVICES

A woman and a boy came over to watch him fish. "Oh, no," he thought when he first heard their approaching voices, but they walked right up, as if they'd spotted him from across the park and made him their goal. The woman just came right out and asked if it would be all right if they watched.

"I haven't caught anything," he said to dissuade them, but it didn't.

"He's wanted to do this all summer," she said of the boy, "but I couldn't handle the worms. And I mean *handle*—no."

Roberts stretched his lips. She was shorter than he was but heavier, in a long red T-shirt, mid-calf cargo pants, and shiny plastic shoes with heels made out of springs. Except for bruises on her arms and shins her smooth skin was caramel-colored, her own smile pleasant but crestfallen, as if she'd come to terms with being overlooked. Roberts was white, fit, younger-looking than he was. The boy examined him.

"Do you have a worm on there now?"

Roberts was surprised at how high and pure the boy's voice was. The boy stepped up onto the thick bottom rung of the iron railing to peer over the top rung. The seams of one of his shoes had split.

"Yes I do." Roberts lifted his line to show. "Look in that little box over there and you'll see more. Greenworms, the guy at the bait shop called them. Growers put something in the soil that ordinary earthworms eat to turn them that bright green color, which apparently catches the fish's eye. He knew all about it. I asked."

The sound of his own voice surprised him, too, as did the way it went on. He tried to remember the last conversation he'd had, the last person he'd talked to face to face. Before the bait shop, it had been several days.

"Yeew," said the woman over the boy's shoulder when he'd jumped down to open the Styrofoam box.

"Look here." Though Roberts had just put his bait on he reeled it in and pinched it off, flicked it out into the current, and opened his pocket knife to cut off a third of another worm.

"*YeeEW!*" The woman turned away.

"Is that part his face?" said the boy, un-revolted. "Or his butt?" He didn't laugh at the word, just looked up at Roberts for an answer, his eyes dark and bright, and Roberts, who had never thought about worm anatomy before, looked back. He didn't know kids or how to tell their ages. This one's head came up to about his stomach, and he was missing his front teeth; when he talked, his lips stretched out over the gap, and Roberts could see tiny pink ridges of gums, where teeth should or would be. The boy's skin was a shade darker than the woman's, like milk chocolate, and he was slightly pudgy. Six or seven, Roberts guessed.

"I don't know," he said.

The boy accepted that. "Look at those boats," he said. "Is it a race?"

Roberts felt a pang: sailing was one of the things she'd wanted to do together that he'd never made time for. What was going on out there now must in fact have been a regatta: some thirty or forty sails of many colors had almost reached the lighthouse. He thought they'd been closer to shore when he'd arrived, though they hadn't really registered on him until the boy mentioned them aloud.

"I'll bet they're going to circle the lighthouse," he told the boy. "First one back to the harbor wins. Last one's a rotten egg."

The boy looked down as if embarrassed for him. Then his small hand reached out to touch the bright-yellow fiberglass rod of Roberts's brand-new pole, which he'd bought with reel, hooks, sinkers, and worms for under twenty bucks. The bait shop was between his house and the park, a walk of fifteen minutes, though this was the first time he'd walked it in the fifteen years he'd owned the house, the first time he'd stopped in the shop—his first time fishing, in fact, since he'd been not much older than the boy.

"Can *I* try?"

"Why not?" Roberts said. Smiling with cautious gratitude the woman faced the harbor, forearms on the railing, thick fingers clasped. A breeze lifted her bangs, and her eyes narrowed. Towers of flat-bottomed clouds over the sailboats, dark below, billowed up the color of cantaloupe flesh, and Roberts figured another two hours of daylight left. He wished he'd brought a jacket. Temperatures had been on the cool side all summer.

"It's nice here," the woman said.

"Can I?"

"All right. Here. Hold it like this."

Roberts was amazed at how delicate the dimpled fingers were that he positioned above the reel and on the spinner handle. He'd bought an open-faced reel, with which he'd had to get used to casting again himself, and now when he opened the bail and tried to show the boy how to do it, his forefinger was too short to hook around the line. "Here," Robert said, taking the pole back. "I'll cast, and you hold it. Then reel in when you've hooked a big one."

You'd be such a good father was almost the first thing she'd told him, and she'd said it often, later using *will*. He tried to remember the last time that was, realizing that it must have been before she'd met the new guy. He pursed his lips and let the line go, banishing the thought.

"Now we just wait. That's what fishing is mostly about. Patience."

The boy seemed glad of the lesson, peering through the rungs to where the bait had splashed just a few feet out. Roberts closed the bail with his finger and ceded control of the pole. The boy began reeling in for all he was worth.

"What are you *doing*? Don't break the man's fishing equipment."

"If I break it, I'm responsible," said the boy.

"It's OK," Roberts said. "But easy does it. That's better. That's good. Just keep the line straight, with just a little tension on it. That way, you'll feel any fish that bites."

"He's biting already. I can feel him."

"Probably weeds. That's why I don't cast too far: they'll scrape your worm off." Roberts thought he'd learned this already, though he'd been here only an hour. "But the fish do like to hide in between them sometimes." Or so he'd figured; maybe good parenting would just mean making things up with conviction.

The boy was holding the pole with both hands, his elbows wide and high to steady it on the top rung of the railing.

"Here, let's try this. May I?" The mother watched him take the pole back, lean over the railing to lower it out over the river, then prop it on the middle rung and hand it back. "More comfortable?"

The boy nodded. "But if I break it, I'm responsible." The word seemed to give him some sober satisfaction.

"Or drop it in the river!" The mother laughed. "He might be responsible but who do you think's going to pay for it?"

"Nobody's going to drop anything," Roberts told her. "Boy's a natural. Boy knows how to *fish*!"

He was grinning, but they both looked down. He'd said it with a trace of jive, a remnant of his Maryland boyhood and the first such in any of their speech; he'd been cautioned before against unleashing it too suddenly, with too much relish, in front of listeners he didn't know. She had cautioned him about that. She'd explained the dynamics of class condescension to him, and as in all other matters he could think of except her last decision, he had found her to be right.

"Are you all right?" the woman said.

At her tone, the boy peered at him, too, the line sagging off the end of his pole. Roberts stepped to the rail.

"Try and keep a little tension on the line," he said. "That's it. That way the sinker's on the bottom, and you'll feel it when the fish takes the hook."

"Keep it straight up and down," said the mother.

"I can feel him," said the boy. "I think I got a fish."

But the worm looked intact when he reeled it up. Roberts flipped the bail open, hooked the boy's finger over the line just out from where it wound off the reel, and tried to coach him into swinging the sinker, then releasing at the end of its arc, so that it would fall three or four feet out. But this proved to be too complex a maneuver, and the sinker swung back and nestled against the cement embankment.

"Good," Roberts said. "That's fine. That's excellent."

The boy seemed to believe him. The woman looked over as if she would reserve judgment. "Question for you," she said. "You know that S-curve on Hampshire?"

Roberts blinked, reconfiguring for the topic shift. He could think of several places where Hampshire Drive curved, but he nodded. "Yeah?"

"What kind of fish are those in there? Because I was by the other day, and they were . . ." She held her hands two feet apart, then another foot. "And thick, too. I was crossing the bridge and just looked over and saw five or six of them."

He asked if she meant the bridge by the cemetery or the one by the museum, and they went back and forth several times trying to pinpoint on which side, whether in pond or canal, but before Roberts could visualize the exact spot she meant, a ringtone of a tune he recognized but couldn't place went off, and she reached into one of the many pockets in her pants, the precise pocket the ring came from. Roberts, new to cell phones, usually had to slap all his pockets several times.

"Hi…No…Fishing…Down by the *water*, where do you think? Are you done? . . . Come on down when you are done, then." She snapped the phone shut like a castanet and told the boy, "Your mom's team's winning."

Roberts looked into the water, reconfiguring again. He couldn't look at this woman he'd assumed was the boy's mother, another thing he'd been wrong about. He recalled passing two or three baseball diamonds at the entrance to the park, where figures in matching shirts played: yet another sign of a world he'd paid so little attention to he felt he had no knowledge of it yet.

"I already lost *my* game," said the woman.

"I got another one!"

The woman laughed, and Roberts did look over now. She was having fun, and the boy was, though this time the hook was entirely bare, and the three of them speculated on why, whether crafty fish or weeds or simple wear and tear on worm flesh. But by the time the boy's real mother called again to say that her team had won and she was on her way to join them, they *had* caught a fish, a three-inch rock bass that the boy threw back with both chubby hands, shivering with the sheer prickly thrill of it, and Roberts could envision a foreseeable future with a certain amount of possibility in it after all.

They shook hands all around. The mother was tall, dark, and graceful, maybe twenty, with big white eyes hard on Roberts at first. As the first woman told her about the fish they softened, and both women thanked Roberts profusely. As the three walked off toward the baseball diamonds, the boy between the women, he chattered up excitedly to his mother, and about halfway there he turned to sing out over his shoulder across the field, "HEY MISTER! If you be down here tomorrow, can we come fish with you?"

GRASP AT THE FAR TURN

We thought we'd tear the old carpet up before my train left so that Sarah could get started on the floors, but underneath we found this ugly brown linoleum and, under that, dry rot like cocoa, just cupfuls of it. We'd been expecting oak or maple.

"What are we going to *do*?" Sarah says.

Well, I didn't *know* what we were going to do. This was our first house. Supposedly, the engineers had checked everything out.

"Harold? Harold? What are we going to *do*? Does this mean our *beams* are going to cave in?"

Ordinarily I'm Harry; at parties I'm Hair, but I'm Harold when she's having a panic attack. Nell could sense her mother's tension, so she poked her brother, and they both began to cry, running towards us with their arms up.

I had a good mind to call him right then, but he was already on the road, and he doesn't have a cell phone.

I kissed Billy's forehead, set him down, and pulled a tarp over the crumbling linoleum tiles we'd torn up, which had orange specks and grooved swirls in them. They looked like the frosting on a store-bought cake, I pointed out.

Sarah laughed obligingly, crisis waning, and said it might be a better day to take the kids to the park, anyway. After a week of humidity, the morning was perfect, blue and gold. I reassured her that nothing was going to cave in over the next two days, requested Nell's special smile until she gave me the better part of one, and ran three blocks to catch the F train to Penn Station, then an Amtrak upstate to deal with my brother.

He was always the guest, he'd complained, never the host. So we'd arranged to meet at Saratoga at first post time, on the trackside apron. "Close as we can get to the finish line!" he'd exclaimed on the phone. I just assumed he'd been drinking. "So we can see the noses cross!"

For some reason, at first I visualized two horses' heads in an X, on a shield, like an emblem for our family's coat of arms. As usual, by the time I figured out what my brother was saying, he'd hung up.

The trains were air-conditioned, but I felt grimy from my trot to the subway. I'd worn a seersucker jacket over my T-shirt, nothing so fancy as to upstage Terrill but nice enough to let him know I considered the occasion special, then smeared hinge-grease on my sleeve in a cab from the station that I split with four other guys, each of them deep into his own superstitious ritual. One guy wanted only clean bills in his change, so the cabbie had to thumb through a wad the size of a balled-up pair of socks, then got a five-dollar tip for his trouble; another guy tipped seven dollars on a three-dollar fare. "Is it always like this?" I asked the cabbie. I'd ridden the backseat hump, the last to get out.

"Always," he said. "They want to bet on a horse with my wife's name, or they want to give me a sawbuck for my hat. December through February, we can live in Florida." He was an old, hump-shouldered guy in a fresh haircut; his hat was a shellacked-straw number with a narrow brim and a high crown.

"Here," I said. "And I want every goddam cent back."

He laughed, and I tipped him a couple of bucks, holding back a comment about how much grease he used on his doors. If I was going to have to write off these two days anyway, the least I could do was relax.

And if you can't do that at Saratoga, you can't anywhere. I hadn't been up there yet. It was the second weekend of the meet, and the weather was as beautiful upstate as it had been in the city. The crowds, the colors, the sundresses. What's the harm in looking? No harm whatsoever. At the track, I had a cup of chowder and bought a cigar and looked so much I didn't worry when post time for the first race approached with no sign of Terrill.

I started out cautiously, with $5-to-show bets on Jardin Salad and Sara's Folly, horses I picked on the basis of their names: Sara's Folly for obvious reasons, suitable for the house and me, too, according to her friends, and the other after our new neighborhood, Carroll Gardens. The first race was a steeplechase, which I'd never seen live; the inside turf was too difficult to see from the rail, so I just watched the screen. Jardin Salad was in the running but came in fourth; Sara's Folly finished dead last. "Well, tough," I said to a fat kid who was pitching his ticket in the basket at the same time I tossed Jardin Salad, holding onto my Sara's Folly ticket for some future apology or make-up note.

I gave the real Sarah a call. In the background I could hear Nell's squeals of delight.

"She's on the swings. Billy's pushing, being so careful. I wish you could see them. She thanks him for every push."

In my mind's eye, I could. Billy pushing had been an all-summer preparation, and now he was handling it. Even no Terrill and the smells of beer and pizza and bare feet couldn't ruin the pride I felt.

"He'll be there. Just have a good time." She was the one reassuring me now.

I stayed out of the second, then the third, in favor of ambling around, wondering with increasing irritation where the hell he could be. The second went to Smarmy Marnie over Rasputin by a length. The third I saw on a big screen on a rotunda, Seabreeze over Salahaldin or Jerry Minetti, depending on the results of a photo finish, then an inquiry that went on and on. I waited as long as I cared to, turned around to head back out to the apron and all but ran into an orange-and-blue Hawaiian shirt I remembered from a previous summer.

"*There* he is!" Terrill said with such exaggerated astonishment I thought he'd spotted me earlier. We embraced with an arm apiece, both of us holding a cup in our other hand. His aftershave smelled like cough syrup; or maybe it was cough syrup I smelled on him. I asked when he'd arrived.

"A few minutes ago. 'They . . . were off!'" His grin was a checkmark shaped under dark teardrop lenses. He wasn't really fat, but it seems like every time I see him he's put on more weight. He's got my eyebrows, my nose. His chin is bigger, but I'm taller and slimmer. He's the older by seven years. It's just the two of us out here. Back in Michigan, Mom has Alzheimer's; Dad's had to put her in a home, where he's figuring to join her soon. *Another year*, he'll shrug. *Maybe two. Don't worry about us. We've had our fun. You want some nuts with that wine?* With high blood pressure and diabetes, he can't have either himself, but he likes to watch others partake.

Terrill, though, had no such reasons for looking me up and down the way he was doing. I don't know what you'd call the look on his face.

I do know. I'm sorry, but it's *grasp*: he's grasping at what's come to me but eluded him, neither of us knowing quite why. When the second-place decision was announced, he grinned eagerly and said, "Did you win anything, Bob?"

The eagerness breaks my heart and at the same time infuriates me. It's like a foot in the door of my life, and he hasn't wiped his feet. He's my brother. But am I my brother's keeper? I keep forgetting what the answer's supposed to be, and every time I see him I feel the battle over which will win out; moment by moment, the results surprise me as much as anyone. I held up the ticket I'd saved from the first race, still wrapped around my thumb like a tube.

"Two horse," I lied, pointing at the tote board, where Salahaldin had placed to pay $23.60. "I put five dollars on him. I'm going in to collect." His face sort of sagged, and I couldn't resist a second shot. "What can I bring you, Terrill? Beer? Bloody Mary? Brandy? Vodka? Gin? Rum drink? Keep 'em coming, I know that much."

His lips got taut the way mine do when the kids are acting up, if Sarah's mimicry is accurate. He held up a cupful of the first thing I'd named.

"I'm still good yet, thanks. Hey, nice to see you, too, little brudder."

I winced. He used to be able to give me fits, calling me that.

But we've shared more good times than bad, all told, and my mythical pick in the third was the only thing either of us hit that day. In the fourth I liked a long-shot named Onashingle, but I didn't place a bet, so when it came in at 30:1, "what's unsaid" became our theme for the afternoon. We share a sense of humor developed in the dark between bunks (mine the bottom) and can riff off of nothing until one of us gets tired of the game (usually me) or goes too far (usually Terrill).

"Well, there goes another two bucks down the . . ."

"Hatch? What'd you do *that* for?"

"No, no, you silly . . ."

"Goose? Rabbit? Billy?"

"Hey, you're talking about my . . ."

"Wow! Would you look at that woman's . . ."

I know, I know, but by the eighth race the muscles across my diaphragm hurt from laughing. Direct sunlight cooks the apron, and between the heat and the hooves and the mix of people displaying festive sportswear and emotions it was hard to nurse anything, resentment or beer.

Not that Terrill had more than that first one, a good sign. And he seemed in relatively good spirits, relatively good shape. I'd worn my Yankees cap, and he bought a bright red one with a racetrack logo and an extra-long visor that caused women to smile, and he smiled back. Since the debacle with Wendy, he hadn't mentioned any other women, and I didn't want to ask; I was just glad I hadn't heard about them on the news.

But after the ninth I came out of the john, and he was standing with a tiny, deeply tanned woman in a tight beige pantsuit with a six-inch-wide belt. She had long streaked hair with bangs to her eyebrows that couldn't hide the creases at the corners of her eyes, though her body was like a prototype, with possibly a negative percentage of body fat. Before I got there, she touched his arm, squinted up at him, and walked back toward the betting windows, smiling.

"Do you know that woman?" I said at his elbow. Something in his posture as they talked, back on his heels with his head half-turned down to her, had made them seem close, and the thought of some kind of sting entered my mind, me the mark. The horses for the tenth race were being led out onto the dirt track in front of us behind their unmarked training partners; in a minute they'd all come back the other way so we could see the ones that were going to run.

"Norma? I just met her. Why?"

He glanced down at me as he said it, and I felt a helpless flood of what I used to feel when he'd wake me climbing the ladder at three in the morning, back before I could drive. *Shhh! Tone dell Tad!* he'd whispered once, a joke that had lasted until we'd both finished college—me before him, by the way, something that for years I'd actually been ashamed of, not for him but for myself. I thumped his damp back.

"Better watch out, Terrill. She might be a . . ."

I gaped over in mid-yuk, but for once he was the one who'd tired of playing first. He kept his eyes on the track, his forearms on the top pipe of the chain-link fence, a rolled-up *Post Parade* in his thick fingers. His nails were long and shiny, either greasy or polished, another question about him I didn't want to ask. He yawned.

"Four horse has the jiggle," he said, indicating a black with its nose over its partner's neck. "I think she's ready."

I opened my own program. Four was a three-year old filly named Private Energy. On the board she was 8:1.

"Are you going to bet her?"

"I already did. Fifty to win. Norma's placing it."

He said it so casually I was studying my program again before it registered that he'd given fifty dollars in cash to someone he'd just met. That was so exactly Terrill that all his more recent trouble returned: from bankruptcy and divorce to attack, arrest, trial, and acquittal on a technicality. The attack was actually driving a stolen backhoe into a bar named Dew Drop Inn, where Wendy was dancing with somebody else; I think the technicality was that no one could actually be that trite and stupid. *It's worth a few thousand every so often not to have him come back here*, Dad said the Christmas after it happened, when I flew Sarah and the kids out to see him—to see them, except you can't tell whether Mom sees you back. *It's just too bad he picked your state to settle in, if you can call anything about that boy settled.* Admittedly, Terrill's had it rougher than I have on the father front: same father but a different front entirely.

At the track, I tried to focus my dismay.

"Terrill. Let me get this straight. You gave fifty dollars to a stranger?"

The horses were approaching the gate. Private Energy was prancing, whinnying, and bucking, all but being dragged into the starting gate.

"Norma's no stranger," he said and raised his arm just in time for her to tuck in under it. Teeth appeared in her burnished face like the edge of a porcelain sink buried in sand. "Are you, darling?"

And . . . they were off.

Norma came to dinner with us. I was giving up two days with my kids so a guy with nothing wouldn't feel like a guest, and he invites this odds-on bimbo to Fiorelli's, a white-tablecloth pasta place on the main drag in Saratoga Springs. The only reason Private Energy hadn't come in last was that My Life Savings fractured a leg so severely it had to be put down. OK, I made up the name.

One of two bow-tied girls at a podium told us there'd be a half-hour wait for a table.

"Oh, but it's worth it!" Norma said, then with a deferential look at me, "unless you'd rather try somewhere else, sir."

Terrill laughed. His cap was on backwards by now. The man's forty. "Call him Harry." He laughed again.

On second thought, it was good she was there, for my brother's safety. This was like dealing with Billy at bedtime, for crying out loud.

"Half an hour will be perfect," I told the girls at the podium. "That'll give us time to walk around your charming town."

Terrill and Norma perceptibly stiffened, but the bow-tied girls smiled in unison, and I left my name—Terrill's and mine—while Norma went to the restroom. Terrill and I didn't speak until she returned. I saw her pause to say something to one of the girls—about soap or towels in the ladies', I assumed vaguely—and when she'd swiveled between tables back to us, I gave her the same cheerful "Ready?" I use with the kids, and the three of us set out.

I paused at shop windows to let them get ahead. Saratoga's strip turned out to have surprisingly good stores, not your usual crammed resort shops, and I saw a pair of shoes worth a closer look in Manhattan. Streetlamps flickered with flame-shaped filament, and everybody was out strolling. A backless dress with cabbage-size roses that I'd noticed at the races caught my eye again, the woman inside slim and elegant and accompanied by a white-haired man in linen. Workhorses with reflector tape around their hooves pulled white carriages. The air was cool, petunias spilled out of pots hung on light-posts, and nobody hollered or whooped. The smells were of oregano, almonds, and curry, not french-fry grease. Even the tattooed here seemed well bred. I was taking mental notes for Sarah. We've talked about a summer place upstate, someday, after I make partner and a lot of other *afters* that would constitute a whole different story.

In this one, Terrill was waiting for me to catch up.

"Do we have time to do the other side of the street?" he asked me. "Or shall we retrace our steps?"

At his *shall*, Norma looked up at him curiously. He'd stuck his sunglasses in his breast pocket, where they ruined the hang of his shirt, and his jeans had the kind of ground-in dirt that boutiques approximate with paint, though you can tell the difference; the soles of his running shoes had worn to the thickness of cardboard. But what got me was the look on his face: he was *loving* this stroll. Back in Brooklyn, it was about bath time, and as we ambled, I called Sarah to remind her to give Nell her Amoxicillin, because even though her ear's gotten better, you're supposed to finish out the week. Sarah said fairly tersely that everything was under control, but in the background, Billy sounded wound up again, and I was wishing I were there—and here my brother was dancing on and off the curb and swatting at the petunias, his eyes moist, as if he'd mistaken this ordinary pleasantness for some kind of grace. He said it again: "What *shall* we do?"

This time Norma patted his hand and waited for my answer.

"Let's just go back."

I turned and walked ahead, listening to my brother and his pick-up date murmur and laugh in the kind of carefree moment that these days Sarah and I would have had to schedule weeks in advance. So sure: add a little envy into my emotional mix.

"Table for four. Right this way," said one of the bow-tied girls when I'd given her our name.

"Three," I said, stepping aside to let Norma and Terrill pass, "but thanks."

"Oh?" She looked like a Skidmore student and spoke with the pique of the unjustly accused. "Then who is . . . ?"

At a corner table stood a thin, dark woman with teased curls in a squarish hairdo that hung over her eyes, like a poodle's. She was as remarkably tall and pale as Norma was short and tan and in a similar fatless condition; across the tabletop I could see the triangular hem of a fringed skirt between long, slim thighs. A little later I was to notice high, matching boots, heelless but also fringed.

"Sybil! *Sybil*! It's my friend Sybil."

Norma beamed up at me and swiveled her way through to give her friend a hug. I turned to Terrill, who'd just stepped on my heel.

"Did you help set this up? *Terrill*! Did you know about this?"

Diners within earshot paused, angel-hair pasta dripping from their forks, which they lowered, waiting for us to pass. But not even my dread of public scenes quelled my fury.

"*Answer my question*!"

"She said she might call a friend." He removed his cap to show me hound-dog eyes. The two women were smiling in our direction, eyelashes batting like the brushes in a carwash. "It's just a dinner, Harold. Just conversation. Do it for her sake, if not your own."

"*Her* sake! I don't even *know* her! I don't even *want* to know her!"

He looked around as if *I* were the one with the behavior problem, but I had to admit that by that time he had a point. Nearby diners were glaring alternately at us—at me, actually—and their cooling food.

Then I realized what was going on: Terrill and Norma were hoping I'd offer to pay. In a wrought-iron cage outside, we'd all seen the prices, but I hadn't given them a thought. *Fine. Let's go in*. Now I figured a hundred and fifty dollars, tops, including tip and a decent bottle of Chianti, not that bad . . . in fact cheap thrills for all concerned, now that I knew what this little junket was about.

Over our noodles we talked about horses, of course. Sybil's own brother was a trainer, and Norma had worked at a stable until her arthritis got too bad—only then did I notice her golf-ball knuckles, which she covered with a napkin as she spoke. Terrill had introduced me as a lawyer, which clammed the women up until I admitted I never went to court. "What's copyright?" Sybil asked when I told her what I did instead, and when I said *books* she nodded sympathetically and said her ex was doing five to ten but would probably be out in three, plus he'd been able to keep some of his accounts going from inside. She was one of those dames too smart to show it; when Terrill laughed, she feigned surprise.

Norma poked him and said, yeah, well, what did he do for a living? This was yet another topic I hadn't wanted to broach.

"I'm in wheat these days," he said. "Wheat and transportation, essentially."

We ate our salads and tried to imagine until my brother drained his Chianti, took Norma's fatless biceps in his sausage fingers, wiggled his eyebrows, and added, "I drive a bread truck. Any type, but my specialty is rolls."

Both women loved this to a point where people scowled over at our table. Another hour, I told myself. The ginger-and-sesame dressing, anyway, was delicious. Sybil looked over both shoulders, at a wall and a latticed window, then leaned over the table confidentially.

"Jeff swears he's got one in the eighth tomorrow that's ready."

Terrill paused in the middle of buttering one of his special deliveries. "Oh?"

"Hold the Phone. That's its name. Bet heavily, he told me. All I know." As if to stop herself from saying more she fit a forkful of salad the size of a carnation into her mouth. When she'd chewed it down a ways, I asked what kind of information her uncle usually came by. "All legitimate," she said. "All based on his faith in a horse he knows and has watched its workouts. And I can't remember when I've seen him as excited as he is about Hold the Phone."

I'd have expected more interest from Terrill, who seemed to be practicing some trick involving nostrils and eyebrows. He said, "I don't know. Even if it were to come in, I wouldn't feel as if I'd earned the money."

Sybil looked at Norma, and they both laughed. Norma poked my brother with a talon the color of our wine.

"None of it's *earned*, Terr. It's a bet, not a job."

"All I know is, I'm putting my Baysider on this horse," Sybil said.

I hadn't realized you could bet a boat. What would the payoff be: a yacht? A supertanker? It would depend on the odds, of course. Terrill finished buttering his roll and popped half of it into his mouth, all with his elbows on the tabletop. He had the worst table manners my father had seen in his life, as we'd both heard repeatedly for almost two decades. Out of old habit I tried to deflect attention from them.

"My brother actually makes an interesting distinction," I said, making conversation. "If a winning bet is unearned, is it un*deserved*, too? And is a losing one *deserved*, then?"

Terrill dropped his elbows back, his hands loose fists. "Will you stop calling me 'my brother'?" he snapped. The women became alert.

I laughed. "*Aren't* you?"

"Not so as anyone could tell."

That's when I noticed how red his face had become. His eyes looked like something had scared him.

"*I* think you look *very* similar," Sybil said so quickly and sweetly I could have kissed her. She smiled back and forth between us, then at Norma. "Look at their eyes, their noses. Look at the way they work their lips."

"They do look like brothers." Norma's tone was careful, her eyes fixed on Terrill. "Anybody on the street could tell. Out of a crowd, you could pick them."

An excessively energetic waitress in a black apron arrived with our pasta. "Yours? Yours? Yours? Oh, *yours*," she chattered, her eyes like that tape on the horses' hooves as she rattled and knocked our plates against the tabletop, but she was a distraction we all welcomed.

Terrill's color faded a bit, but he kept his eyes on his plate. For a while we just ate. I'd ordered scampi, Norma linguini Alfredo, Sybil penne primavera. All these were good.

"Terrill?" I said gently. "How's the Bolognese?"

He held a fork in one hand and a tablespoon for twirling in the other, his cheeks puffed. The thumb of the spoon hand shot up.

"The differences," he said then and finished chewing leisurely, "are minor. The differences are infinitesimal, if you look any depth at all below the surface. They're not a matter of character, morals, or even work ethic, if you're talking about effort and man-hours or any kind of hustling ratio. Maybe there's a little difference in smarts. I'm prepared to grant you a small brain-power gap."

"What's he—what are you babbling about?" I said jovially, but I knew.

"The difference between winning and losing, what it takes to win versus what it takes to lose. The difference between one going up, the other going down. Between law school and union dues, property and rental, happy family and a wife who fucks around. Between a three-hour train ride while the other drives four and a half in a twelve-year-old Chevy, drops his muffler, and has to pay what he's asked for repairs on the road."

We'd all stopped eating, Sybil with her mouth full. Norma's hand rose slowly to her lips, ceiling lights reflecting off her nails like sparks. "Cain slew Abel," she murmured behind her fingertips, but everybody heard.

The coked-up waitress reappeared.

"How's everything? Good? Good? Want another bottle of wine? You guys really zipped through this one, my goodness! Whoops! I didn't mean it that way! Sorry! *Sorry!*"

In about ten seconds, a very long time, Terrill eased back in his chair and handed the waitress the bottle she'd begun to reach for, then drawn back when she sensed our tension stretched over the table like a razor-wire grid.

"Same again, darling. Thank you. Maybe I can get some of my friends to help me out a little more with this next one."

He was looking at me more directly than he had all day, even when I told him I'd won on Salahaldin. But I didn't sense the grasp or even the hostility now so much as amusement. I had the idea he was daring me to correct his diction, that it wasn't just for the waitress's sake I'd been demoted from *brother* to *friend*.

That's when I made my decision, actually a series of them, mostly logistical.

Terrill wanted to pick up the tab, probably to show off his credit card; apparently his rating had been restored. I wondered how many bread-company paychecks it would take to pay down our dinner debt, but any protest seemed likely to risk ticking him off again, so I just thanked him. The four of us walked to the end of the block, the three others happily planning where to meet the next day for race number eight. Norma rose on her toes when Terrill bent to kiss her cheek. I held my hand out to Sybil. Her soft palm was cool and smooth and *waiting*, it struck me, her grip so unlike Sarah's firm one I felt a twinge, and deep in the cave of dark curls her bright eyes glinted before the heavy lashes came down. I turned and watched a carriage driver dismount to help a customer. It was the white-haired man in linen, his flowered companion already seated. The carriage driver wore pointy boots repaired with duct tape, and when he'd climbed up onto his own perch and faced front his smile turned off, and he snapped the reins.

"Norma said to say she enjoyed meeting you," Terrill said. Both women were gone. "You'll see each other tomorrow, anyway."

The best I could do was grunt. We headed for his car, where he held out the keys to me, the closest he came to apologizing or admitting anything.

"Drive?"

The car was so quiet I could believe the muffler was brand new.

We were staying in a Howard Johnson's in Schenectady, since every place in town had been booked weeks in advance, but before we left Saratoga, Terrill asked me to stop at a Stewart's. He came out with the next day's *Racing Form*, clicked on the overhead light, and during the short trip down 87 read out loud the stats on Hold the Phone, conversing with himself.

"And will she be covering more distance tomorrow than in her last race? Yes, she will, from seven furlongs to a mile. When did she last do a mile or more? Not since last season. Where, and what were her times?"

He knew more about handicapping than I do, and in our room, I watched CNN while he did the rest of the card, though I was able to point out one or two considerations he seemed to find valid, like Beyer speed figures.

"Well, good night," he said suddenly. He'd dropped the paper on the floor and was sitting on the edge of the bed in his red-plaid boxers, his heavy thighs pasty, looking in my direction but not at me. The skin around his eyes looked gray. His face was thoughtful and tentative, as if he might have been willing to say more if I went first.

But I didn't, and when he'd finally slipped into a heavy snoring rhythm I got up, dressed, and repacked as quietly as I could, which was very quiet, as I'd laid things where I knew they would be. Downstairs I woke a night clerk to pay for the room, including Terrill's breakfast. He liked French toast and preferred bacon to sausage, and recalling those things made me want to go back up to the room and slip into bed, but again, I didn't. From a card in my jacket pocket, I called the company of the cab I'd taken earlier before remembering I was in an entirely different town now. But it was only money, and by the time I realized, the car had arrived.

Talk about odds: the driver was the old man who'd brought me in from the station, looking like this must have been his last fare of the night. Even his hair looked to have grown.

"All the way to Brooklyn?" He craned around, his eyes bloodshot, his hat back on his head. "You've got to be kidding. I just happened to be down here. I was told this was a local. You'd have to pay the return fare, anyway. But not with me."

"I'll pay triple. Please. Just get going."

I looked back at the hotel, trying to remember which side our room was on and whether a light in the middle of a floor about halfway up could have been Terrill's. Now that I was so close to escaping, the danger seemed acute, though I didn't know exactly what the danger might be: Terrill barreling out of the lobby in his boxers to reach in and yank me back and . . . and what? Pummel me with a rolled-up *Post Parade* until I agreed to swap lives? Make me admit I'd wanted Sybil just the tiniest little bit, or that I didn't deserve my life any more than he deserved his? Or just stoop over the windshield and peer in, his face full of accusation, envy, and rue?

None of those things happened, of course. Nor would the cabbie agree to take me home for any price. But he did drive me to cab central in Schenectady, where the fresher driver of a yellow Mercedes was willing to negotiate a fare to Brooklyn. By two o'clock in the morning we were rolling.

Later—in the months since, when Terrill hasn't returned my calls and now, while I'm telling this—I've felt bad. But all the way home, watching the winking green and red pinpoints on the Hudson, my lap filling with amber that leaked away with each passing lamp post, I wasn't feeling bad at all. I knew I'd be back in time for the kids' rising, my favorite part of any day and Sarah's, too, and I felt great.

FOREIGNERS, SPIES, AND ENEMIES: A Love Story

"Oh, Asole," her father would say. "Do you think that people like that can really love?" (Alexander Grin, *"Scarlet Sails"*)

Emmett met the first woman on his first full day at a coffee shop across a canal from a big dark church. The shop was so busy that the only place to sit was at a tiny round table by an open door, and Lena had just introduced them when the church bells began to clang, loudly, in a steady two-tone cadence the likes of which Emmett had never heard before, multiplying in number and volume, building to a crescendo that he could feel in his temples and cheeks and the pit of his stomach. He held one flat hand high over the other to show the scampering waitress who finally did stop how much black coffee he needed, Lena translating into Russian that sounded like a cough, but by the time his tiny cappuccino arrived, a delicate design like brown herringbone in its foam, he didn't care about caffeine: the pinging, steel-drum sounds of the bells were tapering off into echoes like amplified drops of water in a bucket, and Emmett, who had never given church bells back home much thought one way or another, felt brand new. The whole thing lasted maybe three minutes tops, but it was like coming out of some fantastic solo, like Duane Allman's "Whipping Post" at the Fillmore East, which to Emmett's mind was still the all-time best. Not because of what the song was about, either, even if it had turned out to be pretty much his own life story, at least the parts of it that featured Noreen. But now the Emmett Tessich story, thanks to the five thousand miles he'd come at almost a dollar a mile, so far, was about to change.

"Wow!" he told his date, grinning at Lena, too, in case she had to translate. He'd brought a little phrase book but hadn't had to crack it yet. "What a funky way you've got to pray over here. You didn't order any?"

This last was to Lena, who said she was going to leave them to get acquainted; she flashed peach-colored nails at them, and in a remarkable gymnastic feat clacked down the steep marble steps to the street in her stilettos and tight skirt without losing any poise. She wore the same pink-leather jacket he'd spotted across the train station yesterday before he knew who she was, walking beside the guy who turned out to be Gleb, and through the latticed coffee-shop window, Emmett watched the sunglasses in her white-gold hair swivel this way and that, then cross the canal on a little arched bridge that had huge cats with golden wings posted at its four corners. *Far fucking out*, he thought, still not quite believing he was finally here. Back home, everyone from his mother to Jay Leno had a judgment to pass, if not come right out and say, on why guys like him came over here, and after over a year of email correspondences, weeding out the gold-diggers, and paying a lawyer to check out Gleb's agreement, not to mention all the logistics of passports and visas and travel itself, Emmett still didn't know whether this was the lowest he'd sunk or the best thing he'd ever done. But if even one of the dozen women he'd contracted to meet turned out to have half as much ease with her own femininity as Lena, let alone all-around foxiness, he'd have made the right decision.

The one yesterday he'd been too jet-lagged to judge, and his first impression of the one across from him now was mixed. She had an OK face, not beautiful but striking, with cheekbones as advertised and a jet-black pageboy haircut; she was wearing a black corduroy version of a denim jacket over a pale-yellow tank top. In the picture he recalled, if he'd kept them straight, she'd been looking up over one bared shoulder, with the same bangs but her hair swept off her neck, piled up. When Lena had said "Tanya" she'd looked him in the eye and held her arm straight out with no coyness but nothing to prove, either, her grip firm but not too hard, her smile open but light. She was listed as thirty-five, which looked about right. In his pocket Emmett had a little chart he'd drawn up so that he could keep all twelve straight at a glance, though he realized now that at the times he needed it most, he couldn't exactly whip it out.

"So," he said. His mind went blank.

"So. You have come such a long way. How was your trip?"

He could tell her that. To save money (though he downplayed this), he'd taken Trailways from East Lansing to Detroit, where he'd *walked* across the Ambassador Bridge to catch a Canadian bus to Pearson, then a charter flight to London, Sterling Air to Stockholm, and a ferry to Helsinki. In a hostel there he had a "SAHoona," which he did stress, then caught a midnight train to the Finland Station, across town. He pointed to where he thought that was.

"Ah." She raised eyebrows like black thread. "An adventurer."

He didn't like the eyebrows, but he liked that.

"I guess. Hey, Tanya, are you hungry at all?"

He hadn't ordered anything himself because everything in the case looked like cake, but it was already ten o'clock, and he wondered when breakfast would be. Food and drink were on him, according to the contract, but the schedule was theirs.

"Thank you, no. As well for the coffee, which is wonderful here. Do you not find?"

Her English was better than Lena's, and he liked the direct way she looked at him, curious but not too eager. But coffee was coffee, and again his mind went blank.

"Here," he said, patting the pockets of his new travel vest for the pins he'd brought, then setting hers between their saucers in its tiny plastic bag. Searching for easy-to-pack gifts they wouldn't already have, he'd settled on Pistons brooches, the logo with the flaming horse's head, which was really pretty cool-looking, though he hadn't intended to offer it quite so early. "Those are tail pipes," he pointed out. "Motor City, you see. They make cars there. I live sixty-five miles away, in East Lansing. Actually, I live in Charlotte, almost halfway to Battle Creek. Fifty miles a day round trip to work. In East Lansing, see?" It all spilled out less smoothly than he might have liked.

But she beamed at him as if NBA jewelry was the perfect thing on a first date here, and she thanked him several times. She was accepting his help in affixing it to her lapel when Lena clacked back up the steps and pulled a chair over.

"How are you two?"

"We are fifteen minutes older, Lenochka. What do you think?"

Lena's laugh sounded the way her neck looked, healthy and full. Tanya added more Russian, which came out in a lower key than her English, and while they went on in their own talk, Emmett took a break, finishing off his lukewarm coffee and looking out at the street beside the canal and the big boulevard they'd come in on. Both were filling up with teenage kids, dressed-up ladies, old women in headscarves, bums, soldiers—in a square beyond the church he saw one without legs, on a low wooden wagon—and beefy guys in lemon-colored suits, their shoes about three sizes too long. No Black people, Emmett realized. He was white himself, but it seemed weird, for a city the same size as Metro Detroit (which he knew because he'd done his homework on the Internet). No better or worse, just *foreign*, which he had to admit made a lot of sense.

Then Tanya and Lena were on their feet, kissing three times on the cheeks, and Tanya put her hand out and said, "Pleased to have met you," her smile neutral, and that, apparently, was that. The contract called for a brief meeting first, then perhaps a longer one later, by mutual consent; but now he regretted the Pistons brooch, and after he'd paid and was out on the street again with Lena, he asked her if it had gone all right.

"Oh, sure-sure," she told him over her open cell phone, but because he'd showed up a day late, some huge celebration was in full swing, and everything was up in the air. They had other appointments to keep. Now come on.

First they had to find Gleb in another café, this one with washing machines and computer booths instead of coffee and cake, and down a few steps from street level instead of up. Gleb was a small, fit guy with thick sideburns and a baseball-sized bald spot, which Emmett got a good view of when Lena drew back the curtain in one of the booths. On the computer screen, Emmett recognized the site by its colors and the number 14,000, which was the number of Russian women who wanted to meet you, though now the words had those frat-house letters mixed in with the regular ones.

"My awfice," Gleb said, rising from a metal folding chair to shake his hand. The site said he grew up in Daytona Beach, which from his accent Emmett believed: half Boris from *Rocky and Bullwinkle,* half Deputy Dawg. "Now you know."

"Our real office is remodeling," Lena put in.

"We will go to breakfast in a 'jiffy.'"

Gleb winked—winked!—and drew the curtain behind them, and Emmett stepped back into the aisle between rows of booths. Maybe half of them were occupied; he could hear the click of keypads over the chug of washers in the next room, then the swish and tick of Lena and Gleb's whispered Russian. *They must have secrets to keep from everyone,* Emmett thought. "Secrets are their way of life over there," a guy had told him right before he left, a guy in a bar who'd been over here many times on business. "Secrets are part of their culture. Under communism they were spying on each other as much as they were spying on us, so if you wanted a life here, you had to keep it secret."

Emmett wasn't that into politics. The only other time he'd been out of the USA himself was when a band he'd had with Joe LaNova, the Rockaterros, toured Belgium fifteen years ago, and that had been a whole different thing from being a tourist, which is what his visa this time said. He remembered a song by a folkie act that had opened for them once, not on the tour but at a club in Detroit, maybe Teddy's, where they'd been the house band for almost two years: "Oh, I am a lowly tourist, and they treat me like a schmo . . ." When Lena and Gleb came out of the booth all smiles, and then on the way out the young guy at a counter smiled at them as if he knew and liked them but at Emmett as if the opposite, he felt that for the first time he really understood what that line meant.

Breakfast, however, at another place below street level, was good: eggs and salmon with all the mayonnaise and dill you could pack away, though you had to order your potatoes by the gram, plus big cups of strong coffee, at last. He'd insisted that Gleb and Lena eat with him: what, was he going to let them order his food and then just watch? "Dig in," he said, and they had.

At one point Lena said the other Tatiana he'd chosen had had to back out. "Got married," she added at the same time Gleb said, "Appendicitis," then, with his mouth full: "Plenty more where she is from! Don't worry!" Lena was biting a peach-colored lip, but Emmett had a little white secret himself, not that he'd told them anything but true facts; so he let their discrepancy go, a trade-off. According to the contract, who they might find for any last-minute drops was up to them, so he'd let them worry about it.

Outside the window above their table, a show was going on, a parade of footwear passing by: loafers; army boots; more high heels than you could shake a stick at, including on a thigh-high pair of musketeer boots;

paint-spattered oxfords; black high-top Keds; then a pair of crude contraptions with no stitching, tongues and vamps strapped to the ankles, hobbled slowly past. A week ago on the Internet, Emmett had learned that *peasant* over here meant more than a way for Noreen to get him to stop chewing with his mouth open, which, sitting across from Lena, he was glad he'd learned. She popped a tiny triangle of toast into her mouth, nails flashing, and scrunched her nose at him, her eyes like crushed ice.

"Nice and stuffed?" Gleb asked, rising. "Thanks so very much. Now we must take care of your slight problem. Very slight." He winked and held out a forefinger an inch from his thumb, narrowing the distance by half.

Emmett's migration card had gotten fucked up when he arrived on a later train than he'd declared on his visa, so they had to return to the station he'd come into yesterday. But before they could flag a cab, the first five notes of "Climb Every Mountain" rang out, and Lena fished her phone out of a pink pocket and coughed into it, then handed it to Gleb, who also coughed.

"Hold everything," he said in a minute, snapping the phone shut and handing it back to Lena. "First, would you like to meet Bachelorette Number Two? She's the red-headed Katya Petrovna Borisenko, who came to Peter as a small child but still thinks of herself as a Muscovite. After graduating from the Finance and Economics University—"

"Right over there," Lena put in, aiming a nail across a curving canal to a group of young people outside a lemon-yellow building with wrought-iron gates.

"—our Katya will be wanting a career in moving-picture or music industry. Or bar maid, she hasn't decided yet. She is not too far. We will walk."

Emmett tried to chuckle along with the "Dating Game" routine, which the two others kept kicking like a can down the eight-lane boulevard, alongside a park and over another canal; but he couldn't listen and look and keep his boots on the pavement, which was not exactly flat. No shit, there must be some kind of celebration going on: it was like a Tigers game at the end of a good season around here, except nobody was running around or yelling, just walking slowly and looking happy, mostly.

Then they came to a bridge with statues of wild horses and tamers in the corners, and clinging to one of the pedestals he saw a woman with a rip in her fish-net nylons and hair like a three-alarm fire. She wore matching lipstick, her mouth almost square in some harangue she was delivering to other pedestrians, who marched on past. Lena and Gleb had stopped halfway across the bridge, shoulders hunched in urgent conversation.

"Was that Katya?" he called when he'd caught back up to them. "She looked like she could have used a hand."

"No."

"Not Katya."

Across the bridge Lena stuck a pink arm out into the traffic, and when a small, boxy cab swerved to the curb, Gleb bundled him into the backseat. Through the back window Emmett saw the redhead on her feet, one elbow high to light a cigarette. From this distance her face, with the sneer wiped off it, did not actually look that bad. "She was a . . ." Lena peered around the headrest, turning an imaginary knob back and forth a few inches away from her ear, "vodka person."

Gleb sat back from speaking to the driver, pulling off his best wink yet. "Change in *change* in plans. *Now* we can go to the station."

Emmett nodded, beginning to wonder how many slight problems and possible fibs he might be in for. At over seven hundred dollars a day, two busts out of three tries this morning was not a great rate (though if the first one was a complete bust it was his own fault, for breaking out the Pistons brooch; in fact he thought he might just shit-can those suckers in the next shit-can he saw). If things went well, there'd been talk—nothing contractual, but talk—about his doing a video for the web site, a satisfied-customer testimonial, and now Gleb, surreptitiously watching his face, seemed to realize he had to do a little better. Ticking a fingernail against the half-open window, he began acting like a somewhat underpaid tour guide, naming buildings as they passed as if he'd named them many times before, and Emmett too realized something: contract or not, for the time being he was pretty much at their mercy. He looked out.

"Gostiny Dvor, for when you want to go shopping" was a round, sand-colored building with arcades. Kazan Cathedral was the dark one with the bells. "And this pink one was a palace of the Romanovs . . ."

Within the next few blocks, Emmett saw more pastel palaces, statues, and golden domes than the whole state of Michigan probably even had. They went over a long bridge across a river called the Neva, then another over the same river. Among gleaming spires on the banks stood huge neon signs against the sky; one was for a brewery, Gleb said. People were streaming out of parks and across the bridges, most of them walking the same direction. When Emmett wondered aloud what the occasion was, Gleb passed his hand in front of his face as if at a fly, and what he said sounded so much like "asshole" that Emmett didn't know how to ask again without cracking himself up. None of this shit was what he'd come for, but he had to admit it was some pretty amazing shit. Even the small shit was. From a stoplight he watched a guy with a long cane pole and no reel pull up such a tiny fish Emmett figured he'd throw it back, but no: before the light changed he carefully unhooked what he'd caught and put it in a zip-lock baggie with several other miniature fish already swinging in the bottom, enough for a good-sized meal.

When the cab stopped in front of the Finland station and Gleb leaned forward to pay (according to clause 4B, transportation costs were his), Emmett looked out and saw a big statue that alarmed him at first. He knew immediately who it was, because the Rockaterros' last bass player, a college kid who could lay a steady line and thump a little, was one of these guys with opinions he'd let everybody know with T-shirts: they'd have pictures of Che Guevarra, Mao Tse Tung, Hunter Thompson, or this guy in the statue, whose name Emmett couldn't think of right this minute. He knew they weren't Communists over here anymore or he couldn't have gotten in, so he would have expected something like this to be torn down, like Saddam Hussein's had been. But here the guy was on huge bronze feet, giving the city either the finger or a thumb's up, hard to tell from this angle, his other arm cocked back by his chest, goatee soaring out like a hang glider. People strolled around a fountain in front of him, laughing and chatting, normal as you please; Lena and Gleb paid the statue as much attention as they had those bells and the holiday crowd.

What a fucking trip, Emmet thought, meaning more ways than one. He stood in the shadow of the big square station and waited for Gleb or Lena to tell him where to go.

It looked as if another guy than the one who'd taken his migration card the day before was there now. Everything had been confusing, but the first guy he remembered as skinny and pretty decent. This one looked like a butcher who had to take a wicked leak.

"Greetings," he said in English, with a slight lisp. He was smiling, barely, his voice wet and unpleasant.

"Where is Vasoline?" Lena said. "May we see Vasoline, please?"

"Vasoline has a headache," said the butcher-looking guy. "Today, I am Vasoline."

He was in a dingy room with a few pieces of luggage on steel racks, sitting behind a nicked-up wooden desk with ink stains deep in the grain. His thick-fingered hands were clasped like a nine-pound roast on a blotter the size of a placemat, which looked to be as old as he was, maybe sixty. Before he'd return Emmett's migration card, which the first guy had been almost apologetic about holding back, the new Vasoline wanted to hear again about the ferry in Stockholm. Emmett had already explained it twice the day before, plus had his duffel searched to within an inch of its life. He'd been allowed to keep it afterwards, however, and now he was nervous.

"I missed the ferry," he said, trying to think of convincing new details. He'd been eating a reindeer sandwich, which he'd seen a sign for and walked up to this other dock to get, because he'd never tried reindeer before, but the second dock was further than it looked and by the time he got back to the *first* dock, the ship was pulling out. He was aware of speaking too fast, though he'd said nothing but true facts.

The guy looked fairly pissed off. Under his left eye was a birthmark the size and color of a concord grape, and under his right a mole of about the same size and shape, for a total effect that suggested *clown* in a way he seemed to appreciate while at the same time daring you to. The ice in these eyes wasn't crushed but in blocks.

"Why did you not fly? Jets leave New York, even now Chicago, and from Moscow there is train, very easy. I know Chicago, may I say here. Two years on West Division Street."

Lena and Gleb smiled a little frantically. Emmett didn't know street names but had been to Chicago several times, most recently for Spring-steen in Comiskey Park, with Clarence Clemons and the whole E-Street Band, an awesome show.

"Go Sox," he said.

"*I am asking you: why?*"

Smiles cut out like throwing a switch, three breaths sucking together. Emmett had been arrested before, pulled over for moving violations with small quantities of illegal items in his glove box, but his heart had never hammered like this. Lena and Gleb stood as straight as that statue, noth-ing on their faces but respect for the butcher-looking guy. Emmett licked his lips and tried the same ploy he'd used on the East Lansing PD and the Michigan State Patrol: tell the truth, which had worked pretty well (one stop was thrown out, the other reduced to a two-hundred-dollar speeding fine).

"Cheaper." He retraced his route, with prices. "Took a while but cost me about half what a direct flight would have."

The man watched Emmett the whole time he was talking, one eyebrow or the other twitching every so often, never together. "And these Russians are your friends? Family members?"

"Tour guides," Gleb said, extending a booklet. Lena did too, with some loose papers that they laid on the desk.

Vasoline poked at the paperwork as at ashes, with a pencil point. "He can't fly direct, but he hires two personal tour guides."

Lena shot Gleb a stricken look, and Gleb for the first time Emmett had seen looked at a loss. After a few seconds he stepped up himself.

"Hey, sir. Mr. Vasoline. Look."

"Vassily," the man hissed. "But I am. . . ." He shook his head and sighed.

"Mr. Vassily. The trip was how I can afford them. If I'd flown direct I could only stay two days, with no guide at all. I did the math."

The new Vassily examined them all through narrowing eyes. When they were almost closed his head dropped down between his bull-like shoulders, which began shaking. Then his head came up, and he was laughing.

"Okey dokey," he said in a tone like Gleb's and lifted his clasped hands off the migration card, actually a quarter-sheet of paper with a fresh blue-inked seal on it. "And you, the licensed tour guides: make sure he enjoys our cultural treasures, right?"

Lena and Gleb couldn't even hail a cab, handing their cell phone back and forth to make multiple urgent calls at the curb. Eventually they all walked back across the bridge, which didn't work so well, either, because the sidewalks were packed. "Avoid large crowds" had been one of the State Department cautions his mother had told him about, but the six young girls linking arms ahead of them in short black skirts with flouncy white aprons, like French maid costumes, didn't seem to constitute much of a danger. He asked if this holiday was anything like Halloween, but Gleb either didn't hear or pretended he hadn't.

"We have an idea," Lena told him in a relatively quiet stretch, linking her arm through his in an easy way that made Emmett swallow. "How about for your next date in the museum?"

"What, you think Mr. Vasoline had us followed, maybe?" Gleb stiffened, and Lena looked down, as if suddenly fascinated by the stitching on Emmet's boots. His only experience with museums was an eighth-grade class trip to the Henry Ford in Dearborn, and he left his lunch on the bus. "Also, the contract says no weird stuff."

Lana stopped to laugh, people streaming around her with no apparent irritation. Emmett was glad she'd relaxed but sorry she'd let his arm go. Gleb laughed, too.

"Not to worry. This change of plans is a good one. A surprise I think you'll like."

Emmett said he guessed that one museum wouldn't kill him just as a group of kids almost did, squeezing him off the sidewalk into traffic. "On one condition," he added when he'd clambered back. "Tell me what's the deal with all these people in the streets."

It was more or less the whole country's high-school graduation, they explained to him in a huge square behind the museum, an olive-colored palace-looking building with all kind of fancy white columns and windows that was famous, apparently, and also as it turned out closed, because the square was too clogged with high-school graduates to open the doors. The maids' outfits turned out to be school uniforms, which Emmett figured must take care of truancy problems, though platoons of serious young guys waving short poles with big flags—some white, blue, and red and some all red with crossed white anchors in the center—looked less interested in girls than in their own posture. More people were coming off more bridges in swarms like U2 in Comerica or even the first Woodstock, which he'd been one year old for but had seen the movie nine times (plus driven nineteen hours to Woodstock '94 to see the Allman Brothers at last).

But the expressions on these faces were different than in crowds back home. A lot of the faces there were either too excited or too laid back, too happy or all fucked up. These—not all of them kids' faces, either—looked happy enough but in a calm way, somewhere between cautious and proud; others looked sad or even angry but resigned, as if whatever the emotion, they weren't going to take it any further. At the same time everybody looked alert, as if waiting for something.

"It's the red sale," Gleb and Lena told him between cell phone calls. "Tonight will be the red sale." All Emmett could think of was the color that bass player's T-shirts had usually been; if old Communist flags were going to be auctioned off, he wouldn't mind a souvenir. But you could ask only so many questions, and feeling like a small boy he followed along to another museum they thought might be open.

In the shadows of tall, dark trees stood a thin woman in a white blouse and pearl-gray slacks; and when she waved, Emmet's heart did, too, like a small boy's again, though he didn't even know she was waving at them until Lena waved back.

It was almost noon, the sun warm, and as they approached, Emmett saw the woman's folded jacket on the concrete bench beside her, satin lining out; her high-necked blouse had no sleeves, and abruptly matured, liking the look of her angular shoulders and thin, muscled arms. She kissed Lena three times on the cheeks and shook Gleb's hand, then swiveled toward Emmett, her hand angled like a goose's head, the nails short but polished. Her head too was slightly bent, the enormous blue eyes she raised to him somehow shy and bold at the same time: curious but contained, steady, and unafraid.

Possibly bingo, Emmett thought. It was only his first full day. Her name had been too complicated to catch.

"Coming to the museum?" he asked her. This museum was in a smaller, yellow palace behind them; they were in its gardens.

"Of course. I happen to be tour guide by profession. Real one." She gave Lena and Gleb a mock withering look. "They wait here. We will have date and art lesson. Two for one." Her eyes twinkled, and when she leaned to pick up her jacket, her knees stayed straight.

Very possibly bingo.

True he was no museum fiend, but Noreen used to buy art books at the mall to leave around on the furniture, so he knew Remington's cowboys, the couple with the pitchfork, that Dutchman's ear. Here though he didn't see a single thing he recognized. Even obviously old paintings were entirely new to him, from the artists to the people in them and the landscapes, until he read one of the brass plaques with English translations that identified two guys in pointy hats on horseback as Boris and Gleb.

"Look!"

Yes, yes. They were saints, said his new date, bringing a finger to her lips. He lowered his voice.

"No kidding. Gee, I knew he was a nice guy, but . . ."

Her smile showed she got his joke, and she walked him slowly through the rooms, touching his elbow here and there to point out some exceptional beauty or fine point, an expression on a face or a moonlit river so green it looked lit. On the parquet floors his cowboy heels sounded like claves, but when a woman in a doorway between rooms scowled and snapped something, his date just responded in mild-sounding Russian and touched Emmett's thigh until he lowered his step, her gesture so natural it was a few seconds before he felt the thrill.

Her own practiced heels, wine-colored velvet-looking ones not quite as high as Lena's, ticked softly as a clock. She drew close to some paintings, back from others, her face intent but relaxed, as if she were stringing a guitar. Emmett couldn't tell which to do when, but he tried to look as closely at the artwork as she was doing, and he began to see more in it. In one painting that covered a whole wall, soldiers on horseback were sliding down a snowy cliff, all but three obviously scared; but those three, in a shaft of sunlight, were having such a good old time that Emmett laughed out loud.

His new date turned back to him with a quick smile that showed gaps behind her front teeth, as if her incisors had shrunk; almost immediately she raised a loose fist to her mouth, knuckle under her septum. "That is General Suvorov," she said, extending her other pinkie at one of the grinning three, a man in a tricorn hat. "He was fighting *Napoleon*!" Her own eyes had become as excited as the general's. She put her jacket back on and, hands clasped behind her back, strolled off like a butler in a pearl-gray morning coat, her brown-blond hair drawn back with a ruffled band the same color as her shoes and a small pouch purse that dangled from her shoulder on a long strap.

The paintings got newer and hipper looking as they moved through the rooms: a portrait of a lady on a couch with a naked back and rings on her toes ("Jewish. But have you ever seen such a lovely spine?" He hadn't); a guy's face with the muscles exposed, except up close you saw tiny designs inside them; a factory worker in a canteen, watching a serving girl in the way Emmett must have looked at his date when she murmured, "More your type?"

Then a mountain like the moonlit river but in glowing gold, and he could tell it was by the same guy: they were back in the first room. Hands in his back pockets, Emmett stopped in front of a painting he'd just glanced at before: under a sky the color of buttermilk, a helmeted knight dangling a red spear sat on a white horse, looking down at a tombstone surrounded by skulls. The paint was so thick it looked like clay; you could see the brush strokes.

"Get a load of this one," he whispered, pointing but being careful not to touch. "Wouldn't that make a perfect heavy-metal album cover?"

His date glanced at him as if he'd said something bright, though he knew better than that. She pointed, too, out a window.

"Get a load."

Gleb and Lana were waving at them.

For a long time after that, it seemed that everything was happening in some kind of slow-motion Prince video, except now Emmett was a fan. Throughout the garden, people were drifting mostly in one direction, toward the river. At the concrete bench Gleb asked him how he'd liked the museum, and he said fine, thanks to the guide; Lena smiled from him to Zenka, it sounded like she'd called her, and asked for their ticket stubs for some kind of reimbursements, he thought. When Lena asked, Zenka said no, she didn't have to go right away, and Lena and Gleb looked at each other for a second, their faces careful, then smiled all around and stood up, and the four of them joined the flow.

Emmett did want to ask about lunch. By now it was almost two o'clock, and he wondered if they'd missed it or what. But the others seemed perfectly content to amble, smiling in the sun, and Emmett did his best to cool his jets. *Controlling*, Noreen had always called him. Whatever he'd tried to give her, new dress or exercise bike or tickets for the Supremes at the Joe Louis, three months later it would come back at him as evidence: *You're so controlling. You've always got to direct.* So he tried to go with the flow.

True he had to get used to this pace. They strolled across the canal, and they strolled down some packed-gravel paths, and they strolled around a church with multicolored onion domes like huge stalks of asparagus on acid, a visual version of the bells. They strolled through another garden or park, a bigger and more wide-open one with fewer trees, more shrubs, and more criss-crossing bright-yellow paths, which they strolled. Lena and Gleb stayed twenty feet ahead or behind Emmett and Zenka, calling over every once in a while or swapping partners for a few steps.

"She is nice, no?" Gleb murmured, as if remarking on a breeze.

"She's fantastic."

"I thought you might like her."

"Is Zenka her real name?"

Gleb appeared briefly annoyed, then explained patronymics, diminutives, and her full name, Evgenia Kasyanovna Porshutinskaya.

"Whatever," Emmett said, and when she'd crossed back beside him asked her, "Can I call you Ginny?"

She looked away, then shrugged. "You can call me Ginny." She slipped her arm through his the way Lena had, matching the stride of his Noconas, now and then lightly bumping her hip into his.

Could be it, Emmett thought. *This could be fucking it.*

"At home our crows are all black," he said, pointing at the two-toned ones he'd noticed also in small parks off the eight-lane boulevard, big black-and-tan mothers that hung out in packs around trash cans, hopping up curbs. Ginny'd removed her jacket again and had folded it over her arm in front of her, satin lining out. She gazed off toward an open place he thought must be the river again, her free hand on her hip, blowing from her lower lip at a wisp of hair over her forehead.

"I am not an orphan," she said.

He waited. In spite of the crawling pace, this was going to be like six dates crammed into one now. They faced each other.

Her father had worked in an office, for a gas company; in one of the crises he'd been paid in vodka. "Fine to laugh," she said. He had died when she was twelve; her mother worked in a hotel, at the front desk; she had a brother in the Navy. Ginny had intended to be a teacher, too, but had had to leave the university when her mother needed an operation.

He couldn't ignore that "too."

"I'm sorry about your father," he said. "So's mine. But I've got to tell you: I'm no teacher."

"Oh? Lena said you work for university. Architecture director, she said."

Here it was.

"I'm director, yes, but of Buildings and Grounds. The work is cut the grass, sharpen mower blades, clear the walks, lock the doors during breaks, and supervise guys you hire to help do all that. Used to cut keys too before we went to cards, which I got a week's trip to San Diego for retraining, everything paid. I'm pretty far up the pay scale by now, and you're working for the state, so the security's pretty good. You get health insurance and can take courses if you want to, which I have, but no degree. By inclination I'm a musician, you see. Only it's been a while since I played."

He licked his lips. He hadn't meant to spill all this out; the others already knew some of it from his emails. But talking was either feast or famine with him. Sometimes he'd be giving out work orders Monday mornings, after seeing no one all weekend, and could read it on guys' faces: *Just gimme the slip and shut up.* Gleb must have just looked at the work address on his visa was how this teacher business likely started, but Emmett had never corrected him. Now he wished he had.

But Ginny looked neither dismayed nor delighted, and he felt like he'd done the right thing by telling her right away. Back when the Rock-aterros were playing the worst kind of commercial crap at frat parties, he'd learned that even so, if you played the notes correctly, you could give people a reason to say, "That guy's good," which was more or less how he'd tried to run his life. Except when Noreen was in it, when he'd basically done whatever she wanted.

"What do you play?"

Ginny, too, had said the right thing. He told her, and she shifted her jacket to the arm with her purse so she could dangle her free arm through his again as they walked, his boots scuffing up yellow puffs in the gravel, and he felt like a million bucks. Wisps of hair neither blonde nor brown fluttered against Ginny's neck, and she led them off in a new direction, toward a monument like a handball court around a giant flame licking up out of the ground.

"Look," he said, meaning *Listen*, intending to say something about how awkward this moment was, so that then they could get past it. But when her head came up with a light smile on her lips, he realized that for her this was not that awkward. He might have come five thousand miles, but she'd probably come across town on a subway, if that. "You probably do this all the time," he finished like some virgin after a prom, with the star quarterback, on the fifty-yard line in the dark. Jesus.

"In fact," Ginny said beside him, waggling his hand back and forth, once with each word, "I don't."

The flame was translucent, about two feet high. Small bouquets were strewn on the packed dirt around it like colored toothpicks, their long stems wrapped in cellophane. Beyond it, Gleb and Lena were pretending not to watch, Gleb staring down as if entranced by the fire, thumbs in his belt loops; Lena was facing another way, head back as if to search the sky. *Spying*, Emmett thought fondly. *It's in their blood.* He had never liked to double date, though Noreen had, so he'd been on a million of them.

"I sent the picture a long while since. Many girls do so. It is for us a"—her eyes searched his—"happy bird. Paraquette?"

"Lark," he said, stretching a smile over the sink of this reminder of the kind of dreamer he would always be, especially about people. Joe LaNova was still getting royalty checks from songs Emmett had written, including one he'd recognized on WKSG years after Joe broke up the Rockaterros to move to LA. And Noreen. At the end Emmett had come in on her in the brand-new sauna he'd bought her, her breasts floating on the waterline and bubbles all around; then once he, too, had stripped, Joe's head broke the surface. Now Emmett would be setting himself up for disappointment again, if he wasn't a little careful with his heart.

He took his hand back, not too abruptly, but Ginny glanced over and in a concerned tone said she'd had a friend who'd sent in a picture at the same time.

"Now she lives in Springfield, Missouri. One goes, one stays. Who can tell? We were their age—oh!" Indicating a group of dressed-up celebrators taking each other's picture, she'd noticed what they were posing with: a moldy-looking bear cub that a ragged man in a leather vest was holding by a leash of woven rags. "I wish they'd leave alone the bears," she said with feeling.

"Bears should shit in the woods," Emmett said with some residual feeling of his own, immediately hoping she hadn't understood him. "What's the flame for?"

Gleb and Lena were facing their way now, and he smiled and waved, wondering how he might signal a query about food. "Keep a low profile" was another State Department travel tip, which probably didn't include spooning imaginary soup into your open mouth from across the quad. That was what this park reminded him of: the north quad, which took half a day to mow. Ginny said it was named after a war god and had been used for troop maneuvers for three centuries—longer than the whole U.S. of A. had existed, Emmett thought after double-checking his arithmetic. The monument was to the dead in their civil war, a stop on a tour she gave. This year she was working for a new company, which meant having to start at the bottom again, but she thought this job might last. Her smile reflected her hope and re-sparked his a bit, too, though he kept a grip on it.

He asked when their civil war was, exactly.

"After the revolution. So many dead, so many wars. In peace so-called, too, in my country. Starved. Killed. Every family touched."

He wanted to say something but didn't know what. "Ours was north and south. Yours?" As if now he was the one who didn't know what shit meant, she waved a hand.

But then she reached again for his.

"Do you like kids?" No way to slip it in: he just came out and asked.

"No. I mean yes, *like*, but *want*, no. Not now, for me."

Want was what he'd meant, all right. With a woman like this you not only could be honest, you'd have to be. He was getting too old for kids himself, but Noreen had said she hated them, and he'd never liked to hear that. Other guys came over here looking for mother material, he knew, and he figured the women did, too. *Rank your concern for family values* was one of the "14,000 Girls!" site's first question. Two, he'd put, out of possible high of five, hoping not to be disqualified. But here he was. He was not a modern man, he told her. Not back where he came from, not anymore. For example: Noreen was the only woman he'd ever slept with. True! Oh, sure, he'd passed out with, others aplenty: chicks, bitches, stray animals of all sorts. Blow and hand jobs by the hundreds—well, scores—and he'd fucked and been fucked. But sleep—peaceful, easy, unguarded, dreaming sleep with a woman, never before or since Noreen, and during their last year together, not even with her.

Some of this he wasn't saying aloud.

Even back in the glory days he was only a weekend warrior. No wild man he, no Feel-good Freddy. A stand-in sax player had once given him a few white crosses to make it through a gig he wasn't up for, and the tiny pills in his palm looked to him like babies' teeth. "With water?" he'd said and when the guy'd mocked him Emmett threw them over his shoulder, tucked into the set, and cranked it out like a man.

"I have old-fashioned values," is how he put this one for Ginny.

"That's nice," she said. "The older fashions are the best. Wide lapels, creased slacks . . ." But she squeezed his hand: she knew what he meant.

She didn't ask him anything. Her way was to point out things they saw, inconsequential things she made seem otherwise by pointing them out. About marks in the gravel where it looked as if a two-wheeled cart had changed course a few times: "DNA." About a couple in wigs, hoop skirts and apparently knee-high boots, pointing at the man's feet: "Adidas." About an orchestra warming up in folding chairs on a flatbed stage three semis wide: "Turkey farm."

She didn't seem to expect responses. At home he would have felt obligated to crack back, sit-com like. At home they'd be on their way somewhere, to dinner reservations or a movie or roller blading or mini-golfing, which was usually about the least amount of activity he could stand. But now Ginny, as she'd done with the paintings, was *teaching him how* to stroll, look around, walk beside someone.

"Too bad for fireworks." She indicated the milk-colored sky. Emmett hadn't noticed when the clouds had rolled in. They were indeed low, but the light hadn't changed much; warm as it was, the sun had looked tentative all day, as if cowed by all the gold domes. On the flatbed stage a woman took shiny brass pieces from a case and fit them together to make a trombone, then played a low note. When he felt something at the side of his left foot he looked down and saw Ginny's needle-nosed pump burrowing into his boot. "Like our crows," she said, meaning, he understood in a second, his Noconas, which were full-quill ostrich skin with calf's-leather uppers. Twenty-five years ago, before the Belgium tour, they'd set him back five hundred bucks; re-soled and -heeled many times since, they'd been worth every penny, suitable for stage, riding mower, and now bridge, ferry, Airbus, and train. But when he'd finished telling her about them, she said, "Rockaterros?"

"Didn't I tell you about that?" He did now, bringing a light hand against her back to guide her toward where he thought he'd spotted Lena's pink jacket. The park, or field or whatever it was, had filled even since they'd arrived, but more people were coming in, all moving toward the river. Ginny said that soon a scarlet-sailed ship would arrive, bringing good luck when you saw it, the high point of the celebration.

Oh, sails! He told her about the price-slashed bunting and flags he'd imagined.

"Scarlet *Sails*," Ginny explained, was a fairy tale involving a magician, a prince, and a little girl named Asole—*ohhh!*—who waited years for the prince despite discouragement and ridicule from family, friends, and *townsfolk*. The word amused Emmett but he didn't laugh, because from the way Ginny told the story, he thought it had meant something to her and maybe still did. At the time of his own high-school graduation he could not imagine any story that would have meant anywhere near what a six-pack or a new amp or Noreen in a bikini would have meant to him, but in the young faces around him now, he could see that innocence, though they seemed somehow wise, too. He wished he could put his finger on what-all he saw in all these faces.

From what Ginny said, it was probably fatigue. "They've just finished exams." At least one of them was drunk: a red-faced guy with the huge hoop of his stretched-fabric uniform cap back so far on his head it looked like a gray halo. Guys in identical caps but wearing them right, shiny black visors to their eyes, seemed to be looking after him. Ginny saw what Emmett was watching and moved him along.

"Righteo," she said, or "Why so slow?" or maybe "Let us go," whether to rejoin Lena and Gleb or to a late lunch or to bed: it didn't seem to make much difference, once she'd reached for his hand again, and the loose clasp of her fingers around his own kicked his heart in a way it hadn't moved since childhood—his heart, not his dick, and he thought, Yes.

The crowd was not exactly rowdy but had gotten louder. He listened to the talk like flipping through the dials on I-69 on his way to work, in the same way he'd leaned toward the paintings. Russian wasn't really a cough but a combination of cabasas, bass, and a jew's harp, of all things. He'd played jew's harp himself on "Cripple Creek," back in the day—way back, when he and Joe LaNova were going to call themselves The Foreigners, until "Cold as Ice" came out. Then it was going to be The Enemies or Enemies—this was years before PE or hip hop of any sort—but they couldn't agree on the "The," which was typical. Then their first frat gig came along, and they had to come up with another name quick. "Emmett Tessich and the Rockeroos," he'd said, thinking of Buck Owens, but Joe had left his name out and scrawled the rest wrong, anyway.

He noticed a place on Ginny's suit jacket that had been neatly darned with pearl-gray thread, like a sock, and he imagined her in downtown East Lansing, pushing a cart at Kroger, taking courses if she wanted to, all of which he was prepared to offer.

Then he noticed something he couldn't believe across the street.

"Hey, Ginny," he said, reaching for her elbow but missing. "Wait a sec."

At eye level, in a guitar stand on a flatbed stage, was his own guitar: the black-and-ash Stratocaster Deluxe that had more or less stayed under his bed for the last six years, though he'd paid for it approximately what he'd paid for this trip.

He ran over, dodging strolling hordes, and got as close as he could, all but rubbing his eyes. It had the abalone inlays and the stainless-steel saddle, plus cobalt pickups that he hadn't sprung for, with a capo on the second jumbo fret. Apparently, it belonged to a heavy guy in a muscle shirt who was napping in a folding chair beside it.

Ginny had missed it, so he ran after her.

But he'd lost her. He didn't see Gleb or Lena, either.

An hour later, he had to quit scanning the tightening crowd. People were holding him up in a press like the only time he'd ever swum in an ocean. The voices had risen an octave, and somewhere a symphony orchestra played a tune he finally placed: from *Apocalypse Now*, the scene with the helicopters and napalm that smelled like victory. But familiar as it was, the music sounded to him now the way it must have to the rice farmers in the movie, and thousands of arms that stretched in unison over the embankment to point down at the river made him think of *The Invasion of the Body Snatchers*.

A big slope-eyed man beside him grinned over, and at Emmett's blank look he said something two or three times, then reached over to take Emmett's head in thick fingers and turn it, scaring holy shit out of him until he saw approaching, from downriver, the ship with the red sails.

The man's wife beamed at him, too.

"Asshole!" they exclaimed.

Heart still hammering, Emmett grinned and nodded back that he understood. "*Spaseeba!*" Where had he picked that up?

Then, as the ship passed below, two smaller scarlet-sailed boats following like ducklings, he recognized or thought he did the strange, excited calm he'd been seeing in faces all day long. It wasn't really calm, and it wasn't innocence, either. It was more complicated than that but not so foreign, after all. In fact, it was familiar: it was the very reflection of his own face in his computer monitor when he'd shut it down after studying the 14,000 girls, the way you look at a put-on that you know is a put-on that you also know is being put on just for you.

Later yet, so much later yet—after the ships had passed; after the orchestra had finished "Ride of the Valkyries" and the sky had dimmed, though it never got too dark; after the fireworks had made the cloud cover glow; after the three-girl pop band in black pleated skirts; after the giant torch in the Neva had been lit and Emmett had crossed one bridge and then another; after he'd managed to buy red-caviar *blini* at a wooden stand and a drink like cola and beer to wash them down with; after he'd crossed yet another bridge and gotten his bearings by the lit fountain and the extended bronze thumbs-up, as it turned out to be, of the statue by the train station; after crossing the big bridge back, his cowboy heels biting the pavement, his own adventuresome self now the blackest motherfucker in miles; after he saw Gleb on the palace steps by the port-a-potties scanning the crowd for him, and after Gleb had spotted him, too, and darted through to pound him on the back and deliver Ginny's thank-you/good-bye note, and just after reading, by the flickering river-torch light, "And play your music, my American friend"—after all that, Emmett Tessich had an idea for a song.

It would be the first one he'd written since Noreen left. It would owe something to the tunes he'd composed with Joe but would be entirely his own. At his side, Gleb was talking up the girls scheduled for the next day, and across the square, Pink Floyd notes from the Stratocaster were snaking out over the lit Neva; but in Emmett's head he was onstage with the new band he'd be putting together when he got back to Michigan, playing his new song. They'd play it at the Car Bar and Teddy's, at the Box on Westwood once it got some airplay, and maybe even some day Comerica, why not?, where Noreen would be down in the first row with whoever's life she was running at the moment, and Emmett would be tuning up, taking his time, jabbing a full-quill toe at his fuzz pedal and fussing with the knobs on his amp, and when he got good and ready he'd lean forward until his lips grazed the microphone and look down and announce: "*Issa* lil thang, caw, 'Ginny.'"

He thought he'd set some steel drums to it.

SOFT POWER

Natasha'd often thought that the key to this culture was rock 'n' roll, so she agreed to go, even though she'd told Oleg she'd call around nine o'clock. Usually what she did after finishing the dishes and other chores (like last night's project: fishing out a button her husband had dropped down a climate-control grate, then sewing it back on his jacket) was yawn and say maybe she'd take a walk. On her cell phone, she'd call Oleg from the southwestern end of the complex, which was as far as she could go unless she were to leave and head down one of two busy highways—exactly where she felt like heading, sometimes. Often she'd call her mother, too, or her sister back home, talking long enough to circle the compound several times. When she returned, her husband rarely even looked up from the TV. Sometimes by way of greeting, he'd raise his beer can.

Tonight was a little different: he'd called from work to tell her about an extra concert ticket his brother had and asked her if she'd like to go along, though he himself would have work to do at home. But it had been so long since he'd asked whether she liked anything that she was surprised and touched as well as excited at the prospect of going out. Then immediately she thought of Oleg and felt guilty. Oleg wasn't his real name, of course: he was American, too, just a more refined and interesting one than her husband, as she'd learned enough language by now to realize. These last six months had changed her already-changed life. She and Oleg met twice or three times a week and talked daily at least, texting or emailing every couple of hours, of late. But one night without hearing her voice wouldn't kill him, she hoped. She texted him where she was going, thinking maybe she'd get a chance to call from the concert after all but not saying so, as she didn't like to promise what she was unsure of being able to deliver.

"Get down," he replied. "Idiom mng have a great time at rock concert. Lublu."

She loved him too, so much. Her husband just would have asked what time she'd be back. *To get down*, she wrote in her little address book under *to get even, to get an idea, to get in trouble, to get into or get out of*, not exactly opposites, and *to get frisky*. With so many ways to use a single word, she despaired of ever keeping them all straight. Oleg was not always so reliable *in the bag*, but he was excellent for her English—for correcting all the mistakes her husband had taught her!—and he loved her, and he was learning Russian. And every time she visited, he had fresh flowers and cake or other good things to eat, just for her.

The concert was the first one of the season at the big outdoor music park where her husband had taken her to see the band with the long beards two summers before. She couldn't remember its name, but Oleg had recognized it when she described them, and they'd been so stirring and deep that sometimes even now she found herself humming one of their songs. The park was north of the terrifying city where she'd once gotten lost by herself, on her way to a job interview, the very first week she was eligible to work; the brother-in-law would drive.

Last year his wife had divorced him, and he showed up with a thick woman named Deb, whose graying peach-colored bangs hung over the rims of huge sunglasses. She looked back at Natasha climbing into the back seat as if at a stranger who'd rung her doorbell, her jaw working on what seemed like several hundred grams of chewing gum. Through the driver's window the brothers were grunting back and forth. Natasha extended her slim hand to Deb. "How do you do?"

"Good. You?" Deb considered Natasha's beautiful nails, then reached to squeeze her knuckles and let go.

Natasha sat back and waved at her husband as the car backed across the gravel, reflecting not for the first time in the last four years that in the land of milk and honey, she seemed to have fallen in with citizens of single syllables.

She saw the exit to Oleg's house and out of habit reached for her door lock. He lived on a street with grass and trees, which made the city seem less treacherous, though to get there from the exit she still had to cross several blocks that made her grip the wheel and hold her breath. "They are people," Oleg would tell her, and she knew that, but still she was relieved each time she made it to his driveway, his face in the window or the open doorway, his arms open.

"So, Tosh," said the brother-in-law, his sunglasses aimed at her in his rearview mirror. *Tosh* was what their parents called her, too, a family invention. Like his younger brother, this one was an even-featured man, but from the back seat she could see a shiny bald spot the size of a teacup, a bad omen for her husband. "This is a pretty famous band we're going to see. It's not a reunion, either. They've pretty much been going nonstop since the seventies, touring and recording both. I can't believe you never heard of them over there." He and his girlfriend exchanged a look through their lenses. The brother-in-law's shades were thin dark ones, very fashionable. Otherwise, he dressed like a homeless. To the wedding he had worn sport shoes, as her husband would have too, if she hadn't *put her foot down.*

"I know Pink Floyd, Joe Cocker, Government Mule," Natasha said, sitting up. She was not some peasant, though some of her forebears had been serfs (others, gypsies; only Oleg had been interested in the album in which she kept their brown photos). She knew many things they should learn over here as well as much of what they knew, every day a little more. "Rolling Stones, U2, Sonny and Cher, Darkened Sabbath—"

The two in the front seat laughed hard, not with her, and began chattering happily, not to her. This was the other side of the émigré's freedom that had seduced her into staying as much as her husband had: the freedom from small rules and conventions she couldn't be expected to know or observe. By now, however, she'd come to learn that they could be enforced at any time, often with rigid fines.

But outside was a beautiful evening, the first real warm one this year, even the muted green slightly shocking after the long, hard winter. More familiar were the floes of ice still floating in the river, which she could see from a bridge they crossed, then another. Onto an island, she guessed. Then she recognized the music park, its huge gravel lot more than half full of cars gleaming in the sunset.

The engine died, and the brother-in-law's face appeared between the seats, one inverted triangle of dark hair below his lower lip; otherwise he'd shaved so recently she could smell his Old Spice, exactly as his brother wore. "Here's your ticket, in case we get separated."

The very possibility caused her a clutch of panic. Why would they be separated? Why had he said it? Then, when she tried to take the ticket from him, he pinched it so that she couldn't, his lips curled in a smile as if he hated her, though without his eyes she couldn't tell. Her first impression had been that he was a joker, so maybe he was just playing: a mean game but a game nevertheless. His divorce had been difficult, and then he'd lost his job; so she tried to understand, as her husband had asked her to do. *My brother's sucking it up*, her husband had said, another idiom she'd written down, next to "*sucks*: verb, intransitive, 'to be no good.'" The woman Deb was staring out the windshield at a stream of concertgoers with lawn chairs, coolers, food, and grills, naming everything she saw and asking the brother-in-law if he'd remembered to pack theirs. "Yes," said the brother-in-law, still facing Natasha. "Yes, yes, yes." Finally he let the ticket go and *got out* to unload the trunk.

"Thank you," Tasha said, wondering, also not for the first time, what she had *gotten herself into* now. She had married for love and adventure, but the proportion had turned out wrong, and the quality of both had changed, her delight at the world's possibilities turning often now to dismay. "Thank you both for this opportunity."

She tucked a lawn chair under one arm and two under the other, trotting to catch up, on tiptoe so that her high heels wouldn't penetrate the earth. The brother-in-law carried the grill like a tray with the charcoal and lighter fluid on it, his long legs extending in front of him like denim pistons, boot heels digging into the grass. The woman Deb, in jeans with polka-dot pockets, carried plastic containers of food. On her feet she wore flip-flops with thick, wedge-shaped soles; from behind, she and the brother-in-law looked like Sancho Panza and Don Quixote, which Natasha had read in school, in Russian: he was tall and thin, and Deb was middle-sized and stocky, though not as fat as so many here were. Both of them wore T-shirts with different writing and designs on the back, his with long sleeves and writing on those, too. Natasha, the same height as her husband but not quite as tall as this brother, wore her royal-blue blouse with the ruffled collar and cuffs and her new gray gabardine slacks, proud to be wearing a size two now. The chairs under her arm were light but awkward, with their curved aluminum piping and plastic straps. One chair kept slipping down.

"Please," she called at one point, smiling up at them. "Just a sec," as she had heard a woman in a similar situation say in the parking lot.

They half-turned and paused, but just as Natasha got close enough to wonder at their scowls, they began moving again. "Thattaway." The brother-in-law ticked his head toward a sparsely populated slope. From a stage in a valley, music rose. "Not far. Look for us." And they left her struggling with the chairs. In about ten meters the woman said something that animated the brother-in-law, and as they walked they engaged in spirited conversation about something they did not seem to like.

Natasha took advantage of their preoccupation to send Oleg a message. Her new gabardine slacks fit so perfectly that she had to stiffen one leg back to remove her cell phone from the tiny watch pocket where she kept it, being careful of her nails. As always in public many men were looking at her, and when she'd selected the camera function and raised her arm to snap a photo of the stage, a man in a clean ponytail and a shirt that showed off the tattoos on his arms looked her full in the face. She did not like tattoos or ponytails on men, but his muscles were nice, and his teeth were white and strong, and she smiled briefly before lowering her lids. Things with Oleg had begun with less, so she walked on as quickly as she could. When she'd arrived in this country, she'd been heavier in the bottom, with short hair and spectacles instead of the contacts she wore now, and she knew that from now on she needed to be careful, because she was not going back to the eyeglasses and the weight.

"Rock & roll 4 ever!" was the message she sent Oleg with the photo of the stage.

He didn't reply right away. She hoped he was not jealous. More likely he was busy, exercising or reading *The Master and Margarita* or studying his Russian, anyway making better use of his time than waiting for a band whose name she kept forgetting, though it was on her ticket stub if she cared to look. She had tried to describe to him, but Oleg did not really want to hear what it was like to live in a small unit with a husband who did not care about you in a complex the color of cement between a gas station, a McDonald's, and a donut store. Also nearby was a lumberyard; if she called too early, she had to repeat herself over the whine of saws. From the trees at Oleg's house you heard birds, another reason she loved him. When she'd told him that, he laughed and kissed her.

She saw Deb and the brother-in-law stop and look back her way, conferring, so she slipped her cell phone back into her pocket and got a good grip on the chairs and set off. Oleg would reply when he had something to say; he was not fond of sending texts with no purpose, as he put it, though to let her know he was thinking of her would have been purpose enough. *The point* in this culture was highly overrated, she thought. It was something her husband often asked about, or used to, when they talked: "What's your point, Tosh?" Or "And your point is . . . ?" *I am my own point*, she'd told him once. *You are yours, and we are ours. Truth of life is the point.* He'd looked around as if the walls spoke more sense than his own wife did. It was the last time she'd tried to explain anything to him.

By the time she reached Deb and the brother-in-law, the band onstage had stopped playing and the main one was setting up. Natasha unfolded the chairs and set them out where indicated when she inquired. The charcoal glowed around the edges.

"Quick-light briquettes," said the brother-in-law, pointing out the words on the bag, which was how she understood what he was talking about. As she stooped to read, he watched her face closely the way so many here did, as if in her cheekbones and the shape of her eyes they might find clues to disturbing mysteries they'd long left undisturbed.

"How interesting!" *Not!* From her notebook months ago.

She rose to resume her excellent posture, pushing herself up from her thighs, and smiled at him. Dust from the bag had smudged her fingertips black. In her purse was a packet of tissues, but she couldn't operate the clasp with her left hand, and the fingertips on her right had the dust on them, which made them slippery. Though it went against everything in her nature, she wiped them on her new gabardines, which were only a slightly lighter gray, along the inside seam of her right thigh. Deb, seated in one of the chairs with a can of beer in one hand and a cigarette in the other, faced the stage, her legs crossed, the fabric of her jeans tight around her thighs; her bare feet were pale, their stubby nails painted dark green. When Natasha smiled at her, Deb's top leg began to bounce, the flip-flop flapping off her solid heel. The brother-in-law forked patties onto the grill, pulled a beer for himself from the cooler after Deb shook her head, and tossed Natasha a one-calorie Coke. Everyone in the family knew she didn't drink, and she was the only one in the family who didn't. Holidays were bacchanalia. Every New Year's Eve, the most important holiday of the year, led to stupid men and Natasha in tears, her husband the stupidest of all. Every New Year's Eve except the last one, when she'd spent several happy hours with Oleg.

Tiny figures on the stage were adjusting equipment. Halfway up to where Natasha sat was a huge oak tree that wouldn't have been shamed by those at home. The nearest speaker tower was twenty meters away, tuned to the same radio station that was on in her husband's car and the brother's, too: Z104, "Your Oldies Are Your Besties." Natasha smelled what she thought must be drugs, though what the brother-in-law had lit came from a red-and-white pack, Deb a white-and-green one. Natasha didn't smoke, either. She watched several girls who couldn't have been much older than twelve throwing twigs at the one boy in their group, who wore faded jeans with shoulder straps and no shirt; he had ridden up on a tiny bicycle that lay on its side nearby. They were all smoking.

"So tonight Harmon had to fix something on your computer," said the brother-in-law suddenly. Harmon was the husband, a computer man, and Natasha's stomach dropped. On *their* computer? This was always the way here: as soon as she relaxed, someone would point out something for her to worry about. The next band had begun, but the brother turned away from the stage and pulled his chair forward, toward hers. He was examining her reaction.

"Oh?" she shrugged. "It seems to be working fine. An upgrade, perhaps."

The brother-in-law's eyebrows peaked over the rims of his dark glasses. He swigged his beer and set it back down on the arm of his chair, his posture identical to Deb's, down to the jiggling foot. At the same moment, both of them crossed their arms.

"Per fucking haps," he said.

When Deb grinned, Natasha's mind began running very fast: had she logged out? Would the URLs of her servers appear? Which one had she been using with Oleg? Could her husband *get to* her inboxes? Periodically she cleared them, but Oleg's messages were so sweet that she saved them to reread, and it had been several weeks since she'd erased any. Remembering certain recent exchanges, she panicked. The thought of one in particular from last week, about favorite parts of each other's bodies, brought heat to her cheeks. They'd gone on and on until they'd named them all, even silly ones. *Nostril*, she'd sent. Oh, why hadn't she been more careful? She was breathing rapidly, and the thought that her companions might notice quickened her heartbeat, too. She tried to smile, head spinning. *Like a top*, she remembered even at a time like this, calming her down somewhat.

"Aren't they?"

The brother-in-law had said it twice. The band had finished another song.

"Yes! So good!" She was clapping, fingers to fingers and thumb to thumb. "Those guitars are marvelous! And the drums!"

He grimaced and leaned back in his chair as if thinking her *full of shit*, one of the very first idioms her husband had ever taught her, and in desperation and as a kind of penance, she recalled those giddy days. She had loved him, once, as even Oleg knew, just as she had loved this country's promise. *Oh, please*, she prayed. Maybe there was nothing to worry about.

"They are excellent!"

But Deb cast her a hard look before turning to the brother-in-law. "I just hope they do 'Reaper.' 'Reaper' is all I really care about."

"They're gonna do 'Reaper.' How can they not do 'Reaper'?"

"They better. Seventy-five bucks, they better do 'Reaper.'"

"They will."

From a purple-lined leather case the brother-in-law had taken a gigantic pair of binoculars, which in a few minutes he handed to Deb. Her sunglasses were almost as big, and she took them off to look through the binoculars. When she finished she held them up by one barrel in Natasha's direction, less offering than showing them to her, but Natasha was so preoccupied they didn't register at all until Deb waggled them. Natasha smiled as sweetly as she could and thanked her, no.

"I rely on my eyes," she said, touching her cheekbones, realizing even as she said it that she'd failed to make a joke or even much of a point. You didn't say things here for the simple pleasure of saying them, she knew.

"Whatev," Deb said and raised the binoculars to her own eyes again.

Natasha couldn't stop wondering what Harmon was doing and worrying about what he might find. *Invasion of privacy* was a phrase she had heard: wasn't there a law here, as with everything else? Not within a marriage, probably. Each of them had a separate access code, but from his talk about his job, Natasha thought that codes would be no obstacle for him. Many things he did not know, but *he knew his way around* a computer. Oh, *why* was she never satisfied with what she had? *Why* had she done this? Oleg would have been happy to remain simply friends, or so he'd said at one point, though she hadn't believed him. Oh, why not? Her green card still had not arrived. She did have a letter from the INS saying it was *in the works*, though that was not the letter's phrase but her husband's translation of it—but all it would take would be another letter to them from him, maybe just a phone call, and Natasha would be on a plane. "Back to Russia, Baby!" was an old joke between them, a threat they could both use, but recently neither of them had, as if it held too much truth, or *cut too close*. Regardless, if the marriage went, her part-time job at the department store would not be enough for a green card or to live on, either. All her years here, all she'd learned at such effort, sacrifice, and expense would be *down the drain*. Not to mention returning home disgraced, with her hand out. To her mother who could scarcely pay her own bills.

Her hamburger tasted like mud.

"Mmm, delicious!" she said, holding it up, first to Deb and then to the brother-in-law, nodding her appreciation each time. She could not even tell anymore whether their lack of reaction was the usual distance from which they looked at her or whether, indeed, something serious was afoot.

The band took a break, and this time the radio stayed off. Natasha asked Deb if she was going to the ladies', though there was just one mixed line for the row of portable stalls, and the line was quite long already. Deb smiled as if Natasha had said something silly and said she'd wait, then as Natasha moved off, called out to the brother-in-law, who was dumping out the coals and scraping off the grill: "Wadn 'Reaper' great? Wadn it friggin' great?"

Natasha knew *friggin'* as well as its tougher cousin, and she'd heard a familiar tune or two, probably including this "Reaper." Didn't that mean death?

"'Reaper' was awesome," the brother-in-law agreed.

"I knew it would be."

"'Reaper' was great."

They were still talking about "Reaper" when she left, but in the line she felt them watching her, and when she turned they were, in fact, watching her, Deb through the huge binoculars; so Natasha put her phone away without calling Oleg. Of course she could be calling anyone, but if they asked she'd have to lie outright, and she disliked a lie.

Avoidance and deflections were one thing, but a lie was a lie, a sin, and she needed to keep her sins to a minimum. She hadn't more than sipped at her Coke and didn't really have to go to the bathroom, so at the first revolting whiff of fecal matter from the toilets she stepped out of line.

Then wondering how that might look down below she changed her mind, but people all dressed in black behind where she'd stood wouldn't let her back in. She turned around several times very confused to see the binoculars still trained on her, by the brother-in-law now. *What the fuck was her problem?* She imagined her husband's favorite question in the brother-in-law's voice.

It was when she returned, still in the relative silence between sets, that Oleg replied, the "ding" of his incoming message in her pocket showing on her face and echoing like a stone dropped in a well. The brother-in-law's eyes glinted. With his sunglasses off, the grin was hatred, no mistake, with triumph mixed in.

"I don't do cell phones myself," he said, "or I'd call Harmon. But I think he's had enough time by now, don't you, Deb?"

She wore an equivalent grin. "*Oh*, yeah. Sure do."

Enough time? Harmon? For *what?*

But Natasha knew. She pointed down at the stage. "What about the second half?"

"Oh, please," Deb said. "What does she think this is, football?"

They hadn't even let her carry the chairs back. In the backseat, she was afraid to take her cell phone out and read Oleg's message, because if they grabbed the phone, it could be more evidence. She couldn't delete it, though, without even reading it! She was still in this quandary when they passed his exit, and she thought of pitching herself out the window, rolling down the embankment, scrambling to her feet, running through those desperate blocks where this time she'd *fit right in*, bruised and in torn clothes. In her mind she screamed his name until they were out of earshot.

Neither Deb nor the brother-in-law spoke or even moved until they were south of the city.

"We'll have you back in a jiffy now, Tosh," the brother-in-law said then, to the windshield. His voice sounded tired, almost kind, though with his sunglasses still on in spite of vanished sun, his eyes in the mirror were impenetrable as ever.

Deb peered around her headrest, suddenly—amazingly—smiling sadly. She'd taken her dark goggles off, and the eyes in her plump little face were a surprise: they were as blue as Natasha's. "That's a cute blouse," she said. "Is it from Russia?"

It was off a rack at Marshall's, and Natasha, astonished but hopeful, named its price, an American habit she had joked about with Oleg. "When we arrive at my house, I hope you will come inside for a drink," she added, trying to think what she had to offer: her husband's Michelob, vodka, a little wine from Easter left. Maybe she'd imagined everything! She wanted to kiss their hands, their feet, the lids of their eyes.

Driver and passenger exchanged a look, and then Deb resumed her position and her goggles. "I'm just gonna say this. Did you guys meet on the Internet?"

"We did not," Natasha said. "I am not an Internet bride. My first visa was a student's. I had a scholarship, and in my last years I tutored other students. Harmon I would help with his papers. His spelling was very poor."

"Hold on," said the brother-in-law. "Did you say when we arrive at *your* house?"

They were almost there, passing the lumberyard. In fact, the answer was yes: because of previous legal problems of her husband's, the lease was in her name, like the titles of both cars. But Natasha realized her mistake. "*Our* house. Our *home*."

"Her *happy* home," Deb hooted as they pulled up in front of it: S2.

"I do hope you'll come in."

"Not likely," growled the brother-in-law.

She didn't want to *get out*, but both of them did, immediately, each pulling their seats back for her in an illusion of choice.

"Thank you profusely for this experience," Natasha said. "I'm so genuinely appreciative. Ever so much."

The brother-in-law churned gravel in reverse. When the car was gone, she stood in her entranceway like a wet cat, stooped and trembling and gasping for breath. She poked around in her purse for her key. Then, remembering Oleg's reply, she took her cell phone out, and when she'd read his message and replied—"UNFORESEEN ACTIVITY, MY DARLING. MORE LATER"—and deleted both message and reply she drew her shoulders back, straightened her blouse, breathed deep and smiled, fluffing her hair. She held the key in her hand like a knife, thumb over the shaft with just the point showing beyond her bright nail. Then she rang the bell to make him open the door for her, so that when the battle began she'd have that edge.

Ten weeks later he'd quit drinking and rented her a little white house on a tree-lined street with no curbs, and they'd been baptized together in a cloudy green river in a state park, where in a gazebo afterwards they'd renewed their vows. In between events, she'd called Oleg tearfully from time to time, when her resolve to be good gave way to various doubts.

Toward the end of summer her green card arrived, but before she could fully absorb what new kinds of freedom this would allow her, the band America came to play at a baseball park in the city, and her husband won a raffle at work for backstage passes; then, after the concert, they got their picture taken with Gerry Buckley and Dewey Bunnell! These were names Natasha was hearing for the first time, but the night was such a thrill that she suggested the picture for the centerpiece of the digital photo album they made in October to email friends and family, including her husband's brother and Deb and relatives of hers who had a computer; some of these were people she'd occasionally called in hysterics during the very same months when these shots were snapped. "What a roaler coaster its been 4 us but now we are very happy," she tried to help her husband spell correctly in a heavy font underneath the display of pictures, but just before she hit Send he took her hand from the keys, looked at her strongly, and asked her to add Samsaun73 to the recipient list.

"Oh, absolutely, Baby." Natasha swallowed. Sam Saunders was Oleg, as her husband had learned all about on that horrible night. Her heart hammered, and she didn't reach to key in the address until her fingers had steadied, just the pads of them touching so as not to chip her nails. Her husband watched her face the whole time, but she smiled well at him. "You took the words *right from my mouth*, Baby!"

NATIVE TONGUES

Early on, she told him a joke from her country. Two friends have a falling out, one thinking himself betrayed by the other in some way. But it turns out to be a misunderstanding, and they straighten it out and shake hands. Still, in the ensuing weeks the friend who'd thought himself betrayed keeps his distance, and finally the other confronts him: *Now that our problem's been cleared up, why can't we resume our previous close friendship?* The first guy looks at him with distaste. *I know you're blameless,* he says. *It's the residue.*

Her husband wouldn't have gotten it, but this American laughed, and they became lovers, though not on the spot, of course, or even for a while yet. She was open about her dissatisfaction with her marriage but circumspect about how to proceed. "You are very nice, but I don't want to make another mistake," she'd say, interrogating the lover about himself, his values, his past. "Do you believe in love?"

He was a generation older than she was, and yes, yes, he believed in love! He answered as fully and truthfully as he could. How did he define it? Why had he never married? She wanted to know about his previous relationships. *Another one?* she'd say, impressed but leery, too. *Tell me about her. What happened?* She'd listen carefully and nod when she was satisfied.

His breadth of experience came from years more than from any particular prowess, and the first time she disrobed, her graceful body looked so lovely to him he went soft, more compelled to investigate than to penetrate; he fell back on his lingual skills, which she said later were new to her. When he mentioned certain medical matters he'd let slide she insisted he get a check-up; both of her parents had been doctors, and she had great faith in the profession, knowing even the names of tests he should have done. What she called *sharing love* fixed itself, but he went ahead with the tests, which showed he was fine: no spring chicken but fully operational and more, as she enabled him to confirm over the next several months. "One," she'd say, raising a graceful finger from beneath him when they'd stilled (her hands, at once slender and plump, had fascinated him from the start) and then, from above him, "two," then "three . . ." Another of her jokes was that sex in her country had been illegal until she was out of college, and he felt himself the great beneficiary of a politico-cultural as well as personal revolution made from some new blend of velvet and silk, like the sheets she brought to put on his bed on the days she would visit, and with the onset of winter, micro-fleece.

Then the husband intercepted one of their emails. The frank terms of endearment that had filled the spaces between their native tongues and the vacuum of days between face-to-face meetings made the nature of even their most mundane written communications hard to mistake, as in "Here's a link to that article we discussed, oh my heart."

"He knows about u," she texted in the early hours of the crisis, which happened when the lover was out of town. And a little later: "He found ur number. Dont ansr calls." Then, after hours of silence: "Disregard email to come. Will b 4 his sake."

His alarm was heightened by her abbreviations, which because of a shared care for language that had first allowed them to bridge their separate ones, they'd forsworn long ago. "I am pining for you," they'd thumbed out in better times, and, "Can we see each other Tuesday afternoon?"

Now he replied between meetings at a conference, his fingertip trembling on the tiny keys of his rudimentary cell phone, pressing "ignore" for repeated calls from a number he didn't recognize. Over a call originating from her number he hesitated, then answered. Her voice was strained and flat, and she identified herself with an Americanized pronunciation of her name, not the pure form she'd taught him.

"My husband is here. Will you talk to him. Please."

The lover was in an air-conditioned hotel lobby with floor-to-ceiling windows and doors through which he could see palm fronds waving in an ocean breeze. Back home, there'd been a late snowstorm, a big one; he'd seen footage on CNN. "All right."

The husband's voice quavered in a way that made the lover think of the neighborhood kid whose main contribution to whatever game was being played was strident knowledge of the rules.

"I've got phone records and . . . oh, *so many* emails"—the voice dropped in dismay, then picked back up righteously—"but I want to hear it from you, mister: exactly what is going on?"

The question took the lover aback. He'd assumed that "knows about u" had meant "knows everything," but the standards for communication in this marriage were so low that apparently she'd had to admit nothing, even in the face of evidence. Could the husband not even read? She'd met him when her English was rudimentary, and he seemed not to have recognized how well she'd come to speak. The lover said something lofty and vague about the woman he'd fallen in love with, this man's wife, calling what they had a friendship. Across the lobby, his next conference session was starting. "We do the same kind of work," he said into his phone; this too was true. "So we share those concerns."

"I don't care about that." The husband's voice tightened. "Did it go sexual?" *Seck-shwull*: both the phrase and his pronunciation sounded thick, adolescent. *He's a BOY*, his wife had once said of him, though he was more successful in his career already than the lover had been in his, and he knew he couldn't provide, should the husband kick her out now. The voice rose: "*Did* it? *Tell* me!"

The lover couldn't answer. He was loath to lie but even more loath to deny the best hours of his recent life. A no might have saved his lover pain—might even have saved the affair itself—but he couldn't get the word out. Across the lobby his supervisor raised a hand, tapped a wrist. "Look," he said into the phone, but he couldn't think what might bear more examining here, and he snapped his phone shut.

Forgoing breakfast the next morning to check his email again in the hotel's business center, he found the message she'd warned him about, sent at three o'clock that morning with the subject line "Us." In the body she'd written, "I cannot continue this relationship with you. Do not contact me in any way. My husband is a good man, and I do love him very much."

In spite of her forewarning, the lover was hurt. Her husband's overall goodness she'd conceded before, sighing in bed over their quandary, and "love him very much" could have been dictated; but the "do" seemed spontaneous and genuine, a contrast to her wooden voice on the phone, even with the Americanized spelling of her sign-off. What had happened in the intervening hours, between husband and wife and in her heart? The lover shuddered to imagine. The conference was scheduled to run several more days, his own panel in the very last time slot; he had to prepare, but he could barely concentrate on the presentations of others, let alone his own. Complicating her marriage were her immigration status (her green card was still pending), various legal issues of her husband's, and common property in her name, all tensions the affair had helped her escape. More than once she'd called her husband's behavior crazy, and now the lover couldn't discount the possibility she might be in danger.

So the next morning he answered her email with wording he'd worked out on the notepad that had come with the conference program. "Just this 1 reply then. OK since its what u want. Its what u always said about yr hzbnd any ways. Pls don't tell him abt my damajd testicle & r failed attempt at sex." He thought the better of a couple of the errors as too obvious, but for good measure he signed off with a formal version of his name that he'd never used with her. In a burst of regret for the openheartedness that had characterized all their communications up to that point he added, "I wish you well."

He sat through the day's conference proceedings second-guessing his diction and punctuation, fending off visions of a husband's jealousy compounded by suspicions he was being made fun of. That night the lover slept little, beseeching all the gods he could think of for her safety, rising every so often to go down to the business center to check his email. In the mirrored walls of the elevator car the shrunken sight of himself in the thick white terrycloth robe the hotel provided reproached him for his folly, as well as for failing to keep up with phone technology.

Finally, during the lunch hour before he was due to give his presentation, in his inbox appeared "Re: Us."

"I do not know how to thank you," she had written. "For a second time you have saved me. You will always be in my heart. Please do not reply. He controls my email now."

This time she'd signed no name at all, and it was the last time he heard from her, even after returning to town.

But in a hot and humid week toward the end of summer he saw her in the parking lot of a mall where he'd driven to pick up a window fan at a franchise hardware store. She wore short shorts and dangled huge bags from department and shoe stores; from across the lot, before even recognizing her, he'd admired her long legs, and he recognized the car whose trunk she stopped to open before he recognized her. In fact, they'd used to meet in a similar parking lot, so the moment echoed and echoed, but he doubted his eyes, because she'd often said that shopping for recreation was an American habit she could not abide; and now her energy as she arranged and rearranged her packages in her trunk looked like a skilled shopper's, beyond satisfaction and well into pleasure.

When she finished and looked up, the mouth and chin he could see beneath gigantic sunglasses hammered his heart. Her hair, longer and lighter now, veered away from her cheeks like fenders sprung loose from her clavicles; a slight stoop to her neck, which pitched her head forward in a posture he'd searched out in silhouettes behind steering wheels in that other parking lot, seemed to have deepened.

He changed course so as to approach without startling her and called her by the name she'd taught him. He had to say it twice, and when she turned, her mouth was tight with caution. Though she'd been about to close the trunk lid she held it up with the plump heel of her hand, hunching under it a bit, as if to block a view. He wondered if her husband had kept her under surveillance or threatened to; remembering *seck-shwull* made it seem possible, even likely.

"How are you?" he said in her language, a phrase she'd taught him also.

She straightened. Her head tilted to one side in the pleased way it used to when he'd present her with chocolate bars, chewing gum, a Clementine orange: their every meeting had begun with an exchange of small gifts. But she didn't smile, and behind her bug-eye lenses it was hard to tell what she thought or how she felt. Her poise was the first thing he'd noticed about her, even before her hands.

Her upper lip raised a bit.

"I am fine," she said in brusque English, as if it were a matter of no importance. "You are not. This is evident."

He shrugged: also a matter of lesser importance, it seemed to him now, in her presence again. In this wing of the mall was a franchise café, he recalled. His gesture in that direction felt wild, grandiose.

"Cup of tea?"

Green tea, he knew, but he knew, too, what her answer would be, not from memory but from his recent return to futile dating, online and otherwise, with defensive or overeager women his own age, scornful younger ones, the tentative in-between. Even hard-eyed women who knew all about him from his first utterance might negotiate a wary shot at it until the daily weight of the world or the culture—he never knew which was heaviest—flattened any brief pleasure or feeling or possibilities they might have been able to work up together. Love as logistics, as sit-com, as game show. Love as a hobby like gardening: it might not be for everyone, but it could offer certain rewards for that left-over time in your life, if you weren't too proud to get down on your knees in the dirt.

As if aware of such options she said no, then dipped her head to peer at him over the rims of her glasses, her gray eyes bright as ever. *"Don't get me wrong."* She made sure he caught her use of the idiom, smiling with small pride. "I am glad to see you, briefly. It's the residue."

When he laughed she did, too, then slammed her trunk, got into her car, and drove off, tires squealing a bit.

DESPICABLE

Yes, I slept with your wife. We didn't actually sleep much; sometimes we dozed. Monday and Wednesday afternoons, some Saturdays, from the darkest days of winter until the time you spotted us at the ballgame. I don't know how much she's told you, but I very much doubt you know the WHOLE story, as you say. It was not "despicable." Certainly for me, it wasn't. That little mole on your wife's abdomen, just below her rib cage on her left, was the most beautiful, redemptive thing to have brushed my lips in years, healing for all concerned (not you, at that point). The way she'd draw her knees up afterward, laughing at the ceiling in sheer delight at sensations and possibilities she'd begun to despair of in the life you'd given her . . . also very beautiful. "Ooh, I am going to be soooo BIG," she said once.

Actually, that gave me pause. I knew she wanted children. Her mother had told her she'd better hurry up, and my urologist concurred. Our first conversations were that serious. At the café corner in the grocery store where we used to meet at first she was making faces with an infant at the next table who was enthralled with her face in her sable collar, not so different from the way I had been. "Will you have children with your husband?" I asked. She'd admitted she was married over our first cup of coffee—green tea for her—but had agreed to meet again. True, I'd suggested it—I "pursued" her, as you put it, but as *she* put it when we began meeting at my place, "Oh, you are a man, and there is nothing wrong with that."

And in the café corner, answering my question, "Not with my husband. He is a *boy*, not a man. I must do everything." She raised those luminous blue eyes and arched one eyebrow. "*Every*thing."

But apparently you've learned how to get a restraining order. Did you tell her you'd have her sent back if she didn't sign it? That's the power she implied you always held over her. Now I suspect she didn't tell *me* the whole story about the delay with her green card, though it might have been true at the start. When we crossed the border for a day in Toronto, I saw the letter that she carried instead. She showed it to the customs on the way out to be sure she'd be able to get back in. I was all prepared to do her explaining for her, but there was no need. You could see that the customs guys were impressed with the way she knew the rules and handled herself. "When I first got here, I was so afraid of them," she said, but now she walked right up and told them what was what, hand on her hip like a haggler at a marketplace.

Sometimes I'd offer to intervene. I offered to pay the fifty dollars consultation fee for an immigration lawyer whose offices I noticed coming home for one of our rendezvous. Her eyes glazed over at the complications until she noticed the fresh flowers I'd bought, and in her pleasure the subject was dropped. "I don't know how to live," she said one of the last times I heard from her, before you found her second cell phone. In some ways this was true. Once, not long before the ballgame episode, I asked her what she wanted from me, what she expected. She drew herself back and up in her formal way, one hand to her breast and one extended, as if to hold me off. "I *can't*," she said, "expect anything from you. I cannot allow myself to." She reflected, then signed and said she wanted to walk. She liked to see the homes for sale; we'd peek inside, check out the backyards. One, down the block, had a brightly colored swing set, and more times than not she'd slip her arm through mine and steer us that way until the red SOLD tag was added to the sign.

The truth was that after those first heady months I had doubts I'd be able to give her what she wanted any more than you had. Not just because of our ages—in her seventies, her grandfather had fathered a son with a woman of thirty-eight, as I guess you know, and you must know how proud she was of him, though in the last weeks I knew her she'd received word from other family members that his wife had turned against him in ways that she, *your* wife, was maybe beginning to empathize with more than she wished she could. Once when we were about to go out I'd misplaced my glasses, and I was walking around from room to room searching and muttering impatiently as is my wont when I saw her by the door with eyes wide and mouth agape, as if I'd grown a tail. And all the parts of her daily life with you—*beyond* you—your neighbors, your friends (at least their wives), even your insurance agents and repair-men—gratified her in ways it would have taken years to replicate.

And maybe she saw my face at her remark about how big she'd be. What skidded my heart was the gap between what was on her mind and what was on mine, after the silence of our closeness the previous hour or two, not one of the times we even dozed. Her skin was so soft I often couldn't tell where it stopped and my breath began.

Maybe she knew. I don't remember exactly what I said, no doubt some mild, inadvertent-seeming deflection like hers when I'd brought up the immigration lawyer, but with that tungsten-like intelligence she reacted immediately, though it's not until right this moment that I realize it was a reaction. The weather had warmed enough that for the first time, my window was open. She lowered her knees and rolled onto one side to watch the gauze curtains fluttering. "I have never seen," she said in the tone to which I'd learned to pay close attention so as not to miss the implied request she was leading me to, "an American baseball game. Is not the season to begin soon, I think I read?"

Of course it was, and of course—it dawns on me only now that I've heard from you again, after increasing success at holding off thoughts of you both over these last three months—she'd have known you and your friends had box seats. That's why she offered to go online from work to select ours. "At the ballet," she said, "it makes a difference where you sit. How different can this be?"

I didn't know, no fan myself. But I loved being out with her, the upright way she walked and sat, which she must have known you'd recognize before the game was over, the way she'd positioned us between your box and the field, the way she nestled so close. Who knew it would be on the big screen, with all your drunken buddies pointing? And you the drunkest of the lot, in the next shot your red and bawling face in the 14,000 bulbs on the big screen.

What's happened between you two since then I can only guess; and I've guessed plenty, these last three months. But in these photos you've sent me is a woman I never knew. Your wife, I guess. She does look pleased with that house, though her smile seems strained. With me she was someone else, someone *you'll* never know. And you'll have to live with that just the way I'll have to live without her now. I don't think she was right, that she doesn't know how to live.

I think she's learned exactly what living takes.

PART THREE

WHAT HAVE YOU GOT? WHERE THE WORDS ARE

I have an elderly neighbor, Jim, though the word "elderly" already seems a miscue. Jim's an old man, in the classic sense. I don't remember when I first became aware of him, but in the first memory I can call up now, he was out in the street in one of those four-wheeled walkers with hand-brakes like a bicycle's, sitting backwards on its shelf and trying to corral a garbage bin that had blown across the street after pickup. A veteran, which I know from seeing V.A. trucks stop in front of his house, and a former sheriff, as I've heard from other neighbors since, he's physically big, gone to fat now as well, and pasty-skinned Irish, a green, white, and orange flag on his porch along with ours. The Irish are still considered a voting bloc in this ethnically defined city where I moved for two part-time jobs that constituted almost a full one, and in my first conversations if not very first conversation with Jim, he lyricized about the red hair and freckles of the woman in the next apartment to mine, expressed disgust at his sister's having married an *Italian*, and complained about a doctor he'd just seen, "a big BLACK guy" who'd kept Jim waiting and then taken his seat in the examination room. I'm of significant Irish stock myself, percentagewise, though I've never quite fathomed what perks or obligations that's entailed, and I was sufficiently put off by Jim's assumptions to pay him little further mind for a long time. When coming and going I was aware of him listening to ballgames on the radio from deep within his front porch, with its trellises and peeling dark green paint and taped-up patriotic and sports decals—bumper stickers on windows and walls—and I'd noticed the distinctive way that several large stones and a vented iron pipe lid in his front yard were whitewashed. And there's no ignoring the smell that wafts out to the sidewalk or the occasional rat literally high-tailing it to the street like a plump woman on high heels. But otherwise, for the first two or three years after I moved into the cheap apartment where I still live, it was live and let live between me and Jim.

Then one spring day he called out as I passed. He had a job for me, he said. He'd lived in this house for eighty years, he said, and every summer since his father had called it a Victory Garden, he'd planted tomatoes. But this year, maybe because he was getting less mobile, he couldn't get out to buy the plants, and would I take this ten dollars down to a deli a few blocks away—he located it by landmarks nearby I hadn't known by name until he said them—and buy as many tomato plants as I could? "Mix them up," he said. "Beefsteaks, Big Boys, whatever he's got this year."

I knew the place, out of business now, a small hit-or-miss store on the edge of a parking lot with a collection of ball caps in the window behind a hand-lettered slogan on cardboard taped to the glass, a new one every week that always seemed slightly off, as if another week of revision might have helped: "You are what you eat, so try our ingredients!" The stock was sparse and hours unreliable, and I used to stop in only for the odd head of lettuce or potato or iced tea when I was doing laundry at the coin-op nearby, but out on the sidewalk now was a fantastic selection of tomato plants I'd never noticed before, the ones Jim had mentioned and heirlooms, dwarfs, paste and cherry tomatoes, and one called "Ace." At two dollars apiece I picked five varieties, and the deli owner, a perpetually harried guy though his shop was usually empty—no matter the time of day when I'd stopped in before, he'd always seemed to be swabbing the floor, about to close up—came alive, telling me what to expect from each variety in terms of number, height, and sweetness, how often to water, how fast they'd grow, and how big and red they'd get.

Such was his enthusiasm and Jim's appreciation when I showed up with the plants in my street bicycle's panniers that I began to think tomatoes might be my key to this city and my neighborhood, where although the jobs had solidified a bit I was feeling pretty much like a renter still. Of course, I *am* a renter and always have been, only partly out of a desire to live within my means. The whole idea of owning property to me seems like more than an economic or even a lifestyle decision: it'd be like a personality change. I have friends for whom the idea of paying a sizeable percentage of one's income month after month and never having anything to show for it is as loathsome as is to me the thought of spending my time mowing lawns, waiting for plumbers to arrive, and being unable to pick up and go. Not that I often do, but for me, it's the possibility of leaving that makes the concept of home. The idea of being so personally invested in a roof over your head is something I can't get my head around: what do you do when the mortgage is paid, sit around and admire your walls? An otherwise interesting-looking woman down the block from me walks her small white dog past every morning and every night. As with other neighbors, we nod and speak briefly as the distance warrants, but once I saw her at a nearby event, introduced myself, and by way of conversation asked if she lived in that distinctive red house (it's just one story but has a mansard roof). "Yes, I do," she said, beaming. The occasion was a book fair, but she didn't have anything to say about the books. "It *is* a great house, isn't it?" Her smile might as well have shown missing teeth, though I mean no offense to the cavity prone.

But as the years pass and I collect neither house nor family nor wealth—only the occasional small career achievement and even more occasional romantic connection, the hour-by-hour satisfactions of read-ing and writing, three bicycles, a cat lost to feline diabetes—notions like neighborhood and community are beginning to register a little more.

I can't say *appeal*. But when Jim's delight in my selection of tomato plants bled into a request that I plant them, then maybe throughout the summer water them every once in a while, just walk back there any time, and if it wasn't too much trouble yank up a handful of weeds every now and again, and by Labor Day I'd have more of my choice of tomatoes than I could eat . . . well, I didn't say no, and I'm not even that partial to tomatoes.

I tended his tomato garden the next summer, too, and at some point over the next couple of years painted the peeling dark green trim over his garage and whitewashed the stones and the vented iron cover and replaced fuses that blew at nine or ten at night and, entrusted with his EBT card, even made trips to the grocery store. He gave me a precise circumstantial reason for his every request: his son, who lived in a sub-urb fifteen or twenty miles north, had to work overtime, or they were feuding, or the landlord was coming to make a sudden inspection—at a daughter's bidding Jim had sold the house, but only on condition he be allowed to live in it until he died—or Meals on Wheels was late or he'd lose the money in his EBT account if he didn't spend it by the end of the month. And he always insisted on giving me something in return—the change from a five for a purchase of batteries or milk or two on-sale loaves of the white bread he threw into the street for birds, his coupons finger-torn out from a circular—or for the bigger jobs a barely legible check for five or ten dollars, none of which ever cleared. Once around Christmastime, I received by UPS a box of cheeses and sausages from Wisconsin, my home state, as I'd told Jim when I was leaving town for few days. He'd seen these items in a catalog and thought, "Oh, boy, Steve will love this," he told me with such pleasure I couldn't tell him that I'd given up eating cheese. And when he calls to say he's left a new "sports book"—usually *ESPN* magazine, when he's done with it—under the chair on his porch, the next time I pass I climb his steps and pick it up, bring it home, and add it to my pile of newspapers and magazines to take out to the curb on recycling day. An article or two on tennis or bicycling and a 17-year-old who sailed solo around the world have caught my eye, but—maybe ongoing fallout from my early interest in literature in the middle of Packer country—I couldn't care less about mainstream sports. But I've never said so to Jim.

So maybe when this arrangement broke down it was my own fault, for introducing this note of dishonesty. If Jim has a virtue, in the limited scope of my knowledge of him, it's saying what he thinks and feels: he's true to his own heart. If I express impatience at some errand he's asked me to run when I'm late for work, he won't let me run it, and I won't hear from him again for a couple of weeks. Since he told me in tears one humid August night when he was wearing a colostomy bag that he didn't think he'd make it to morning, I've learned he has other resources on the block: a high-school teacher across the street, my landlord around the corner, and others on the block, in fact anyone who passes by. Jim's not shy, maybe another virtue. But my only virtue in the realm of our relationship is the kind of small-scale generosity and compassion that these people or anyone else might exhibit, if as next-door neighbor I fulfill more requests: "You're the best, Steve! You're the one who always comes through for me!" But maybe it's in compensation for what I've held back, and maybe too because I don't have more in my own life. My mother, back in Wisconsin, uses a walker like Jim's, though not to chase blown-away garbage bins, as her Parkinson's has reached a point that keeps her inside. My father takes care of her, a strain on them both, and though neither one of them has ever asked anything from me and I visit and help when I can, I often feel bad not even so much at not being able to offer more as at not having lived in a manner that's allowed me to. My renter's worldview—which in its adolescent inception and at its grandest still is a kind of Buddhist nonattachment—has led to an obligatory regret, like missing something you never had but probably should, by now.

In Jim's backyard, I saw when I was painting the garage trim, he has a shrine—to his wife, the woman across the street said—a statue of the Virgin Mary and some plastic flowers and whitewashed stones, maybe a plaque. I never looked too closely at it, and when Jim's blessed me with his thanks or asked God to, I've taken it as a figure of speech, thanked him and moved on. But when a woman came into my life talking about children and marriage, permanence and attachment began taking on a whole new appeal for me. She was from another country, another culture, and a younger generation than mine, too, such that her old-world outlook combined with one formed by a world of changing borders and rules. Wearing running shoes anywhere but a gym, for example, was abhorrent to her, but until the crisis that brought about the end of our relationship, she was fine about coming to my apartment to betray her husband three afternoons a week. In between times we texted; she lived on her cell phone. And she liked walks, when she'd slip her arm through mine as we strolled the neighborhood, often enough past Jim's house.

If honesty's his virtue, discretion and respect for privacy aren't. I know more about the rest of our neighbors from Jim than I ever learned from them or observed myself. From his porch or a back room whose window faces my house, Jim sees all: a beer can on a lawn, a hibachi left out in the rain. I keep my bicycles in the basement, the door to which is across a lawn from Jim's screened window, which is where he often called me from to do his bidding. He could see me, but I couldn't see him, just hear his voice as soon as I appeared or came home, if he'd been waiting for me. And when the woman across the street had a low fence put in to keep dogs off her lawn, or the young doctor and his wife next door to her had a child, or the house on the other side of him was painted yellow,

Jim had plenty to say about the changes and the people in whose lives they were occurring. But he never mentioned my girlfriend, and over the six months of our affair he called me less and less with requests, as if he understood that I had other things on my mind now.

But within a week after her husband's discovery of certain evidence and her precipitous return to him, Jim was calling me again. Would I trim a vine that blocked his view, buy him Pepsi and a certain canned ham he'd clipped sale coupons for at the Rite-Aid? Also, in the same ad they had some winter gloves on sale that looked pretty good, so would I pick him up a couple of pairs in case he made it to another season? And some gum, too, for when his mouth got dry.

In the past, I'd balked when his requests seemed to stem more from loneliness or the pleasure of having someone do his bidding than actual need, and he'd agree, saying, "Oh, whenever you get time!" or "Forget it!" But now, preoccupied by missing someone in my life who in another while might have become a more permanent part in it, had we been able to control events better, I was susceptible to Jim's requests, if not happy to comply. And I didn't really notice that they'd escalated—from milk and bread and batteries to a certain cough syrup, anti-itch ointment, and on-sale plastic Adirondack chair that I actually went to pick up, then realized Jim wouldn't fit in it and invented a more diplomatic reason I hadn't brought it back. I didn't realize that my own involvement had escalated, too, from doing what I was asked to stopping by on my way home from a circuit of the park or the bicycle-path loop to see how he was doing, every time I passed his porch, in fact—until the time he hit me with a stale biscuit.

It was a mistake: he was pitching them out for the birds, leaning out of the shadows from his overstuffed chair, and I'd pulled in from the side of his driveway before he could stop his arm. I don't remember where I got hit—arm or chest, bouncing off my helmet—and it didn't hurt, but Jim got such a hearty kick out of it I was embarrassed, then furious, and after the open-palm wrist-flick that's the international sign for "Screw this" I rode off across the lawn, put my bike down in the basement, and went in. For all the times he'd telephoned me—within minutes of returning from a trip or a weekend away (the pattern: "Steve, how you doin." "Good, Jim. How you?" "No good. Refrigerator's out again. I need ice.")—the phone never rang for a "Steve, I'm sorry I hit you with a biscuit."

This happened the day before I was to leave on a visit home. I'd stopped by, in fact, to ask Jim if he needed anything and tell him I wouldn't be available for the next week, and the next time he *did* call—within five minutes of my car's pulling up after my twelve-hour return drive home—I told him not to ask me for anything again unless it was important. On the telephone, maybe due to some amplification feature he had, he never had the problems hearing me that he usually did when I hollered up from the sidewalk to his porch ("I'm deaf, pal," he'd shrugged once). Now there was a longer silence than I'd heard from him before. Then: "OK" and a click, and that was the last I heard from him for at least a month. He stopped hollering out at me from his darkened window when I brought my bicycles in or out, and he stopped shouting me down in the street when I passed, and I had a few weeks of peace, when I could step out into the world and begin to look at it before a voice from it would shout my name. Jim was on his porch—I saw a guy up the street on his steps once, getting his instructions—but we didn't speak. I felt bad, but not too bad. "If it's important," I said—up to him to make the judgment.

But it was a judgment of my own—sparked by something about his posture beside his door, in not his overstuffed chair but the heavy wooden ladderback he used to weight down sports books, his hands on his knees, looking straight out into the street—that caused me to stop the other day. I was on my town bike, on my way to the post office before work, and when I asked how he was doing he answered in the mid-stream whine of frustration that had been building up inside him for some time, a common enough tone from him. In his hand was his phone bill, with his account number and a service number on it, and he was waiting for someone to call the latter, because a gas main had cut the line. Somehow Jim had talked to his son earlier that morning, but his son hadn't called. "I said, 'Christ, you got the cell phone right in your hand!' What if a guy has a third heart attack? How's he gonna call 911? He's *not,* buddy. He's *dead,* that's what."

Well, this qualified as important—in fact, on my recent visit, I'd complained to my parents' phone company for just such an interruption in service—but the mention of the son, whose responsibility I'd invoked to myself often enough, kept me from offering to make the call until I returned with some groceries that, due to a short line at the PO I'd had time to stop for, though I had my cell phone in my pocket.

By that time I really did have just a few minutes to get back to work, and I felt some of the old aggravation as Jim hollered the service number at me and I relayed the operator's requests for information back to him—"Jesus, twenty questions!" he bellowed in my own kind of impatience at corporate telephone procedures. "GET SOMEONE O-VER HEEERE!"—before she was able to process his request for emergency service. Even so, it would probably be the next day, she said, though there were one or two tests he could try. "I awreddy *did* that!" he yelled when I gave him a short version of the procedure she'd given me a short version of in the first place, in deference to our obvious communication difficulties. I told him to sit tight, but I didn't want him panicking if the sun went down and no one had come, so I made sure he understood it might not be until the next day. "Aw, you gotta get goin'," he said. "Thanks a lot. You always come through."

I haven't seen or heard from him since. The weather's gotten cooler, so that might be what's kept him inside. And the other night, three months since I'd seen the married woman or heard from her husband, my cell phone rang, and it was her husband again, dialing from a restricted number. "What you did is despicable," he said.

But it wasn't. It was as beautiful as she was, and he'd been neglecting her, and the time I spent helping her get his attention were some of the sweetest days I've had since moving to this town. In the meantime they'd been baptized together in a state park, where they'd renewed their wedding vows afterwards, then visited several cities and gotten backstage concert passes to have their pictures taken with vintage rock stars, all according to an online photo album emailed to me a couple of weeks before this call. And now somewhere between the pinch of his still-angry voice—"I'm mad," he said in case I missed it; "I'm very mad"—and the whine in Jim's helpless one with his phone bill in his hand, I felt glad to recognize at last my own particular frequency, the territory I've staked out for myself, the zone in which I'm going to have to live and make my way: neither mean nor entirely compassionate, attached nor entirely transient, of a place nor gone too long from it, foreign nor entirely domestic, clueless nor absolutely sure, happy nor entirely sad.

DELIGHT FOR THE WRETCHED

If the barrier-busting presidential campaign indicated how far the country's come, the headlines about Obama's win showed how far we've still got to go: even *The New York Times*'s June 4 banner couldn't get over "FIRST BLACK CANDIDATE TO LEAD A MAJOR PARTY"; its November 5 subhead "Racial Barrier Falls" seemed slightly less amazed, but of all the hot issues of the campaign, race was still front and center. Conversations about race might be crucial, but does every conversation need to be about race, even—especially—every political one? The term "post-racial" is an oxymoron, guaranteed to bring race to mind when you hear it. So in the days after Obama's win, when (again according to a *New York Times* article) its significance was reverberating in the African American community, the effect it was having on me, a white supporter, was a step backward: the guy in the apartment upstairs became the Black guy in the apartment upstairs, and the two people in the oil-change-place waiting room became two African Americans. As it happened, Clinton's concession speech was just then breaking news on Fox; I kept my eyes on my crossword puzzle; when one African American looked up at the screen and asked the other what had happened, the answer was terse. Chairs were against two walls in a corner, and when a white woman came in she sat on my side. Then another white guy came in and crossed the room to sit with the white woman and me. My oil change and tire rotation took forty minutes, and except for the TV, that waiting room was silent.

It was not necessarily a tense silence, though. We were, after all, in the second poorest city in the country, according to the 2007 Census Bureau figures; it has a 50% poverty rate, according to Barbara Ehrenreich's formula of doubling the official estimate, and a long history with race. When I first came here over a decade ago (when its ranking was eighth), I got driving directions in ethnicities: go through the Irish neighborhood, past a Black neighborhood with Polish street names, hang a left after a street full of Italian restaurants, then ask. One of our several nicknames is "City of Good Neighbors," over a logo of two hands emerging from differently styled cuffs to clasp, and you know what make good neighbors, Robert Frost notwithstanding.

So by the time I headed to a car wash on my way home from the oil-change place, I was already in a more optimistic frame of mind. I'd stopped for a light when a pedestrian across the street leaned forward as if to peer in at me with evident interest and pleasure, calling out "How you doing?" My first thought was that this was a post-Obama-victory moment, if not a fully post-racial one: the man was about my age, maybe even grayer haired, and I was in a Black neighborhood now. I waved back and called out, "Good! How you doing?" (This is the basic Buffalo exchange.)

In fact, around this particular intersection, race itself is not as apparent as the shopping carts outside a mission door or the legless men who line their chairs up along a certain sidewalk to catch the sun, taking turns wheeling across the potholes to a store with a hand-lettered sign to buy cold drinks. The oil-change place was in a wide commercial strip, as impersonal outside as in that waiting room, but the street here was livelier, with its lost shoes in the gutters and Burger-King bags in the wind and graffiti on traffic signs and shouts over music from the huge digital marquee of a Pentecostal church that's kitty-corner from a rent-to-own outlet and a muffler repair shop. And before the light had changed, I heard laughter, too, gleeful laughter, and into my vision on the other side of the car from the man who still had his hand up appeared two toothless-looking dark-skinned women carrying bottles in paper bags, the intended recipients of the wave I'd returned.

"Good! Good!" All three people involved were doubled up.

I drove on laughing myself, at myself: if I hadn't made their day, they'd certainly made mine, not just for the chuckle but for reminding me to wonder again what makes us assume, once we get even just to the point of paying others to change our oil and wash our cars, that the way we see the world is the way it is. More than economics must be involved: maybe in order to function at all in the world we need to believe it'll hold steady, at least until we're ready to take our next step. But I wonder if the particularly American notion of success as necessarily stepping *up* doesn't contribute to the perpetuating of our own particular national curse—our spin on race—as well. As it happens, though I can spend $50 on basic car maintenance with less attention to the price than to strangers in the waiting room while the work's being done, I don't earn much: I'm a part-time teacher in a public education system geared toward tenure. I have health insurance but no job security, and though for twenty years I've made enough to pay my bills, I've never had a change in title or known beyond a few months whether I'll have more work. Of course I complain a good deal about all the benefits my job doesn't provide, but what I do get instead is an enforced daily adjustment to the predominant assumptions of the institution in which I spend most of my time. When you're rewarded by a system—by a paycheck, approval, increasing status, etc.—you don't question its values as much as when you have to locate them by and for yourself, either within the system or outside it.

But other values are there when you look, all systemic indicators to the contrary, just as are other characteristics than race in Senator Obama, you, or me, despite headlines that either dictate or reflect (same difference) the priorities of sensibilities nationwide. You had to have heard the rich laughter of the women with the bagged bottles to sense the complex ironies that occasioned it: cold beer on the first warm day of spring, white man driving through, old Harold grinning our way as usual, that white man grinning right back: *one* Black candidate, and this man thinks we *love* him, now!

Even from my own relatively lowly vantage point, as a relatively well fed white person, I need this kind of reminder that the true nature of the world is such that even the wretched can find delight in it, that delight doesn't equate with money or come with it, necessarily, and that lack of money doesn't obviate it. Credit-card ads to the contrary, life's not a perk; accurate perception of life isn't, laughter isn't. Broad strokes and easy categories, abbreviations and approximations—these are the tools of mass media, not truths of human existence itself.

It is true that abbreviations can work wonders, though. Since about January, I wore an Obama button to work, unobtrusively on my collar. Part of my job is in a drop-in tutoring center, where students I don't know come by with essays their regular instructor has graded lower than the students want. Many of them are students of color, and whether it was the button or the fact that tutors don't grade, speaking of barriers, these students began opening up in a quiet, trusting, natural way that's rarer in other student-teacher contexts I'd known. Though I could earn per year three times what I earn now and still be shamed at college reunions, this proximity is what I take home instead: not just the indications of trust and appreciation and barely credulous relief that these students showed but the times when the two of us, tutor and tutee, were focused on a common task, their paper—perhaps the formula for overcoming mistrust of all types—and the way these kids would often then start spotting their own mistakes, correcting them, suggesting ideas, new wording . . . improving their papers, i.e., in many cases along the very lines that the instructor had written before on the paper itself, which students would have dragged in behind them like a favorite pet that had been drowned by a mean neighbor. But then in the space of fifteen or twenty minutes I'd see them come alive, eyes bright, sitting up straight, correcting *me* when I'd misread their work.

This is not to claim any great sensitivity, empathy, or tutoring training of my own; my training and main interest are in another field, really, albeit a related one; I've just recently learned that tutoring as a profession has its own textbooks these days. And, like I say, I don't know what role my Obama button played. What I think helped most was the physical proximity of our heads, two of us alone in a small room with no windows, our four eyes peeled for commas.

And in this exciting new time in America, such closeness needs factoring in—along with money, career, or prestige in a community—to any formula for success. Post-"Mission Accomplished," if not fully post-race yet (or post-*Jackass*, post-Larry Craig . . . pick your cultural milestones), both Obama's victory and this tutoring room seemed to operate in a similar way: as a surprising, uplifting indication to people who'd previously had no faith in the system they lived under that it could, in fact, serve them in ways that increased them, and not only could but had begun to. And what these two situations had in common was not race but proximity. How does Barak Obama deal with resistant populations? Well, he goes to meet them in small groups. You've got to look into a face to see more than its color. Then it's easy, because the person there is obvious.

A fictional narrator of James Baldwin's wrote of reaching out to his estranged incarcerated brother only after losing his own daughter to polio: "My pain made his real." Do you have "to expose thyself to feel what wretches feel," as Lear said and did, to fathom the fundamental paradoxes—the non-Black-and-whiteness—at the core of all human existence? Do you have to have the limitations of an unjust stereotype imposed upon you to avoid stereotyping?

I don't know. Certainly plenty of people have devoted more of their lives to living closer to the world's wretched than I have, and benefited more of them more substantially, often without diminishing their own achievements or comfort levels; look at Bill Gates. But I just saw a posting for a job in another, more heterogeneously white state that calls for my exact credentials. It's a perfect fit, really: it's near where I grew up, near family who still live there, and it almost certainly pays more—but I'd rather live in Buffalo.

TAKE THE BUS

I'd lived in what the Census Bureau has now called the second poorest city in the nation for five years before I took a bus. My own income's below the local family median, but I've been employed since I've been here, and I own a car and three bicycles, which I prefer to the car. But one day I found myself with none of them, for some reason, so I waited for and climbed up into a bus that runs along one of the busiest north-south thoroughfares, a street on which it's said, among a certain segment of locals, you're bound to run into everyone you know sooner or later. (I haven't, myself, but, as I say, I moved here from elsewhere.) In fact, according to one of these locals, another recent assessor ranked about an eight-block stretch of this street, along with surrounding residential blocks, among the most desirable in the country: it's a street with boutiques and restaurants and bars, coffee and ice-cream and bicycle shops, churches, foreign-language and yoga centers, tattoo and piercing and pizza parlors, antiques outlets, pet and crafts and music and convenience stores . . . and plenty of people appropriate to each place. It's vibrant, i.e., with its own streetlamp banners and its own kicky name, E______ Village; you can get an EV bumper sticker, black block letters on a plain white oval, like a nation's. I live a block away in a cramped apartment, and though I've bought holiday gifts at a nearby sweatshirt boutique, I generally only go to the same few places—Chinese and Italian take-outs, a laundromat, a convenience store, and a bagel place. But I don't think about moving. E_____ is not exactly Easy Street, but it's an easy street to live near.

Then, this late-winter day, I got on the bus, and through the tint of ad-wrapped windows, the view was completely different. We passed the same Blockbusters, tea room, garden shop, Damsel in a Dress, but the atmosphere was shut out, beyond those of us in the fiberglass seats, our boots on the grainy rubber matting. The mood inside I'd call tired, and the borderline festivity outside, everything that gives the street its distinctive flavor, seemed irrelevant. Not even silly or frivolous or indulgent, though it's certainly—admittedly, proudly—all of these: Spoiled Rotten is the name of a gift shop here. But nobody in the bus seemed resentful or angry or contemptuous. In fact, what struck me most was what can strike Northerners who've crossed the Mason-Dixon line: how polite everyone is. If they spoke at all, people spoke low, and they moved their boots to let you pass. How familiar yet strange, a new world for sure. As with other new worlds, any discomfort or threat it might have seemed to pose at first soon gave way to an impression of normalcy. I was the only one looking around, whether out the window or at fellow passengers. Most of them just seemed glad to be sitting down.

All told, that hour and a half—both riding and waiting beforehand, in a shelter to block the wind—to go eighteen blocks, from a vantage point of maybe four feet higher than my usual one along the same street, was real travel. It gave me new eyes, and in the hush whenever the doors folded shut after a stop and the bus accelerated, I felt the same sort of alert calm that can set in abroad, when you're on your way to another culture's holy sites, along with a kind of startled thankfulness that I could see this. It was a trip indeed, in the perspective it gave me on my own place in life, and it cost only a dollar and a half.

LETTER FROM BUFFALO: The Shrines of Summer

All over the West Side in the summer you come upon street-side shrines: piles of stuffed animals, religious candles, liquor bottles, beads, and other memorabilia where kids, whether gang members or mistaken for gang members, have been shot. The first one I noticed this year was on the curb by the entrance to the fenced-in parking lot of a refugee agency where I do volunteer work. I'd read about it in a random browse through the *Buffalo News*: a teenager shot on that corner at around 1 AM, assailant or assailants unknown yet. Inscriptions were burnt into a wooden post: nicknames, messages like in a high school yearbook.

A few weeks later I was fishing in LaSalle Park when three Latin high school-aged kids shared my bench, talking aimlessly between them of this and that, me eavesdropping just as aimlessly while reading and checking my line, and when the oldest-looking girl burst out suddenly "Oh I miss him so *much*! We used to have so much fun!" and the others fell silent, I wondered if she meant one of these victims of gunshot. I can still hear the way she drew out that second "so."

"What's moving is their paucity of expression," I started to write about the shrines, but it's not paucity but range and unexpectedness, their symbols of tribute drawn from all over, desperately. On these curbs is piled anything that might offer meaning: candles in tall frosted glasses, Christ figures with clean feet and hair like a Clairol ad, empty Gallo magnums and V.S.O.P. bottles, dirty stuffed Dalmatians and pandas that the victims weren't ten years past needing as much as they needed a pistol of their own on the night in question. Two kids were sitting out by the first shrine I noticed, the Monday morning after the early morning shooting that Sunday: a heavy girl and a sober-faced boy in a flat-brimmed Yankee's cap, the girl quietly crying in the thin, half-forced and half-hysterical way of kids whose emotions haven't developed to the magnitude of their circumstances. I locked my car and went over and told the guy I was sorry about their friend. He nodded up at me, seeming to appreciate the gesture without entirely trusting it.

Since then I've seen other shrines west of Richmond Avenue, which I live a couple of blocks east of; several have been closer to my place than that first one, shootings I hadn't read about first, so I've come upon the shrines with surprise. The other evening I saw two new ones on 19th Street, a route I often take home from Grant Street or Ferry, the last leg of my habitual jaunt to the Erie Canal on the Riverwalk bike path. One shrine was directly across the street from another, both at the base of trees, the stuffed animals roped to their trunks like lynchees. Below were the liquor bottles, the religious pictures, the candles in frosted glasses, one burning on the curb as I passed; its wick seemed unusually long, a stem coated white from the wax it rose from, as if it had just been lit. People were around: in peripheral vision I'd noticed a guy sitting on a front porch, and I'd smelled dope, unmistakable even from a moving bicycle. The street on that block is narrow, its small houses close together, very living-room-like.

Of course the big violence story here this summer is the eight people shot at the City Grill downtown, some of these thirty-somethings but also speculated to be gang-related. As I write, the perpetrator's still at large. Early on, pastors of churches with challenging names urged the perpetrator to turn himself in, as one said in the local press, for his own good, because friends of the victims are very upset. People in line at convenience stores turn and comment on the ongoing headlines, deploring the violence: no one's as resentful of such disruption to law and order as the people who live on these blocks.

But what strikes me isn't the threat to public safety or the moral shock, either, remarkable as both are. It's the disparity of assumptions between populations that walk the same streets, the gap between realities that occupy the same real space. My jaunt down 19th Street was on the way home from a coffee shop that closes at 6 PM, occupying as it does a West Side corner where covered women walk behind their husbands, thin-tired SUVs shake and boom past, and skinny, spaced-out looking guys in Timberlands and hankies under their hats amble past wrought-iron lawn furniture where people like me are connecting to the Internet via WiFi over $4 cups of iced coffee. Inside the café that afternoon, a half-dozen young people with musical instruments had been promoting a play about coal miners at a new theater called the Subversive. They were tuneful and earnest, inventively bearded and clad, and between songs a strong-voiced young woman in flowing skirts talked about Mother Jones, promising more info "on these issues" at the opening. Later they congregated outside with friends and supporters and talked. "So nice to meet you finally," I heard, and "Yeah, Jennifer's back, and I saw Aaron at Wegman's, but in another check-out line," and "Oh but of course on the other hand we've that big stage to work with, haven't we?" and "Do you want to come up for a minute, after?"

Among the excited voices I recognized the vibrant one of the woman in flowing skirts, who'd been so confident and pure in her passion for the coal miners I wanted to turn around and look again, but just then a movement across Grant Street caught my eye, a tiny procession: a stocky black-haired woman walking close behind her two teenagers, I presumed: a thin boy of twelve or so in basketball clothes and an older black-haired girl in sky-blue drawstring pants with white flowers on them. The three moved solemnly and evenly, not exactly slowly but in a *stately* way beyond the traffic, their backs straight and their heads up, eyes straight ahead. They weren't smiling, and it was with something between fascination, obligation, and reverence that I watched them coming my way as the actors' and musicians' voices behind me bubbled off.

RUSSIAN TO EAT: Fast Food and Common Decency in St. Petersburg and Moscow

If it's your first time in Russia, chances are you'll be thrown by the Cyrillic, even if you've diligently studied the alphabet charts in your guidebook beforehand. The mix of recognizable Roman and Greek characters and the Russian ones with no English equivalents will be charmingly baffling for about four hours, or until you get seriously hungry. Then it'll be frustrating, not only to identify a restaurant as such and read its menu but to identify the dishes themselves. Even simple staples like *kulebyaka*, a bread with white mushrooms or cabbage baked inside, or *moiva*, a small dried fish served whole as an appetizer, or the traditional fermented rye beverage *kvass*, a sort of peasant's pop like a dark near beer, are hard to translate, let alone order at first. Never mind delicacies such as pickled garlic or pike-and-perch soup (though borscht is borscht, a force of life, by force of dill; I had it because I could say it, though I hadn't touched beets since some unpleasantness at age five, but I'm a borscht lover now).

The restaurants in or near or advertised in your hotel might offer one solution, fancy-to-fine places you can come to call the Georgian place or the Armenian one as you return again and again throughout your stay, the food problem addressed, if not too varyingly resolved. These establishments tend to have either menus in English or English underneath the Russian describing each dish, much like in nouvelle cuisines back home, as well as prices per size of portion in grams. Also, you'll probably hear about or stumble across charming neo-tsarist places like Zoom, a St. Petersburg café where the check arrives in a novel or volume of poetry—in Cyrillic, a necessary reminder that you're not in Soho, Monterrey, or some upscale mall in Des Plaines.

But what you really wanted was to pass your GREs, your Genuine Russian Experiences, not to mention, once you've been up and down Nevsky Prospect or the old Arbat for a few hours, something solid in your stomach right now. A meal at these places, or just getting the check for one, can take several hours or seem to, given intercultural variations on the concept of time (and/or of going out to dinner, perhaps) and a visitor's limited amount of it. So can carefully constructing your schedules and routes in order to plan lunch and dinner at restaurants your guidebook lists that are close to the monuments and museums you want to see in morning and afternoon. And that risks turning your stay into something very like a workweek, even if traffic and transportation and other variables go as hitchlessly as they rarely do anywhere. But if you're like me, the best travel guide is Chet Baker. After all, itchy feet are not called dailyplannerlust or knownquantitylust, are they? The rewards of travel are in the surprises when you get lost. Within reason, of course. And whether you know where you are or not when hunger hits, the stomach can't be ignored. What's surprising is that the ordinary quest of trying to fill it can lead to nourishment of a longer-lasting sort, as well.

One of the best plain meals I found in Russia was at a chain called Kroshka Kartoshka, which looks something like KPOWKA KAP-TOWKA in Cyrillic. On the logo, those letters appear in a circle around a cartoon chef hoisting a giant potato, which is what's served, baked, with your choice of sauces, in stainless-steel bowls you can point at through Plexiglas: mushrooms, greens, fish, meats. I pointed to green-and-brown, pink-and-yellow, and another I forget, all flavorful beyond the chili and broccoli-and-Kraft I've had at similar establishments here (though it's a great idea anywhere, isn't it?). Maybe the scenery helped the flavor: in the lively Sennaya Plochad (Haymarket Square) location where I first noticed these in St. Petersburg, I took my dressed potato outside on a tray with a draft Boshkarov beer to eat at pine-green plastic furniture (pine green is the color of Kroshka Kartoshka) set out under umbrellas just across from the wishful new monument to international peace, a column made of a metal that looks like ice.

In Moscow, I saw a pine-green cart with the familiar round logo in the old Arbat, across fruit- and vegetable-stands from the McDonald's at the end of the pedestrian mall nearest Smolensky Bulvar and the Foreign Ministry, furthest from the end near Arbatskaya Plochad and the statue of Gogol. Keep your eyes peeled, and forget the KGB: it's the Kroshka Kartoshka that are all over.

So are—in St. Petersburg—the fast-*blini* chain Teremok (looks like "Tepemok," in script-like letters). Don't be put off by the lit plastic, orange-and-blue burger-chain-like facades and ordering systems: the upside is that the food is pictured, so you can point (and smile, remember). It's also good, reasonable, and Russian, ranging from ham-and-cheese to soups, salads, *kvass*, and, of course, *blini*. These are pancake-like crepes, griddle-fried for each order—so the lines can be slow, particularly on Nevsky Prospect around weekday lunchtime, but the wait is worth it; they're filled with salmon or red caviar. Salads, often a bit heavy on the mayonnaise, come in the kind of clear plastic cups used for sundaes at Dairy Queen. *Kvass*, on tap like soft drinks, can be bought to go, in a plastic bottle.

A note about the mayo: if you don't like it, visit a different country. A piece of meat, maybe veal, that I ordered once in a restaurant like those mentioned above arrived under a puffed layer that looked like breading or melted cheese until cautious prodding revealed it as maybe half a cup of mayonnaise, possibly baked, the closest this traveler came to a complete cultural balk, though of course the goo was easily scraped off. And the mayonnaise for take-out salads comes in packets, so you can set your own limits.

These I found in a refrigerated display case at one of the small stores identified by sidewalk signs that read, more or less, "24-YACA," ("chasa," or hours)—not a chain, just a sign, also generally circular. Think Mom and Pop meet 7-11. At a step-down 24-chasa behind white latticed doors and windows on the Kazanskaya in Petersburg, what look to be dozens of varieties of vodka (including horilka, a Ukranian hot-pepper vodka best treated with care and respect) in interestingly shaped and labeled bottles share shelf space with breads and other goods that women behind the counter will hand down to you one by one, sighing, as you point (and smile). My salads were in a trailer of a 24-chasa parked at the angle of Zabovsky Bulvar and Burdenko in Moscow, near the Leo Tolstoy statue and the Moscow Home HI hostel, in round clear-plastic containers that make the contents visible. And the contents do need identifying, because in Russia anything—from fruit to cucumbers to pasta to pickles to fish and meat—can qualify as "saLAHT" (looks like "calat"). It's healthy food, the ingredients neatly cut or cubed and stacked by kind in the container, though it did take two salat to make a meal for this overindulged American appetite.

One such two-salad meal, along with a bottle of BonAqua "bez gaz" (or "still"; i.e, no bubbles) mineral water, cost 55 rubles, some $2.25 at that point, an indication of why I didn't keep stricter accounts of other meals, which were on a similar scale. For a Boshkarov I paid between sixty and 120 rubles. I'd spent over a thousand dollars to get to Russia and back, so who I was I to quibble while there?

Also in the 24-chasa—or in supermarkets like the St. Petersburg chain identified by a big red dot on its sidewalk sign—you might ask for yogurt. Not "yo-GOORT" or "yo-GOOR" or "you-HOOR," as I somehow felt obligated to try out until that last brought my mistake to my own ear—but "YOgurt," our very sounds, a cognate. Sometimes Russian, like travel moments anywhere, can be as suddenly and astonishingly easy as lifting a trunk you'd thought was full but wasn't.

More often, though, we travelers need help. And the best source of it, in these Russian places where you want to lose yourself right up until the moment you find yourself lost, is Russians themselves. The magic words are please and thanks: paZSAlusta (the middle syllable pronounced as in Zsa Zsa Gabor) and spaSEEba. Just as important is to breathe, smile, and look your server in the eye. You might not always get a smile back—like Kroska Kartoshka, the grumpy are all over—but you'll eat. The transaction beforehand can become complicated, even its successful conclusion quite humbling, as when I had to eat rice and salmon with a soup spoon because I didn't know how to say that a cafeteria's fork bin was empty.

But I count a renewed awareness of life's complexity among the substantial rewards of travel. Modern Russia, no matter its sins or problems past or present, is a society growing from of a core value of solidarity, among other similar ones in the revolutionary ideologies of ninety years ago, and hunger, especially in the formerly besieged former Leningrad, is a great leveler. I made few friends trying to order food, but I was fed. And the smiles when they did come were glorious: fleeting and curious, delighted and kind. Call it insight into oneself or the Russian character or grace itself: travel might well be the Great Romance, as a 1920's poster for a cruise down the Nile put it, but unrehearsed mealtime can be the Great Reality, which turns out not to be so grim.

"Nyet," croaked a woman I was trying to pay for a red-jelly pastry in a pedestrian underpass in Moscow, shaking her head slowly with the grave, deadpan gaze Russians seemed to favor no matter the issue at stake. The pastry was some fourteen rubles, and I'd given her two bills totaling sixty: a fifty and a ten instead of the two tens I'd intended. These times I could have been taken but wasn't (even a drunk who'd accosted me turned down five rubles, wanting only to share a sentence he knew in English: "The city is very beautiful") filled me with a sense of gratitude and love for people anywhere who, strapped though they might be, live by more than immediate gain. To travel well, you have to believe in these people, literal strangers, and put your faith in them and the world itself, wherever you might insert yourself into it. For every story you might hear about a pickpocket or marauding bands of trained gypsy child-thieves, you'll experience dozens of these small gestures of honesty, generosity, respect, and automatic principle—if you look for them.

A cafeteria can be another find, a great place to smile and point. One called Kapmaro on the east side of the Gribadoevar Canal in St. Petersburg (on the right as you turn in from Nevsky Prospect toward the Church of the Spilled Blood), promises "quick service" on its orange signs outside, and inside offers nature videos on twin TVs and, among other dishes, salmon whole or in patties, pastries, and borcht served hot or cold. In another, a step-down with an Arabic name on the Nevsky Prospect just above the M. Morskaya Ulitza, another Western traveler, judging from his new "So-and-So Properties" shoulder bag, and I ate well and in peace. But you'll make your own discoveries, eat your own meals, and have your own insights and fun, once you get out in it. Don't be afraid.

WHOSE BAD? MOCKERY IN MANY LANDS

Virgil was telling me about the double sets of locked doors on the apartments of his Russian friends even as they'd explained to him that their lives were relatively stable now. "But they lock both doors!" He held up two fingers, then two hands he held flat and vertical, one behind the other with a few inches in between, to show me the security arrangement. Virgil was a Frenchman, and I'm American; we were speaking in his language, and he wanted to make sure I understood. "Everything's fine, everything's fine, but—!" He flipped his hands to turn imaginary keys, clicking with his tongue, then sat back from the table with his national shrug.

We were eating on the lamp-lit patio of an Uzbek restaurant just off the old Arbat pedestrian mall in Moscow, in the street behind the statue of the folk singer Bulat Okudhaba, at about ten o'clock at night. At our hostel, six blocks away, were a Taiwanese girl who hadn't wanted to have anything to do with either one of us, and seventeen Venezuelans, members of the entourage of Hugo Chavez, who was just then concluding a visit to Putin with characteristically anti-US vitriol. I'd been on the road long enough that travel euphoria had become a sort of status quo, but I knew signs of tension when I saw them. Virgil's excitement about the locks made me think again about the forty-two ultranationalist protesters who'd been held after anti-gay violence in Moscow's Slavyanskaya Plochad just a week before, as I'd read in *The St. Petersburg Times*, and about the charge of government critics that such measures were a too-feeble response to a growing threat. It made me think about my own Russian friend, Masha, mother of a five-year-old son born in America; when I'd asked conversationally about her future plans, her face had darkened, and she'd said they depended on the elections (in 2008: this was before then, of course). Her answer shocked me: despite apocalyptic-sounding rhetoric and hope for any given candidate, who in America, except candidates themselves, holds off on life decisions pending the results of a Presidential election? And just that afternoon, when I'd gotten caught in a thunderstorm on a long walk to Gorky Park and taken refuge in the doorway of an anonymous office block somewhere around the doorway of an anonymous office building, a towheaded young man in work clothes had emerged to peer at me with such a glitteringly contemptuous look that I'd caught a chill from more than the damp. So as Virgil and I waited for our food to arrive, I felt it again now.

That was when I noticed the table of men in the shadows behind Virgil's shoulder and the merry attention they were paying to us. Virgil wore his frizzy hair in a pony tail with the sides clipped to his scalp, a remarkable enough style, though less so than his story: he was returning from two years in what he'd found to be an unfriendly Korea, he'd told me, capped off by six days on the Trans-Siberian Railway from Vladivostok with a stomach bug he hadn't been at all sure he was going to recover from. Crossing the Urals seemed to have done the trick, however. "How good to be back in Europe!" he'd exclaimed every few minutes since we'd left the hostel, *à propos* of nothing but the cool of the evening, the soft yellow light on the patio, and the murmur of strollers on the Arbat. But now he, too, seemed aware of the commotion from the shadows behind him, with enough of an inkling about its cause that he lowered his voice and didn't turn.

Our bib-aproned waiter, waiting by the door from the restaurant to our patio, was watching the table behind us, his head hung, his expression loaded with at least three kinds of unhappiness: in his grim face I read his recognition of this situation, if not of these particular guys than of their kind, his embarrassment for the rest of us, and his inability to do anything about either. A glimpse over Virgil's shoulder showed one of the men leaning back to angle a camera toward us, his neck stiff with a sort of stagey surreptitiousness for the benefit of his chortling buddies, and my blood ran cold.

I thought they were Muscovites: maybe vodka-primed businessmen, owners of struggling shops, ill-paid office workers, and/or bored former KGB goons in some fraternity of the misbehaved. To look too closely would be at best to take their bait and at worst to invite a confrontation I'd have no taste for in my own hometown. Anyway, by this time a close look was beside the point: no matter where these guys were from and what they did for a living when they weren't out cutting up in public, there was no mistaking them as members of that class of people whose confidence in the absolute rightness of their perceptions is like artillery. And the shells when they land affected everyone in the vicinity: me, the waiter, and other patrons who turned twice, once to see the problem, then back to their plates, eyes down. Even Virgil had fallen silent.

That was how I finally made out my own language, in my own accent: "But, hey! I wouldn't like to meet that one guy in a dark alley," I suddenly and distinctly heard. Whether because of an overactive auditory imagination or the mind's instinctive reach toward meaning, I've often experienced false cognates abroad, but up until now as some buried phrase that startles and delights with its sudden incongruousness: "bumma bumma bumma jump rope," from an elderly lady to a bus conductor or, from one of two kids on a playground, "Winna winna wit's the *wine*!" But here a whole sentence more or less fit the situation, and when I did look now I saw the face of the speaker, a golf-looking guy in a dark golf shirt, ducking away from the one he wouldn't like to meet in a dark alley . . . me!

I'm fairly beefy, I guess, and was bearded then, but to think of myself as a physical threat to anyone, much less to this rowdy bunch who'd worried me just a few moments before, constituted the kind of rug-yank astonishment that in another context can be one of the highest rewards of travel, if not its whole point. Each of our misunderstandings and misplaced fears—mine of the group as possible thugs, golf-guy's of my fists and Virgil's haircut—seemed to evaporate, for me at least. But, international as ignorance is—as hatred is, as ridicule and discomfort are—it was only the particular injustice I'd committed myself, attributing the snickers to factions within a country I knew superficially yet, that I could do anything about.

"They're Americans, aren't they?" I asked Virgil, checking my own impressions as I looked directly at the table for the first time all night. The man who'd held the camera looked old enough to be the father of one of two other men. The fourth might have been one of their sons. *Teach your children well*, I thought.

Virgil, though he'd given no indication earlier of how much he understood what was going on behind his back, answered immediately. "It would seem so."

Our food came: grains and kabab and a delicious side dish of greens whose name I'd have written down if I hadn't still been a little rattled, and on the whole the tension was broken. The chortling group—a subgroup, I guessed, who'd escaped from a bus tour like the one I'd seen earlier filing into the rest rooms in the McDonald's a little ways up the Arbat—lost interest in us, and the sounds of talk and laughter of a healthier kind filled the patio again. Virgil and I found some more digestive topics of conversation.

I did toy with the idea, when we'd finished our meal, of approaching the men's table slowly, leaning on it with my dark-alley knuckles and arms, then zapping them with a "How you boys? Enjoying yourselves?" But I lacked the nerve to pull it off, and I wouldn't have wanted the resentment I still held against them to be drowned in any backslaps and grins and outbursts of "Where you from? Jeeze, fella! You really had us goin'!" Nor would I have wanted to disrupt the other diners again with what, from their point of view, would have now become a family squabble. What I *would* have wanted to do is to point out that everyone in the restaurant resented these chuckleheads' behavior, as if my country's image abroad needs any more tarnishing these days. But who learns anything from a scold?

Still, I wish I'd done it. Unforeseen human connections across cultures are often a good thing, what the thoughtful traveler hopes for. So to recognize ignorance and poor behavior so far from home, not to mention misattributing it, was something of a comedown. As everyone from mindfulness-meditation advocate Jon Kabat-Zinn to country singer Clint Black have reminded us, "Wherever you go, there you are"—and that includes our bad and our ugly, unless we can shine a light on them.

TALK-TALKING THE TALK-TALK

A faculty-lounge conversation led to a year's full-time appointment, then another two at a state-university branch where I'd taught as adjunct for several years. When the department underwent a change of leadership, the new chair was a Joyce scholar. I'd seen him in the halls, but we'd never met. I introduced myself on a day I was teaching "The Dead." In class, I'd shown parts of the John Huston film.

"Yeah, but it doesn't really come off," said Dr. Squirrel, as I'll call him because he liked to eat nuts, which he brought in small plastic bags and kept in the refrigerator. "I have serious problems with the casting—Gabriel should be older—though the cinematography is downright brilliant in spots."

I was drawn up a bit by his language and tone, which seemed to owe more to "Sneak Previews" than to the critical traditions of an English Department, but I told him how much I loved the story itself. Sharing that love with undergraduates—instilling it, if possible—was our job, I thought.

"Yeah, but all that *romance*," said Dr. Squirrel, popping a nut from his fist into his mouth. His upper teeth were shorter on one side than on the other, somehow, giving him a smile like a guillotine. "I mean the rain, the fog, the tubercular teenage *lover*—come *on*. It's almost *fun*ny, isn't it?"

"Oh, hahahahahaha!" I said, and the next conversation we had was a phone call at the end of that summer, when discretionary funding had come through for him to hire full-time, fixed-term lecturers, to be deployed however he saw fit.

We had another conversation at a departmental function that spring, when I sat at a linen-draped table with him and his wife.

"Larry," he said at dinner's end, leaning forward to pitch his napkin on his plate (Larry Lecturer, not my real name), "did I ever tell you about the time we hired a chair over a chest of drawers?"

The appearance of his teeth clued me in on the intentionality of his *diction de meubles* and sudden confidence. The story was that he and several others in the department used to collect antique furniture, and during a previous search (back when Ernest Emeritus had served as acting chair, if I remembered Ernest, not this last time he served but his *first* time, another interesting anecdote the good doctor promised to share with me some time) they'd all gone out to an estate sale in the country, where by chance they discovered that the auctioneer had a Ph.D.

"'Can you teach Chaucer?' we asked him, because we needed a chairman who could teach Chaucer, too. 'Yep,' he said, and that was it: I had Sara [Sara Secretary, administrative assistant still] draw up the papers and send them on over. Plus a beautiful cherrywood three-drawer bureau with a matching commode for fifty dollars, I got." Dr. Squirrel leaned toward me to draw a pipe from a side pocket of his jacket, though no building on campus allowed smoking, and with his thumb in the bowl lowered his voice so his wife couldn't hear. "Of course *that* was before Affirmative Action."

"Oh, hahahahahaha!" I said again for my second year's contract, though my middle name (my real one), has three syllables and ends in 'a'.

By my third year Dr. Squirrel had caught on, so it was a more difficult year for both of us and my last on a full-time contract, but what I'm getting at has less to do with my own particulars than the particular way in which Tip O'Neill's remark about politics being local applies in academia—even in a department that purports to preserve language in its noblest forms. If you're in such a department, you need to watch your own carefully, because the nature of the job dictates that language must be used in different ways, high-minded and low, at different times. Using one when the other is called for can result in a painful torque.

Naturally, members of every profession, like any group, speak differently to each other than to outsiders. Plumbers use a different vocabulary with other plumbers than with their customers, as do doctors and insurance salespeople. But education is not insurance (particularly in the humanities), and teachers must also address a third group: students. Despite economic imperatives that can make schools seem otherwise, students are not just customers, and they're not complete outsiders, either, so they tend to know when they're being sold a bill of goods. Therefore they need to be spoken to in the language of truth, curiosity, compassion, and possibility (if schools do offer a commodity, that last is it, isn't it?). And that's as it should be.

Unlike students, however, colleagues—especially superiors, and especially during these times of retrenchments and lawsuits—don't need to be delighted, surprised, or amazed. What they need is reassurance that everything's going, if not fine, at least relatively smoothly, just like in what's called the real world. On a local public-television special during a recent economic crisis, a prominent businesswoman was asked for job seeking advice. She finished up a list of common-sense tips with one that seemed to have just struck her, offering it in the hushed language and voice of a good teacher, earnest and bottom-line honest: "And don't worry so much about competition. Don't try so hard to be the best.

People want someone they can work with, someone they're comfortable with, not necessarily the best person for the . . ." Her voice trailed off.

Not necessarily the way things should be, but the way they often are. For the same reason these phrases, drawn from faculty meetings, hold meaning for people who've successfully risen through the ranks of institutions of higher learning to positions of personnel decision-making:

"Just didn't fit in with our . . . just . . . I don't know, just didn't fit. You know?"

"'*We* want *you* to become *our colleague.*' *That's* what a job offer means!"

"The Union serves pretty good chili, but watch out for their tacos."

Students will forgive and even appreciate the occasional lapse into the practical language of the difficult world, but the opposite lapse—addressing professional colleagues with imagination and delight, for example—can spell trouble.

"Flaky flapdoodle."

"Who hired *that* guy?"

"Get with the program."

But your chairperson also wants to know your students will sign up for more of your department's offerings, so you need to be able to move back and forth between the two kinds of language. A useful bridge can be dry wit—but not too dry, and not too witty. The safest course is caution: rein your language in. Even in the classroom, don't make it too sharp, even if it's sharp language you've been hired to teach. Has a novel turned out to be more challenging than it seemed when you put it on the syllabus, its ideas too weird, its images too unpleasant, its prose too difficult? A convenient phrase can be "I think by now we've gotten the idea of what Salman Rushdie [or Arundhati Roy or James Baldwin or Isaac Babel or Guy de Maupassant] is trying to say," as if writers are really some sort of pathetic stutterers, as students and many faculty suspect anyway. The most useful phrase of all might be "The less said the better." Tenure-track colleagues many years my junior, people far smarter than I with specialties from Emerson to Asian literature to Hollywood musicals—men and women, Jew and gentile, white and non, people of various temperaments—have seemed to share one trait as they settle in toward review: an increasing tendency toward platitudes, if not silence. Some of them have families, wives or husbands or long-term partners, households, young kids in school. You can't entirely blame them.

"Just *fine. Very* well, thank you. And how are *you? So* good to see you!"

One needs to say something. So if silence is unavoidable, stick with the tried, if not the true.

I used to wonder how the tenured talked. They seemed either secretive and remote or hearty and fleeting, but finally I got a chance to observe one in an unguarded moment, a sort of natural habitat: conversing in an office doorway with a colleague whose tenure hadn't come through yet. I approached cautiously, feigning absorption in a memo, impressed and a little awed by their stolid postures and grave tones. Then I made out their actual words.

"That's exactly what we got, too," said the older colleague. "We looked at the two-door, but I just didn't think there was going to be enough room."

"The mileage looks great—on the sticker, at least. Do those estimates hold up?"

"As I recall we got thirty-two on the highway, the last time we kept track. That was when it was new, mind you. What color did you get?"

Of course, nothing indicated any tenure, retention, or promotion decisions being made here. But, hey—as you couldn't go two steps in the real world without seeing or hearing in some form or other a few years ago—it happens.

HEY! HEY! HEY! HEY!

I am nobody, but I need to tell you that after fifty-six years of tri-al-and-error, just within the last two weeks I may have figured out how to live. No doubt if I make it through many more months I'll fall back into old habits of doubt, frustration, and complaint, but often over the last two weeks, and more and more strongly, I've sensed the shimmering absolute rightness of all the familiar Buddhist-like dicta my own culture's co-opted about moments and how to live in them: I've felt brand new. This seems to have come on not long after the interruption of my latest cancer therapy, which after a year of variously effective others, I guess I'd developed high hopes for in spite of myself. Or maybe it's been due to lack of sleep, though that seems less like pathology than symptom of this newfound joy: three o'clock in the morning, and my breakfast menu's all planned.

Everything's fun: errands, newspapers, the radio, sun, rain. Like Lyle Lovett, I love everybody, even when they don't love me. A guy just now behind me in line at the donut shop commented to a friend on our changeable Buffalo spring-summer, looking out the plate glass at the way the sun lit up the damp pavement: "Ain't gonna rain today after all?" "Not this minute," I chirped. Same thing buying a burrito for yesterday's lunch, making cheery remarks to the beleaguered woman who slid over my order for minimum wage. She scowled back.

Rightly so, because for me now everything's easy, because I'm off work. I taught last semester and will later in the summer, but for now

I'm off, with enough to live on and more, thanks, too, to money my mother left me when she died midway through my first treatment, which at that point was working. More on this legacy's effects on me in a minute, but for my family, this year has been the emotional equivalent of tornado season, though in ways even beyond this selfish financial one, my mother's death has been a good thing, not immediately, but all told, after the increasingly difficult twenty years she lived with Parkinson's disease. And people's concerns for me and my father afterwards have helped to spread out the grief, if not thin it down entirely.

In other luck—including my own foresight and fortitude, to be fair to myself—I have none of the health-insurance worries that aggravated my first onset, twelve years ago. Now, I'm on a sort of early retirement plan that my employer, the State of New York, offers to employees who've worked ten insurable years and are on the payroll when they turn fifty-five. After holding my breath through low per-course pay and insecurity for over a decade at four SUNY campuses, I took that deal immediately, three months before my cancer reappeared, even though I had a contract to teach the next year, this past one. HR personnel wondered why I wanted to retire but keep working, which no one on my campus had ever done before, but I insisted, as if subliminally aware of what was brewing in my body. Luck, foresight, and ESP, maybe.

Because sure, spirit is part of this new sense of well-being. I've always liked the notion of faith but never had any, in spite of trying. When news came to me via Facebook the other day of a childhood friend whose son was hit on a bicycle and is in a coma, one of the family's posted requests was to pray. Horrified as anyone, I posted my best wishes only after deliberating over my wording to avoid the hypocrisy of agreeing to pray. "I'll keep a good thought for you" is a line I adopted from one of my first writing mentors, John Clellon Holmes—who actually might have asked for me to keep one for him as he was dying of cancer himself in Old Saybrook, Connecticut. Now I wish I'd just posted, "I'm praying.

My God." I was a bicycling kid myself, never in a helmet. I fell off once, knocked myself out, and I still only sometimes wear one. There for the grace, you know. But "I love Jesus" is like an algebraic equation to me still, or new software: I lack the basic concepts for it to compute. "Have a blessed day," said a clerk at the 7-11 just now. I ground my teeth.

But it's the clichés that capture my new outlook, an antithesis, not to say an anticlimax, to a life spent vilifying and bending myself out of shape to avoid them, in my behavior as well as my work. Raymond Carver's characters were "at the end of their rope but doing wonders with the last few inches," as I recall a blurb on *Will You Please Be Quiet Please?*, one of those early books I read trembling with the certitude it was one of the most significant experiences of my life to that point—and I feel that, both ways, all the time now; that this is the most significant time of my life and it might be the end. Never a dangerous drinker but always a steady one, I haven't had a drink in six months—only now do I see that that coincides with my mother's death, but at the time it was more of a health consideration, as absurd to mix alcohol with the vemurafenib I was on then. Anyway, the simple clarity of sobriety's another possible reason for my frequent euphoria, of course. But unlike a Carver character, what I'm doing with the last few inches has less to do with desperation than its opposite: this is about all the small, quiet, unexceptional moments identical to moments that have bored, frustrated, embarrassed, and/or angered me for years. Now I see them for what they are: great moments.

Actually, it's more complicated than that. It's paradoxical: I'm speeding up and slowing down at the same time. I have a million things to do, and one by one, I'm getting them all done: errands, will arrangements, getting a tattoo (small, tasteful, inside left forearm—so that the phlebotomists have something to look at when they draw my blood, because thinking of others is part of this newfound wellbeing, too) not to mention hectic logistics for moving to a new apartment across town.

Yes: I signed a lease. *Prepare to live* is my two-week old motto, possibly another tattoo (larger, around the elbow). Bucket lists: sky diving, dune-buggy racing, seeing the Alamo at last—well, fine, if the opportunities arrive, but just living—taking out the garbage, reading a thick book, being awake to hear the first bird at dawn, a twenty-minute walk—all these are enough to make me bust. I'm cooking, finding my own meals delicious, chewing slowly, listening to music I've never understood. I am *OK with everything*.

I still get down. I get sick of myself, discouraged. I worry how much pain there'll be. I remind myself that at any moment the pleura around my left lung, where the primary tumor has been (it's been a while since I've been scanned, since this most recent treatment is a long-term one) can fill with fluid again. I sense or imagine gasps, pains, gulps—and try to distinguish which I've done, sensed or imagined. I wonder if there'll be pain, where and how much. I recall the chest tubes from ten months ago, the talc injected in the lining to close it up and leave the fluid nowhere to go. I remember the talk of hospice, the statistics of Stage IV. And sometimes I'm dismayed by the remote attitudes of friends and family, even when they're trying to be sympathetic or thinking they're being supportive. Few beyond the medical staff are like Gerasim to Ivan Ilych (the nurses are actually very like him in their matter-of-fact compassion, though I can't imagine Tolstoy's taught in nursing schools); and I get resentful. "Well, it must be tempting to overthink it," said my brother to a recital of options and contingencies I trotted out while deciding on a course of therapy. He'd offered to listen and had done so helpfully before, but I was stung: he was doing what I've sometimes suspected my overworked oncologist of doing, too: going for the quickest, lowest-common denominator answer. All my oncologist wants to hear about for a colitis I've developed as a side effect to ipilimumab, the therapy now on hiatus, is how many bowel movements I have per day, but according to the fairly meticulous log I've been keeping at his own doctorly urging, the picture is so much fuller and richer than a poop count! Time between poops, what I've termed "clusters," or movements within a quarter of an hour of each other—count separately, he says, but I disagree!— consistency, urgency, force of emission, color and smell . . . but all he wants is a number, and if it's too high, he won't restart my immunotherapy. So I get angry, suspicious, susceptible to all my old bad attitudes.

But not for long at a stretch, now, nothing like the days, weeks, months—hell, years when I was stuck in one predominant mode of mind or another, years when I lived on generally accepting terms with such bad attitudes and lousy, self-defeating outlooks. Now it's about facing the light, so easy to do I can't believe all that time I couldn't tell where the sun rises from where it sets. Of course, both can be beautiful. But "combat strips away the bullshit," thinks James Houston in Denis Johnson's fine, fine Vietnam novel *Tree of Smoke*. So does cancer, and so maybe this, after fifty-six years of what's so often felt mostly like struggle, like anyone's daily life—is combat.

In James Dickey's great poem "The Firebombing," the pilot reflects, from the vantage point of twenty years later: "One is cool and enthralled in the cockpit," entranced by the power of beauty, while the children die below. My combat is mine alone (there are limitations to every analogy) but this is something of what it is like. From his suburb, Dickey's pilot says he can't imagine the people he napalmed, though he's done it for us if not himself; from my life I can't imagine my own death, for you or myself, either, the paradox that enlivens my days.

As Dickey's pilot reflects,

> *I still have charge—secret charge—*
> *Of the fire developed to cling*
> *To everything . . .*
> *the apotheosis of gelatin. . . .*

Death will not be what it should;
Will not, even now, even when
My exhaled face in the mirror
Of bars, dilates in a cloud like Japan. . . .

when those on earth die, there is not even sound;
One is cool and enthralled in the cockpit,
Turned blue by the power of beauty
In a pale treasure-hole of soft light
Deep in aesthetic contemplation,
Seeing the ponds catch fire. . . .

It is this detachment
The honored aesthetic evil
The greatest sense of power in one's life,
That must be shed in bars, or by whatever
Means. . . .

Absolution? Sentence? No matter;
The thing itself is in that.

How else could it be? It's all life, all good, including the clichés, like finding a perfectly good short-sleeved yellow Arrow business shirt at a used clothing store, the kindness of the poor in line and behind the counter both. It's like grace: floating over, like the pilot's view of beauty over the horrors below that have everything to do with him or, as he realizes, should. Stripping away the bullshit.

Now everything's interesting but my own regrets. The years I've spent in doubt, worry, sadness, ruts, self-hatred and irritation at others, locked up and blocked . . . these aren't worth a thought. Senate races in states I've never been in; AAA baseball, Russia, where I spent a month years ago, that ever enigma-wrapped lover of truth, beauty, and strength; the new multicolored strobe in the jammed plate-glass window of Hu's Discount Store; drones; clams; the tandem shifts of Afghans working the Sunoco on my corner, speaking Pashtun, one told me grudgingly but pridefully one day, and the fact they're out of Raisin Bran but not of Froot Loops and Frosted Flakes, possibly an indication of a new health consciousness among the convenience-store clientele? Even this feels like a speculation worth entertaining.

And everything works out. The Raisin Bran had been on my menu since 3 AM, my recent time of first waking, though I read *Our Mutual Friend* until dawn, but as it turned out when I got back from my walk I have some oats left from winter, and it's fifty degrees this morning. Chores, errands, tasks, treats . . . there's time for everything or seems to be. They all get done.

Of course, time is exactly what I might well not have that much of. That's the paradox that illuminates, the conundrum that clarifies, the urgency that strips away the bullshit, as Johnson's Pfc. Houston said, but it doesn't feel urgent or frantic; it's not like that. It feels like grace.

Yet I could see my mother's death, and I feel it still, but I think of her alive: how else? Life is what we must assume.

Today I'm walking straight and true, my back straight. Monkey mind, as the Buddhists say: swinging and grabbing at thoughts and images as they pass, but who's more at home than a monkey in the trees?

Mom's money doesn't bother me the way it did when she was alive: then she'd have been supporting me, it'd still have been hers; now it's her gift, my good fortune in memory of her. "I think you ought to live *well*," she said once, when I wasn't, when I felt obligated not to. It was more important to me to live on my own than well, at that point. Now I'm surprised at how enjoyable—more, how easy, how guilt-free—living well can be. I still do my own laundry. But I've moved into an apartment building with washers and dryers on the premises: no more laundromats!

Abundant life. All these concepts and terms from *religions*, for crying out loud, are clicking for me now. The names of the Christian principles, the standard injunction, admonitions, and reassurances all remain worn out, thank God. But *glory*, for example, spoken with a tremor and shine I never could fathom—these days, I get it.

The vocabulary of faith might be algebraic to me, but moving out from my old apartment on a recent Sunday morning, all my electronics packed except for an emergency transistor I keep in my car trunk, I listened to the only station that came in at all, WBLK, which was broadcasting services from a Baptist church on North Fillmore, on Buffalo's predominately African American East Side. I'm white, and the radio was white noise for me as I wrapped dishes in newspaper and fit them into boxes, duct-taped the boxes shut: announcements about socials and other upcoming events, free school-support programs that would pick kids up and deliver them back home, introductions of honored members of the community to say a few words, all interspersed with the standard expressions of faith, thanks, and praise that have been anathema to me. Their offense is not only in their opaqueness to those of us not steeped in Christian lore—they might as well be *Star Trek* references, recognizable but unknown—but in their hackneyed quality.

But as I was listening, after the announcements and the guest speakers and I'd moved on to the medicine cabinet in the bathroom, I became aware that one voice had been talking for an extended stretch, a man's, the main preacher of North Fillmore Baptist, and I began to listen. I hadn't at first, because his tone was more talkative than sermonesque, so

I hadn't noticed a shift. But preaching was what he was doing, though in no way I'd heard from clergy before: he exhorted but empathized. "We have been so drunk, many of us, that we didn't know where we were when we woke up." Well, I empathized, too. Not since I'd sat on the hard dark pews of the church my mother took me to four decades hence had I listened to a sermon in its entirety. And closely, moving on to the huge miscellaneous pile in the front room that I'd been putting off—more: intrigued, compelled. His theme, and I admit my mind hydroplaned over the biblical verse that focused it, was old age, from the mildly contemptuous expression "my old man" to what we can gain as we leave behind the follies of youth. His larger theme of course was living right, and sure, loving Jesus, but his tone was never scolding, never dour, and mostly he spoke with a calm excitement, using practical terms I listened to as I went through nine years and more of my accumulated possessions, throwing as much as I could onto an old sheet in the center of the room so that I wouldn't have to cart it to my new apartment across town.

Only after I'd returned from a second trip to the dumpster outside did I realize the voice on the radio had risen with a new urgency. The content had changed, too, to full-bore faith talk about the power of worship. Pure algebra, but I listened: "The power of worship. The *POWER!*" The rhythm of the voice was pleasing, and the conviction behind it was, and I listened closer, packing automatically now, my mind on the radio first. Worship led to full living—as a duty, somehow, or an effort one must make to reap the rewards he was trying to convince us of. "Don't live like you're reading about it," the preacher said, striking a nerve, as many's the experience I'd rather read about than live through, just as many's the experience I've lived through but only understood later, when writing about it. But I didn't feel admonished, just urged: *Try looking at it this way, my man*, though by now the voice was crashing like surf, reasoning beyond reason, explaining but celebrating, then, in the middle of a sentence—

"Hey! Hey! Hey! Hey!"

The hair on the back of my neck stood up, unless it was chills down the spine. I forget, just as I forget the point he was making—still the power of worship, maybe, and the good it could do you—but dusty and tired in my barren apartment as I was, I was thrilled. In a few minutes the preacher tapered off, signed off, and ceded the airwaves to good R&B standards and more, from Marvin Gaye to Bob Marley to Ann Peebles's original "I Can't Stand the Rain," and I was in tears, sobbing, not born again or cleansed or loving Jesus but brand-new, glad, once again loving everyone, though no one was there, just sobbing and laughing on my bare floor. It was some time before I could quit, though every last one of the tunes that kept coming until I turned the radio off to replace in my trunk I'd heard before.

Reporting symptoms to my oncologist, I described my weeks of well-being, downplaying the spooky-dooky side of it. I told of feeling great, rising at three to get a jump on the day, feeling in many ways the best I'd felt in my life.

"Oh, that's the steroids," said my highly informed nurse. "That'll pass as you taper off."

Sure enough, I'm down to forty milligrams a day now and waking at six, rested but non-euphoric . . .

Soon to be less than nobody, maybe. Even euphoric, I know the odds. Actually not, as this go-round I've eschewed numbers, but I know what they say, that the possibility is a probability. At times I face it, I admit it, sometimes making myself, though more often I'm reminded by strangers, when they treat me not as one retrieved but one among them, the living, and not just among them but in their way, another pain in the ass. In a dispute with a retail cashier the sudden dislike on her face even as she apologized brought me down from the articulate triumph with which I'd told her how wrong the store's policy was. *Just get out of here,* her face said, and I did, suddenly sick of myself, sure that after all and no matter what, you just shouldn't be so happy, so fine with everything.

But that, too, was a kind of relief, and cranking my ignition in the parking lot I was thinking in Ralph Stanley's mournful voice, suddenly mine: "Oh, Death. Ohh, Death. OHHH, Dea-eath. Won't you spare me over for another year?"

Everything is so sweet.

About the author

Steve Moncada Street, after receiving his MFA in fiction from the University of Arkansas, taught for four years at the American University in Cairo, then for thirty years at a dozen American colleges and universities. A noted academic labor activist, his commentary on the crisis confronting adjunct labor appeared regularly in the *Chronicle of Higher Education*, *Inside Higher Ed*, and numerous other venues. His fiction, book reviews and personal essays were published in *The Missouri Review*, *The Quarterly*, *Cimarron Review*, *Palabra*, *Another Chicago Magazine*, *Exquisite Corpse*, *Great Lakes Review*, *Rain Taxi Review of Books*, and *Intima: A Journal of Narrative Medicine*. He died of cancer in 2012.